Stella Quinn has had a love affair with books since she first discovered the alphabet. She lives in sunny Queensland now, but has lived in England, Hong Kong and Papua New Guinea. Boarding school in a Queensland country town left Stella with a love of small towns and heritage buildings (and a fear of chenille bedspreads and meatloaf!) and that is why she loves writing rural romance. Stella is a keen scrabble player, she's very partial to her four kids and any-thing with four furry feet, and she is a mediocre grower of orchids. An active member of Romance Writers of Australia, Stella has won their Emerald, Sapphire and Valerie Parv awards and was a finalist in their Romantic Book of the Year award.

You can find and follow Stella Quinn at stellaquinnauthor.com

The VET from SNOWY RIVER

STELLA QUINN

mira

First Published 2021
Second Australian Paperback Edition 2022
ISBN 9781867254102

Published by
Mira
An imprint of Harlequin Enterprises (Australia) Pty Limited (ABN 47 001 180 918), a subsidiary of HarperCollins Publishers Australia Pty Limited (ABN 36 009 913 517)
Level 13, 201 Elizabeth St
SYDNEY NSW 2000
AUSTRALIA

® and TM (apart from those relating to FSC®) are trademarks of Harlequin Enterprises (Australia) Pty Limited or its corporate affiliates. Trademarks indicated with ® are registered in Australia, New Zealand and in other countries.

A catalogue record for this book is available from the National Library of Australia
www.librariesaustralia.nla.gov.au

Printed and bound in Australia by McPherson's Printing Group

For Brother, Ash, Soph and Jen.
And Rosie, who loved to snooze under my writing desk.

CHAPTER

1

The cat was back.

Vera stood, bin in hand, at the kitchen door of the old Federation building she'd just signed a lease on and met the cat's stare with one of her own.

'Scram,' she said, as she tipped the rubbish she was carrying into the alley skip bin. She was too tired to put much heat into the word. The cat paused in a puddle of spring sunshine then settled into a brick of fur.

Excellent. She'd have no trouble at all running kitchen staff, a barista, and a team of waiters if this was how a stray cat responded to her commands.

She lowered the rubbish bin to the ground and took a second to ease the knots in her back. What had she been thinking? She knew nothing about running a café, particularly one in a small tourist town in the Snowy Mountains. All she knew was that she needed an income to pay for her aunt's medical bills, and cooking was the only skill she had left.

A horn tooted from the street out front of the building and had her checking her watch. Ten o'clock, bang on time. She hurried back inside, stripped off her rubber gloves, and peered through the plate glass windows that formed two sides of her shopfront. A delivery truck stood by the kerb, and two tradies were untying ropes and hauling drop cloths from the huge sign resting in its tray.

Vera felt a prickle of emotion deep in her stomach. It took a moment to recognise the prickle for what it was, it had been so long. She opened the front door and stood in the entryway as the last of the cloth was lifted, and her excitement grew from a prickle to a roar.

'You want us to hang it now, love?'

Yes. Hell yes, she wanted them to hang it now. She may be about to make a monumental financial blunder; she may be unsure, and nervous, and sick with worry about whether her daft, outrageous idea was going to pay off, for her *and* her aunt. But by god, yes, she was ready.

'Let's do it,' she said.

The two men reached into the truck's deep tray and hauled. She caught her breath as the sign came clear: glossy chocolate background, pale cream writing in a stylish font she'd agonised over. The border of wildflowers had come up so much better than she'd imagined, with the yellow billy buttons plump and cheerful, and the delicate stems of pink triggers providing some old-fashioned whimsy. THE BILLY BUTTON CAFÉ, PROPRIETOR VERA DE ROSSI.

She pressed a hand to her heart. She felt a little wild herself.

A slow clap sounding from the park on the street's far side distracted her as she signed the delivery invoice.

'Noice.' The broad country accent drew her attention to a buff-looking guy on the denial side of fifty staring at her with his arms crossed.

'Um, thanks.'

He stepped onto the road. 'I'm your eleven o'clock,' he said, as he walked past her and into the dimly lit chaos that was currently the interior of the café. 'Crikey. Lots to do, lucky I'm early.'

Vera felt a frown forming and willed it away. She was a café proprietor now—she needed to be friendly. 'We're not open yet, sir.'

He turned to her, offered her a hand to shake and a grin that was all manicured beard and charm. 'Graeme Sharpe. I responded to your newspaper ad for café staff.'

Hell's bells, where was her head? She was supposed to be a detail person, and she had totally forgotten she had an interview booked for later in the morning. 'Of course. Sorry, I lost track of the time.'

The man eyed the clutter, and she followed his gaze as it moved about the room. The chairs were piled high in one corner, still wrapped in plastic. Tables needed legs attaching, copper urns and drooping ferns formed a pyramid in the middle of the floor. 'Vera De Rossi,' he said. 'Proprietor. That's you, I take it?'

'Yep.'

'Uh-huh. You run a café before, Vera?'

'Nope.'

'You serious about making this one work?'

Vera pursed her lips. Who was interviewing who, here? This Graeme guy wasn't lacking in confidence. 'I'm deadly serious about making The Billy Button work.' Understatement of the year. If the café didn't turn a profit, her Aunt Jill's safe haven in the dementia ward at Connolly House would be gone before she'd had a chance to change into her slippers.

'And food. You buying in from suppliers, or making your own?'

'Making it here. Cakes to eat in and take away, big breakfast menu, light lunch menu. Maybe dinner down the track. You know, my bank manager didn't ask me this many questions.'

He smiled. 'Just checking if you and I are going to be a good fit. If you're interested in hiring the best barista north of Fitzroy, I'm your man. Only, I have to warn you, I *do* have experience in running cafés and I'm fussy, bossy and opinionated. But in a totally good way.'

She drew in a breath. Hiring a man with the razzle-dazzle of a talk-show host had not been what she'd envisaged, but she was here in Hanrahan to remake herself, wasn't she? Rigid and fussy, that was the old Vera. This new Vera had to be flexible.

She could adapt. 'Barista, you say.'

'My lovely, I can make you a latte that would make an angel sing.'

She fought down a smile. 'That's quite a claim. Do people outside of the city know how to make decent coffee?'

He threw his hands up in mock horror. 'Such prejudice. Skinny flat whites, iced long blacks, affogatos—show me your machine, lady, and I'll show you caffeine heaven.'

She grinned. 'Sheath that indignation, Dundee. I believe you. Unfortunately, the espresso machine hasn't arrived yet.' She eyed him, wondering if he really *would* suit. Graeme the barista was clearly a small-town people person—she'd need that, because she sure as hell wasn't any good with small towns. Or people. She could barely run her own messed-up life. 'Do you have references?'

He winked. 'All sorts. What skills are you needing referenced?'

'Coffee-making, obviously. But I'll be needing more than a coffee that can—um—show me heaven. I need a front of house person. Like a maître'd of a restaurant. Someone who knows the customers' names, keeps the peace when someone decides their skinny-soy-half-strength-with-a-quarter-sugar isn't hot enough. Someone who can keep an eye on young staff and check the milk order when it arrives and balance the till. Who isn't above giving the loos a quick swab when the waitstaff are slammed.'

'Oh,' he said, nodding his head. 'You need a miracle worker. The answer, then, is yes. I can do all of that and more.'

Graeme sounded too good to be true. She frowned. This café was the only way she was going to be able to keep an income coming in if the worst happened and her lawyer couldn't keep her out of prison. She couldn't afford to not ask tough questions, not when so much was at stake. 'If you're such a hotshot, Graeme, how is it you're out of work? And why are you burying your barista awesomeness in Hanrahan?'

He shrugged. 'Love and lust, Vera.'

Did he just say—

He must have read her look of befuddlement, because he laughed. 'I know, right? Who would have thought Hanrahan was such a hotbed of romance for middle-aged guys like me? I moved here to be closer to my partner Alex about a year ago, but it's well past time I found myself some gainful employment. And Marigold—have you met her yet? Town busybody? Heart of gold and impervious to snubs?—well, she showed me your advertisement and said fate was giving me a gentle nudge.'

'Fate?' God, she hoped not. She was hoping the disastrous string of events which resulted in her placing the advert in the local paper had come to an end. She'd had quite enough of fate for the time being … especially as her own never seemed to arrive as gentle nudges. Her fate felt like it was being flung from a distance by a vengeful goblin.

Graeme smiled. 'Marigold is a bit of a hippy. She throws words like fate and karma and mindfulness around like she's throwing frisbees for a pet dog … I blame it on the yoga.'

They had moved deeper into the room, to where tape marks on the old floorboards marked where the new timber veneer counter would be installed, and she did a survey, wishing the hard work was done already. To her right, tall sash windows looked out over Paterson Street to the small park, and a soot-stained fireplace of dark brick soared from floor to ceiling.

To the left, more windows framed the view of lake and mountain that had driven the monthly rent up to a worryingly high amount.

This café was a gamble, and one she couldn't afford to lose: if fate had truly brought Graeme to this moment of decision, desperation had been what had brought her. She shouldn't employ the first person she interviewed, no matter how sweet he seemed. She had a lot riding on this café, and so did her aunt.

She racked her brain for another employer-like question to ask. 'Have you been out of work long? I'll be needing someone who can put in a full working week. There'll be some early starts, too.'

'I know the drill, Vera. The thing is … I get a bit antsy when I have too much alone time. I've been building an extension on our house which has kept me flat strap, but I'm happier surrounded by a bit of bustle.'

Alone time. Sounded like bliss to her, and she was hoping for plenty of it herself now she'd moved to Hanrahan. She didn't know anyone, and no-one knew her. She'd learned her lesson: getting involved brought nothing with it but hurt and betrayal, and she was so done with that. Her relationships from now on were going to involve her, her battered pile of recipe books, and the never-ending list of tasks she had to complete to get this café up and thriving.

She made a snap decision. Graeme didn't look like a bad bet, and she needed a barista. A fun one with charm to spare was just icing on the cake. 'Okay. Why don't we say a four-week trial? I'll pay above the going rates, but only just, because I'm pretty much broke. I'm hoping to open a week from today, and there's plenty of work if you want to start sooner.'

Graeme held out his hand. 'You're making the right decision, boss.'

She grinned at him, because really, who wouldn't? He was one hundred per cent adorable. And besides, she had a good feeling about this arrangement. Her new (and only) employee was like the fire to her hydrant, the dazzle to her drab. The more he kept the customers entertained, the more she could devote herself to her pots and pans in the privacy of the commercial kitchen out back.

'When you say I can start sooner ... I do have a few ideas.'

And so it began, she thought. Her café was no longer a one-woman dream. 'Ideas? Like what?'

'Are those bentwood chairs I see, tucked under all that plastic?'

'Yes. Mahogany stain. I was hoping for some club chairs in a cigar-coloured leather, but my bank manager was starting to look pale and sweaty whenever I asked if I could extend the overdraft.'

Graeme moved forward to lift the plastic and inspect the exposed wood. 'Now, where's the fun in getting it all perfect at once? These chairs will look lovely ... old school, to suit the building. What's the age of this place, Federation?'

'Nineteen ten, according to the lease I signed.'

'You'll be wanting to capture a little of that charm, I expect. What are your other decoration plans?'

She felt a little rush of affection for this stranger who had, within the space of a few minutes, grasped the importance of getting The Billy Button Café right. This wasn't some hole-in-the-wall take-away joint she was trying to create. She took a breath. 'I'd love to talk over my plans if you have time. I had a graphic designer help me with the sign, but everything else'—she gestured to the clutter of stuff she'd dragged in or had delivered—'is a collation of ideas I've been gathering in a scrapbook for years.'

'Scrapbooking? Oh, goody.' Graeme said it like he was a kid at a party who'd just spied the pile of party bags to be given out. 'Can I see? Is it here?'

'Er ... sure. It's in that box over there along with the paint rollers and drop cloths.'

She waited until he'd pulled it out and spread it open on one of the round, iron-footed tables she'd set up.

'Oh my,' he said. 'Stylish but warm, I love it.'

She shrugged. 'Look at this place. Those huge sash windows, the fireplace, the decorative swirls in the ceiling. Anything else would seem, I don't know—'

'Sacrilege?'

She grinned. 'I was going to say a wasted opportunity, but sure, let's scale it up to sacrilege.'

Graeme gave a chuckle as he turned the page. 'Girlfriend, scaling things up is my special skill. Oh ... these deep green velvet banquettes, I love them. You could pop a corner banquette there, near the inner room.' He spun on his heel. 'Perhaps another by that window.'

'Way ahead of you. A carpenter down at Cooma is whipping them up as we speak. Should be here in a day or two.'

'Lighting? Please tell me these abominations are going.'

Vera looked up to the strips of fluorescent tubing lining the stained ceiling. 'I've found some simple fixtures at a disposal store. Copper rods that bring the lights down low, a simple glass fitting that has an amber glow to it. If I had an endless budget I would have tried for some vintage fittings but ...'

'In time, Vera. Lightbulbs are an easy change. Who do you have in mind to do the painting? What is this current wall colour, anyway, apricot jam?'

She laughed. 'I know, right? Hideous. You should see the kitchen, it's like a tree frog exploded in there. I'm doing the painting. That's today and tomorrow's job, along with retiling the fireplace surrounds and waxing the floorboards. Once that's done, I can start placing the furniture and have the counter delivered.'

Graeme walked over to the stack of tiles leaning against the decorative skirting board lining the room. 'These are gorgeous.'

Yeah. They ought to be for the work she'd put into them. She'd found them advertised as a giveaway from a house renovation in Queanbeyan. Glossy, deep-green handmade tiles a century old that had enough of a ripple in the surface shine to give them whimsy. She'd spent an afternoon chipping them off an unwanted kitchen backsplash, breaking as many as she'd managed to save. They were magnificent—and so too would the fireplace be, if she could somehow get it to look like the pictures she'd gathered in her scrapbook, with her vintage tiles set subway style about the cast-iron firebox. The timber mantel was already perfect. Made from a blackened hardwood, she liked to imagine it had been polished by the people of Hanrahan for over a hundred years.

'I should have enough for the fire surround,' she said.

'Does the chimney work?'

Hell, she hadn't thought to ask the landlord. She'd been daydreaming about serving mulled wine in front of a snug fire once autumn arrived in the mountains, and hadn't given a thought to the state of the chimney. 'I have no idea. I'll add it to my list.'

Graeme made a *hmm* sound and continued inspecting the bits and pieces she'd assembled.

'Maybe you could help me find a local florist, Graeme. I'm hoping to use local wildflowers as centrepieces on the tables. Fresh or preserved, I don't mind.'

He grinned at her, a smile that was as wide as it was wicked. 'Oh, have I got a florist for you, Vera.'

'Um … thank you, I think.'

'About these tiles. I can do the fireplace for you, if you're willing to trust me with it.'

She'd disappeared into a daydream imagining The Billy Button Café beautifully dressed and ready to party, plump yellow wildflowers adding a little sunshine to every table, but Graeme's words pulled her back to the dusty drop-cloth reality.

'Excuse me? Did you just offer to do a DIY project for my fit-out?'

He shrugged. 'Sure. Why wouldn't I?'

'Um … because people aren't usually that nice. Not where I moved from, anyway.'

Graeme gave her the full benefit of his megawatt smile. 'You're in Hanrahan now, Vera. Besides, I am one fussy renovator. If I'm going to be looking at that fireplace all day, I'm going to be needing some precision grout lines.'

'Huh,' she said. 'I don't like to boast, but I've watched three online tiling tutorials. I'm pretty much an expert now.'

Graeme grinned. 'I think we're gonna make a great team, boss. You got an apron hiding in that pyramid of stuff?'

Aprons she had. They were works of art, chocolate brown and piped with cream edging. There was no way in hell she was letting one of her new aprons anywhere near a DIY tiling project.

'I can offer you a plastic garbage bag or a grease-stained old tea towel?'

'Ew. Why don't I pop home and get into my overalls. I'll be back in an hour.'

She reached out and touched her new café manager on the arm. 'Are you sure you want this, Graeme? Building something from the ground up like this? It's going to be a lot of work.'

Graeme rested his hand over hers and turned to give the interior of her café one long look. 'Girlfriend,' he said, 'this place is going to be a sensation.'

She hoped so. She really hoped so. She looked through the smudged glass windows, to where The Billy Button Café sign swung in a breeze curling up from the narrow northern arm of Lake Bogong, and squared her shoulders.

She couldn't afford to let *anything* get in the way of this café being a hit.

CHAPTER

2

Josh Cody slid a loop of gut into his hooked needle and carefully knotted the last suture.

'How many?'

He looked up at his sister, who'd popped her head in round the door of the surgical room. 'Eight. Three black, one chocolate, four yellow. You owe me ten bucks.'

Hannah flashed him a grin. 'You've got mad diagnostic skills, Dr Cody.'

He ran his hand over the chest and stomach of the plump labrador on his stainless steel table. She'd been exhausted when the man who'd found her in his shearing shed had brought her in—luckily, he'd performed more than one emergency caesarean by now. The operation had gone smoothly, which made being called Dr Cody, Veterinarian, feel less like the dream of a moron who'd screwed up his chances and more like the hard-earned truth.

'Did you find a microchip? I can run it through the database.'

'Nothing. Her fur's in a poor state, nails are brittle and torn up, and she's a little long in the tooth to be having a litter. She's not underweight though. Hard to say if she's a stray, or just has owners who haven't got a clue how to look after a pregnant dog.'

He glanced down into the plastic tub on the bench, where eight furry lumps the size of vegemite scrolls snoozed atop a pink fluffy heat pack. The cause of this morning's drama, the chocolate pup who'd tried to enter the world sideways, lay on his back, a tiny pink tongue poking from his snout.

Hannah moved in next to him and reached a hand into the bucket of pups. 'Poppy's going to go nuts when she sees them.'

He sighed. 'I hope so.'

He'd not seen his daughter for weeks. And her absence from his life had chiselled a hole in his heart that even the excitement of his new vet career couldn't fill. She was mad with him for moving from Sydney to 'the boonies', as she called it, and kept finding new ways to make him suffer. The first time he'd brought up the idea of relocating to Hanrahan she'd flounced off back to her mother's, returning a week later with a second set of ear piercings. Dragging her feet about visiting was Pop's latest brand of torture.

Sure, he got it, school and assignments and Year Ten exams mattered ... but didn't he matter too?

'Give me a hand with getting her off the table, will you, Han?' he said, turning his attention back to a problem he *could* do something about.

'Sure.'

They lifted the sedated dog and carried her through to a pen. 'You written up the chart yet?' said Hannah.

'No time. She looked ready to pop when Trev carried her in.'

'Trev? The old bloke from out near Stony Creek? Wow, I haven't seen him in yonks. I thought he hated the hustle and bustle of town.'

He snorted. 'Hannah, I hate to be the one to break it to you, but Dandaloo Street in Hanrahan can in no way be described as hustle and bustle.'

'That is so not true. You haven't seen the fuss and bother going on in the old bank building. Some fancy new café is opening up. Hanrahan is cosmopolitan these days, big brother.'

He rolled his eyes. 'Noted. I'd also like to point out that the only hustle and bustle we need to worry about right now is the fleas on this dog. I'd better find the old girl a flea collar.' He rested his hand on the brown dog's head. 'You've got fleas as big as bandicoots, Jane, you know that? Don't worry, we'll get rid of them for you.'

'Jane?'

He shut the pen gate and returned to the bench to collect the pups. 'Jane Doe. Isn't that what they call unidentified people in cop shows?'

Hannah put her hands on her hips and gave him the you're-an-idiot look she'd been sending his way for nearly thirty years. 'Only the dead ones, moron.'

He pulled her long brown pigtail. 'My case, so I get naming rights. I say it's Jane Doe.'

He put the pups into the whelping box next to their mother's cage. She'd be waking soon enough, and once he was sure she wasn't so sedated she'd roll on the new arrivals, he'd pop them in with her. One happy family.

Just like he and Poppy could be if she ever condescended to pay him a visit.

'Before you get into the paperwork, I want to show you something.' Hannah dug into a pocket of her navy scrubs and pulled out a thin card. 'A box of these arrived this morning. What do you think?'

He read the card in her hand and flashed his sister a smile. Finally. *Finally.* 'I didn't know you were getting these printed.'

She punched him in the arm. 'I don't have to tell my new partner everything.'

He read the words a second time: JOSH CODY, CODY AND CODY VET CLINIC, CNR DANDALOO STREET AND SALT CREEK FLATS ROAD, HANRAHAN. It had been a year since his little sister had invited him to buy into her growing vet practice in the historic mountain town where they'd grown up. He'd still been a student then, Poppy living with him every second week, and working construction on weekends to keep the bills paid. It had taken him three seconds to decide that was the move he wanted to make, but it had taken another three months before he'd told Poppy his move to Hanrahan was no longer a dream but reality.

She'd been so thrilled she'd moved all her belongings out of her bedroom in his apartment and taken up residence permanently at her mother's.

'Just getting used to be being abandoned,' she'd thrown at him.

Happy days.

What Poppy didn't understand was how much Hanrahan was a part of him … of all the Codys. His grandparents had lived here back when the Snowy River still flowed in all its glory from the mountains to the Southern Ocean, flooding pretty much everything in its path when the snows melted. Despite her current refusal to reside with him, Poppy was as much a Cody as he was, which meant she needed to know that city life wasn't the only type of life she could have.

And then there was the other thing. The personal thing. Fifteen years in Sydney, scraping and saving and working his arse off to get by had just about done him in. He needed this. He needed respect, and he needed to be valued. And—he rubbed his hand over the Poppy-sized ache in his chest—he needed his daughter to be the one doing the respecting and the valuing.

Maybe then he could finally quit beating himself up for blowing his chances.

As he slipped the card into the back pocket of his jeans, he choked down the lump in his throat. 'I love it. Thanks, Hannah.'

She grinned. 'You can thank me by sweet-talking Sandy into opening a pack of the good biscuits. I've got surgeries back-to-back this arvo, and if I don't get some chocolate into these veins, I'll be too weak to cut the boy bits off Mrs Grundy's dalmatian.'

Josh winced. Why was it women vets always said that with such relish? 'Enough said.'

Hannah moved to the workbench and started assembling gear. 'Before you disappear, there is something else I need to tell you.'

Josh studied his sister's face. 'Why do I get the feeling this other thing isn't as fun as a shiny new business card?'

Hannah pulled a mask off the storage shelf, gloves, a canister of the jerky treats they fed to the furry patients to remind them that their vet visits could be fun, despite the needles and indignities they might suffer. 'It's in the mail-in tray. The local newspaper.'

'Why would the local newspaper put an expression of doom on your face?'

'Remember the community section? The Hanrahan Chatter?'

'Sure. Someone hit a birdie at the golf course. So-and-so got married. Garage sale on Brindabella Avenue followed by bingo at the community hall.'

'Not this week.'

He clamped a hand down on the sterile dressings she was layering on a tray. 'Just spit it out, Hannah. What are the noisy miners twittering about now?'

She flicked him a look. 'Maureen Plover took it over some years back. Remember her?'

'No.'

'Sure you do. She used to work in the pharmacy.'

'Lots of hair? Gimlet eyes? Stood guard over the condom display?'

'Wow,' his sister said, with the deadpan inflection his daughter had also mastered. 'That's what you remember, huh?'

He shrugged.

'Well, these days she keeps herself busy nosing around everyone's business and writing a column for the Chatter, and this week, you're her hot topic.'

'Crap.'

'Uh-huh. High school hero returns ... some titillating backstory about Beth, none of it true ... finishes with a plug for the vet clinic, as though that makes it all friendly and sweet.'

He closed his eyes. When would this town let it go?

'I'm sorry, Josh.'

He sighed. 'Yeah, me too. We got any wood out back in the shed? I'm feeling a strong urge to drive an axe through something, and firewood would be a better option than finding Maureen Plover's home office and trashing it.'

He left Hannah to prep for her afternoon list and stepped into the cluttered office out back where they kept their case notes and work desks. He tapped out a quick *Have You Lost Your Dog?* flyer, then frowned at the social media logo on the screen as he waited for the printer to rev up. May as well use the internet for good as well as evil, he thought, and posted a message on the clinic's community page. *Found, one chocolate labrador, aged 8–9 years, contact Josh.* Thank god the gossips of Hanrahan hadn't been switched on about social media back when he was making waves on the town's news radar; the backlash then had been bad enough.

He had to ignore it. Gossip in the local paper was no reason to sour his return to Hanrahan. Poppy's passive-aggressive texts were a different matter, but he couldn't blame the old biddies of Hanrahan for that.

He looked at the text message he'd received that morning in response to his reminder that her two-week school holiday was about to start, and she still hadn't said when she'd visit.

It's not all about you, Dad.

True. But couldn't it be a little bit about him? He was two biscuits into a self-pity snack when the idea struck him. Assurances and pleas and begging hadn't worked ... maybe it was time for a new strategy. He'd been busting a gut to make everything work for her to visit him, offering to book train tickets, pick out a new doona cover, coordinate with her mum and her school term and whatever activities she had on so it would be easy for her.

Maybe that was part of the problem?

He picked up his phone before he could overthink it.

She answered on the second ring.

'Shouldn't you be in class?' he said.

'Hey, you called me, remember? Anyway, I've got a spare this arvo.'

'Phones in lockers. That's the school rule.'

Her sigh carried with it the weight of teenage girls everywhere who had to put up with dorky dads asking them tedious questions. 'I can hang up, Dad, if you're concerned about the minutiae of phone usage rules at Rosella State High.'

She was right. He didn't want her to hang up. 'About Hanrahan,' he said.

'Can we not get into this again? I've said I'll come out sometime, all right? I've got a lot on so I can't commit. I only get two weeks break in October, and I don't want to waste half of that time on a train.'

'Cooma Train Station is five hours from Sydney, not five days.'

'Whatever.'

Ouch. The sting of that three-syllabled word was worse than a snake bite. He should know—he'd had someone's pet python latch onto his arm twice in the last fortnight.

'Anyway, the reason I was calling …'

'Yes?' she said.

He took a breath, then worked at injecting a note of frazzle into his voice. If this strategy was going to work, he needed to give it some heft. 'I've kind of lost the plot with getting the flat ready.'

'In what way? You didn't pick some gross colour for my room, did you?'

'Baby pink, just like you asked for.'

'I so did not! Bloody hell, Dad.'

He chuckled. 'Just winding you up. I haven't got around to paint yet. I only just got the planning notice sign erected out front.'

'What do you need that for?'

'It's a formality for council. Gives the locals a chance to make comment before council approves the plans. The building is heritage listed, you know.'

'Huh. Like I care about old buildings.'

'Oh? Well, that's too bad, because it's *your* heritage. I don't want to mess it up by making a dumb building decision.'

'What … *my* heritage?'

'Well, the building will be partly yours one day. And it's part of Snowy Mountains history. Not everybody gets to restore a three-storey Victorian stone building built during the gold rush.'

'Wow. I had no idea it was so old.'

Was that interest he was hearing in his daughter's voice? She delivered her comments with such a chilly tone, sometimes it was hard to tell.

'Plus, I'm no good at choosing sheets, or any cooking appliances besides a sandwich maker, and the tiling in the bathroom's only half done.'

'You do make epic toasted sandwiches, Dad.' Yeah—she was definitely warming up a little.

He sighed. Mournfully. 'I don't know, Pop. It's so difficult making all these decisions all by my lonely lonesome self.'

Silence pulsed down the phone line for a long moment.

He broke first. 'Poppy? You still there?'

'No. The deputy principal just saw me on my phone, so I'm currently being dragged off to the interrogation room to be torn apart by alsatians.'

He grinned. 'So, what do you think? Could you spare a teeny-weeny bit of time over your break to help your old dad out?'

'If this is your idea of bribery, it sucks.'

'Will you think about it?'

The silence dragged out again, but this time Poppy was the one to end it. 'I'll try,' she said.

'I love you,' he said.

'I know,' she said, and the line went dead in his ear.

CHAPTER
3

It's done, Jill, Vera wrote on the letter pad she had perched up against her knees. *Our café is open.*

Her thoughts wandered as the bubbles in her bathtub made gentle popping noises against her skin. Her aching feet felt better now she had them submersed in hot water, and the lavender oil she'd dolloped into the tub was doing wonders. A half-hour in the tub relaxing, a quick dry of her hair, and she'd be out at Connolly House to see Jill for a sunset tipple of the monstrously sweet sherry her aunt was partial to.

She could call the egg supplier on the drive down to Cooma. She'd need to double her order for the coming week if their first day's sales were any indication, and she'd need to go visit the local butcher, too, and start prepping the more substantial meal menu she was hoping to offer.

She tapped her pen against the porcelain. Kitchen logistics could go on hold for now, she had to think how to describe today—opening day of The Billy Button Café—to her aunt. She'd been so busy working her butt off, the details were a blur.

How many business openings had she attended in her old life? How many dry, emotionless little articles had she penned for the *South Coast Morning Herald*?

The old bank building in the small town of Hanrahan has been given a new lease on life this week with the opening of The Billy Button Café. Vera De Rossi serves Italian-style sweets as well as some old-fashioned country favourites, and plans to open—

'Blah blah blah,' said Vera, and grinned, surprised at herself. Journalism had been her life, once, and she'd prided herself on her cool, dispassionate prose.

She took a sip of the green tea she'd perched on a stool by the tub. That was the old her.

The new her baked fancy tarts and made epic beef bourguignon and could use whatever flowery words she damn well chose.

'Opening day at The Billy Button Café was frazzling and glorious,' she announced to her imaginary audience. 'It was nerve-racking and frantic. It was'—she hunted for the perfect word to capture how she was feeling—'empowering.'

She smoothed the top page of her notepad, where lavender steam was making the corners curl, and continued her letter to her aunt.

I hope you've settled into your new room and you're enjoying the garden. Such a pretty view! So much better than that gravel carpark your window at the old place looked out on. Have the local birds found you yet? I wonder how the butcher birds of Queanbeyan are coping without your toast crumbs keeping them plump?

I've not got very far with unpacking all your storage boxes, Aunt Jill, but they're in the spare bedroom of the apartment I'm renting in Hanrahan. If I unpack anything fun, I'll bring it in to show you.

She sat bolt upright in the bathtub.

The De Rossi brush! Of course, that's where it must be! She must have slung it into one of those storage boxes instead of packing it in Jill's suitcase for the move from Acacia View to Connolly House. No wonder she hadn't been able to find it.

Tossing her notepad onto the stool, Vera hauled herself upright, ignoring the protests from her sore feet. She dried herself off in a hurry, flung herself into jeans and a t-shirt and the softest, flattest shoes she owned, then went into the spare room.

Cartons stood in a higgledy-piggledy row, their bland brown sides neatly annotated with words like *books*, and *winter outfits* and *useless knick-knacks with sentimental value*.

She swallowed. Jill—the old, fun, hippy Jill—would have hated to see remnants of her adventurous life packed so neatly away.

So boringly away.

Vera could do something about that. Not this second, perhaps, or even this month, because she was up to her eyebrows in café jobs as it was—but soon.

For now, finding the family heirloom her aunt had used to brush Vera's hair when Vera was a little girl would have to do.

She ripped into the masking tape until the flaps of the first carton flopped open, revealing the jumble of memory within.

The brush was there, right on top. Vera smiled. Maybe fate really was going to be on her side from now on.

When she arrived an hour later at Connolly House, her aunt Jill was seated in a wicker chair beneath the speckled canopy of a grevillea. Her face, once so quick and lively, stared into Vera's with interest, but no recognition. So, today was going to be one of *those* visits.

She set the sherry bottle and two tiny crystal glasses down on the picnic table, and gave her aunt a kiss. 'Hello, Aunt Jill. It's Vera. How are you settling in? Your room looks lovely, and someone has popped a rose on your bedside table. How sweet is that? Fresh flowers!'

Still no response. The visits where Jill struggled to formulate thoughts into words were becoming more common. 'Do you like it here, Jill?'

She hoped so. The gardens were beautiful—as Jill was, colour in her cheeks from the crisp mountain air, the soft fleece she wore newly laundered. Nursing staff and residents could be heard chatting and laughing in the gardens behind them, and she could almost feel the late afternoon sun gilding the place with peace and serenity.

She felt hope loosen the tight knot of worry that was her constant companion. Maybe this hospice would slow down her aunt's demise. Slow down the loss of memory, the loss of speech.

Maybe Connolly House really *could* be a home for Jill.

She poured a full nip of sherry into a glass for her aunt, and a scant splash into a glass for herself. Jill's favourite tipple was the rock bottom of adult beverages, so she only ever pretended to drink it.

'Jill? A drink for you?' She held out the glass, ready to assist her aunt to hold it if need be, but her aunt had turned her face to the mountain range which was never out of view.

Not sherry, then. Perhaps Jill was still confused about where she was. She could do something about that, she thought, and tried to recall some snippets of local lore.

'This close mountain you can see is called Old Regret by the locals. Rock climbers love it, and there are horse-riding trails, and a few privately owned properties that farm on its lower slopes.' Now, where had she heard that? In the online material when she was researching homes who had room for her aunt, perhaps. 'Behind it are the eastern ridges of the Snowy Mountains. People ski up there, in the winter.'

She'd skied herself a little, growing up. On school trips and occasionally with friends.

'I wonder how Hanrahan got its name, Jill? Maybe the gift store in town has a book that will tell us. I know Lake Bogong spills into a creek system that ends up in the Snowy River. Sounds romantic, doesn't it? A ribbon of water, winding through the mountains for thousands of years, snow gums shadowing its banks. Sadly diminished now, of course, since the dam went in. Progress, I suppose they called it back then. You'd call it an environmental tragedy, Jill. You'd have been painting signs and chaining yourself to snow gums.'

'Snow gums,' murmured Jill. 'So lovely.'

'Yes!' This was progress! 'I could bring you in some leaves from one of them next time I visit. We can rub them in our hands and smell them—that would be fun, wouldn't it? Like we used to smell herbs back in your garden.' Vera opened her bag and pulled out the heavy hairbrush. Now Jill was responding, perhaps she'd remember the old family brush she'd held so often in her hand.

'Shall I brush your hair, Jill? Then you can look lovely too.'

Her aunt's face grew confused. 'Let me see that.'

She handed the brush to her aunt. 'It was your mother's, remember?'

'No, Barb took it from me. She was always taking my things, wearing my clothes. She was a pest.'

Vera sighed. 'It's mine now, Jill. You gave it to me.'

A tear ran down Jill's cheek. Sadness for the past, or sadness for not being able to remember the past? She gave her aunt's hand a squeeze. 'Don't be sad, Jill,' she said. 'I can do the remembering for both of us. Come on, let me smooth these tangles for you.'

She began to draw the brush's stiff bristles through her aunt's wiry grey hair, and the motion was bittersweet. It was her aunt's brushed hair—or, rather, lack of brushing—which had begun the descent into hell which had taken up the last year of her life.

She'd thought it such a simple question at the time. 'Excuse me,' she'd said to the duty nurse on the desk at Acacia View, 'my aunt … her hair's quite dirty, I noticed, and unbrushed. Has she been difficult about washing herself lately?'

'All commentary and complaints about patient management are to be in writing,' the woman had said.

She could recall her surprise. 'I just wondered if there was anything I could do—'

The duty officer had tapped a laminated sign sticky-taped to the counter. *Zero tolerance*, the sign had read. *Aggressive and abusive behaviour will not be tolerated.*

Vera kept sweeping the De Rossi brush through her aunt's hair, up–down, up–down. If only her bitter memories could be swept away and detangled as easily.

If only she'd not involved the other residents' family members, asking them if *they* had concerns. If only she hadn't joined that social media group for relatives of Acacia View residents.

If only—

Crap. There was no use wishing *if only*. She'd done what she'd done, and now she had to live with it … or pay for it. A courtroom of strangers would decide which.

As though fate had heard her thoughts and decided to mess with her just a little bit more, her phone buzzed in her bag.

Hell. The one person she never wanted to hear from who she still had in her phone's contact list.

'Well well,' said a voice that was three parts gravel and one part schmooze. 'What do you know, telephones work up there in snowy woop woop.'

'Hi, Sue. I've moved to the foothills of the Australian Alps, not Antarctica.'

'Is there a shoe shop within a five-minute drive?'

'Er ... no.'

'Antarctica it is. I got a little something in my in-tray today. You checked your mail?'

Vera held her breath. 'Don't tell me they've dropped the charges?'

'I applaud your optimism, Vera, but this is not my good news voice. This is my serious voice, the one I use when my trusty timesheet is billing you for every minute of our time.'

Crap. 'Just tell me quick, then. How bad is it, this thing you've received?'

'Court appearance notice.'

'When?'

'Six weeks.'

'Six *weeks*? I thought you said these private prosecutions dragged on for months.'

'I was wrong. You might want to buy a lotto ticket, because that doesn't happen often.'

Vera pressed her phone to her cheek for a moment. 'What else do I need to know?'

'Here's the gist of the short particulars listed on the notice: Acacia View are bringing a charge against you, they've lawyered up with some hotshot from Sydney, and they're ready to turn their threats of prosecution into the real deal. Arraignment, trial, verdict.'

Prosecution.

It was really happening, then. The countdown on her time as a free woman had begun.

Bile rose in Vera's throat. 'It's ridiculous. Since when was looking out for a vulnerable person a crime?'

Sue's voice was brisk. 'Since the Surveillance Devices Act was introduced into New South Wales in 2007 and put limitations on what is considered okay to record. You planted a camera with a microphone in your aunt's aged care home, and now you're facing the consequences.'

Yeah. She sure as hell was … all thanks to her former boss (and boyfriend) Aaron who had sold her out. She was facing consequences all right, and a potential prison sentence was just one of them.

She eyed the inch of sherry she'd poured her aunt and wondered if this situation qualified as rock bottom.

'Vera? You paying attention?'

'Yeah. I was just thinking about alcohol.'

'You and me both. You, at least, have an excuse. I just paid a hypnotist a hundred and eighty bucks to convince me that five booze-free nights a week would make me a happier person.'

'That's … a lot of money.'

'Yeah, I could tell he was spouting claptrap while I was listening to him drone on, but his recliner was epic and, wowza, he was easy on the eye. Not my worst buy for a hundred and eighty bucks. Where was I?'

'Prosecution. Lawyers. Hotshots.'

'Right. The court appearance notice says you've been mailed a copy but I'll scan this in and email it to you so you can read the details. It lists place of offence, statutory provision breached, summary of charges.'

'It's all sounding very serious, Sue.'

'Of course it's serious; it's the law, but that doesn't mean we need to be quaking in our Italian leather heels.'

'What about this hotshot they've hired?'

'Hotshots don't scare me.'

That, Vera could believe. Sue would be more likely to be slipping them her phone number on a cocktail serviette. 'What do I do now?'

'Keep dusting flour off your hands and pinning your apron on, or whatever it is professional women do when they abandon their careers and go on a mountain change. I'll be in touch.'

Vera frowned. 'Sue, I run a caf—'

Too late. Her lawyer was gone.

Taking a breath, Vera reached forward, lifted the glass, and tossed her aunt's nip of sherry down her throat like she was an outlaw in the Wild West. Rock bottom it was.

Sighing, she dropped the phone back into her bag, then moved to tuck the rug in a little more firmly over Jill's knees. Her fingers paused as they rubbed over the bland beige of the hospital-issue blanket. Her aunt hated beige. She loved colour, loads of it, all clashing and lurid and loud as squabbling parrots. When she got home, she should dig through those boxes once she had the evening's baking in the oven, find something a little more fun to keep her aunt warm.

Keeping busy was the best way she knew to keep her mind off her problems.

Her aunt patted her hand and the gesture was so missed, so very very welcome, she felt tears rush to her eyes.

'Thank you, Barb,' said her aunt.

Vera, she wanted to yell. I am *Vera*. Instead, she stretched her legs out in front of her and crossed her booted feet. 'Shall I read you your letter?' she said in a voice of forced calm. 'It's from me ... I mean, it's from your niece, Vera.'

Jill didn't answer, just continued to stare up at the mountains darkening the late afternoon sky.

Vera pulled the folded sheets from her bag and started reading. Maybe some part of her aunt's brain was listening, and enjoying hearing what the niece she'd given up her independence for was doing to rebuild her life.

'*Dear Aunt Jill,*' she read. '*It's done. Our café is open …*'

CHAPTER

4

The pups woke him.

Josh stared, bleary-eyed, at his watch and winced. He'd dropped onto his bed at two am after a callout to a calving, and unless he'd strapped his watch on upside down—always a possibility when you were cleaning yourself up in a paddock using the beam from your ute's headlights to see—the hour hand was on the wrong side of seven.

Way too early to be getting up after a night on call.

The pups must have had a different agenda, because he'd barely shut his eyes again when their fretting sounds moved from mild to miserable. Who knew eight little snouts no bigger than thimbles could generate so much noise? Where were earplugs when he needed them?

'All right,' he muttered. 'I'm coming.'

A brown face with tired brown eyes was peering up at him from the bottom of the stairs when he left his flat.

'Jane Doe,' he said, heading down to her. 'What are you doing out here?'

The old dog thumped her tail against the newel post in reply.

She gave a groan of appreciation as he ran her ears through his fingers, then trotted off in the direction of the sleepover room, turning after a few steps to check he was following.

'I'm coming,' he said, his curiosity piqued. 'Have you got something to show me?'

Jane Doe's chocolate rump disappeared into the gloom of the room where they housed their overnight guests, and the yipping noises of her pups went up an octave.

Considering their eyes and ears were not yet open, Jane's young hooligans were adept at knowing when their mum—and the comfort of their next feed—was close.

He peered into the whelping box, smiling at the cluster of anxiously squirming bodies. 'What are you waiting for, Jane Doe? I'm counting eight little fluff-bundles pretty keen to latch—'

Wait. Not eight, but seven. Where was the jumbo brown one?

'Bloody hell, Jane, well spotted.' He went to the door and flicked on the strip of overhead lighting, ignoring the outraged hiss from the recently neutered cat in Cage Six. Where could one plump, barely mobile pup get to in a metre-square box?

Jane had climbed into the whelping box and was pointing her nose into the back corner, where the plywood rim bumped up against the mesh of the large cage. 'Down there, is he?' he said, and he dropped to his knees and crawled his way into the box to have a look.

Aha! One missing pup. He dug his fingers into the crevice until they'd surrounded the furry lump and levered it upwards. 'You okay, buddy?'

A pink tongue lolled out of the pup's mouth, and it yawned hugely.

'Getting stuck seems to be your favourite thing to do.'

He plopped the pup down with its brothers and sisters, and Jane rewarded him with a lick to his hand.

'You're welcome,' he said. 'And don't worry, I'll whack a bit of timber beading down that hole so we don't lose him again.'

He settled on to the shredded paper next to them and Jane rested her head on his ankles and looked up at him lovingly while her puppies fed.

'You're doing a good job, old girl,' he said.

'Talking to your extended family?' said a voice from behind him.

He turned to see Hannah standing in the doorway, buried in bright orange polka dot pyjamas that he didn't think his retinas could deal with before coffee.

'Lost pup drama. It's all sorted now.'

'Good. Because I was counting on at least another hour's sleep.'

'You and me both. I was up half the night delivering a calf out past Crackenback.'

Hannah grinned. 'God, I love having a junior partner.'

'Remind me to smirk next time you're on call and have to spend the night in a freezing ditch.'

His sister laughed. 'It's a deal. Whose calf was it?'

'The Lyndon place. Hobby farmers, so they were a little anxious about letting their pet cow go into labour without a vet on hand.'

'Hobby farmers,' snorted Hannah.

'Now now, we didn't all have the luxury of growing up in gumboots.'

'Yeah yeah. Maybe I should send them a bill this morning while they're still feeling like proud hobby parents.'

He grinned, and took his time checking on the pups and refreshing their bedding before leaving them to snooze in the sleepover room and following his sister to the office. He'd take middle-of-the-night calvings over doing the bills any day of the week. By the time he got there, Hannah was rifling through files in a way guaranteed to raise the ire of their receptionist.

'I'm ducking out for a coffee, Han. You want one?'

'I'd love one. You want to take those lost dog flyers with you? They're cluttering up the printer and you know I can't deal with mess.'

'Excuse me? You're the messiest person I know.'

'True. Okay, I can't deal with other people's mess. I have a system; it just looks like chaos to the uninitiated.'

He took the pile of flyers Hannah handed him and the photo of Jane Doe stared up at him. Maybe he should pick her up a bone from the butcher while he was out. Take her for a walk down to the lake later, so she could sniff at tree bark and chase ducks ... have herself a well-earned mumma-dog break.

He patted his pocket and the jingle of a pile of coins rewarded him. 'My budget would stretch to a sausage roll or a lamington. You hungry?'

Hannah groaned. 'Don't tempt me with naughty stuff. I'm revving myself up into a health binge.'

No problem. He'd be sure to dust the crumbs from his shirt before he returned.

The old timber door closed behind him and he dragged in a breath of country air. The first day of spring had come and gone, and the promise of warmth hung in the breeze. God he'd missed this place—the perfect peace of early mornings in the shadow of the mountains. Gossip be damned, he'd made the right choice coming home. He just hoped like hell it was the right choice for Poppy too.

'Joshua Preston Cody, bless my heart, it really is you.'

He looked up, met the inquisitive gaze of a tiny little woman wearing a pink and white flowery dress, and groaned inwardly. Trust him to time his outing to run into Mrs LaBrooy, who was the undisputed Hanrahan gossip queen despite the fact she lived a forty-minute drive out of town. She was also one of his favourite people in all the world.

'Mrs LaBrooy, you've not aged a day.'

She let him kiss her cheek then held him close while she gave him the once-over. 'Still charming the ladies, Josh. There were hearts aplenty broken when you left Hanrahan.'

He patted her hand. 'One of them mine, Mrs LaBrooy. I never forgot you.'

She chuckled. 'Or my apple pie, I'll be thinking. You come visit when you're settled, I know Tom'll be itching to see you. Bring that sister of yours with you. I miss her since she quit visiting the stables.'

He took a step back when Mrs LaBrooy paused, and zeroed in on her face. 'Hannah used to visit Ironbark Station? I didn't know she was looking after the stock horses.' He certainly hadn't seen their files. Or, now he thought about it, any plump cheques being deposited from the deep coffers of the Krauss family. He cocked his head. 'Is there something going on I don't know about?'

'Oh, pet, just forget I said that, will you? Tell me about yourself. Where's that precious little babe of yours?'

Fine. He'd grill Hannah later. If she wanted her junior partner to keep doing the daily coffee run for her, she could tell him what was going on between her and the up-country station where Mrs LaBrooy was housekeeper.

He slid his hand under Mrs LaBrooy's arm and walked with her down Dandaloo and across the pretty park that formed the town's centre. 'Poppy's no little babe anymore. Fifteen now.'

'Fifteen? Never say it.'

He grinned. 'I know, right? Her last birthday clocked over and it was like the gates of hell opened. Sass, eyeliner and obnoxious music all arrived in my life at once.'

She chuckled. 'Josh Cody, brought to his knees by his teenage daughter. Lordy me, how happy am I to see this day. And ... um ...'

Here it comes, he thought.

'And Beth?'

'Poppy's mother's doing fine. She's married to an architect, and they have twin sons that just started school. She's even back teaching.'

'Really? Teaching high school students? I would have thought that—'

He stopped her right there. 'Beth is my very good friend, Mrs LaBrooy. No-one criticises her in my hearing, is that clear?' He kissed her on her plump, vanilla-scented cheek. 'Not even dear old friends who've promised to bake me apple pie.'

She turned watery eyes on him. 'Josh, my love. You are so right. Accept the apologies of a foolish old busybody, won't you?'

He tucked her hand back under his arm. 'It's forgotten. I'm just on my way to get coffee. How about you take pity on a lonely thirty-something bachelor and join me?'

She giggled. 'Like a breakfast date?'

He laughed. 'Like I even remember what a date is. So, you're the expert. Where do we go to get the best coffee in town at this time of the day? Last time I was here, I was more of a chocolate milk from the servo kind of guy.'

Mrs LaBrooy gave his arm a squeeze. 'I know just the place. Remember the old bank building?'

He looked over at the lake end of the park, to the corner of Paterson and Curlew. 'Sure. Mr Pidgin, wasn't that the bank manager's name? Always wore a bow tie.'

'Fancy you remembering that.'

Josh ambled beside Mrs LaBrooy through the roses growing in their neat beds of mulch, past the pale marble cenotaph. There was Cody history there, too: Preston Wilfred Cody, his grandfather's uncle, lost to the Great War on the other side of the world when he wasn't much older than Poppy was now.

'I never forgot Hanrahan, Mrs L.'

'You must notice some changes, though.'

He smiled. 'Well, sure. The tourists, for a start. Who knew the place could be so busy either side of the ski season? There's always a bus or two parked along the road out to the Alpine Way, and people snapping photos of the ducks down along the Esplanade.'

'Have you seen the new development down on the southern out-skirts of town? Fifty houses, I heard. City people buying them up as weekenders. House prices have skyrocketed too.'

'I haven't driven down that way,' he murmured, his eyes on the distant ranges. This northern arm of Lake Bogong was narrow enough for him to see the grass plains on the far side of the lake, the stands of eucalypt hunched together like old men around a camp-fire. And above them, stark and rugged, the towering peaks of the Snowy Mountains. Snow still shone white in crevices and crags, and some huge raptor—a wedge-tailed eagle, perhaps—soared serenely from peak to peak. No-one who'd grown up here could have forgotten these mountains. This view.

'Here we are,' said Mrs LaBrooy, squeezing his arm. 'The Billy Button Café. The new owner used to be a big-city journalist. She's having herself one of those tree changes, I expect.'

Trust Mrs LaBrooy to have all the inside goss; this town didn't need a community section in its newspaper.

The café stood on the end of a row of terraced Federation-style buildings, with tall windows and deep stone windowsills. Aged red brick that had seen a century of summers gleamed behind the wrought iron of the upper storey's railings. The terraces looked like the shorter, younger siblings of the Victorian stone buildings on the opposite side of the park where the clinic was. Hanrahan had the gold rush to thank for the money that had been spent on the town's infrastructure in the late 1800s ... and fate to thank for being high enough to escape the flood when the Snowy River was dammed nearly a century later. He should take some photos, perhaps visit the local Historical Society museum; make sure the renovation plans he had for the Cody building were sympathetic to the era.

As they pushed open the heavy timber and glass door, Mrs LaBrooy leaned in to him.

'You're going to want to try the sourdough butterscotch donuts,' she said. 'I don't know how the new owner dreamed them up, because they're not like any donut I ever saw. Like a sugared ball, with a dimple, and that dimple just oozing with sticky sweet good-ness. Tom brought some home with him the other day. Are you listening to me, Josh Cody?'

But Josh wasn't listening. Hell, he wasn't even sure if his ears still worked. His thoughts had scattered, too, details of architraves and Federation fretwork and gyprock driven out by the vision splendid before him.

'Mrs LaBrooy, who is *that*?'

'Who is who? Oh. That's the new owner. Vera, she calls herself. Moved up here from Canberra, I think. Took up the lease on this place and had it all kitted out like an olden-day film set in no time at all. She's a worker, and boy, can she bake.'

Boy, could she catch the eye. His eye, that was for sure. Her face was pale, like an antique cameo, and he rather thought her eyes might be grey. She was lean—almost too thin—like an athlete who'd run herself too hard for a season, and her hair was a deep, chestnut brown.

As she turned, her eyes met his, just briefly, for one long breathless pause of looking, before she returned her attention to her neat, neat rows of cake.

'Good morning, welcome to The Billy Button Café. Would you like a table?'

Josh dragged his eyes off the woman placing food in the glass-fronted cabinet and settled them on the waiter by their side.

'Umm,' he said.

Mrs LaBrooy answered for him. 'A table for two. This handsome young man's invited me out on a date.'

The waiter grinned. 'In that case,' he said with a flourish of the white napkin in his hand, 'allow me to place you at our honeymoon table in the window. I'm Graeme. I'm the café manager.'

Whipping two menus from his catering apron as though he was performing a magic trick, he set them down on the starched tablecloth and whisked away a fallen petal from the table's vase of flowers. He held Mrs Labrooy's chair for her while she took a seat. 'I'll give you a minute to choose what you'd—'

'We're having the donuts,' said Mrs LaBrooy. 'And a latte for me, young man.'

'Well, aren't you a lamb. It's been a decade or two since anyone called me a young man. You come back again. Something for you, mate?'

Josh craned his head past the waiter, but the dark-haired woman had disappeared through swinging doors into what he presumed was a kitchen.

'Coffee? Tea? Table water?'

He felt the not-so-subtle point of Mrs LaBrooy's shoe jabbing him in the ankle and snapped his attention back to the waiter. 'I'll have the same.'

'Lattes and donuts coming up, Dr Cody.'

Josh tilted his head, took the time to look properly at the man serving them. Somewhere between his age and Mrs LaBrooy's, who had to be pushing seventy if she was a day. Fit, tanned, bald, neat. 'Do I know you?' Maybe the bald head was throwing him—he'd been gone for sixteen years, after all; a lot could happen to a guy's hairline in that time.

'Graeme Sharpe,' said the waiter, holding out his hand to shake Josh's. 'I've lived here in the district about a year. We've not met before, I just read your name tag: DR CODY, VETERINARIAN.'

Josh touched the badge buttoned to his work shirt. 'Call me Josh,' he said, shaking the manager's hand. 'And this is Mrs LaBrooy, housekeeper out at the Ironbark Station. She's also the town flirt, so guard your heart, Graeme. She's left a string of broken men from here to the coast.'

Mrs LaBrooy batted his arm, clearly enjoying the attention.

'You can flirt with me any day, love, I promise. I'll have those coffees and donuts with you in a tick,' said Graeme.

Half an hour later, as Josh wandered back into the vet clinic to see his first scheduled appointment for the day, he was still thinking about the dark-haired woman behind the counter. Mrs LaBrooy hadn't overstated the case about the new café owner's baking skills—he should have brought a batch of those sugary donuts back to the clinic for later—but it was the woman's face that had stayed with him. Not grey, but green, he thought. Her eyes had been the quiet green of alpine grass.

Too bad he didn't have time for romance. He'd have liked those eyes to rest on him a while longer.

He let himself in the door and there was his sister, hands on her hips, looking like a patient had just sprayed a hefty dose of cat pee on her top lip.

'Well?'

He frowned. 'Well what?'

'Where the hell's my coffee, Joshua Cody?'

Crap. *And* he'd forgotten to deliver the lost dog notices.

CHAPTER
5

'Hot vet alert.'

Vera was running a wire cutter through a plum and crème anglaise tart when Graeme sauntered behind her.

'Second visit today. But is it for the cakes or the cake baker?' he murmured.

She didn't need to look over her shoulder to know her café manager was waggling his eyebrows and doing a little shoulder shimmy. Graeme had missed his calling as a comedian; she'd laughed more this week since they'd opened the doors of The Billy Button Café than she had in months.

'He's all yours,' she said.

'Not this one, lovely. Had his eyes on you like gum on a shoe this morning.'

Her thumb slipped into the hazelnut crumb, and her eyes shot to the footpath they could see through the café windows. Surely not. Besides, it would be a dark day in hell before she'd be getting involved with a man again. A betrayed, bitter woman with a café business to build up and a prison sentence to face down did not chat up customers.

Not after the last disaster.

Graeme wasn't wrong about the hot factor, however ... even a people-challenged, down-on-her-luck café owner could see that. The man entering her café for the second time that day was hotter than her new six-burner commercial stovetop.

The vet was tanned and outdoorsy looking, as though he spent his weekends logging timber with his bare hands, or rock-climbing the famous escarpment on Old Regret. His tan didn't go at all with his close-cropped hair, though. The trim style made her think of the big-city lawyers who'd spent the last year screwing her out of virtually every dollar she'd saved, and most of her dignity.

'I'm the kitchen person; you're the people person, Graeme. That's why we make an awesome team. I'd rather peel potatoes than do the meet and greets.'

'Vera. If you want The Billy Button to be a success, you're going to have to play nice every now and then.'

Graeme was right, damn it. She lived in Hanrahan now, and this wasn't the outskirts of Canberra, where residents and tourists outnumbered coffee shops a zillion to one. Her café would need regulars to thrive during the off-season, which meant she needed to stop hiding behind her pots and pans and engage with people. Gritting her teeth, she kept her place behind the counter. She could do this.

'Hi,' he said.

She worked up a smile and hoped it looked genuine. 'Hi. I'm Vera. Would you like a table?'

'No, thanks.' He grinned, and she felt a little dizzy by the onslaught of all that handsome smileyness being directed straight at her. He was older than she'd first thought. Friendly eyes the colour of chocolate sauce, lashes the same hazelnut blond as his hair.

'I'm Josh Cody, from the vet clinic across the park.' He held his hand out over the counter.

She hesitated. She'd have thought nothing of shaking hands with strangers back when she worked at the newspaper. Executives, stay-at-home parents, small-business owners, sporting celebrities— she'd have shaken their hands, grilled them within an inch of their lives about whatever story she was pursuing, and marched on back to her desk to bash out an article without batting an eyelid.

But that was before.

She huffed out a breath, annoyed with herself. She was over-thinking this. She reached out and gripped his hand, then gave it a firm shake. Definitely spent his weekends hefting man tools, she thought. His hand was warm, strong, steady. Like a stone hearth in a homey country cottage.

Her skin clung to his as she drew away, and she realised too late her fingers were covered in powdered sugar and hazelnuts. She really should have stayed in the kitchen. 'Sorry. Sticky fingers ... it's an occupational hazard.'

He smiled, and her heart did that pit-a-pat thing she'd read about in novels.

'No problem.' He dug into his jacket pocket and pulled out a few sheets of paper. 'We've a lost dog at the clinic. I wondered if we could post a flyer in your window?'

She smoothed the paper out on the counter. A photo of a dog, contact information and phone numbers, and—shouting out loud and clear from the bottom of the flyer—the words *Cody and Cody Vet Clinic*. Oh, a husband-and-wife team, which was just as well ... she had no time to be having hot thoughts about Snowy Mountain vets.

Pull yourself together, Vera, she chided herself. She was exhausted, what with running out of coffee beans on opening day, and having the grease trap in the kitchen blow a fuse, and baking late into the night all week. The drama of the café's first week in business was clearly playing amuck with her brain function. She'd sold everything she owned and ditched Queanbeyan to work hard, find a new solitary life, and a place of peace and tranquillity for her aunt.

A clean slate.

Sizing up random married guys over cake crumbs and coffee grinds was an absolute no-no.

Taking a breath, she gave him the best customer relations smile she could muster. 'Sure. I'll put this straight up.'

'Appreciate it.'

She pulled some sticky tape out of the cubbyhole beneath the till, and made to walk around the counter, thinking he'd leave, but he perched on a stool and fixed his eyes on hers.

'How are you settling in?'

'Er ...' She tried to think of a response. It had been so long since she'd engaged in small talk, she almost blurted out the truth: she was anxious, she wasn't sleeping, she had to check her bank balance before every five-dollar purchase to make sure she didn't go into the red. 'So far so good,' she managed. 'This late September weather is a little chillier than I'm used to.'

'Yeah? Where did you move from?'

She swallowed, and wondered if she should edge past him towards the front window to bring this conversation to an end. The less anyone knew about where she was from, the better. 'The coast,' she said, waving her hand towards the front door as though that was an adequate answer.

'I just moved back myself.'

Yep, she was going to make a break for it to the window. She waggled the flyer in the air. 'That dog's owner could walk past any minute now. I'd better, um—'

His eyes crinkled in a way which ought to be banned for married guys, because now she was so flustered she'd dropped the sticky tape. She reached down for it but the chatty vet beat her to it. He dropped it into her hand, and she scooted past him to the window before he noticed the colour she could feel heating her cheeks.

He stopped in the café doorway as he headed back out into the sunlight. 'Welcome to Hanrahan, Vera. I'll see you around.'

'Sure,' she lied brightly, mindful of Graeme's instruction to play nice, while making a mental note to keep a wide distance between her and all the distracting vets in the district. 'See you.'

Vera successfully resisted the urge to watch Josh Cody disappear up Paterson Street.

'You see?' she said to the cloth she'd pulled out of her apron to polish the pane of glass beside the front door. 'This is how you stick to your goals. Discipline, hard work and averted eyes.'

She pushed the vet out of her thoughts as she fussed about with the flyer, wondering what the optimum height was so as to not interrupt her customers' view out. A noticeboard would be better for community flyers—something timber and ornate, maybe in the alcove on the side wall by the fireplace—with a bookshelf below it. A fern in a copper pot above the books would match the copper light fittings, and perhaps she could source some vintage photos of the historical buildings lining Hanrahan's pretty park ... create a fireside nook to encourage customers to linger.

The local school could pin up its fete notices, and maybe there was an amateur dramatic society who put on plays, sang Christmas carols in December, that sort of thing? The ski season on the upper slopes had come to an early end with the snowmelt a few weeks ago, but there'd be more events on the town's calendar. If she was still a free woman at the end of October, Halloween would be fun.

Pumpkin scones, she thought, as she taped the vet's flyer to the glass, would lure the Queensland tourists inside. Was that straight? She eyeballed the square edge against the windowsill. Nope. She peeled off the tape, adjusted the paper, tried again. The local kids might enjoy cupcakes decorated as little monsters, perhaps some olive and egg spiders.

She caught herself smiling at the thought of whipping up a batch of mulled wine, with dry ice and scary ping-pong eyeballs floating about in it. Maybe this café caper really was beginning to soothe her ragged nerves.

She jumped as a face popped up on the other side of the window and eyeballs, real ones, smiled at her from beneath an old-fashioned cloth cap.

'Bloody hell,' she muttered. Beside the elderly man towered a handsome woman wearing the largest and pinkest and dangliest— was that a word?—earrings she'd ever seen.

'Incoming customers, Graeme,' she called over her shoulder as she tucked the sticky tape into her apron pocket and made her way to the doorway. 'Look welcoming.' Like he had to be told. She plastered her happy café-owner face on and took a breath.

'Hello,' she said to the pair.

'You must be Vera. Let's take a look at you,' said the woman, reaching out and taking both of her hands. 'Isn't she a peach, Kev?'

'Ah, hello. Yes, I'm Vera. Welcome to The Billy Button Café.'

'Marigold Jones. I expect you've heard of me.'

The woman disconcerted her by batting eyelashes which might have been fake. It was hard to tell, what with all the green eye-shadow and the arthouse earrings and the acres and acres and *acres* of flowing leopard-print frock. The name did sound familiar though. Where on earth could she hav—

'Call me Marigold. We are going to be such friends, Vera. I knew it as soon as I saw your lovely sign. Wildflowers are my favourites, especially yellow billy buttons and pink triggers. You, my love, have taste. This is my husband, Kev.'

'Pleased to meet you. Are you … er … needing a table?'

The steamroller's attention had been claimed by the interior of the café, and she swooped from table to table, inspecting the cut-glass vases, pinching the white linen tablecloths, for all the world as though she was at an estate sale and wondering what to buy.

'I'll be taking a seat, Vera,' said Kev. 'Where do you want me?'

The café was empty, the last lunch-goers having left their empty plates and generous tips behind just moments ago. 'Take your pick, sir.'

'Now don't go calling me sir, you'll have Marigold thinking I'm getting old. Kev will do fine. Don't mind my wife, she's as nosy as she is good-hearted, and when she's finished deciding which of those fine-looking desserts she's going to let me buy her, she'll be right over.'

'Vera, my dear,' called his wife, 'what are you doing with this other room through the archway?'

Vera hurried from Kev's side, bemused. Small-town living took some getting used to, that was for sure. 'I haven't decided. The big table was already there when I took over the lease, but the area is a bit dark, even with the fresh paint. Maybe a private dining room eventually for groups of twelve or so? I thought I'd settle in to coffee and cake, breakfast and lunch, until I get a feel for how many people in Hanrahan are dropping in. Start simple, maybe build up a little when I know what I'm doing.'

'That's a good plan.'

'Thank you, I—'

'But it's not a great one. Now, you go and cut me and my Kev a slice of that fancy cake—the one with the layers and the toasted coconut—and bring us over a cuppa. I've got a new plan for you, and mine *is* a great one.'

Vera headed over to the counter and found pretty plates, a teapot. What was it about this town? 'Look out,' she muttered to Graeme. 'This new customer's even bossier than you.'

'Hush your mouth. *That* can't be true.' He looked over her shoulder and grinned. 'Ah, yes. I see you've met our prophet. Excellent.'

'Excuse me?'

'Marigold Jones. She was the one who told me I should apply for the job here. She's got the personality of a wind turbine, but she's a gem, Vera.'

'She's certainly talkative. I can see why you didn't say no when she suggested you get a job; you wouldn't have had a chance to.'

'Coffee? Tea? Milkshake? What's their poison today? I can make it for you while you get acquainted.'

She gave him a quelling look, which he waved away. 'Tea, Graeme, thank you. Two teacups. And would you mind making me an espresso? Something tells me I'm going to need it. Marigold's invited me to take afternoon tea with them ... and when I say invited, it was more like a commandment from the First Testament. She says she has *a plan*.'

'Go you, girl,' said Graeme, tamping down a dose of ground arabica beans, then sliding the portafilter into the machine. 'Mingling with the locals. You'll get the hang of this café business yet.'

'Mmm,' she muttered, and slid two slices of hummingbird cake onto the gold-rimmed plates. She debated for a mini-moment then shrugged. What were a few hundred calories here or there anyway? She cut a third slice, set them all out neatly on a tray. Worrying about her waistline was way, way down on her current list of worries.

'You'll have to let me know what you think of the cake,' she said, as she set the tray down on the table in the inner room where Marigold had settled herself like a CEO at a board table. 'It's my aunt's recipe.'

'Your aunt?' said Marigold. 'Now this is just the sort of detail I like to know about my new friends. Tell me more.'

Vera could feel frown lines dragging her eyebrows together and cast about for a way to deflect this line of questioning. She had no interest in filling in her life details for some random woman.

'Er ...' Poop. Where was a change of topic when she needed one?

Kev stepped in. 'Mags, my love, eat your cake and stop being nosy.'

She threw him a smile and relented. She could share a little, couldn't she, without the sky falling down? 'My aunt was quite a cook in her day, but she's elderly, and doesn't bake anymore. Using her recipes is a way for me to connect with her.'

'That's wonderful,' said Marigold, from around a mouthful of cake and cream. '*This* is wonderful.'

Vera felt her throat backing up and took a scalding sip of the espresso Graeme had slipped in front of her. 'You may know the aged care home she's just moved into,' she said when she could trust her voice. 'Connolly House, on the outskirts of Cooma.'

'A hospice.' Marigold reached across the table. 'My dear, I'm sorry. It's a lovely home for the terminally ill. Kev and I pop out there quite frequently, don't we?'

Kev gave her a wink. 'Mags is sizing me up for a room, I expect.'

Vera choked on a mouthful of toasted coconut shreds.

'Now look what you've done, Kev.' Marigold passed her a glass of water. 'Have a sip of that while we tell you our plan.'

'Hold your horses, love. Let her finish her cake.'

Vera took stock of her two eccentric guests. Kev was clearly older by a good margin; his skin had creased into leather the shade of aged pine floorboards. Close-cut grey hair curled tightly beneath his dark green corduroy cap. The clothes he wore hadn't been in fashion for thirty years—a wide-legged brown suit, a cream shirt ironed to perfection, a tie that a seventies hippy would have been proud to wear to a revolution.

Marigold was only slightly less dramatic looking when seated. Her massive updo had streaks of grey through it, but the streaks were theatrical, as though an artist had painted them in with a flourish. Vera couldn't remember meeting a woman oozing more personality than Marigold Jones.

'So,' she said. 'What's this grand plan?'

Kev puffed his chest out. 'It was my idea.'

She smiled. 'Okay, and it involves …?'

Marigold reached across to his plate and spooned up the last inch of his cake. 'It's true. Kev pretends he's the quiet one, but there's a lot of action going on beneath that old cap.'

For a second Vera wished she was a teenager again, so she could roll her eyes. 'And yet, here I sit, still clueless.'

'It's a long story,' said Marigold.

'Give her the short version,' said Kev. 'Girl's got a business to run.'

His wife nodded. 'You're right. Okay, here's the thing. Kev and I are on the committee of the Hanrahan and District Community Association. We have a hall down at the southern end of the

Esplanade; it's one of the oldest buildings in town and dates back to 1870. It's in the parkland beside the historic town cemetery, and council leases the building to us on the condition we keep it restored. The community hall was the courthouse back when this district was a gold rush town, and we've all put in a lot of work refurbishing it back to its glory days. The cemetery, too ... it has some treasures we look after: notable headstones, a few pioneers, even a woman who legend says was hanged for bushranging.'

Kev cleared his throat. 'Even more exciting than the bushranger ... there's the roses.'

His wife patted his hand. 'Yes, Kev does the roses. Problem with historic buildings, though, is they don't keep pace with change. We've just had to close the hall to functions while we get some emergency repair work done. Turned the lights on yesterday and you'd have thought Lucifer himself was tap dancing in the wiring.'

Kev nodded. 'Sparked like diesel chucked into a bonfire.'

'The electrician says we can't use it until we've had the ceiling down and the lights rewired.'

Vera nodded. 'Okay. You can't use your hall.'

'Mrs Juggins is the problem.'

She pursed her lips. She should so have let Graeme handle this. 'Mrs who?'

'Hold your horses, Marigold. The girl's not a local; she doesn't know about the Jugginses.'

The woman gave her husband's hand a pat.

'Mrs Juggins is tucked up in her coffin at the funeral home waiting for us to send her off. She was one of ours, a community hall regular who ran our craft stall for, golly, I don't know how long. Ever since I sold up the florist shop, and that's been a goodly number of years now.'

'Umpteen, shouldn't wonder,' said Kev.

'Is umpteen a number, love?'

Kev scratched his head. 'More than ten, at any rate.'

Vera coughed, just gently, and forced herself not to look at her watch. The lamb shanks in her kitchen crockpot must be calling her name by now, begging to be rescued. 'Mrs Juggins in her coffin,' she prompted.

'Funeral's next week to allow for her daughter to get back here from London,' said Marigold. 'Thursday, half past ten. The tea-and-cake afters should have been in our hall an hour later, but the wiring's thrown a spanner in that idea. We need a venue that can cater a function after the funeral. And all the functions coming up until our hall gets the devil stripped out of its wiring. Your back room is perfect. We move the table to the side and set up a buffet, bring a couple of chairs in for the folks who aren't so steady on their pins, the rest can stand. We'll fit thirty in here at a pinch.'

Vera nodded. Next Thursday gave her a chance to set up a menu, think through her supplies of milk and tea and heaven knew what else. And what an opportunity to bring some locals in to sample what The Billy Button Café had to offer! 'I might need to borrow some of your hall's cups and saucers—I'd struggle to keep thirty sets clean and have customers in the main room being served too.'

Kev gave a satisfied humph. 'Knew this was a great idea.'

'Now then, Kev. Save your bragging for when you've brought a load of crockery over here in the ute. Maybe the big urn, too. Some of our regulars can drink tea like it's bingo juice.'

Vera needed a pen, paper, maybe a spreadsheet. She'd need to bring forward her plan to secure a waitperson, too. Perhaps a teenager? 'Chicken ribbon sandwiches. Mini lamingtons, mini quiches, perhaps a fruit cake and a gluten-free slice. That sort of thing?'

'Perfect. And don't you be thinking we'll be skimping on payment. A hardworking girl with a business to run needs cash as well as the next person. Kev can go rustle up some crockery while you and I crunch numbers.'

Vera smiled. 'Marigold, I'm beginning to see why Graeme was so happy to see you drop in today. You were right. My plan was good, but your plan is way, way better.'

CHAPTER

6

'The complaint says *what*?' Josh looked into the cup of coffee he'd made for himself and wondered what was off: the milk, or his culinary skills. He'd worked ten-hour days for a week straight and been called out during the night a half-dozen times. His pantry was so bare, soon he'd be eating microwaved rice for breakfast. And lunch. And dinner.

'Some by-law about farming chickens in urban areas within five metres of another dwelling.'

'Farming chickens? Here at the vet clinic? Is this some sort of joke?'

The receptionist, Sandy, poked her head through the door of the back office, where he and Hannah had been holed up since what felt like dawn having a read-the-mail-and-make-decisions meeting. 'Hannah? Your seven o'clock is here.'

'Thanks, Sandy, I'll be right there.'

His sister shoved the letter into his hand then plucked a stethoscope from the shelf and hung it around her neck. 'Here, you read it. It's from the local council, official letterhead and everything. I don't know what they're on about. The only chicken we've had here in months has come in a takeaway box from House of Fu, wrapped in a blanket of hoi sin sauce and nestled in a bed of steamed pak choi.'

'Maybe it's a mistake.'

'Can you contact council? I've got a full surgical list from now until the funeral.'

He frowned. 'What funeral?'

His sister made a snort-like noise that sounded remarkably like a pug sneezing. 'Josh! It's on the calendar. Today, ten-thirty, Mrs Juggins. You better be free.'

He raised his hands. 'I'm free.' He'd been hoping to catch up on some much needed sleep, or at least get a head start on the drafting plans for the building renovation, but Hannah was giving him the look that suggested he better be free or else.

He followed her into the main treatment room. 'This complaint, is it a one-off? Any other trouble with council I need to know about?'

'No. We're model citizens ... although, better check the date on our business licence, Josh, before you call. It's in a frame behind Sandy's desk. I think it's current, but we don't want to send you in to council to shoot the lights out only to end up with egg on your face.'

'Wow,' he said. 'That's about five clichés in one sentence, Han.'

She chuckled. 'That's why I studied science at uni, big brother. Words are so not my thing.'

'I'll go see them. Don't worry, I've got this.'

'I knew I hired a junior partner for a reason.'

He pulled her ponytail and left her to it. Visit to the council office, power nap, funeral. Looked like his day off was filling up.

Vera twisted the posy of daisies so their yellow heads nodded towards the sun streaming in through the window, then looked up as the bell on the door jangled.

Ah. Marigold. The whirlwind herself.

'Good morning,' she said. 'We don't usually see you this early.'

'Rushed through my yoga class, my love,' said Marigold. 'Busy day, lots to do; thought I'd pop in and check all was in order for our little function later.'

Jeepers. Marigold looked like she was about to whip out a clipboard and start doing a food and safety inspection. She'd triple-checked everything, hadn't she? Food handling certificate on display, bathrooms pristine and ventilated, premises thoroughly clean. Sure there was a cat who occasionally rested his paws on the step to the back alley, but she'd never let it in the kitchen.

She couldn't afford a fine. Or notoriety. Or another brush with the law. She felt her heart rate skip into overdrive. 'I'm pretty sure we have everything ready. Come through to the back room, Marigold. We're just about set up and we have all the appropriate licences, I assure you. There's wheelchair access on the—'

'In a minute, my love.' Marigold was hovering over the display cabinet. 'First, tell me about these delicious-looking bundles of goodness.'

Oh! Heavens … Vera forced herself to relax. Marigold wasn't here to judge her. 'Er, sure,' she said. Talking about her baking was something she could totally do. 'Up top we keep the staples the tourists gravitate to, the old-fashioned favourites: chocolate caramel slice, vanilla slice, ginger slice. The shelf below is where we get a bit adventurous. There's a paleo slice with carob and nuts, a baked plum and crème anglaise tart, Portuguese custard tarts. Savoury items are at this end: pork pies, zucchini and feta muffins, tomato galettes. Which takes your fancy?'

Marigold fussed about in her pockets and brought out a handful of gold coins. 'I stopped listening when I heard the word ginger, so it had better be that one.'

'I'll plate it up. Do you want to take it through to the back room so you can see the preparations we've made for the wake?'

Marigold waved a hand. 'My love, I just wanted to make sure you didn't need a hand. If you're sure you're okay, I'll just perch here at the counter, that way I can eat and talk.'

Vera was pretty sure Marigold could eat and talk no matter where she was sitting, but she slid a piece of ginger slice onto one of the vintage plates she'd bought at the local op shop and set it down in front of the woman. 'Cup of tea, too?'

'Better not. The funeral service is at ten-thirty, and the old bladder isn't what it was. The bereaved get a bit testy when the celebrant ducks off to spend a penny halfway through the ceremony.'

Wait ... what? 'You're doing the ceremony, too? I thought you were just organising the wake.'

Marigold's bangles jangled on her arm as she lifted a forkful of ginger slice. 'I'm a celebrant, Vera. I'm performing the ceremony.'

'Oh! For some reason ... gosh, this is awkward, I thought—'

'You thought I was retired? An elderly lady of leisure, just puddling about in Hanrahan putting my nose into everyone's business because I'd run out of socks to darn?'

The wink Marigold dropped in her direction took the sting from her words, but Vera reached down into the cabinet and pulled out a slice of tart for herself. She needed a calorie fix.

'I suppose I did,' she said. 'Pretty ageist of me, wasn't it?'

Marigold chuckled. 'I think you need to pop on down and join my yoga class, Vera. Every morning at dawn, spring through autumn, on sunrise. Keeps me young at heart. But, you aren't totally wrong. I *did* retire. I had a florist shop in Cooma back in the day, which is how I became an expert on weddings. And funerals, now I think about it.'

Something was tugging at Vera's memory. 'Graeme told me he knew a florist; he must have meant you. Do we have you to thank for the fresh flower delivery he organised?'

'That boy is almost as cunning an operator as I am. I put him in touch with the couple who bought my business. Mates rates,' she said. 'I send bridal business their way, so they like to keep me sweet.'

Vera smiled. 'I'm very grateful. The tables are so pretty with the touch of pink and yellow. Do you do much, er, bridal business?'

Marigold scraped her fork over her plate to gather up the last crumbs. 'One a month, I suppose. Funerals the same. The weddings tend to be out-of-towners who fancy a wedding in the alps. The funerals are locals. Usually people Kev and I have known for donkeys.'

'That explains ...' Vera paused.

'What, honey?'

'Oh, it's just, when we first met, you mentioned you and Kev visit Connolly House a bit. Where my aunt is.'

Marigold rested a ring-heavy hand on hers. 'I do funeral services there, yes. There's a chapel for those that like a reverend to see them off, and celebrants are welcome to use it. I potter about with the relatives of the deceased, and Kev takes roses from his bushes at the hall and does a bit of flower arranging with the residents who enjoy that sort of thing. Is this going to be difficult for you today, Vera? Having a funeral wake here? Is it too close to home?'

'No. It's fine, really.'

'Because we can farewell Joyce in the park; you just say the word.'

Vera blinked away the sting in her eyes. 'You're very kind, Marigold.'

Marigold gave her hand a squeeze. 'You just remember that later when I'm bossing you around.'

CHAPTER

7

Josh knew the power nap wasn't going to happen the second he walked back into the clinic. Sandy must have heard him come through the private foyer which led upstairs, because the door to the reception area flung open and she was standing there, with a pleading look on her face which did not bode well for his plans.

'Josh, best boss ever, you got a minute?'

He supposed he did. And being called boss did still send a thrill up his spine. 'Sure, what's up?'

'I need to run to the bank, and Hannah's tied up, and—' She angled her eyebrows to the waiting room behind her, to where a chubby-kneed kid sat huddled in a chair. 'We have a goldfish emergency.'

'A what?'

Sandy lowered her voice to a whisper. 'Might be dead. Kid's used half a box of tissues already trying to stop snivelling.'

'Seriously. A fish.'

'Yeah. Ovoid in shape, has a tail, breathes through gills.'

Josh narrowed his eyes. 'Snarky remarks mean I get to have a jellybean from the reception jar; you know that, Sandy.'

She winked at him. 'The crying fish kid beat you to them. Go on, see what you can do, can you?'

'But I'm so inexperienced,' he said. 'Surely this is a job for our most senior vet?'

'Nice try, hotshot.' She turned her head and called over her shoulder. 'Sarma? This is Dr Cody. He's going to take a look at your pet.'

He sighed. 'There better be some more beans in that jar when I next come out here, Sandy, that's all I'm saying.'

She gave him a pat on the shoulder like he was a truculent toddler. 'Bank and jellybeans, you leave it with me. I won't be long.'

She headed out to the street with the haste of an army retiring from battle, and he turned to the kid, who'd stood up, and was now looking at him with hope in her eyes and a plastic bag clutched to her front. When had Poppy last looked at him like that ... like he could solve every problem and would never disappoint her?

Had it been weeks? Months? Certainly not since he'd first brought up the idea of moving back to Hanrahan. He had to believe he'd made the right decision, moving home. It would just be a hell of a lot easier to believe if Poppy would agree to pay him a visit.

'Can you fix my fish, Dr Cody?'

He gave the kid a reassuring smile. 'Call me Josh. I hope so.'

'I put my moneybox on the counter. I dunno how much is in there, because my brother took the key when he was torturing me.'

'Oh? Your brother torture you often?'

The girl rolled her eyes. 'Do sheep have dirty butts?'

He grinned. Sarma, whoever she was, had a flair for the dramatic. 'You know, I have a sister, too. I used to play all sorts of pranks on her when we were little.'

She stopped sniffling long enough to look up at him. 'Oh yeah? Like taking her teddy bears and tying them to pretend train tracks and sending her ransom notes? That kind of stuff?'

He steered her into the last treatment room and wrestled the plastic bag from her sweaty grip. 'Exactly that kind of stuff.'

'Huh.'

'You know what my sister did to me once?' he said.

'No. What?'

'Put a lizard in my bed.'

She giggled. 'No way.'

'Yes way. Not that I'm recommending you do the same, mind you. Now, what,' he said, holding the bag up to the light, 'seems to be the problem with this fish?'

'Starsha.'

'Excuse me?'

'That's her name. Starsha. She's not eating her food, and she's just doing nothing.'

'Let's get her out of this bag. Fish breathe oxygen out of the water, and there's not enough water in this bag to keep her going for long. We can use a glass snake tank for the time being, but this is where we need to have a serious talk.'

'About dying?'

Josh cleared his throat. He'd forgotten how direct young kids could be.

'Yes. Your goldfish—Starsha—is not my usual kind of patient. Fish are tricky to treat because we can't take an x-ray of them, or feel their muzzle to see if they're dehydrated, or listen to their heart with a stethoscope … that sort of thing.'

Did fish even *have* hearts? He wondered how unprofessional it would look if he turned to his computer and googled *How to tell if my goldfish is alive.*

'Just do your best, Josh.' Sarma sat herself in a chair and looked at him expectantly, her eyelashes wet with tears.

He sighed. Water. Neutralising agent. No sudden change of temperature. That would have to do for a start. He ran his eyes over the row of textbooks and science journals stacked in the shelving above the desk and settled on the battered copy of *The Australian and New Zealand Vet Companion*.

He flicked the child a look. 'Can you read, Sarma?'

She frowned at him in a way that made him think fondly about strapping teddy bears to fake train tracks. 'Of course I can read. I'm *nine*.'

'Look up goldfish in this index, will you, Sarma, while I fill the tank and get the temperature adjusted. Let's get Starsha a new clean home with plenty of oxygen in it. We can work on her lack of energy and appetite later. You cool with that?'

Sarma slipped off the chair and marched up to the desk like a warrior preparing for action. 'G for goldfish. That comes after F, right?'

He had to resist the urge to give her a hug. Plucky and cute. Just like Poppy used to be.

'Yeah,' he said. 'That's right. Let's see what we can do for your pet.'

❧

An hour later, Josh was staring at his reflection in his sister's new bathroom mirror. The bevelled glass fixture was a fine piece of work, rising from the hip-height marble counter to disappear into the decorative plasterwork of the cornice. He should know— he'd nearly broken eight fingers installing it.

'Tell me why we're going to this again?'

'Mrs Juggins's sausage dog, Henry, was one of my first customers. And, owing to the ridiculous quantity of biscuits, sausages and well-buttered vegemite toast triangles she kept feeding him, he was one of my fattest customers, which meant he was a frequent visitor. His vet bills probably paid for the x-ray machine.'

Josh's fingers paused on the blue silk of his tie. 'The bunny ran under the tree. No, down the hole and over the tre— Damn it. Where's YouTube when you need it? I can't believe I've forgotten how to fasten a tie.'

'Come here, you big lump.'

Hannah swivelled him round to face her. 'Crouch down a bit.' She flipped the tie into position, then pulled his collar straight above it. 'Any luck at the council office?'

'Some clerk made me wait for an hour, then let me fill in a form and cut me loose. The local councillor's out of town for a few days, so I've booked an appointment for next week.'

'Barry O'Malley? Our local member?'

'Yeah. I grabbed his business card and stuck it to the noticeboard in the office.'

'I guess that's something.' She smoothed the top buttonhole in his shirt then stood back. 'You scrub up okay, big brother.'

He grinned. 'That's more than I can say for you. Do you even own clothes that aren't made of denim?'

'Some. Maybe. I think. Why?' She looked into the mirror, fussed a little with the neckline of her no-nonsense navy blouse.

He pulled her ponytail. He should have known better than to poke fun at Hannah for what she wore, so he covered his gaffe with a comment guaranteed to annoy her so much she'd forget the clothes question.

'Wonder if Tom Krauss will be there? Haven't seen him since I moved back to town.'

Hannah suddenly grew very busy fixing a string of bright orange beads around her neck. 'What are you doing in my bathroom, anyway? You've got your own flat. Downstairs.'

'I don't have a mirror. Or hot water. Or furniture.'

She snorted. 'Heaven forbid Hanrahan's prodigal son should rock up to an elderly lady's funeral with his hair mussed up.'

'Ouch,' he said, grinning. 'Come on, let's get outta here before someone brings us another depressed goldfish.'

Hannah giggled. 'That was so sweet. I had to get Sandy to pinch my arm to stop me from laughing.'

He grimaced. 'The dizzy heights of a small-town vet practice. And me just a first year, too. I'm surprised you let me handle such a tricky case as overfeeding.'

His sister clattered down the stairs ahead of him. 'Well, Sandy said it seemed like more of a kid issue than a pet issue. And you're the expert there, Dr Dad.'

Yeah. Such an expert his own daughter was giving him the run-around. School holidays had started and still no word of a visit. 'Don't let Poppy hear you say that. Ever since she turned fifteen she's developed this epic expression of utter disdain. Let's not give her an excuse to use it.'

He grabbed his jacket from the hook by the door. 'You want yours?'

'No thanks. It's warm enough out.'

'I heard the wake's on at the new café. Hopefully no-one will call before I get to sample the buffet. I'm starving.'

'Thinking with your stomach. How very like you. Come on, we don't want to be late; Marigold will give us The Look if we interrupt her service.'

'Marigold Jones,' Josh said with relish. 'Kev still kicking?'

'Of course. The two of them still gambol about like spring lambs. Love or yoga—one of the two—is keeping them young.'

'Which one, I wonder?' said Josh, as he held the back door open for Hannah.

'I wouldn't know,' she said as she passed him.

'Yeah,' he muttered to himself. 'I wouldn't know either.'

❧

The funeral was sweet. From the heart, as anything was when Marigold Jones officiated, and poignant. Sadness emanated from the bowed shoulders of Mr Juggins, alone in the front row but for Kev, who had the knack for knowing just where he was needed most.

The Jugginses had run the garage out near the local primary school for years. He could remember George Juggins as a younger man in green-stained overalls, rolling out from under a car to offer up some old-fashioned service at the fuel bowsers. His wife had managed the store and sold soft drinks and hot pies to schoolkids passing by who were lucky enough to have a few bucks in their pocket.

By the time the small crowd had made it from the cemetery down near the lake to the private room of The Billy Button Café, the general air of decorum had dissipated, leaving the older towns-folk to resume the chitter-chatter and story-swapping of people who'd known each other half a century or more.

He'd missed this. The sense of belonging, of being known. He'd thought Poppy had finally been willing to give it a try, but her school holiday was about a third over and there was still no sign of her.

No phone calls, either, and even the surly text messages had dried up. She was ghosting him, and every day she didn't arrive, his hope grew dimmer.

He hadn't missed all the country-kiss greetings, though. He'd been kissed by so many old biddies in the last hour, he was sure he had coral lipstick stripes on his cheeks: the wife of his old Scout Leader, the lady who ran the bowling alley where he'd hung out after school some nights, even Marigold had cornered him, demanding to know why he'd not found the time to drop by. She'd slipped him her yoga schedule for dawn stretches in the park.

Yeah. Like that would happen.

The one pair of female lips in the room that hadn't made their way to his cheek were currently on duty by the tea urn. He let his eyes dwell on them for a minute. Soft. The colour of pinot noir in a glass held to the sun. Kissable.

'If you're sick of the tea, mate, I can make you a coffee that'll strip the hairs from your chest.'

Josh turned to the waiter he'd met the other day. 'Graeme, isn't it? Better not. I've already had about six cupcakes. I won't fit into my scrubs.'

His eyes wandered back over to Vera. She stood apart from the crowd, looking … he thought it over, tried to find the right word. Unsettled? Anxious?

'Girl can cook,' said Graeme in his ear.

'Mmm,' he said, but before he could wonder if he was embarrassed about being caught staring at the waiter's boss, Vera picked up a plate of salmon blinis from the buffet table and began passing them around.

The crowd shifted, Graeme disappeared to collect glasses, and before he knew what was what, she was standing right before him.

She was even more breathtaking up close. Colour warmed her cheeks, throwing the paleness of her skin into sharp relief. She'd tied her hair back into some sort of braid, but wisps of it had escaped, softening the formal black suit she wore.

'Blini?' she said.

'Josh.'

'Excuse me?'

'Just reminding you what my name is.'

She sighed, a quick in-out-in that made him wonder if she'd noticed him in the same breath-seizing way that he'd noticed her.

'I know your name. I really should keep serv—'

Before she could move on, Marigold began tapping a teaspoon against a pink and white floral teacup.

'Can I have your attention, everyone. Everyone! George thanks you all for coming here today to celebrate the life of his wife, Joyce.'

Josh surreptitiously glanced at his watch. He was due back at the surgery in ten minutes, and Marigold Jones wasn't famous throughout the whole Snowy River region for her brevity.

'Our friend, Joyce Juggins, was unwell for some months, but still found time to worry about how George was going to cope after she passed. She and I planned out this gathering between us, and she asked me to read a little something here.'

'Oh boy,' muttered a voice behind Josh. He turned to see Kev right behind him. He raised his eyebrows at the old man and received a wink in return. What was Marigold up to now?

'*Dear George,*' she read out. '*I want you to look around you today and see all the lovely folk of Hanrahan who've come to see me off. They're here for me, but they're here for you too, and they're getting my sincere thanks for it. You make note of all these faces, George, and when you're feeling lonely, you know who you can go visit. I've baked some casseroles for you and they're in the freezer—*'

The crowd gave a laugh, and even Mr Juggins seemed to see the funny side of his beloved wife still caring for him from the grave.

'—and I want you to promise me you're going to take up a hobby. You can take on my role up at the community hall, or join the Men's Shed down in Cooma. Something with people, okay? Pottering about with your tomato seedlings doesn't count. Promise me now, out loud, in front of all these good people.'

Marigold looked up at old George expectantly. 'Well? What do you say, George? Have we got your promise?'

George cleared his throat. 'Bloody women.'

'I know, pet,' she said. 'And I'm taking that as a yes, and don't worry about deciding on your hobby, I've decided for you. I've had an idea.'

A bony finger poked Josh in the back. 'Really, it was my idea,' whispered Kev.

He heard a little snort beside him, and caught Vera hiding a grin behind her hand. So. The new café owner had a sense of humour, did she? If he didn't have Poppy and Hannah and the future of his just-started vet career to worry about, he would have liked to get to know Vera a little better. He let his eyes rest on her face, on the dark sweep of lashes hiding serious eyes, the generous curve of mouth … yeah, a *lot* better.

He tuned back in to Marigold, who had a head of steam up now. 'The Hanrahan and District Community Association is having a few hiccups at present, as I'm sure most of you know. Our hall is closed for renovations, and Vera'—she smiled her thanks at Vera, who stood beside him, blini tray in hand, reminding him of a roo paralysed by a set of high beam headlights—'has made us welcome. So welcome, in fact, that as President of the Community Association, I have made a decision. I think that instead of postponing our weekly craft meetings until the hall is back in use, we should move it right here into The Billy Button Café's back room. Once a week, like always, Wednesday evenings. And you, George, can bring along Joyce's unfinished craft projects and do yourself and the world a favour by joining in.'

'Oh, hell,' muttered The Billy Button Café's lucky proprietor by his side. He glanced at her, ready to offer a commiserating smile at the way she'd been roped in so sneakily by Marigold, when his attention was snagged by the spectacle beyond her, staring in at him through the street-facing windows.

He'd know that kilt anywhere. Hideous orange, with a broad black plaid, teamed with stockings you could use to catch fish and a blouse that had so little fabric it'd struggle to catch a butterfly.

The tortured goth look he could cope with, but there was something new, something glinting silver amid the heavy eyeliner and powder plastered on his daughter's face. Christ almighty, Poppy had a ring sprouting out of one of her eyebrows.

Oh, hell was about right.

The door to The Billy Button Café swung shut behind Josh and he inspected the glowering face of his daughter.

'Hey,' he said.

'Six hours and fifty-eight minutes,' Poppy fired at him. 'You said it would take five hours tops.'

'Do I get a hug? Or are we moving straight into the bickering? I'm fine with either.'

'Idiot,' Poppy said, and then she stepped forward and he wrapped his arms around her.

'I missed you, too.' The prickle of cheap metal dug into his bicep and his mouth kept talking before his brain had a chance to caution him. 'I'm not loving that eyebrow ring, Pop.'

She stiffened into a plank of outrage and drew back.

'Too bad,' she said. 'You won't like my tattoo, either.'

'Tattoo? Wait, it's illegal for kids to get tatt—'

Her eyeroll silenced him. 'You're winding me up, aren't you? Come on, let's get over to the clinic and I can show you around. You were a toddler last time you saw your great-grandparents' building. Hey, where's your luggage? And come to think of it, how did you get here? The train ends in Cooma.'

'My luggage is on my back. I caught a bus. I have no interest in old buildings. I do, however, have a keen interest in doing a pee, so maybe you could continue your interrogation when we get to wherever we're going.'

'That eyebrow ring has made you very stroppy, Poptart.'

She shrugged, but she didn't pull away when he reached down to tuck her hand in his, so he left it at that. The backpack she was wearing was more like a decorative handbag with crisscross shoulder straps than actual luggage—clearly, his daughter wasn't planning on a long visit to Hanrahan.

Well. He'd have to do something about that.

He headed across the park to Salt Creek Flats Road. 'What are your thoughts on helping out with the clinic animals while you're here?'

'You keep animals now?'

'Sure. We have a sleepover room with cages which connects to a grassy area out the back. Dogs recovering from snake bite, rabbits with hotspots who need to be on antibiotics, that sort of thing. Your Auntie Hannah runs her practice more like an animal hospital than a day clinic, so there's always a house guest or two that needs its ears scratched or its water bowl filled.'

Poppy gave a noncommittal grunt, so he decided to sweeten the bait.

'You'll love Jane Doe and the gang.'

'Who are they?'

'Jane is a lost dog. She was brought in to the clinic a couple of weeks ago and we delivered eight pups. The mum's a labrador, father unknown.'

'I guess puppies are kinda cute.'

'You should see the fat one. He's a heartbreaker.'

Josh stopped on the footpath when they reached the clinic and looked up at the old Cody building. *His* old building … his and Hannah's, and Poppy's, too, one day. The midday sun was shining down on the granite gneiss blocks, making the façade gleam, and the fresh white he'd painted on the windows of the upper storeys gave the building a touch of the elegance it must once have had. Before some butcher architect in the seventies tacked on a plywood storefront to the ground floor.

'Here it is. Home.'

Poppy looked up. 'It's, um … big. I guess.'

'Yep.'

'And kinda bodgy looking.'

He pulled her ponytail. 'I'm working on that. Clinic's on the bottom floor, you and me are in the middle, and Hannah's got the top floor.'

'I do have a bed, right?'

'Bed, doona, pillows.' He wondered if this was the right time to mention he hadn't got the hot water working on his floor yet. Nope. Some news was best delivered over pizza.

They didn't make it upstairs.

A rap on the windowpane from inside distracted him from his building-gazing. A woman was eyeballing him from the reception area, pointing at her watch.

Shoot. His noon appointment had arrived ahead of schedule.

'Looks like you'll have to show yourself around the apartment, Pop. Sandy—that's the receptionist, you'll need to keep on her good side if you want access to the high calibre biscuits—will show you where to go.'

'Whatever.'

'Come on, let's drop your bag inside. Me and Han usually use the side door to get in and out without cutting through the reception room, but you see that woman staring us down?'

'With the big hair?'

He grinned. 'Kelly Fox. Went to school with me. She's a little snippety, but she has a kid not much younger than you. Let's say g'day.'

'I'm not here to meet people, Dad.'

'Whatever,' he said, giving her his best Poppy impersonation. She frowned at him and he laughed. 'Come on, at least come in and meet their guinea pig.'

He pushed open the front door of the clinic and ushered Poppy in ahead of him.

'Kelly,' he said. 'And Braydon, isn't it? Let me just grab your file and we can go through.'

Sandy's eyebrows disappeared under her fringe when he walked over to the counter to collect the chart she was waving at him. 'Is that your daughter?' she whispered.

'Sure is. Poppy, honey, come and meet Sandy.'

'Hi,' his daughter said.

'Hello at last,' smiled Sandy. 'I love your boots!'

He chuckled. 'Don't encourage her, Sandy. Do you mind showing Poppy around while I see to the Fox family?'

'Not at all. You've got a pair of cats in at two, then a break until Pete Harris at five. His border collie's coming in to get the drain out of his ear and a few stitches put in.'

'Gotcha.'

He turned back to Kelly and the kid beside her who had a shoe-box with—he assumed—an arthritic guinea pig tucked up inside of it. 'Come on, team, let's head into the treatment room. Pop, you want to meet Peanut?'

Kelly had made it into the treatment room ahead of him, but she only had eyes for Poppy. 'So *this* is your daughter, Josh.'

Josh frowned. Kelly's tone sounded a little too interested.

'Yes. She's visiting from Sydney. Poppy, this is Mrs Fox and her son Braydon.'

The boy was lifting the lid on the shoebox and Poppy was leaning in to have a look at Peanut, a smile on her face for the first time since she'd arrived in Hanrahan. Animals, Josh thought. The world's greatest source of comfort.

'So, is it true about your mum?' the boy said to Poppy, wiping the smile from her face. 'You know, what we read about her in the paper?'

CHAPTER

8

Dear Aunt Jill

It's me again, Vera, your niece.

I have a little fun news that you might enjoy. You know how you've spent years trying to convince me that craft is fun, not just a chore involving knitting needles or hot glue guns, and I've never, ever, ever believed you?

Well, I've been persuaded (bulldozed, really) into allowing a local craft group to use part of the café as its temporary headquarters.

There's a very bossy woman in town, Marigold Jones; have you met her? She tells me she visits Connolly House pretty often. She's about six feet tall, wears outfits that are sort of half hippy, half Gold Coast muu-muu. She has a deep voice so beautiful it's like she hypnotises you and you agree to anything she suggests. Just today at a wake we hosted here (she seems to have about forty jobs, and one of them is being a celebrant at weddings and funerals), she started off saying a few words, and before I knew what was what, she'd volunteered my café for her craft group and strong-armed the husband of the deceased to turn up for knitting lessons!

The wake was busy, and I took some orders for cakes (your hummingbird recipe is a big hit). Hopefully, the people who came enjoyed their morning tea enough to visit us again.

All that craft talk reminded me of your boxes, you know, the ones we pulled out of storage when we left Queanbeyan.

Vera put down her pen to roll her shoulders. The function had gone well—except for that last bit when Marigold Jones decided to offer up The Billy Button Café's back room for her craft group. Was that what had made her feel guilty about not unpacking her aunt's boxes? Jill had been such a keen crafter in her day ... and Vera's sporadic attempts at unpacking had uncovered a stash of half-finished projects.

She'd barely begun rifling through them when crazy, scrappy fabric things in watermelon red and blueberry blue and paprika orange had surfaced. Half-made skirts, table runners, a plump assortment of patches that was maybe a quilt.

Perhaps there'd be some items in those boxes she could use to add a flourish to the café's interior? Some exotic material that would make gorgeous cushions on the new green velvet banquettes, or an art deco vase or bronze candelabra to perch on the mantlepiece above the fire.

Vera twisted in her chair and tried to imagine the café gussied up with some of her aunt's collection. It would be like Jill had visited The Billy Button Café in person to wish it well.

'I'm off, Vera. Kitchen's clean, windows are locked, till money's hidden in the microwave.'

She turned, waved a hand at Graeme as he pulled his jacket off the peg by the door. 'It went well today, didn't it?'

'Super well. So well, in fact, maybe we think about a waitper-son or two—casual hours—to keep the tables cleared and the food served hot at busy times.'

The calico bag of takings she was going to drop into the bank in the morning was by her hand. She touched it with a finger-tip. Counting up the notes and merchant slips in there had made her start to believe, just a little, that her mad, mad plan to keep her aunt in care even if she wasn't around to earn a living might actually work.

'Vera?'

'Oh, sorry Graeme, I started daydreaming about café profits and drifted off. What did you say?'

'You want me to look into hiring some more staff?'

'Oh, yes please.'

'No prob. Just one thing: Wednesday night is date night for me, so I'm not going to be much use for craft group. I'm sorry. Alex's schedule won't be flexible until the fire station roster changes.'

'You have date night? That is so sweet.' Well, not to *her*, obviously—date nights had been poisoned forever by her ex-boyfriend, along with romance, candlelit dinners and handholding—but she could be glad for Graeme. Only ... oh crap. That meant she'd be the one who'd have to chat nicely about craft with a dozen of Marigold's cronies every week.

Graeme's grin was a little sly. 'You know Marigold will rope you in to making tassels, or decoupage, or painting wild horses on velvet.'

She chuckled. 'You're making my blood run cold. I'll manage. Thanks for letting me know.'

'Don't stay here too late, will you, boss? I can wait, if you want me to walk you to your car.'

What a guy. 'No, Graeme, you get along home. I'm just finish-ing this letter to my aunt while the meringues cool off, then I'll be on my way.'

'Your Aunt Jill who lives in the hospice down at Cooma?'

'Yep.'

'Why do you write to her when you go visit her twice a week?'

She sighed. 'She doesn't recognise me. When I visit, she thinks I'm my mother—her sister, Barb—who passed away a long time ago now. Jill's geriatrician gave me some advice about communicating with her … aim for a peaceful environment, you know, so she isn't distracted by noise and buzz, and use a method of communication that she enjoyed in the past. Music, cards, singing and so on. Jill always loved receiving letters, so I write these and we sit in the garden at Connolly House and I read them to her. I like to think somehow, somewhere in her thoughts, she knows what her niece Vera is up to.'

'You're a sweetheart, Vera, you know that?'

She swallowed. She was pretty sure if she was truly a sweetheart, she wouldn't be facing a criminal prosecution. 'See you tomorrow, Graeme. We can workshop how we're going to run this weekly stitch-and-bitch event Marigold sucker-punched us into.'

'You got it, boss.'

Silence settled in the spotless café when the door shut behind Graeme, and Vera leaned back in her chair.

Things really *were* going well. The Italian-style dinner menu she was experimenting with was receiving compliments, the coffee was exceptional thanks to Graeme's skill at the espresso machine. The locals of Hanrahan were all coming for a look-see and buying a roasted-vegetable tart or a cake, and despite it being the shoulder season between snow skiing and bushwalking, holiday tourists were plentiful.

She turned back to her letter.

We (that's me and my new manager, Graeme, who is a godsend. He's a marvel with the customers and could run this place with his eyes closed) are going to try opening up a couple more evenings a week and test the market for more formal dinners. It'll mean getting some help with food prep, as dinner menus aren't my forte, as you know!

I'll write again soon to let you know how it all goes, but it's getting late, and work starts early in the kitchens here. The apartment I'm renting is just a few blocks away from the café, and the streets seem very safe here in town, but I don't want to be heading home too late alone.

I'll visit when I can,

Love, Vera xx

A bleep-bleep from her phone interrupted her as she was folding the letter into an envelope, and she fished it out of her apron pocket and checked the screen.

Sue Anton calling …

Crap. Sue never called with good news.

'Hi, Sue.'

'Vera. This is not my good news voice.'

'I've given up expecting good news. What's up?'

As much as she liked Sue, the woman charged like a flock of angry emus. She'd learned the hard way to keep every conversation with her lawyer as short and succinct as possible.

'Just an update on your arraignment. The court wants to bring your attendance forward, so we need to make our decisions on your plea. I need to make you aware of your options.'

'What options, exactly?'

'The first option is you plead guilty to the charges and we ask for a section 10 dismissal, which means you are found guilty, but no conviction is recorded, so it won't affect your ability to work or travel in the future.'

'I plead *guilty*? Sue, I've had to sell my apartment to defend my innocence, and now you're saying I just roll over and accept the charges?'

'It's an option. It might not be your worst option. You're paying me legal fees to give you advice, Vera, so listen to it before you bite my head off, all right?'

Vera snorted. 'As though anyone could. I suspect you're made of titanium, Sue.'

'You'd be right. A non-conviction order would see you having to comply with a good behaviour bond. And there'd be certain conditions attached, like steering clear of writing damning articles about the aged care sector in Australia for example … but it might be the quickest way to get this shitshow behind you. To move on.'

She drummed her fingers on the table. 'So if we agree to this— what did you call it?—section 10 dismissal, that's it? I'm guilty, but I'm done with all this?'

'It's not that easy.'

Of course it wasn't.

'The magistrate decides whether or not they'll grant it based on the seriousness of the charge, and they'll take into account your character and criminal history, your concern for the greater good, that sort of thing. We have a solid shot.'

'But no guarantee.'

'Of course not. Where would the legal profession be if this stuff was ever clear-cut?'

Broke and bitter, she expected. Like she was. 'What if I don't want to plead guilty?'

'Then we proceed as planned: we enter a not guilty plea at the arraignment, the magistrate will set a trial date, and we'll argue it out.'

Lawyers in suits, batting words back and forth in some musty old courtroom, and her future on the line. She'd known it was coming. She'd known it would be a burden. What she hadn't factored in was how hard it would be to stay strong for her aunt, for her employees, for the sake of the café's bottom line, when the world was conspiring to bring her to her knees.

'Vera? You still there?'

'Yes, sorry. I was just brooding for a second.'

'You're going to want to give me a decision on your plea in the next couple of days. We don't want to mess the court around, and we want time to work on our arguments depending on which way you want to go.'

Time for her to worry. Spend her last cent on legal fees. Be so distracted she messed up her new business. She sighed. 'Thanks, Sue. I'll think it over and let you know.'

Sue made a long breathy noise through her phone receiver, and Vera could almost smell the gush of nicotine. 'I thought you'd given up smoking?'

'My lungs did too. But then my ex-husband rang and enraged me so much, it was a cigarette or an aggravated homicide charge. I figured a cigarette wouldn't ruin my career.'

Vera laughed. 'You're a funny girl, Sue. Sorry I got a bit antsy before, I appreciate your hard work, really I do. Thank you.'

'You won't be thanking me when you see my latest bill. I just emailed it to you.'

'Yikes. I better get the hell off this call,' she said, only half joking.

She said goodbye and hit the end icon. Those meringues had better be ready. She might need to comfort-eat a dozen or so before she headed home. Tidying up the table she'd been using to sort through her paperwork, she stood up and made for the kitchen. Meringues, home, wine, bath. Maybe she'd have the wine *in* the bath.

The oven door felt cool when she rested her hand against it, so she chanced opening it and had a look inside. Ah. Dozens of baby meringues winked back at her, their creamy tips just blushed with brown colour. She smiled. No matter how crappy things got, there was always something to be glad about in the kitchen. She hauled out the trays and began lining them up on the stainless steel bench, then frowned as a noise caught her attention.

Crying? She listened, then heard faint scuffling—not in the café, but out in the back alley.

She drew back the bolts and opened the door, and there was the cat, perched on the step as though it had just knocked and was awaiting a butler to grant it entree into a grand home.

'Can I help you?'

She really must be tired if she was speaking to stray cats. She went to shut the door, then hesitated. For all its attitude, the cat *was* thin. 'Wait there,' she said. 'Not a paw is to come inside. This kitchen is run by the anxious owner of a safe food handling certificate, and cats are strictly forbidden.'

She rummaged through the cupboards until she found a saucer, then poured a liberal dollop of milk into it from a bottle in the fridge.

'Here,' she said, and sat the saucer down on the step. 'But don't think this is going to happen again. I've no time for relationships, not even with half-starved cats.'

The cat looked up at her with wide grey eyes.

'Do you have a name?'

Its eyes blinked, and her thoughts drifted to the other name she'd heard that day—Josh, at the wake, who'd introduced himself again just before Marigold dropped her bombshell—as though she'd needed to be reminded who he was.

Her head knew she'd sworn off men for eternity, but her hormones were clearly still adjusting. Maybe she should have a cold saucer of milk herself.

The sniffling started up again, but the cat had hunkered down on the step, helping itself to a drink. If not the cat, what ...

While all she could see were the skip bins that lined the dark recess of the alley—one for each of the storefronts that faced Paterson Street—since the sun had disappeared behind the mountain range to the west, the back alley was just a little creepy.

Another noise. Definitely crying.

'Who's there?' she said, staying within the doorway so she could leap back inside the kitchen and bolt the door shut if she had to.

'Nobody. Go away.'

Hmm. Young, female, stroppy. Sounded like a teenager having a crisis. She should leave her to it; god knows, she was no good at fixing a crisis. She'd learned that lesson.

Her eyes fell to the cat who was staring up at her from lopsided eyes. *Well, do something*, its expression seemed to say.

She rolled her eyes. Cats, crying teenagers, and craft groups for lonely widowers all in the one day. She was turning into a one-woman charity shop. 'Would "nobody" like a meringue and some milk?'

There was a long pause. So long that Vera wondered if the crying girl had scampered away in the shadows, then a voice sounded from nearby.

'You got a Coke?'

The girl stood just outside the pool of kitchen light spilling into the alley.

Vera's vision of herself reclining in her bath with Mozart in her ears and a glass of deep velvety shiraz in her hand evaporated. 'Sure, I've got Coke inside. Come and sit in the kitchen with me while I box up my batch of meringues.'

The girl stepped closer, and Vera tried not to raise her eyebrows at the outfit. The boots alone must have weighed as much as bricks, and her skinny legs didn't look strong enough to lug them around. Plaid skirt the colour of a school bus, eyeliner stripes making her look like a sad fairy penguin … so this was the modern-day version of teen angst. How well she remembered her own.

'Just step over the cat,' she said. 'It's easier than trying to encourage him to scram.'

The girl dropped to her knees. 'Your cat's a she.'

'Oh. He … I'm sorry, *she* isn't mine.'

'British shorthair. Expensive cat to be a stray.'

Vera followed the girl inside. 'You know your cats.'

The girl stiffened as though Vera had just said something horribly offensive. She replayed her words in her head. What was so bad about suggesting someone knew something about cats?

'There's Coke in the big fridge. Bottom left, hiding behind the organic stuff. Help yourself,' she said, and started rummaging in a drawer for storage boxes. 'You any good with scissors?'

'With scissors?'

'Yep. I need to layer these meringues into these boxes, and if I don't put a square of waxed paper between each layer, the tops get ruined.' She handed over the roll of paper and a set of kitchen scissors. 'Actually, might want to wash your hands first. That back lane isn't the cleanest place in Hanrahan.'

She paused, hoping the prompt would push the girl into saying why she'd been lurking there. Nothing came, so she tried another tactic.

'I'm Vera.'

'Poppy,' the girl said as she dried her hands on the handtowel.

'Uh-huh. You live here?'

'No freaking way.'

'Oh! Are you lost? A runaway? A time traveller from another dimension?' She watched the girl's face as she plucked a waxed paper square from the pile stacking up on the bench. The girl was neat, fast, and totally adept at snipping. 'Only, I'm just wondering why you were crying in the alley.'

Poppy's fingers slipped on the roll of paper. 'I wasn't crying.'

Denial. Okay, that was a defence she recognised. 'Good to know. Only, I'm new in town. If you're having a full-on teenage crisis, I don't know who to call. Your mum?'

'She's in Sydney.'

'Dad?'

'Like he'd care.'

Aha. She must have had a fight with her dad. 'Sisters? Brothers? A cool unmarried auntie who drives a moped and wears men's clothes?'

The girl's voice was quieter than it had been before. 'I'm new in town, too, sort of, but don't worry because I am *not* staying. Six hours in Hanrahan has been six hours too long. And get this ... everyone here seems to think they know more about me than I do myself. And they don't! They haven't even met me before! And I do have an auntie here who's kinda cool, but she works with my dad.'

Vera sealed off a box then reached for the last few meringues on the baking tray. Okay, that was hopeful; the girl had family in Hanrahan. Maybe Poppy just needed to cool off some, then she'd be happy to go home. A little like her meringues. She picked one up, offered it to Poppy. 'Want to try one?'

'I guess. I've made a few meringues myself, you know, back in Sydney, where everything used to be great until Dad wrecked my life.'

Vera popped one in her own mouth as she studied the girl. She dodged the wrecked-life comment and focused on the other bit. 'Oh, you bake too? No wonder you're such an expert with food storage.'

Her guest gave a little snicker, which encouraged her to think Poppy was feeling a little less blue. 'Anyone can cut paper.'

Vera smiled. 'Maybe. You know, Poppy, as fun as this is, we can't stay here all night. I bet your dad's missing you and wondering where you are.'

Poppy sighed. 'Can you keep a secret?'

She frowned. Sure she could, but she was out of her depth here in teenager land. What if the girl told her something that shouldn't be kept secret?

'I can, yes,' she said. 'Except if it's a personal safety issue. Then, sorry, I'll have to blab it to someone who can help.'

The girl frowned. 'Ew. It's nothing like that. Okay, the reason I was in that dumb lane was I got mad with some dumb kid called Braydon. Like that's even a name.'

'Why? What happened?'

'I'm surprised you didn't hear it from here.'

'Hear what?'

'The yelling. Dad's business is just across the park. He was trying to be all friendly and cute and "you'll love it here, Pops", but really he just wanted me to do some dumb chores, but then this woman with big hair and her kid got all up in my face and it all went bad. *Epically* bad.'

'And there was yelling? Your father shouted at you?'

'What, at me? No way! Dad's the best.'

Oh, this was so confusing. 'I thought your dad had wrecked, um, your life and everything.'

'Well sure, he has, but … whatever. It's complicated.'

'Poppy, maybe I've eaten too many meringues and my brain's clogged up with sugar, but I still don't understand.'

'It all happened when I was looking at the guinea pig and the Braydon kid asked me if it was true what he'd read in the paper and what everyone was saying about my mum.'

'In the newspaper?' Vera tended to avoid the *Snowy River Star*, as well as the national papers. Part of her survival strategy was pretending her old life hadn't existed, and journalism was part of that old life. 'What's everyone saying about your mum?'

'Yeah. Good question. And I was just about to ask him that, but then my dad went apeshit crazy and told Braydon to watch his mouth, and then his mum went even crazier and told Dad it wasn't her son's fault if Dad chose to bring his mistakes back into town and he should have kept his trousers on back in high school even if his science teacher was a cougar and a hussy who should have gone to prison not Sydney, and then Dad went all green-looking and stiff and said in this cold voice *my daughter's not a mistake*, and I was like, what the hell, does she mean me? I'm the mistake? And then Dad says *Kelly Fox, I think you'd better take your son and your guinea pig and your vicious bitchy self the hell out of my office*, and she started crying and then I started crying and I ran out of there and hid in the alley and wished I was dead. Or maybe in Sydney.'

'I see.' Well, that was a lie, because she didn't see anything at all after that impassioned outburst. Mistakes? Trousers? *Guinea pigs?*

Poppy shrugged. 'It doesn't matter anyway. I'm just here because Dad made me come see for myself what this stupid town is like. I'm not staying, I don't care how many puppies he bribes me with.'

'That's too bad. My café manager was just telling me we should hire some casual waitstaff to help us. You know, in school holidays especially.'

'You mean, you'd hire me? Like, if I was up here in the holidays I could work in your café and bake epic meringues and stuff?'

Vera shrugged. Underneath all that mascara and angst, Poppy seemed a sweet kid. And washing dishes and clearing tables was bound to be more fun than crying in dirty access lanes. 'Yep. Here in my café, although maybe the work would start off with kitchen duties and waitressing and we could work our way up to baking.

It's not every day I meet someone who can cut such a neat square of paper.'

The girl almost grinned. She looked shyly up at Vera, then took a big breath in, let a big breath out.

'I've got to be back in Sydney for school at the end of next week, but I've got, like, *weeks* off at the end of fourth term. When can I start?'

CHAPTER

9

Josh pulled his truck into the narrow car space at the back of the clinic and killed the ignition. Wherever Poppy had run off to, he hadn't found the place. He'd checked the movie theatre, the narrow strip of pebbled beach down by the lake, the park, the old cemetery, the shops around the town square … she was nowhere. Only bars and restaurants were still open now, and no barman in town would let Poppy in. Despite the pierced eyebrow and eyeliner fetish, she looked younger than fifteen. Way younger.

Crap. He may as well just get it over with. He pulled his phone out of his pocket, sat there in the dark with it a second before punching in the number.

'Josh, hi. Everything okay? Poppy texted earlier and said she'd arrived.'

Beth Horrigan. His one-time high school science teacher and mother to his daughter Poppy and, more recently, a five-year-old set of twin boy hellions, courtesy of her husband Ron Seeto.

'Hi, Beth.'

'Riiiight. I take it from that tone you've seen the eyebrow.'

'It's not that. She's run off. She hasn't called you by any chance?'

'No. Hang on a second ... Ron, honey? Have you heard from Poppy?'

Josh listened to the rumble of a deep voice in the background, then Beth was back.

'No, nothing here. It's getting late, Josh. And is it cold up there? Did you check the bus depot? Maybe she's trying to get back to the city.'

Hell. No, he hadn't thought of that. 'Good idea. I'll go there now.' He had a sudden mental image of her standing by the Monaro Highway thumbing a lift from some old guy in a beige sedan who looked like a dad but was really a pervert with a secret room under his toolshed.

He dropped his head in his hands. 'This is all my fault. I pushed her to come here, Beth. She's lived her whole life in the city, I don't know why I thought this was going to be a positive change for her.'

'Hanrahan is your home, Josh. There have been Codys there for generations. You didn't want to leave that town; you left for me.'

He did. And he'd do it again in a heartbeat. 'I'm not ashamed of us, Beth. We are good people.'

'We were young and stupid people. You were just a bit younger than me, that's all. And that town was never going to forgive me for destroying the future of their golden boy. First University of Sydney scholarship ever awarded to a student from Hanrahan, thrown away when that same golden boy knocked up his high school science teacher.'

'Trainee teacher. And I'm pretty sure I'd graduated before you let me get my horny teenage hands under your sweater.'

'Bloody hell, Josh. Try and remember I'm on speakerphone, would you?'

Oops. 'Hey, Ron.'

'Hey yourself,' said Beth's husband. 'Speaking of teenagers with, um, hands, you want me to drive up and help you look for Poppy?'

'Give me an hour or so, Ron. There's a few places I haven't checked yet.'

'You got it. Call me if you need me. I can drive through the night and be there before morning.'

'Thanks, man.'

Beth's voice came in over the family room ruckus he could hear in the background. 'What happened? Why did she run off?'

He pulled himself together. There'd be plenty of time for cataloguing his mistakes once Poppy was safe. 'You remember Kelly? My age, curly hair, cried in class whenever she broke a nail.'

Beth's voice was wry. 'I blanked out every face in that town the day they ran me out at the end of a pitchfork.'

He would have grinned if he wasn't so worried. 'Well, unfortunately she hasn't blanked you and me out. She was at the clinic this afternoon with her kid and an overweight guinea pig. Asked Poppy how she felt about everyone knowing her dad got seduced by his teacher and got her knocked up and—'

'Oh my god.'

'Yep.'

He heard Beth's long drawn-out sigh. 'We should have told her.'

He should have. He was the one who'd come back to Hanrahan, stirred up all the old gossip, all the busy eyes wondering just when had his and Beth's affair started. He was damned if he'd give them the satisfaction of setting them straight.

'I'd forgotten how occupied everyone got here with other people's lives.'

'Mmm,' said Beth. 'That's small towns for you. And they never let the facts get in the way of a good story.'

He heard a crash followed by high-pitched screaming and wondered if one of the Seetos had just fallen through a plate glass window.

'Boys! Cut that out. Nick, give Toby back his lightsabre. Toby, get your foot off Nick's head. Josh, I've got to go before they kill each other. Remind me again why I had more children.'

He smiled. 'Because you're a great mum, and Ron was born to be the King of Dads.'

'What a charmer. Call me after you've been to the bus depot, all right? We can call the police together, and either Ron or I will get in the car and drive up tonight. I'll call her friends here in Sydney in case she's made contact, or posted anything online.'

'Will do. Talk soon.'

'Bye, Josh.'

Bus depot. Now why hadn't he thought of that? He reached for the ignition then paused. The depot was up the hill on the main road out to the Alpine Way. He could go on foot, check the streets on the way in case Poppy was loitering somewhere. All he'd need would be a torch; plenty of those in the treatment room.

A deep woof sounded as he let himself into the back office. Jane Doe. The vet nurse would have taken her for a walk before he left for the day, but she'd cope with another. Who knew? Maybe the old girl had sniffer-dog skills hidden under all that fur.

He grabbed a lead from the row of hooks lining the wall by the door and headed into the sleepover room, where Jane Doe was tucked up with her pups.

'How're you doing, sweetheart?'

The old lab thumped her tail against the floor and scampered up, dislodging the pups dozing against her belly.

'Fancy a walk?'

The dog pricked her ears. She knew the word 'walk' fine, like she knew 'treat' and 'sit' and 'nice try but get away from my sandwich'. She was someone's pet for sure, or had been.

He unlatched the gate and led her into the corridor. 'We're going on a Poppy hunt, Jane. You ready to earn your keep?'

'Talking to dogs now, Josh?'

Josh looked up at the man standing in the doorway. Tall. Fair hair worn short and sharp as a seasoned Navy officer, eyes just as ruthless. Shoulders that could withstand a premiership quarter tackle, or at least they could back when they'd been on the same Aussie Rules team at school. 'Tom Krauss. It's been a long time, mate.'

'Same. I hear you're up to your old tricks schmoozing all the ladies in town.'

Josh sighed. Some gifts just kept on giving. 'What do you mean by that exactly?'

His old schoolfriend cocked his head. 'Nothing,' he said after a pause. 'Mrs LaBrooy told me you took her out for coffee.'

Well, that would teach him to jump down the throat of anyone who made a half-baked innuendo about his past. He grabbed Tom's hand, shook it then pulled him in for a back-slap and hug. 'Sorry. It's been a long day. My daughter's run off, and my old schmoozing tricks, as you so tactfully phrased it, are the reason.'

'Hell, Poppy's run off?'

'Yep.'

'Tell me what I can do.'

That. That was the reason he'd moved back to Hanrahan. More than the chance to get into his own vet practice. More than the majestic historic building he could live in rent free, the mountain air he could breathe, the gleaming blue of clear, cold lake water he could see from damn near every street in town, the row of Codys at rest in the cemetery.

Community. Friends who'd grown up with him, known him as a skinned-knee brat freewheeling through town on his battered BMX; sat shoulder to shoulder with him at birthday parties at the old ice rink while they woofed down milkshakes and hot chips and tried to out-belch one another. Friends who were ready now, without a prompt or a prod, to help.

'I'm heading up to the bus depot on the main road. Beth thinks Pop might have booked herself back to Sydney when she ran out of here, and she'd need a bus to get her into the train station at Cooma.'

'Let's go.'

Josh gave the lead a tug and Jane Doe stopped sniffing the hem of Tom's jeans and fell in beside him. As they let themselves out the side door, his brain worked around to the incongruity it hadn't noticed until now. 'What are you doing here anyway, Tom?'

Tom shot a glance up to the top floor, where lamplight shone from behind Hannah's new curtains. 'Don't ask.'

Josh inspected his old friend's set expression. 'If you and Hannah are—'

'We're not.'

Hmm. If Tom had been upstairs, that would explain why Hannah hadn't been answering his calls.

'No sign of an hysterical fifteen-year-old girl up there?'

'No, Josh. She would have been a welcome distraction, I can tell you that much.'

Okay. He could grill Hannah about Tom later. One drama a day was his limit, and Poppy being missing was the only thing he could care about right now.

He flicked on the torch, shone it into doorways and alleys as he and Tom walked down Dandaloo and cut through Quarry Street up to the main road at the back of town. He hunted around for a question to ask to take his mind off his worry.

'So you left the Navy, I hear.'

'A while back, yes.'

'They finally wised up and booted you out.'

Tom gave an easy grin. 'You wish. You're looking at a decorated officer.'

'Uh-huh. So why does a decorated officer ditch the Navy and head on home to the farm?'

'Well, I've been working as a civilian for a few years, so it's not like I ditched the Navy last week. I came back here to be with Dad. Mrs LaBrooy didn't tell you?'

Josh frowned. 'Tell me what?'

'Dad has multiple sclerosis. It was me come home and keep the business going, or sell the horse stud. Easy choice.'

He doubted Tom would tell him if it had been the toughest choice of his life—he was a guy who played his cards close.

'You got a good equine vet looking after those nags of yours?'

Tom punched him in the arm. 'You are such an operator, Cody. And yes, your sister's been known to come and look at my horses.'

'Hey, I topped my class in equine studies. Interned at Dalgety Flats Stables six months last year. Just saying ... there's more than one Cody in town now.'

'Dalgety Flats? The Frasers?'

'Yeah.'

'Heard they had had a winner in the Golden Slipper last year.'

'You heard right. Three-year-old colt named Gondwana.'

The bus depot loomed ahead, an ugly squat building that was a tribute to shoddy council development approvals in the eighties. Jane plodded along beside him, her huffs sending a cloud of mist into the night air.

Beth had been right about the cold. Even now, in spring, the nights could turn bitter. And Poppy wasn't dressed for mountain weather.

He stumbled at the thought of Poppy shivering somewhere in the dark. No … he couldn't think that. He kept up the horse chatter to drive the image from his head. 'You interested in racing stock out there at the Ironbark Station? Or are you breeding working horses?'

'Quarter horses mainly, but I've a few special horses in the mix. You'll have to come out and see my mare, Buttercup. I just paid a fortune for her. She's in foal, a bit early in the season, but there was an opportunity to match her with a good bloodline. She's a thoroughbred, built for racing, or was, until injury ended her career. I think she's going to foal me a winner.'

'A Triple Crown winner?'

'Why not? A bloke can dream, right?'

A bloke sure could dream. Hadn't he dreamed his whole life of being a vet in a large animal practice?

The arrival of Poppy into his world had changed things—he'd not taken up that scholarship. He'd had bills to pay, cots to buy, nappies, mashed up carrots and kindergarten fees to provide. But he'd never lost his dream, not in ten years of labouring on high-rise construction sites in downtown Sydney.

'Yeah,' he muttered. He paused in front of the closed ticket window at the depot. 'Hang on to Jane Doe, will you, Tom? I'll go find someone inside.'

'No worries.'

He pushed his way through the heavy glass door. Bored-looking travellers sprawled across vinyl seats, but Poppy wasn't one of them. He approached the desk and grilled the young man at the only open counter.

'I'm looking for my daughter. Fifteen, grungy clothes, hair dyed black. Here's a picture.'

He pulled up the photo files on his phone. He had hundreds of photos on there, thousands perhaps, and ninety-nine per cent of them were of Poppy. He showed the guy his screen.

'She been in? Sometime after one? She'd have been looking for a bus to Cooma, and then train to Sydney.'

'Sorry. I've been here since noon. Haven't seen her.'

Bloody hell. Where could she be? He headed back outside, and Tom must have seen the despair on his face.

'I know the local police officer. Her name's Meg King, and she's one of the best. Let's get her involved. I can call the old crew. Jacko—remember him? He's driving again now so if we can prise him away from Tracy, we take a quarter of town each; we search until dawn if we have to.'

There was a sob in Josh's chest, bucking just under the surface wanting to pound its way free. He choked it down, nodded.

'Okay, yes, okay. I promised Beth I'd let her know if Poppy wasn't at the depot. Let's head back to the clinic and we can get your police friend to meet us there.' Josh turned to the man he'd grown up with but hadn't bothered to keep in contact with for the last decade and a half. More fool him. 'Thanks, Tom. I mean it.'

Tom just nodded. 'Here, take your girlfriend. I was warming to her, but then she tried to pee on my new boots. She's all yours.'

'Let's walk down the other side of the street. There's a few service alleys we should check.'

'You got it.'

They crossed the street, the light from Josh's torch flickering silver lines across the pavement. Maybe Beth had heard something by now. He dug around in his pocket for his phone.

'Well, well, what do we have here?'

'Hmm?' Josh frowned down at his screen. Beth's message was another dead end; none of Poppy's friends had heard from her. No selfies adorned Instagram with a convenient sign in the background letting him know where she could be found.

'Some new chick I have definitely not seen in Hanrahan before. Brown hair—or is it dark red? Easy on the eye, my friend … and she's not alone.'

Josh ran a hand over his jaw, feeling the stubble there. Police, that had to be the first call. Then Beth. Then Hannah, damn her, could snap out of whatever Tom Krauss–funk she was inhabiting and come downstairs and help.

Tom's last words finally sank into his brain. 'Not alone?'

'Ugly orange skirt. Boots that look like besser bricks. A nose that is one hundred per cent Cody. And I oughta know—I went to school with one of them, and I've wasted a mess of time getting the cold shoulder from the other. I think we've found your daughter, Josh.'

He looked up from his phone and on the dimly lit footpath were two figures walking towards them. Holy crap, Tom was right. He could have kissed him. He *would* have kissed him, except Tom was looking at his watch and muttering blather like *gotta go*, and *now the drama's over*, and *see ya, mate*.

He ignored it all and lunged forward, earning himself a yelp from the startled labrador by his side.

'Poppy? Honey, I've been so worried. Come here and give your dad a hug before he embarrasses all of us by crying in the street.'

And then she was in his arms. All five-foot, eyebrow-pierced, stroppy inch of her. She felt just about as perfect as a daughter could feel.

CHAPTER

10

Oh! Poppy's dad was the big handsome *vet*?

She hauled in a breath. Wait, so Poppy's story about the gossip in town was about Josh Cody? And—she flicked through the kid's story in her head—if he was in business with Poppy's aunt ... then that meant the Cody and Cody Vet Clinic wasn't a husband-wife team, but a brother-sister team.

Not that who he was in business with was any concern of hers.

He met her eyes over the top of his daughter's head, thanks and questions written across his face.

'Er, hi again,' she said. 'Vera. From The Billy Button Café.'

He smiled, a grin so brimful of charm she was able to understand how Poppy's mum, whoever she was, had fallen under its spell.

'You don't have to keep introducing yourself. I know who you are.'

Oh boy. And now she knew who he was: single; too good-looking for her peace of mind; and with daughter-shaped emotional baggage which she had just sort-of employed.

Poppy was peeling herself out of her dad's chokehold. 'Guess what, Dad?'

'What?'

'I'm going to be a waitress.'

'You are?'

'Yep. Vera's offered me a job for the holidays.'

'I see.' He raised his eyebrows in Vera's direction. 'Honey, can you call your mum? Let her know I found you.'

'My phone's dead.'

Josh rolled his eyes. 'Of course it is. When you charge it again, maybe you'll see the three thousand messages I've left for you.'

'Oops. Sorry, Dad.'

'No, it's fine. I'm the one who's sorry. We'll talk, okay? Here, use mine. Your mum and Ron are worried about you.'

He handed his phone over to Poppy then looked up at Vera. She figured some sort of explanation was in order, so stopped running the ears of the dog through her fingers and stood up straight.

'About the job,' she began.

He nodded. 'About that. Listen, you got time for a coffee or something? My place is just down the road. I'd like to get Poppy inside out of this cold.'

Vera hesitated. It was late, and she'd been planning a long bath and a deep-bottomed beverage. She shot a glance at her watch and dithered.

Saying yes would be a mistake. Get involved with no-one and avoid all drama … that had been her mantra as she packed up her life in Queanbeyan.

But … she *had* just employed this guy's daughter. Maybe it was her civic duty to prove she wasn't going to be an ogre of a boss.

Besides, she just had a cold, lonely apartment to go back to, with only her worries about guilty pleas for company, and this reckless spark the vet had lit in her brain felt good. When had she last felt good?

'Sure,' she said, recklessness winning out over caution, for now. She turned with Josh and started back down Paterson Street in the direction of the lake. Poppy's chatter to her mother filled the air behind them.

'You live above the vet clinic?'

'Yeah. We, as in my sister Hannah and me, own the building together. It's been in the Cody family for generations. Our grandparents ran a haberdashery from the ground floor, back when haberdasheries were a thing. There's apartments on the upper storeys. Hannah's on the top floor, I'm the middle floor.'

'That's handy for work.'

He smiled. 'Sometimes too handy. And since I'm the junior partner, Hannah thinks it's my job to deal with the middle-of-the-night pet dramas.'

'So you bought into your sister's practice?'

'Well, "buy" probably isn't the right word. Me and Hannah made a deal.'

'Oh? What sort of deal?'

He shrugged. 'She'd have let me into the business for nothing. But she'd used her savings to fund the fit-out—the treatment rooms, the x-ray machine, the dog run out back—and worked hard the last few years to build the practice up into a profitable business, so I found a way to pay her in kind.'

In kind? What an idea. If only she could pay the rent on the café in cakes and chicken ribbon sandwiches.

'I worked construction when I left school. Ten years. I can knock out walls, lay tiles, plumb a shower. Hannah gave me the idea. The apartments on the upper storeys hadn't seen a paintbrush since about 1920 when we moved in, so I strapped on my toolbelt and worked out my half of the practice fixing up her apartment. My place will be next and then, when time and money permit, we're going to restore the street frontage to its original condition.'

A vision of Josh wearing a toolbelt and a patina of sawdust and man-sweat drifted across her mind's eye, and she tripped on a crack in the footpath. She stiffened as his arm came up under hers and set her back on her feet.

'You okay?'

Vera could feel herself blushing and unglued her fingers from Josh's muscled forearm. What had they been talking about? Her mind had gone blank all of a sudden. Oh, right. Buildings. In kind. *Kindness.*

How messed up was her world that kindness felt like a word from a foreign language?

'Construction to vet school. That seems like a big jump.'

'Journalist to café owner and cake expert. Seems like you don't mind a leap yourself.'

Vera stood stock-still on the footpath. How the hell did some random guy, who she'd barely met, know she used to be a journalist? And if he knew that, what else did he know? Her voice, when it came, was low. 'It's a long story. One I have no intention of sharing. I don't know how you heard that, but—'

Josh touched her arm. 'Hey. I'm sorry. I didn't mean to pry. I've got a few long stories myself, one of which crawled out and bit me on the bum today. Bit Poppy, too.'

She sighed. 'Don't tell me. Small-town gossip. Poppy did give me a mangled version that made virtually no sense. It seems like I was prying, now, but at the time I had no idea who she was or how to get her home without a bit more information.'

He reached his arm around her and gave her shoulders a little squeeze. It felt good. Too good, for a woman who'd sworn off men forever.

'Whatever you did, it worked. This is the nicest Poppy's been to me since I told her I was moving to Hanrahan.'

Vera eased herself away and looked back over her shoulder, to where Poppy was nattering away on the phone about puppies and bus travel and how to store meringues like a professional. Josh was right, at least Poppy looked a whole lot happier than when she'd first seen her, weeping in the shadows of the skip bin.

'I should have guessed when she mentioned a guinea pig,' she said, as she followed Josh across the park over to Salt Creek Flats Road.

'Excuse me?' He was looking at her like she'd lost her marbles. Which, truth be told, she may very well have done. She'd barely been in town a month, and already she was halfway to forgetting her personal vow to never get involved with any guy, ever again— no way, no how. Problem was, when she made that vow, she didn't know she was about to meet a warm-hearted vet with a flirty grin and a kooky daughter.

'Poppy was going on about boys keeping their trousers on, and older women, and unexpected babies, which didn't make a lot of sense, and the guinea pig threw me for a total loop. I should have realised the guinea pig was my biggest clue. Who else has guinea pigs for clients other than vets?'

'Former client.'

She grinned. 'Yeah, Poppy mentioned everyone left the room in a hurry when you went ... what was her word? ... apeshit.'

Josh chuckled. 'Yeah. There's a bill that'll never get paid.'

The light over the doorway of the Cody and Cody Vet Clinic shone a golden circle over the quiet street corner.

'Come in,' said Josh. 'You can fill me in on Poppy's job, and I can thank you for keeping her safe for me. I should probably also mention she doesn't actually live here in Hanrahan full time. I'm not quite sure how a job is going to work.'

She shook her head. 'She told me. School holidays only. About coming inside … I don't know, it is kind of late.'

The vet shrugged. 'I've got wine, frozen pizza, peanut butter and half a loaf of maybe stale bread?'

She raised her eyebrows. 'Wow. That's a dizzying list of food enticements.'

'Please, Vera,' said Poppy, who had bounded up to them after finishing her call. 'If you come in, Dad won't tell me off for running away this afternoon.'

Oh, what the hell. It wasn't as though this was a date. She was just reassuring a worried father that she was going to be a nice employer for his daughter on the odd occasions she was in town.

She nodded. 'You Codys have a unique way of persuasion. But just for a bit. I really do have to be up at dawn.'

'Great.' Josh shoved a key into the heavy wooden door, and let her and Poppy precede him into the foyer. 'Popstar, can you take Jane Doe back to her pups? Make sure she has some water.'

'Okay.'

The dim foyer was quiet after Poppy led the dog away, the clicking of claws on the tiled entry fading as they disappeared somewhere in the house. Quiet and oddly charged, like static had built up in the space between her and the man who stood watching her.

'So,' she said, clearing her throat. Ridiculous to feel this nervous, he was just a guy. Just a concerned father, with a whole life she knew nothing about. Hell, he could be gay, celibate, completely uninterested.

He moved a step closer.

Oh boy. The static charge jumped up by about a thousand volts. Her clothes prickled, her hair felt heavy, her breath juddered in her chest.

'So,' he said, the low echo of her word rumbling in the space between them. He leaned a shoulder up on the wall in a gesture that would have seemed casual if it hadn't, for some crazy reason, also sent her heart rate into a spin. 'This is a little unexpected.'

She pretended to have no clue what he was talking about. 'Not at all. Graeme and I were just talking the other day about having some casual workers on our books. Hiring Poppy for a few hours this week will help us work out when we need staff the most.'

She wondered if she sounded as dizzy as she felt. *Hot vet alert.* Graeme's words rang in her head; her feckless hormones had been on high alert ever since she'd felt the blaze of Josh Cody's eyes on her.

'You want to take off that jacket? It's plenty warm upstairs.'

How had he managed to make an innocuous sentence sound like an indecent proposal? Not gay, then. Or celibate. Or uninterested, if the look in his eyes was anything to go by.

'Ah …' she said. 'Um …'

'You know, I was wondering if I should get to know you a little better.'

She swallowed. 'You were?'

'Yeah. But, you know, I've got a vet practice to build up, a daughter to wrangle, a derelict apartment to renovate in an historically sensitive way. I'd take some persuasion.' His teeth gleamed in the shadowed light. Oh yeah, this guy had charm all right. And it was damn near irresistible. She hugged her jacket about her; perhaps the padded fleece of her old winter coat could deflect some of it.

'Uh-huh,' she said, putting some steel in her voice so it wouldn't sound like she was flirting. 'Well, that's just as well. I've got a café business to build. My aunt to care for. Some, er … stuff left over in the city that can't be ignored. I most definitely could not be persuaded.'

His voice was lower still. 'And yet, I've got this big hungry urge to try.'

Oh, she was in trouble. Sexually charged banter was not the road to a calm and peaceful life alone in Hanrahan while she pulled herself together. Sexually charged banter was the road to ruin.

Josh was—*crap*—was he leaning towards her? Was he going to *kiss her*? She had about sixty thoughts all at once, none of them connected, none of them making any sense. A few were along the lines of *this is sudden*, and *woah there, Vera, you hate guys right now*, but the big clamouring all-caps one was saying *DO IT, DO IT, DO IT!*

At the last second, common sense prevailed. At least, that's what she told herself as she turned her head to the side and his hot, stubble-rough mouth pressed a kiss into her cheek. Chickened out was what she'd really done.

She dragged in a long breath. 'About that wine,' she said, 'not a good idea.'

He held his hands in the air then gestured towards the old-fashioned timber staircase to the next floor. 'Hey,' he said. 'I'm sorry. I thought ... well, it doesn't matter what I thought. What matters is that we're being neighbourly, and to be honest when I said wine, I may have been exaggerating. There's beer, that I can promise. And I wasn't joking about the stale loaf of bread.'

Poppy's footsteps clattered up the corridor behind them. 'Relax, Vera. I can make us a green tea. It'll be like a practice run for when I start making tea for customers.'

The girl looked so pleased, she didn't have the heart to turn her down.

'Sure. Just a quick one, though, I have work tomorrow.'

'Cool! Me too? I mean, you do want me to start tomorrow, right? I've only got a few days, I need to learn *everything*.'

Vera smiled. Crazily enough, this almost felt like fun. 'Sure, tomorrow sounds fine. Six am.'

'Six am?' The girl's shriek nearly splintered her eardrums.

She heard Josh give a snicker of laughter beside her. 'Oh, I am *so* persuaded, Vera De Rossi.'

He wasn't sure what madness had led him to try and plant his lips on Vera's. He could kid himself and blame it on the euphoria of having Poppy safe under the Cody roof, but that hadn't been the reason.

Vera was the reason.

There was a stillness to her that had drawn him in from the moment he'd laid eyes on her standing stiff and uncomfortable behind her cake cabinet; and there she'd been, in his shadowed hallway, light from the dusty bulb turning her auburn hair into flame, and those watchful eyes of hers doing something to his willpower that was, frankly, baffling.

He'd been leaning forward to check if she tasted as good as she looked before he'd had time to consider what the hell he was doing.

Kissing women he barely knew was not part of his home-coming plan.

Family was. Heritage was. Which was why he was at the locked door of the old cottage on the foreshore waiting for Marigold and Kev to get the heck here already.

He looked at his watch. He had a cranky pig with mastitis who was due for another shot of antibiotics before lunch, and an even crankier sister who had filled his afternoon list with more appointments than he could count.

Still. Taking a moment by the lake on a spring morning, with a wide stone step to sit on and a sun-warmed timber door at his back ... he smiled. He'd had worse mornings.

His mind drifted back to the kiss he'd nearly bestowed on Vera, and how she'd tilted her head, turning the moment from sweet to awkward in a heartbeat. So, kissing him wasn't part of her life plan, either, but for a second there? When her eyes were on his and her lips were so close?

He rubbed his hand over his face. Oh yes. For a second there his blood had roared in his ears and his lungs had seized and the look in Vera's eyes had switched from watchful to startled to something way, way sweeter.

She was a puzzle.

If he was a prudent guy, he'd accept the rebuff, sling his stethoscope round his neck and get on with the things he *ought* to be thinking about ... like his vet practice. Like building himself a life in Hanrahan that Poppy could feel proud to be a part of.

But prudence didn't warm a guy's heart, not like the new café owner seemed to. Besides ... there was no rush to decide, was there? He was in Hanrahan, she was in Hanrahan, and neither of them were going anywhere.

'Somebody's looking pleased with themselves this morning.'

He squinted into the sun, and there was Marigold, standing over him in a floaty whatsit that made her look like a giant cuttlefish. 'Hi, Marigold. Thanks for meeting me.'

'Don't thank me yet, my love.'

Ominous words from anyone ... but particularly ominous when they came from the town's busiest woman. He was here to access the historical society's archives, currently tucked up in storage boxes in the community hall while the electrics were replaced, for old photos of the Cody building. If Marigold thought he'd be slipping into some lycra and joining her yoga class as thanks, she was mistaken.

'You bring your hard hat?'

'Excuse me?'

Marigold bustled past him up the stairs and pulled a massive bunch of keys from within the folds of fabric floating by her sides. She jiggled a stout, three-inch-long iron key into the rusty lock, gave the door a heave with her shoulder, and braced herself across the doorway.

'This is a construction zone, Josh. No-one's allowed inside without permission from the project manager—that's me—and appropriate safety gear.'

'I just want to look in the historical archives, Marigold. You *asked* me to meet you here.'

She gave his cheek a pat. 'Safety first,' she said, in a pious tone which was at odds with the wink she dropped him. 'Luckily, I have spares. Here you go.'

She reached in the door, handed him a hard hat, then spent a minute cramming another down over her beehive of strenuously lacquered hair.

'Why do I get the feeling you're conning me?' he said.

She led him inside. 'Because you're not stupid. Of course I'm conning you. Kev and I have been wondering how we were going to get this ceiling replaced after the electrician's done with his rewiring, and then you called.'

'Bloody hell.'

She grinned. 'Bloody serendipity, more like. Come on, at least have a look and give me some advice. It's not every day a brawny young man with carpentry skills asks to be allowed into the community hall's inner sanctum. Most of our regulars are on the shady side of sixty and I could hardly send them up a ladder with sheets of gyprock, could I now?'

'You know there's a mother pig with a ferocious infection waiting for me, Marigold. I may be brawny, but I'm also busy.'

'That's what makes you perfect, my love; busy people get things done. Now, what do you think?'

'Let's see the archives first. If we're striking a deal here, at least let me see what I'm getting out of it.'

She narrowed her eyes at him. 'A man who likes to negotiate. Excellent. Well then, let's see. What are you looking for, exactly?'

'Photographs or mentions of the buildings on the Dandaloo Street side of the square. The front of our building was remodelled in the seventies as a storefront and I'm looking to restore it to its original condition. I'm also interested in any content about the old quarry.'

'Up at Stony Creek?'

'Yes. I imagine local stone was used, and I'd like to know for sure where it came from.'

'This is excellent, Josh. We've a stack of photographs, and old diaries with sketches, land title records, details of the routes used by horse-and-cart traders before the roads went in. Mind you, we have a lot of information so narrowing it down to the bits you need might take a little digging.'

Yikes. 'Digging through paperwork, that sounds like fun.'

'Let's add that into our deal.'

It was his turn to narrow his eyes at her. 'Are you offering?'

'You repair these patches in the ceiling so we can get the community hall opened up again for the good people of Hanrahan—well, and the bad people too, as we are open to all—and I'll get Kev to go through these old boxes and pull out anything he thinks you might need to see.'

He frowned at her. 'It's a deal. On one condition.'

'Coffee deliveries? You need an assistant? No deadline?'

He considered. 'All of the above would be welcome, but no. I'm looking at your ceiling. That plasterboard is a bodgy add-on. What say we rip it out and see what condition the original ceiling timbers are in? There may even be pressed metal up there. This cottage is Hanrahan's history ... why don't we restore it the right way rather than take the cheaper option?'

'Joshua Cody, present me with your cheek. You, my love, are getting a kiss.'

'It's not necessa—'

Too late. Marigold was bestowing him with a kiss and a hug and he spent a moment clawing his way out of the acres of chiffon billowing around him.

'I'll have to do the work at nights and weekends,' he said.

'I know, that's fine.'

'And Poppy's here at the moment, so I'll make a few plans and such, but I won't start the work properly until she's headed back to school.'

'Understood.'

'What's our budget? You want me to rustle up an estimate of costs before I rip anything out?'

'If you would, my lamb. I know I like to swan about as though I make every decision, but the committee approves expenditure.'

He eyed her a moment. 'You're being awfully agreeable in this negotiation, Marigold Jones. Am I missing something? Have you another dastardly plan up your sleeve?'

She chuckled. 'You know me so well, Josh. But in this case, no, I'm not about to spring another surprise in your direction. I'm just so happy we're both getting what we want. Isn't that a great feeling?'

He took a breath. 'When I've got all I want, I'll let you know.'

CHAPTER
12

'Ms De Rossi, can I have a word?'

Vera dropped her eyes to the woman's name tag. 'Nurse Boas, of course.'

'Call me Wendy. We haven't met yet; I see from your aunt's file you often pop in to Connolly House during the afternoon shift after I've left.'

'I run a café in Hanrahan. Mornings can be a little busy.'

'So I hear! My daughter keeps telling me how lovely The Billy Button is. I'm looking forward to visiting.'

'That's very kind of her so say so. Is everything all right?'

'Yes ... and no.'

Alarm rendered her vocal cords useless for a moment. 'Please, tell me what's wrong.'

'Your aunt has been a little out of sorts during the night.'

'Unwell?'

The nurse grimaced. 'Cranky would be a better word.'

'Jill? She's never cranky.'

'It's certainly the first time we've noticed it. It is not unusual for dementia patients to become agitated, so perhaps we're just seeing some progression. When you're with your aunt, you may notice something we haven't that might be causing her distress. A sore tooth, a cramping toe, her hair parted on the wrong side ... perhaps we've missed something.'

'That's ... very thoughtful, Wendy. Thank you for letting me know.'

'Any time.' The nurse gestured to the waxed box Vera held in her hands. 'Is that something from the café you've brought with you?'

'Date scones. I use a lot of Jill's recipes, and this is one of hers.'

'Now who's been thoughtful? You enjoy your visit,' said the nurse.

Her aunt's voice, when she greeted her, was stronger than she'd heard it in weeks.

'Barb? Is that you? You're terribly late and I've been cross with you for *hours*.'

Strong, but still confused. 'No, my love, it's Vera,' she said, resting her hand on paper-thin skin. 'I've brought you a scone for morning tea—the one with dates. Your favourite.'

'Oh. Vera. You must be a nurse. How clever of you to know what I like. I suppose it's written in my file.'

Vera smiled, despite the tug of pain she couldn't help but feel. To be confused with her long-dead mother was bittersweet. To be confused with the nursing staff? She wasn't sure how she felt about that. Wouldn't that be a wonderful world, though, where residents of aged care facilities had their likes and dislikes documented in their files? *Jill De Rossi, vascular dementia and cardiomyopathy, aged 63, prefers date scones over plain ones, won't eat tuna sandwiches prepared with mayonnaise, enjoys classical music for an hour before dinner in the company of her favourite and only niece, Vera De Rossi.*

'Shall we go into the garden? You can hold onto my arm if you need to.'

'I am quite all right to walk,' said her aunt, 'if only this carpet would stop making me dizzy.'

The carpet was grey and nondescript. Vera ran her eyes over Jill's room but noticed nothing out of the ordinary that might have thrown her aunt out of sorts. 'Give me your arm,' she said, leading the way into the corridor. 'The sun is shining and the sky is so blue today, Aunt Jill. I think you'll love it outside.'

'If you say so, dear.'

She settled her aunt into a wicker chair and plumped up the cushion behind her thin frame. 'Comfortable?'

Her aunt's chattiness had waned, so Vera decided to dive straight into the thoughts that had been troubling her for the drive down to Cooma. 'Aunt Jill … I've been wanting to ask your advice about something.' Lots of somethings, really, and who else did she have to ask for advice?

She'd moved here to the foothills of the Snowy Mountains to simplify her life: cook, save money, lick her wounds and hunker down while the tatters of her self-respect re-knit themselves into a shape she recognised.

It had been naive to think her troubles would let her go so easily. The court case, of course. That was the trouble with a capital T that hung like a spectre over every minute of every day.

But then there was the new bit of trouble—the spark that had been kindled in her cold, bitter heart in the dimly lit foyer of the Cody and Cody Vet Clinic.

She didn't want the spark. Sparks were trouble, and she was so over being in trouble.

Her aunt's face didn't change, but Vera kept going. 'You know the great hairy mess of things I made back home? The charges, the arraignment, those hideous articles in the newspaper? Well, I've been given a choice: take an easy way out so I can move on, so *we* can move on, or dig my heels in and fight.'

Her aunt breathed in, and out, and her sparse grey lashes fluttered on a blink. Her earlier vim had sputtered out.

'What would you do, Aunt Jill?'

Her aunt said nothing, but she didn't need to. Vera knew damn well her aunt would have said *to hell with those drongos. Do what feels right.*

She took a long breath in of mountain air. Okay, then, decision made. She'd put this phone call off long enough.

'Sue?' she said as the dial tone connected. 'It's Vera.'

'Finally. What's it to be?'

She took a breath. 'I don't believe I'm guilty.'

'Vera, we talked about this. A section 10 dismissal isn't about you being saintly and earnest and taking a Mary McKillop stance. It's about wrangling through a legislative loophole and getting your life back.'

'I know. But here's the thing, Sue, I don't want to wrangle through loopholes. I do not feel that what I did was wrong, and I am not going to be made to feel guilty for that on top of everything else.'

'Vera—'

She was on a roll now, and even the thought of her lawyer's money clock spinning ecstatically with every word she spoke wasn't going to stop her.

'If I were being charged with selfishness for placing my aunt in an aged care facility that I hadn't thoroughly vetted beforehand, I'd plead guilty. If I were being charged with having lousy taste in men and being the biggest fool on the east coast of Australia, then lock me up. I'm guilty as charged and wearing all that guilt already; it's wrapped around me so bloody tightly some days I can't breathe.'

She took a moment to get some control over her voice. 'That's why, Sue,' she muttered at last. 'That's why I am *not* going to plead guilty to breaching the Surveillance Devices Act.'

She could hear her lawyer tapping on a keyboard.

'Okay, Vera. Understood. We do this the hard way.'

'Thank you, Sue. I'm sorry I'm not taking your advice.'

'Don't be sorry. I love doing it the hard way, it gives me a visceral thrill. You know how hard it is for a woman my age to feel a visceral thrill? Trust me ... you're doing me a favour. In terms of our legal stance on this, now we need to shift our mindset into offensive action rather than defensive reaction. We take these charges *down*. You ready for that, Vera? You'd better be.'

She swallowed.

'Um, yes? How about you?'

'I was born ready; I'll be in touch.'

As the call ended, she let her phone slip to the table, wishing she'd been born with just one per cent of Sue Anton's confidence.

'Well,' she said, resting her hand on her aunt's pale one. 'Decision made, Jill. I think you'd be a tiny bit proud of me.'

Jill's head was nodding, as though she was the type of woman who agreed with whatever was going on around her.

Vera snorted. As if.

Jill—the old Jill—was at her happiest when she was neck deep into an argument about politics or climate change. Jill would have had no hesitation about taking on the legal system. She'd have had no hesitation about flirting in a dimly lit foyer either.

'Cup of tea over here, ladies?'

She looked up as an orderly in navy scrubs approached them. A trolley had been set up beneath the wisteria. 'Oh, yes please. Black for me, Jill has hers with milk and—'

'Milk and one,' finished the man.

She smiled at him. 'I don't think we've met.'

'Tim. You need a little butter for that scone you've brought?'

Vera glanced at her waxed carton and the scone she'd torn into bite-size pieces. 'No, thank you, Jill's not a butter fan.'

'I'll try to remember that,' said Tim. 'Here you go.' He set two cups before them, durable china with a sturdy handle for her, and a sip cup for Jill. 'She can hold this herself, she tells me. Now, can I interest you in some reading material from my trolley? Lots of the residents enjoy having the paper read to them. There are magazines up in the common room, too, if you'd prefer to read something about four-wheel drives or surprise royal babies.'

She raised her eyebrows. 'Er … Thanks, Tim.'

She waited until he'd moved to other residents enjoying the sun, then pulled the letter she'd written from her handbag. No surprise royal babies there. 'Shall I read to you while you have your tea, Jill?'

No answer, so she cleared her throat and began anyway. '*Dear Aunt Jill. It's me again, Vera, your niece. I have a little fun news that you might enjoy …*'

By the time she finished, her aunt's gaze had drifted above the treeline to the smudge of mountain purpling the distant sky.

'Jill?'

No response.

'Is there anything you'd like to talk about, Aunt Jill? Anything you need?'

Still nothing. She glanced at her watch. There was nowhere she needed to be, and she had plenty of time. Perhaps she could put

Tim's advice into practice. Her eye fell on the newspapers he'd stacked on the wicker table, and she rifled through a few pages of the *Snowy River Star*. National politics was a nope, dry as dust; worries about drought; a bushfire out of control in the high country. She turned the page to an exposé on a local businesswoman who'd made a donation to the repertory theatre and smiled. Right up Jill's alley.

She started reading. *Businesswoman and former mayor Isabella Lang is the platinum sponsor of the upcoming Snowy River Region Repertory Theatre summer season. Opera, melodrama, and some new Australian drama is heading your way this year, with a focus on—*

She paused as the name Cody caught her eye on a side bar. She read the heading, Hanrahan Chatter, and realised she was looking at a community page. She smiled. She may have only moved two hours' drive from Queanbeyan, but in some ways it was like she'd moved a century back in time.

Our very own Josh Cody returns to Hanrahan after fifteen years and takes up a role as veterinarian in the Cody and Cody Vet Clinic founded by his younger sister Hannah Cody. Mr Cody is the only graduate of Hanrahan High ever to receive a full scholarship to the University of Sydney.

What a shame he didn't go. He'd sure put plenty of practice in at the school science lab, or so we hear, and—

Vera frowned. Was this the standard of news local readers were subjected to here in the Snowy Mountains? This sounded like the sort of trash Poppy had been subjected to that had resulted in a crying jag in her back alley.

'What a load of rubbish,' she said, moving her eyes up to the date on the paper's banner. Yes. Last week. That poor kid.

'Oh hell,' she said as a thought struck her. What was today's date? Or more to the point, what was *today*?

Wednesday. Bloody hell. Tonight was the inaugural craft group gathering at The Billy Button Café and she'd done nothing to prep for it!

She pulled her phone out of her pocket and texted Graeme, who was on the early shift. *Graeme! I totally forgot, tonight is curtain's up for the first craft meeting. Six o'clock start. I'll be there after lunch to get prepped … would you mind checking milk and egg stocks? I can pick some up here in Cooma before I drive back up the mountain.*

Her phone beeped seconds later.

Milk and eggs in stock. I've set Poppy to work prepping a tea station on the buffet in the back room. Maybe some fresh flowers, if you're passing the markets, would be a nice touch. Might want to buy a bottle of gin and some fresh lemons too, Vera, in case you need a sneaky G & T in the kitchen to get you through the evening, LOL.

She grinned. Her lovely Graeme … always brainstorming the good ideas.

Love your thinking, she tapped back.

You're the only one rostered after five pm. Want me to ask Poppy or Jackson if they can work late?

She hesitated. Having a spare pair of hands was marvellous, despite the pain her till takings felt every time she paid her casual staff their wages. And who knew how many would be coming to Marigold's evening craft group?

Let's ask Poppy. She's going back to Sydney early next week for the start of Term Four, and she's keen to get as many hours in as she can. If it's quiet, I can duck out to walk her home.

You're the boss, boss.

She smiled. Damn straight, she was. She glanced at her watch. There was no need to hurry back. Graeme could run the café with one of his manicured hands tied behind his back, and Poppy had taken to café work like a duck to water once she'd overcome her outrage at the early starts. Vera had plenty of time to work up some sandwiches and cake for the evening ahead.

She leaned back in her wicker chair, held her aunt's hand, and turned her face to the sun.

CHAPTER
13

Seven hours later, Vera was knee-deep in fabric scraps and empty teacups and had a headache playing rap music in her skull. Sixteen residents of Hanrahan were gathered around the big table in the back room of the café, but from the noise you would have supposed there were six hundred of them.

The table bristled with jugs of knitting needles, pots of glue, little yellow wheels which looked like pizza cutters but seemed to be designed to cut fabric into weirdly thin strips. Ribbon making? Hair ties?

Whatever. She'd given up trying to make sense of any of the activity going on. The food she'd prepared had been inhaled within minutes, and she'd be needing to restock her tea caddies first thing in the morning.

Kev caught her eye as she bent down to wipe up some glue that had dripped from a hot glue gun, down her second-hand sideboard, onto the wide floor planks.

'It's going well, isn't it, Vera?'

'Absolutely,' she lied, wondering if she should go get her icing spreader to lever the glue off before it became a permanent fixture.

'Even George turned up. Marigold's set him to work on detangling Mrs J's basket of embroidery threads.'

'Excellent.'

The last of the glue flicked up under her fingernail, and she stood up. Perhaps it was time for that sneaky gin and tonic.

Kev leaned a hip against the sideboard. 'Now, why don't you tell me what's got you in a bother?'

'I'm not in a bother at all, Kev. You need something? More hot water?'

'I need you to take a breath, love. If this is too busy, we can think about a new venue. Just because Marigold loves a bit of crazy craft chaos, doesn't mean you have to love it. Let's go find a table in a quiet corner and have ourselves a minute.'

Vera sighed. She would love to sit a minute. And the rush for sandwiches and cake *had* slowed. She followed Kev to a table tucked between the antique bookcase she'd restored and the fireplace and fell into a timber chair.

'It's not the craft,' she said.

'You want to tell an old man what's got you so quiet?'

She did want to unburden herself. The weight of doubt had been eating at her since leaving Jill so non-responsive in her wicker chair. The truth was, Jill was dying. Soon, too soon, Vera would be on her own, and that future frightened her. Even in a whole room full of chattering, cheery people, she felt apart, like a biscuit that had been discarded on the baking tray because its edges were a little too burned.

'I'm no good with people.'

'People. Well, that's a big word, my love. Reckon if I had to be good with every darn person out and about, I'd be quaking at the knees.'

She smiled. 'I do not believe your knees have ever quaked, Kev.'

'Shoulda seen me the day I married my Marigold. Wobbly as one of your toffee custards I was. Point I'm making, Vera, is you don't have to be good with people all at once. That's the great thing about us. We come in ones and twos as well as in great noisy bunches.'

She blew out a breath. 'My track record with dealing with them in ones and twos isn't so crash hot.'

'You let someone down? Someone let you down?'

'All of the above.'

'You're hurting, Vera. I'm sorry about that. But there's good people here in Hanrahan, ones who won't let you down.'

Kev reached a hand across the table, palm up, like he was waiting for her to place her hand in his.

She twisted the cleaning cloth she still held into a knot. 'I wish I could believe that.'

'Sure you can believe it. You've got me in your corner, haven't you?'

She smiled, and gestured to the nook they were sitting in. 'Literally.'

'You know what I mean. Your café manager, Graeme? He in your corner?'

'I guess he is.'

'Little Poppy Cody's been here working every day since she rocked up to town; she must think you're okay.'

'Well, yes.'

'And my little Marigold's taken a shine to you. She's hoping you'll join her yoga classes down at the park. She salutes the sun every dawn, and it's a treat to see that pink sunrise reflecting off the lake.'

'Okay, Kev, don't take this the wrong way, but most dawns I'm here already with my whisk whipping up eggs in a mixing bowl, and your little Marigold is a six-foot-high tower of intimidation.'

Kev cracked a smile so wide she could see a gold filling glint in one of his teeth. 'That's my woman, all right.'

Vera looked over at the table where Marigold was slicing cardboard into strips: people were laughing and comparing projects, and old George was stirring a heaped teaspoon of sugar into yet another cup of tea.

'One person at a time, Vera, that's all it takes.'

One person at a time. Maybe she could do that. Maybe then she'd work out sooner rather than later if a person she was befriending was as big a rat as her ex-boss Aaron Finch.

'Those people over there, some of them have reasons, like you do, to be shy of people. But they come out anyway, and have themselves a little chitchat and community time, and it puts a spring in their step. You just watch.'

Kev was right. George was clearly happy to be surrounded by chattering women. Everyone looked … content. She should unbend a little, socialise, stop suspecting everyone she met of being the next candidate to betray her friendship. The empty glasses could sit for a second longer while she chatted to Kev—he was as perfect a candidate as she could think of to practise socialising.

'Thanks, Kev. They do look happy, don't they?'

'Happy as galahs in a wattle tree.'

She smiled. 'A success, then. How was the food? Enough? And what about the tea? The orders seem to have slowed down a bit.'

He gave her a wink. 'First night fever, my love. They'll be regretting how much they've consumed when they spend all night shuffling to the bathroom.'

She giggled. Where was Kev when she was busy making bad decisions about guys?

'Marigold's put the word out. Everyone's to leave ten dollars in the kitty for a biscuit and a cup of tea and a contribution to wages.

They order anything off the menu, they'll pay their own. If you find yourself short, you come and find me.'

That would cover it; more than. 'Thanks, Kev. I appreciate it.'

Poppy swung her way through the kitchen doors carrying a tray of the fruitcake she'd sliced earlier into finger-thin soldiers, and began passing them around. The girl had taken to café work like … words failed her. Like a goth to eyeliner? Like a teenage girl to mood swings? She watched on as old George accepted a slice of cake and promptly dropped it in his basket of thread.

'I'll help you, Mr Juggins,' she heard Poppy say.

'Cake disaster,' Vera murmured to Kev and rose from her chair to rescue the rest of the fruitcake so Poppy could help the old man.

'Call me George,' she heard him say.

'Call me Poppy,' said Poppy.

'Poppy! That's a pretty name for a pretty girl. Look out, don't mess up my work, young lady. I've spent an hour sorting out this tangle.'

'Yes, George.'

Vera could hear the girl giggling as she passed around the rest of the cake, filled water glasses, plucked cotton snarls from her black apron.

She smiled. So okay, maybe this community craft caper wasn't all bad. And she'd taken three bookings for lunch next week from tonight's guests.

Her thoughts drifted back to the half-made quilt she'd pulled out of one of Jill's boxes. Maybe she should bring it along to the craft group and try to finish it; gussy it up a little. Take a seat at the table, push through her reluctance to get involved, and do something good for her aunt, at long last. Her aunt should have a little colour draped over her knees, not a bland beige hospital blanket.

Her eyes fell on Marigold. The woman was a dynamo, darting about the table, voicing her opinions as though they were commandments. She and her aunt would have bonded like fondant onto cake. Bringing Jill's quilt along, and setting a few stitches in if the café was quiet, was doable. Winter would be a shock to both her and her aunt, this far up in the Snowy Mountains. She'd love to be able to tuck Jill's quilt over her knees … all she had to do was get the thing finished.

Fabric, cotton, wadding, scissors. If she could make a lemon soufflé, surely she could bang together the other half of a quilt?

The guilt of all the things she *hadn't* done for Jill—like ensure she was in a safe home—came crashing into her mood and she reached out a hand to steady herself.

'Vera, we're out of cake, and that's the last of the sandwiches, too. Do we have any more?'

She stared blindly at the girl for a moment.

'Vera?' said Poppy. 'You okay? You look a bit funny.'

Pretending she was okay wasn't easy, but she'd had plenty of practice. 'I'm fine. Don't worry about the food, perhaps just take the teapot around again.'

'Sure thing.'

'And, um, Poppy? Are you right to hold the fort for five minutes? I just want to duck out back for a second.'

'Wow. I'll be the boss? You know I'm fifteen, right?'

Vera forced a smile, pulled off her apron and set off through the kitchen and out the back, but the second the door closed behind her, she sank onto the back step and felt her dam wall of pretence break.

Shit. Shit, shit, *shit*. Why couldn't this grief for her old life be done already? This guilt over stuffing her aunt into a crappy care home and making a total balls-up of everything? She was tired of crying, and having to make excuses, and run from rooms so she could hide what a total mess she was.

A bump at her elbow made her look down; the cat was there, its round furry face looking up at her expectantly.

'I don't have milk if that's what you're after,' she sniffed. 'And if it's answers you're after, I sure as hell don't have any of those.'

The cat butted her elbow again as though to make doubly sure she knew it was there, then it curled itself onto the step beside her and commenced making a noise like it had a lawnmower tucked away under all that fur.

Was that … purring? Her life was swirling down the plughole into a sewer-stink of regret, and her new bestie thought this was something to purr about?

'You suck at empathy,' she muttered.

But the longer she sat on the step, the warmer her right hip began to feel under the cat's weight, and the more that loud rumble of a purr began to sink into her soul. The tears had stopped. Her breathing had sorted itself out. She felt … a little wrung out, like she always did when her emotions found themselves exposed … but better.

'I suppose I'd better go and rescue my fifteen-year-old employee from those tea guzzlers,' she said to the cat.

It ignored her, but in a very empathetic way.

CHAPTER
14

By the end of the week, Jane Doe had taught Josh that her day wasn't done until he'd taken her out for a late afternoon stroll about the park. Saturday was no exception. When he reckoned the old girl had sniffed enough trees and park benches and rhododendrons, he headed back to the clinic and found Hannah sitting on the bottom step of the inner stairwell.

'Hey, it's the weekend and *I'm* the sucker on call,' he said. 'What are you doing spending your time off sitting here in the dark?'

She leaned back and crossed her arms. Even in the dim light spilling down from the landing upstairs he could see she had her cranky face on.

'If this is about the orange juice from your fridge,' he said, 'I'll replace it next time I go to the supermarket. Pinky promise.'

He held out his little finger but she batted it away.

'I thought you'd solved the city council problem, Josh.'

'What, that silly chicken complaint? I went down there, didn't I? I even booked an appointment with—' Oh, crap. The appointment had been for Monday morning up at the council office on Quarry Street, and with the excitement of having Poppy home, he'd totally forgotten about it.

'Barry O'Malley?' said his sister.

'Yep. I should have gone to see him the other day. Shoot.'

'That might explain the letter that I just got from Barry. Hand delivered, in person.'

'Our local member came here?'

'He asked to see you, but you were out with your girlfriend here, piddling on trees in the park, so he gave me the lowdown.'

'The lowdown on what?'

'Read it and see,' she said, shoving the letter in his hand.

He flicked on the overhead light, then took a seat next to his sister on the bottom step. Jane Doe flopped to the floor with a grunt.

To Hannah Cody and Joshua Cody

Cody and Cody Vet Clinic

Yeah, he knew what their names were and what their business was called. He scanned down until he reached the meat of the letter.

… failed to address the complaint received by council from a member of the public regarding chickens … council is obliged to deal with all complaints … subsequently received a second complaint, details of which are attached.

Josh lifted the letter to reveal the second page.

A complaint has been received by council that indicates subsection 12(1) of the Companion Animals Act 1998 *has been broken by owners and staff of the Cody and Cody Vet Clinic as a result of their continued practice of exercising dogs in the area outside clinic grounds without ensuring said dogs are wearing collars identifying the dogs' names and the owners' addresses or phone numbers.*

'What the fruit?' said Josh. 'This is about the dumbest thing I've ever read.'

'Yeah,' said Hannah. 'Pity you weren't here to say that to Barry.'

He turned back to the cover letter.

… where complaints are not addressed, council reserves the right to deny renewal of, or suspend for a period of 90 days, constituent privilege. In this instance, that privilege would be the veterinary practice business licence on issue to Hannah Celine Cody and Joshua Preston Cody of 36 Salt Creek Flats Road, Hanrahan.

'What was Barry O'Malley's take on all this?'

'He said it sounded like a crock of shit, but he's obliged to respond to all complaints that aren't anonymous.'

'Someone put their name to this bullshit? Who?'

'He wouldn't tell me.'

'Well, hell. It must have been someone pretty close by if they can work out there's no phone number on Jane Doe's collar.'

'It's just so … mean-spirited. Who would do this?'

He let out a breath. 'No idea. Wait, you don't think …'

'What? Who?'

'Remember Kelly Fox? She brought her kid's guinea pig in the day Poppy came to town, and it didn't go so well.'

'I don't know, Josh. Kelly's a gossip, but she's not evil. Besides, we'd already received the chicken complaint before you ran her out of here.'

'Well, someone's messing with us. I don't like it.'

'Neither do I,' Hannah said. 'What will we do?'

'I'll go see this Barry O'Malley guy first thing Monday morning and resolve the chicken problem. Maybe we get a bulk order of collars made so when you or me or the vet nurses are toddling a dog around the park for a post-operative walk, we don't get another of these idiotic complaints. I'll give him a copy of our collar order, take up our records so he can see we haven't got some bizarre secret income stream from harbouring chickens onsite.'

'Good idea,' she said. 'Better print everything up and take copies. We should probably start a file if we're going to tackle this like adults.'

He groaned. 'I hate paperwork.'

'Well, sure, we can find out who's trying to bully us by throwing eggs at everyone who comes too close to the dogs in the park, but is that really going to work?'

'Okay, point taken. I can be an adult. I'll print and file everything.'

'Okay then.'

'Okay,' he said.

His sister didn't budge from her position on the bottom step.

'You got something else you want to talk about?' he said.

She sighed. 'Not really.'

'Nothing about … Tom Krauss, for instance?'

She stood up abruptly. 'Definitely nothing about him. On that note, I'm going for a bath. Don't forget you're on call tonight.'

He held up his mobile phone. 'The devil's instrument is glued to my hand. You going to be here in the building in case I'm gone during the night? I don't want Poppy to be alone.'

'Of course I'll be here. It's not like I ever go out.'

He yelled after her as she walked up two flights of stairs to her flat. 'The world wouldn't stop spinning if you did!'

He looked at his phone and decided it was way too early to be hoping Poppy would have finished her shift at the café. He headed into the office to find an online shop that might fulfil bulk orders of dog collars.

He was ten collars richer and a hundred bucks poorer when he had a brainstorm. If he was heading into council offices on

Monday anyway, that would be the perfect time to check on his development application for the heritage work he intended to do on the outside of the building. Splicing new timber into the unsound verandah posts, repair work to the masonry window trims and the big one—the roof—was going to take some careful thought. The most important part for the renovation, however, would be restoring the downstairs entry to its original state, rather than keeping the cheap but functional shopfront his grandparents must have had built before opening the haberdashery store.

Expensive, time-intensive, and tricky work … but he'd enjoy doing it.

He printed off a copy of his application, so he'd have it handy for his Monday visit, and was just losing himself in some online research into tuckpointing mortar, when the phone out in the reception room rang.

His mobile finally caught the call diversion and trilled in his pocket. Please god it wasn't some farmer from down on the flats needing help with a difficult calving.

'Josh Cody,' he said by way of greeting.

'Mister? My mum's seen your lost dog notice down at the Cooma Markets and she says you've got my dog.'

It took a second for the message to sink in. 'Your dog … do you mean the brown labrador?' He looked down at the fat animal currently sprawled over his boot.

'Yes, sir. My Rosie's been missing a couple months or more, and my brother told me the drop bears done her in and ate her for snacks.'

Josh closed his eyes. 'How old are you, mate?'

'Seven.'

'Uh-huh. You reckon your mum can bring you into the clinic here in Hanrahan so we can see if our lost dog is your Rosie?'

'I can ask her.' The boy's voice didn't sound overly hopeful.

He tried again. 'Maybe your mum can come to the phone and I can have a chat with her now?'

'Oh, she's not here now. She works nights on the new freeway with one of them Stop Go signs.'

'Okay. Well, maybe when she gets home you can ask her to drive you here. Or call me.'

'I guess.'

He wondered if he ought to mention the eight puppies snoozing away in their pen. 'When did your dog go missing?'

'When I was six.'

He grinned. This was like pulling teeth. 'What's your name, kid?'

'Parker.'

'Parker, when you were six, was that just a little while ago?'

'I had a cake, even, from the bakery. Seven candles, so that makes me seven now.'

'It sure does. Listen, you know anything special about your dog? Maybe she can do a trick, or has a scar, and I can check to see if this lost dog I've got here has the same one? Then we'll know if this really is your Rosie.'

'Well, she loves tuna out of a can with an egg cracked over it.'

Yeah, like that would narrow it down. What labrador didn't love food? 'Anything else?'

'She drools when I eat vegemite on toast. Oh, and I know, she used to love swimming and running, but then she got some grey around her snout because she's old and she just sleeps all the time instead of playing footie with me in the backyard.'

A soft snore rumbled out of the dog sleeping on his foot. Grey hair did sprinkle Jane Doe's snout, just as the boy described. 'Get your mum to give me a call, Parker. And if this is Rosie we've got here, don't you worry, because we're looking after her, okay?'

'Yes, sir. Thank you, Mr Cody.'

He slipped the phone back into his pocket. Parker sounded pretty adorable, but still. Jane Doe had grown on him. He looked at his watch. He could go upstairs and put another coat of paint on the bathroom ceiling while he waited for Poppy to finish her shift, or he could go and have one beer at the café. Chat with his daughter *and* get his eyes on the new owner again, just to see if that spark she'd lit in him last week was the real deal.

He eased his boot out from under the snoring dog and headed for the back door. A beer it was.

CHAPTER
15

Vera had spied Marigold and Kev in the café just after sundown, but she'd been procrastinating ever since. Was she ready? Was she filled with courage and swag and all that other confident stuff she'd been talking herself into?

Of course not. Having a noble idea three nights ago about finishing her aunt's quilt was one thing … actually doing it was another.

Her chance to do or die came when Marigold swanned over to the cake cabinet to inspect the desserts in minute detail.

'And what's this pale pink concoction, Vera, my love?'

'Rosewater meringue. It's served deconstructed with strawberries and gold kiwi fruit and crème anglaise.'

'Mmm. And in those tall glasses?'

'Oh, I think you'll like that a lot. Have you ever been to Italy?'

Marigold shook her head.

'My tiramisu trifle will take you there. It's served with a generous tipple of amaretto sluiced over it, homemade ice-cream, and whipped mascarpone.'

'Vera—stop talking, start serving. I'm about to embarrass us all and start drooling.'

Vera busied herself gathering long silver spoons. 'Um, Marigold, I wonder if I might ask you something.'

'Honey child, I am yours. Ask away.'

'I have this unfinished project. My aunt started it, but her fingers gave way well before her mind started to, and I think—if I can finish it—it might bring her a little pleasure. She loves colour so much, you see, and the blankets at Connolly House are very bland.'

'A craft project? Vera, you dark horse. Do you have it with you? Let's have a look.'

She reached down and pulled out the calico tote she'd hidden under the counter for this very purpose. Marigold grabbed it from her and bustled into the back room to the big table.

'Oh my,' she said, as Jill's quilt spilled out in all its dazzling brightness. 'It's the beginnings of a rag quilt.'

Vera frowned. 'Is that a thing I should have heard of?'

Marigold grinned at her. 'You've promised to finish this, but you don't know what it is?'

She shrugged. 'Uh-huh.'

'All quilts are special, but this one is special in the way it's made. Usually we make one enormous quilt top, then worry about wadding and whatnot.'

'Okay.' She was totally lost, but it seemed easier just to agree. Maybe if she appeared totally clueless, Marigold or one of the other crafty types would take pity on her and offer to finish it. She could pay them in jam drops. Or chocolate sundaes with hot fudge brownie sauce.

'A rag quilt is different. You make lots of small squares—scrap fabric on the top, wadding, scrap fabric on the bottom—then when you have enough squares, you stitch them together. The joins ruffle up around each little square to give the quilt texture. It's a perfect way to build a quilt as large as you want even if you only have a very small workspace.'

'Small like a coffee table and one sewing needle?'

Marigold pulled her in and gave her a rousing kiss on the temple. 'Small like one amazing craft group filled with people who will help.' She grinned at Vera. 'You are so bringing this every Wednesday night from now on. Oh! The fun we are going to have. Choosing the colours from a scrap fabric stash is my favourite thing.'

Vera smoothed her hand over the fabric. 'I don't have sewing skills, but I would like to learn. I promised myself I'd finish this for Jill, and so far it's just one more promise I've not seen through.' She flashed a look up at Marigold. 'I'd be grateful for your help.'

'Oh, pet. You're so sad, and you shouldn't be. You're letting guilt get in the way of your life. Come on, let's wrap this up so it's safe, and you and I will put our heads together on Wednesday and get started, okay?'

She smiled. 'Thank you.'

'Now, let's get back to that dessert cabinet before someone snatches those tiramisu things out from under us. My need, Vera, is great!'

She'd no sooner delivered their desserts and tucked her calico tote back away under the counter when Poppy was leaning into her.

'Oh goodie, Dad's here.'

She looked up and then wished she hadn't. Josh had settled at the stool on the end of the counter and his eyes settled on her like a firebrand.

'He ordered a beer.'

'Excellent, um, excuse me I just—'

And like a coward she darted into the kitchen where she contemplated shoving her head into the freezer for a couple of seconds to make sure her cheeks weren't flushing.

'You're chicken-hearted, Vera,' she told the jumbo packet of frozen peas taking up the second shelf. The pea packet seemed to agree. After a moment, the thought of how huge her electricity bill was going to be if she stood in her freezer door every time the vet came into the café made her see how ridiculous she was being.

This was her café, damn it. She marched back out a few moments later with a dish of *tartes aux fraises* to top up the stock out front, determined to be composed. There were a dozen tables she could concentrate on serving, and Poppy could certainly serve any food her father might require.

'Well, well, if it isn't the talk of the town,' said a loud, stroppy voice by the till.

'Oh, golly,' muttered Poppy.

Vera looked up from the dish of tarts she was hoping would tempt the guests who liked to pop in after the early Saturday night movie screening for dessert. 'What's up?'

'You know how Dad's here?'

'Yes,' she said cautiously.

'Well, so is guinea pig woman. She must have been at the movies with her kid, because they've just rocked up. That's her in the doorway, the one with the bulging eyes and the zippered-up mouth.'

Guinea pig woman and son? Oh. The penny dropped. She looked across the servery and saw a pretty blonde woman with a pouty face and big hair marching towards the counter stool where Josh Cody had taken a seat with a beer and today's *Snowy River Star*.

'The woman from the clinic who trash-talked your mum?'

'That's her.'

'You think it's going to get ugly?'

Poppy grinned. 'Here's hoping.'

She frowned at her young assistant. 'Just because you're leaving town on Monday doesn't mean the rest of us can. Let's try and avoid a ruckus, shall we? I'll try and head her off. Think you can do a better job than me slicing this tart?'

Poppy shrugged. 'Maths is my best subject. A hundred per cent of tart divided into eight equal segments comes to twelve point five per cent per slice. Yeah, no probs.'

Vera could feel a wrinkle forming on her forehead. 'Who are you, and what have you done with my favourite fifteen-year-old?' She handed Poppy the knife. 'I'll go serve this woman. Try not to mention the words guinea and pig out loud.'

Poppy's giggle gave her a warm little rush, as did the arm the girl slung around her. 'You're the best boss, boss. I'll stay close in case Dad goes nuts again and has to be dragged out.'

Vera eyed Josh as she came around to the public side of the counter. He'd set his beer down and was looking up at the big-haired woman, all bland charm. Vera busied herself wiping her sticky hands on her apron and hovered closer so she could intervene if things got noisy.

'Kelly,' he said. 'How lovely to see you again. And Braydon, isn't it?' He reached out and shook the teenager's outstretched hand. Maybe she wasn't going to have to intervene after all.

'The kid's kinda cute,' she stage-whispered to Poppy.

'I know, right?'

She glanced at the girl, who grinned up at her. Kids. Who knew they could be this fun? She had a sudden image of a sprightly Jill, walking alongside her teen self on the windswept beaches south of Canberra, her head thrown back, her rich laughter filling the air. She'd always thought she, Vera, had been the lucky one, to have Jill step in and look after her when her mother died … but perhaps her aunt had found herself just as rewarded?

If she hadn't met Poppy, she'd never have understood that.

'Oh-oh,' she heard Poppy mutter.

Events seemed to be heating up at the end of the counter.

'Don't you Kelly me, Josh Cody,' the stroppy woman was saying, and not in her inside voice. 'Not after the way you treated me in your clinic. You've got a nerve, coming back here and talking down to me. The whole town knows why you ran out.'

The newspaper Josh had been reading snapped shut.

'Jeepers,' said Poppy. 'Apeshit alert.'

Vera cleared her throat. Where was Graeme when she needed him? 'Are you allowed to say that word, Poppy Cody?'

'In dire circumstances.'

She could see the girl's point.

'Kelly,' said Josh, his tone even louder than the woman's. 'Getting a job to support your family is not "running out". Now, why don't you stop bitching about ancient business and let me buy you a drink for old times' sake, hey? How about you, Braydon? My daughter Poppy makes a double-fudge chocolate macadamia sundae that ought to be banned, it's so good. What do you say?'

The woman wasn't saying anything nice. 'Don't you sweet-talk me. I've never been so insulted as the day you turned us away from your clinic.'

'Mum. I'd kinda like a sundae.'

Vera knew a silver lining when she heard one. 'That's your cue,' she said to Poppy. 'You get the kid to this end of the counter and start layering up as many sugar-rich calories as you can into a sundae dish. I'll wrangle the mother away from your dad.' She smoothed down her apron, took a deep breath, then glided over in her most Graeme-like way.

'Good evening. Welcome to The Billy Button Café. Can I show you to a table?'

'Oh, well. I'm not sure—'

Vera scanned the café, looking for a table as far from Josh as possible. 'Table six! Right near the bookcase.' She herded the woman in and ransacked her brain. What would Graeme do?

She had it. 'What a heavenly scarf. I love that coral colour on you.'

'Oh.' The woman ran a hand through her hair. 'Well, it's new, I bought it on a girls' weekend in Melbourne, so thank you for noticing.'

'My name's Vera,' she said, and pulled menus from her apron and laid them on the table. 'The dessert special for moviegoers tonight is sticky date pudding, half price if you hand in your movie ticket, or we have our regular menu available as well.'

She shot a look over to the counter where Poppy gave her a thumbs up. Peace had been restored, and it had just taken a little ingenuity and schmooze. Teamwork. Just one of the many skills she'd acquired since moving to Hanrahan. 'I'll be back to take your order in a bit.'

Sixteen mains, the movie-dessert deal for four couples and only one broken glass later, the evening rush was over and just the honeymoon table was still busy: Marigold and Kev lingering over a drunken tiramisu trifle for two.

A deep voice by her side had her jumping so bad she rammed her thumb into the sliding door of her dessert cabinet.

'You slice a neat piece of tart, Vera.'

Josh. She blamed her racing heart on the start he'd given her. And the three coffees Graeme had made her this afternoon before he'd headed home.

She looked up at him, thankful that Poppy had retired to the kitchen to run crockery through the dishwasher. She'd had time to rethink that breathy moment in the vet's foyer, and all the sparks of awareness she'd felt the next half-dozen times she'd laid eyes on her young waitress's dad—and the thoughts had all come to the same resounding conclusion: she didn't do relationships. Period. Regardless of temptation.

She looked down into her pristine display cabinet. 'I like to keep things neat and tidy. No mess, no jagged edges, no getting muddled up with the topping on the desserts either side.'

He grinned. 'You talking about desserts? Or yourself?'

She frowned. Hot *and* perceptive. It was an unfair mix. She hunted for a change in topic.

'We'll be sad to say goodbye to Poppy. She's worked so hard this week, and the customers have grown very fond of her.'

'I'm more thankful than you know. To see her here, surrounded by the community, fitting in … it's just the change from city life I was hoping she would experience.'

She snorted. 'Hanrahan is definitely not the city.'

He slanted her a look. 'Where exactly did you move up from? I asked you before, but I don't think you said. Canberra?'

She didn't feel quite so defensive this time about answering his questions. Why that was, she wasn't sure. 'Queanbeyan.'

'Huh. You support Canberra or New South Wales come grand final time?'

She smiled. 'Not everyone's a rugby league tragic, Josh.'

'So true. I'm more of a museum and jazz club person than a footie bloke.'

She eyed him over the counter. Was he having a joke? Hadn't she heard somewhere that Josh Cody had been a sporting star back when he was in high school?

Kev slid in beside them, his wallet in his hand. 'Now that's the sort of bare-arsed lie my old gran used to say would bring lightning down on my head, Joshua Cody.'

Josh grinned. 'Hey, give me a break, Kev. I don't want Vera to think I'm a philistine.'

He didn't look even vaguely embarrassed at being called out. The opposite. She watched him pat the old guy on the back and ask him about his prize roses, a subject Kev seemed thrilled to be engaged with. She forgot about the fact she was determined to put Josh out of her head, and instead let her eyes linger on him while he chatted.

His dark blond hair was mussed up. His mouth was quirked in a grin as he looked from Kev over to his daughter who had emerged from the kitchen, pride and amusement clear on his face as he watched her bustle about the café wiping tables.

She felt her resolve to deny temptation waver. *Why did he have to be so darned adorable?*

'Did you say something?'

Josh was looking across the counter at her, and that indulgent, affectionate smile was now directed—god help her—at her. Crap. Had she said that out loud?

She cleared her throat and returned to her safe subject. 'How's Poppy liked working here this week? She's certainly earning her wages, she works like a Trojan. Washing dishes, clearing tables ...' She smiled. There was no need to guess where Poppy's people skills came from. 'Cosying up to the old timers. She's a natural.'

He shook his head. 'I'm impressed. Really.'

Were those tears in his eyes? Holy dooley. Why, oh why, now that she'd declared her vow of non-involvement with anyone, good-looking guys in particular, had she run into Mr Perfect, who went all gooey-eyed when his teenage daughter managed to hold down a job for seven days?

She straightened her spine. She had a kitchen to tidy up, and guests to kindly but firmly shove in the direction of the door. Chattering with handsome men was not on her to-do list.

She cleared her throat and turned to Kev. 'You'll be wanting to settle up, I expect, Kev?' she said, running up his bill and swiping the card he held out to her. 'See you, Marigold,' she called over his shoulder, then took a step backwards so this counter chitter-chatter with Josh couldn't turn into a tete-a-tete. 'Well, I'm on the payroll too, in a manner of speaking, so I'd best get back to—'

'Vera.'

She paused. 'Yes?'

'About the other night in the foyer, when I was a little forward, and you were a little unimpressed.'

Unimpressed? Wow, that was not the word she'd have chosen to describe the moment when Josh had tried to kiss her and she'd turned her cheek. Dazzled, regretful, thrilled, ashamed ... all at the same time.

'Yes?' she said, cautiously. She eased out of earshot of Marigold and Kev, who were taking their time wrapping themselves in jackets and patting their pockets for keys and inching at a snail's pace to the door.

Josh didn't seem deterred. 'You want to, I don't know. Go for a walk sometime? A movie?'

Oh, damn. Damn, damn, damn. Vera had a brief vision of another world, where she didn't have a court case hanging over her head with the possibility of incarceration. Where her aunt still knew who she was and didn't need round-the-clock respite care. Where she worked diligently as a newspaper journalist for a benevolent and avuncular boss who valued her worth and didn't sleep with her then sell her out. Where she hadn't lost her trust in people and could accept an invitation to a movie with a gorgeous man whenever she damn well chose.

But that fantasy world was just that: fantasy. And her real world was complicated enough without adding a date into the mix.

'I can't. I'm sorry.'

'You can't? Why not?'

She frowned, and lowered her voice as Poppy moved past with a tray to clear the Joneses' table. 'How is that a tactful thing to ask? I can't, all right, and I don't need to explain my reasons.'

'Boyfriend? Husband?' He raised his eyebrows. 'Girlfriend?'

'None of the above.'

He nodded, as though the information she had given him was what he'd expected. His next comment was definitely not what she was expecting.

'You've got coconut on your cheek.'

'What?'

He reached a big hand over and swiped his thumb across her cheekbone. She felt it the way she imagined a steer at a cattle station might feel a brand. She reared her head back.

'Don't.' Her voice was louder than she'd planned, and she felt Poppy's eyes lift in their direction. Perfect. Now she'd brought attention to herself having a moment with her employee's father. She must be the most unprofessional person alive.

It was his turn to frown. He held his hands up and took a step backwards. 'Hey, Vera. I'm sorry if I upset you.'

She drew in a shallow breath. 'I'm not upset.' Bitter, angry, disillusioned … yes. But not with him. With herself and her own mosh pit of drama.

'Dad, is everything okay?'

His eyes, the curious expression she read there, drifted from her to his daughter. 'Sure, honey. I thought I'd walk you home, if you're finished. Jane Doe's tied up to the streetlamp outside. Poor girl needs a break from those eight hooligans she's given birth to.'

'Vera? You want me to help you tidy up?'

'No, Poppy. You go on home.' And take your handsome father with you. 'I've got this.'

'Cool. Dad, come on. I'm starving. I'm heading back to school on Monday afternoon, Vera, but can I call you if I'm coming up for a weekend? Just in case, you know, you need a super keen waitress for a few hours?'

'Sure, thanks honey. Enjoy school.' Vera watched them leave then turned to the counter and just stood there a moment until a lean, sun-spotted hand reached over hers.

Kev was back.

'All right, Vera?'

She paused. Fixed a smile to her face, then felt some of her stress melt as he brought his other hand up over hers, holding her there.

'I'm fine.'

Kev cocked a bushy eyebrow in the direction of the doorway, where a fat brown labrador was leaping up at her fifteen-year-old waitress. Josh was chatting to Marigold and watching indulgently while the dog and the girl behaved as though they'd been separated by stormy oceans for a decade.

'Your shoulders got all droopy, my lamb. What's got you and the town sweetheart all lathered up?'

She shot her eyes back to Kev's face. 'Excuse me?'

He winked at her, tapped his nose. 'He's a mighty fine-looking fella. Reminds me of me when I was a lad. Something else you should know about him, too. He's loyal. You don't find that very often.'

Vera could feel a blush staining her cheeks. 'You're imagining things, Kev. Now, if you'll excuse me, I've got a stray cat in the alley waiting for her saucer of milk.' She rushed through the swing doors to the kitchen before anyone else could drag her into a conversation and read her all-too-obvious thoughts about Josh Cody.

She was so not ready for life in a small town.

CHAPTER
16

Josh ripped off his tie and threw it into the corner of the treatment room. He'd made no progress whatsoever with his heritage works development application, but that was only the first setback of his Monday morning. 'Next time,' he ranted at his sister, 'you're going to see Barry bloody O'Malley. Two hours I waited before he showed up, Hannah, *two hours*, and he still wouldn't tell me who lodged those complaints. There were about a hundred other things I would rather have been doing on Poppy's last day.'

Hannah had her hand halfway down the throat of a bull mastiff and didn't look up. 'I thought you'd been a long time. Lucky we had a quiet day here; I sent Sandy home after lunch.'

'Yeah, lucky,' he said sourly.

'That bad, huh?'

'Remember Principal Kincaid—made you sit on the bench outside his office for an hour, then when you finally got in to tell your side of the story he actually didn't give a shit?'

'Aha!' Hannah slowly withdrew her arm from the dog's mouth, bringing a broken-off shaft of chicken bone with her. She tossed it into the rubbish bin and turned to Josh. 'Unlike you, I never got called to the Principal's office, Josh. He thought I was an asset to the school. Citizenship Awards five years straight if I recall correctly.'

'Well, if you're such an asset, why don't you take these nuisance complaints up with council?'

'I don't own a tie.'

He snorted. 'You can borrow mine.'

Hannah plunged a needle into a bottle of antibiotics and then injected the fluid into the dog's neck. 'Give me a second, here, will you? Rambo's my last patient for the day, then we can lock up and you can tell me all about it. There might be a couple of beers in the blood fridge if we're lucky.'

'Sure. I'll go check on the patients.'

She looked up at him. 'Hey, did that kid's mum ring back about Jane Doe? Those pups are getting bigger by the day. They're a month old now … we're going to have to think of fostering them out in a few weeks if an owner doesn't show. We can't put them in the dog run out back unsupervised; the other animals will trample them. Or worse.'

'Nothing so far. To tell the truth, me and Jane Doe have got a bit of a thing going. I'd miss her, especially with Poppy going back to Sydney this evening.'

His sister grinned. 'Tell me something I don't know. But no matter how much I love you, which is quite a lot most of the time, and not at all when you've been helping yourself to the contents of my pantry, we're not keeping eight labrador pups.'

He headed next door to the sleepover room where cages lined the walls. Cats ignored him from various small cages on the upper tiers, as did a western black snake who'd swallowed a fake egg, and an overweight mouse doing circuit work on its wheel. The furballs

in the big low pen weren't ignoring him, however. He could hear
their beating tails and their yips from the door.

'Hey, Dad.'

'Popstar! I didn't see you there. You all packed? Only a few hours
'til I need to take you down to the train station.'

His daughter had crawled into the pen and was seated in the
corner, her lap covered in squirming pups.

'All sorted. And … I'm so pleased I stayed until the last possible
minute, because you will never guess what's happened!'

'Try me.'

She spun the fattest pup, the brown male, around to face him.
Sleepy eyes stared up at him, then drifted to a snoozy close.

'No,' she ordered. 'Wake UP, Maximus. Show Dad your new trick!'

She plopped him on all fours, and he promptly splayed on the
ground like a bag of sand.

'Come on, Maxie, you've got this,' she urged, and lifted him up
again. He teetered on all paws for a second, then staggered like a
drunken sailor towards the pyramid of fur that was his brothers and
sisters.

He grinned. 'He can walk, finally. He is the fattest runt ever.
You want to help me weigh them?'

'Sure. Pass me the scales and I'll do it in here. I already cleaned
out the pen and gave them fresh bedding.'

'You're a champ, Pop,' he said, squatting on the floor beside her.

'I know.' She grinned up at him, and he almost commented on
the makeup that was missing from her eyes, the absence of teen-
pouty-face he'd grown used to over the last year, but managed to
stop himself at the last second.

'This one's called Max, huh?'

'Yep. That's his name because he's the biggest, even if he is the
slowest to learn anything besides feeding.' She lowered the pup

into the bowl of the old kitchen scales they used for small animals. 'Eight pounds? Dad, how ancient are these scales? Australia's been metric for about a hundred years.'

'I can convert, Miss Smartypants. Those scales belonged to your great grandparents, so show some respect. You named them all?'

'Uh-huh. The three black ones are Angus, Bingo and Carmelita. The yellow ones are Frodo, Pumpkin, Kylie and Doofus.'

He wrote the weights down in the chart—weighed words in his head while he was at it—each one of them a whole lot heavier than a plump pup.

He'd put this off long enough. Any longer, and his daughter would be on a train heading north and he'd miss his chance. 'Pop.'

'Yes, Dad?'

'I've been meaning to talk to you about what happened in my office that day, and now you're leaving, and well ... I should have said something sooner about, you know, why Kelly was in the clinic digging up old gossip.'

'About you and Mum?'

Boy. No wonder he'd left bringing it up for so long. This was *hard*. He pushed the scales to the side and sat on the floor next to the cage. 'Your mum was a student teacher at my high school when I was in my senior year.'

Poppy made a gagging noise. 'You really don't need to tell me this, Dad.'

He smiled. 'Relax. This is not the beginning of a birds and bees talk. Just hear me out, will you?'

She rolled her eyes. 'If I must.'

Jane Doe stood up in the pen, dislodging the pups clinging to her side, and clambered over the high lip of the gate to settle down beside him. She rested her head in his lap. 'We liked each other. A lot. And when school was out, we got together.'

'Like, *together* together?'

'Yep. And your mum fell pregnant.'

'With me.'

'With you, Poptart.'

'And you were like eighteen? Dad. That is so not cool.'

He chuckled. 'Thanks for the heads up. Anyway, the thing about carrying on like you're an adult, means you've got to start behaving like one. We had to make some difficult choices, both of us, and so I gave up my plan to go to university, and your mum returned to finish her teaching studies in Sydney. I went with her and found a job to set us up as a family.'

'You lived with Mum when I was little?'

'Sure. But after a while we worked out we were going to be better parents, and the best of friends, if we lived separately.'

Poppy was quiet. 'And that's what Mrs Fox was talking about.'

'Yep. Small towns love their gossip.'

'Dad, I've just spent the last week working in a café. I worked that one out before I learned how to ring up change on the till.'

'I just don't like to think you're the target of anyone's loose talk.'

His daughter tucked the pups up against the hot water bottle. 'Why'd you come back here, Dad, if you didn't like the way people talked about us?'

'I didn't come back, at first, not for years and years. Your grandparents always came to us because I was … bitter, I guess. But after a while my bitterness was gone and all I could remember was what I loved about Hanrahan.'

'I guess it's not the worst place I've been to.'

He smiled. 'Don't get all mushy just because you're leaving today.'

'But the gossip's pretty bad, Dad. You wouldn't believe what I hear when I'm cleaning tables. It's like being in Year Nine all over again.'

'True. But still … let me give you an animal analogy. Would you stop loving Maximus if he had a flea?'

'So the flea is the gossip and the dog is the town.'

'Uh-huh. I loved growing up here. I love having Old Regret outside my window just waiting for me to look up at each day. I love knowing people on the street, them knowing me, even if it means they know every darn thing about me, good and bad. I wanted you to know a little of what it's like to grow up here in Hanrahan, before you go away to university or get a job or go travelling and get all grown up.'

'Yeah, Hanrahan is definitely not Sydney.'

He grinned. 'You worked that out too, huh?'

She rested her hand on his knee. 'I don't hate it here as much as I thought I would.'

If happiness was sunshine, he'd have started glowing right there, that moment. 'I'm so glad to hear that.'

'Is this the right time to ask you if I can keep Maximus?'

'Only if I can keep Jane Doe.'

She grinned at him. 'You're okay, Dad. Even if you are a total dork about some things.'

'You too, Poptart. Listen, me and Hannah are having a meeting in the office, but then we can get some early dinner, pizza perhaps, if you like, before we head down to Cooma. If you've got any good-byes to say, better say them now, okay?'

'We could have lasagne for our last meal together at the café? Vera makes the best lasagne.'

He hesitated. After Vera blocked out his date request on Saturday, he was wondering if a little space might be a wise choice. She'd been upset and pretty keen to distance herself from him, and he still hadn't figured out why.

'But pizza's my favourite,' he said with his best fake sad face.

Poppy stroked the belly of the yellow pup who still lay across her lap, and it splayed contentedly under her hand. She looked up at him and pursed her lips. 'Did you have a fight with my boss, Dad?'

'No.' He reached into the pen and flicked his daughter on the ankle. 'I don't fight with anyone. Mr Calm and Cool, that's me.'

'You had a fight with Mrs Fox right next door in your office.'

He sighed. 'You got me there. But no, we didn't have a fight. If you must know, I asked her out on Saturday night, and she said no.'

She nodded her head. 'That's what Kev said.'

He inspected his daughter's face. 'You and Kev were talking about me and Vera? I thought you were paid to wash dishes, not gossip with the customers.'

She shrugged. 'Kev said he bet you'd asked Vera out, and I said no way, gross, my dad never goes out with anyone, he's, like, over *thirty*, and Kev said he was nobody's fool and he could smell April and May when it was carrying on right there in front of him, and I said what does April and May mean, and he said, it means your dad's got the hots for the café lady.'

Josh laughed, he couldn't help it. 'That's quite an analysis.'

'So.' Poppy cleared her throat. 'Do you really have the hots for Vera?'

He groaned. 'Are we really having this conversation?'

'Only, I wouldn't mind. Just in case you were wondering if I did.'

'Poppy. You're the centre of my world, you know that right?'

'Sure I do, only, you'd better cover Jane Doe's ears next time you say that. But I'm going any minute now, and then I might not be here again for ages.'

'I know.'

'What I'm trying to say, Dad, if you'd stop interrupting me, is …
maybe you should ask her out again.'

Yeah. Maybe he should.

❧

Hannah had beaten him to the beer. She handed him an open one
as he walked into the office and snicked the top off another for
herself.

'Cheers,' he said, clinking the glass neck of his bottle to hers.

'Okay,' she said. 'What did our man Barry have to say?'

'Nothing helpful. I showed him our file, suggested the concerned
citizen who was lodging all the complaints must have an ulterior
motive, but I couldn't work out what.'

'Did he agree to that?'

'Well, he spoke at me like a politician for a while, so he could
have been agreeing with me, but it was hard to tell.'

Hannah drummed her fingers on the table. 'You think that's the
end of it?'

'We've dealt with both complaints to his satisfaction—he's going
to send that to me in writing. So we have no reason to think our
business licence won't be renewed.'

'Okay. And if we get any other council problems, we'll have to
jump on it straight away.'

'Agreed.'

He swigged down the last of his beer and lobbed the bottle into
the rubbish bin. 'You know, Hannah, I'm getting the feeling that
there's more to you being all quiet and cranky than this complaints
business.' He leaned forward and covered her hand with his. 'You

want to tell me what's going on? You want me to speak to Tom Krauss about something?'

She skewered him with a look. 'You want to tell me if you started shagging Beth Horrigan before you finished high school or after graduation?'

He winced. 'That was a low blow, Hannah Cody.'

'Yeah, maybe. But maybe it'll teach you to stop mentioning Tom. Okay?'

He wanted to push a little more on the subject, but that little quaver under the surface of her voice decided him against it. 'Okay. But just so you know: he's my friend, but you're my sister. You come first, always. We clear on that?'

She closed her eyes. 'Clear. Are we done?'

'We're done. What ab—'

He broke off as he heard a phone ringing in reception. He looked at Hannah. 'You switched the night calls over to your mobile yet? I can't take this; me and Poppy have to drive to Cooma in a couple of hours.'

'Not yet.'

He heard Poppy's voice talking, then the clatter of her boots on the timber floor.

'Dad! It's Vera. There's this cat that lives behind the alley, and she thinks it's sick.'

He looked at his sister. 'This is a job for you, Hannah Banana. Me and Poppy have pizza plans.'

'Oh, but Dad!'

He sighed. He could read where this was going from a mile off. 'Yes?'

'Can't you see her? I told her to put the cat in a box and bring her straight over. I told her you were the best vet in town.'

Who could resist that plea? Besides, he felt a warm rush at hearing his daughter say it. He shot a look at Hannah. 'You hear that, Hannah? I'm the best vet in town.'

'Please. Don't make me nauseous. I've had a long day.'

'Oh,' said Poppy. 'Sorry, Aunt Hannah. But anyway, Dad's got the hots for Vera, but he had some sort of dumb fight with her, so he really needs to be the one to save her cat.'

He rolled his eyes. 'When did you say you were leaving?'

She grinned. 'You can thank me later, Dad.'

'Okay. You go let Vera in. I'll be in the treatment room. A stray cat,' he muttered to himself as he headed out of the office. 'Worms, fleas, and a bad attitude, I imagine. Lucky me.'

Hannah fell into line behind him. 'I'll assist.'

'Assist my arse. You just want to be nosy.'

'Hell yes. Who knows? I may pick up some skills from the best vet in town while I'm at it. How long have you been a registered vet now, Dr Cody? Nine months? Ten?'

He threw a chew toy at her.

The cat could be heard, but not seen. One look at the scratches crisscrossed over Vera's wrists had him taping closed the flaps of the box she'd carried in.

'Had an aversion to being helped, did she?'

'Seems like.'

He looked up from her wrists and inspected her face. There were shadows under her deep green eyes.

'Hi, Vera. I'm Hannah, Josh's sister. I saw you at the wake the other week for Mrs Juggins, but we didn't get to meet.'

'Hi. Sorry to barge in on you after clinic hours. Poppy said it was no trouble.'

Hannah met his eyes and dropped him a not-so-subtle wink. 'No trouble at all.'

Sisters. Daughters. What-oh-what had he done to be saddled with one of each? He decided to drag the interview back into medical channels before his sister embarrassed him completely. 'What makes you think the cat's sick?'

'I put some salmon out this morning and she wouldn't touch it. Then before, when I was putting out some rubbish, I could hear her making a wheezing noise. Like she couldn't breathe. She let me pat her, but as soon as I tried to put her in the box she went psycho.'

'Uh-huh. Panleukopenia, most like. Pretty common in unvaccinated cats.'

'Is it life threatening?'

He opened his mouth to say yes, but then caught his sister's eye and downgraded his answer. 'Not necessarily. Let's have a look at her and see what we can do. Hannah, you do the box, I'll get the cat. You ready?'

He pulled the longest, thickest gloves the practice owned onto his hands. 'Poppy? Better shut the treatment door. We don't want our friend here to spread her fleas all over the place.'

He heard the door shut and nodded to Hannah. 'Okay, let's go. Better stand back, Vera. Just in case.'

He slid his hands close to the join in the cardboard, and as Hannah lifted the flaps, he reached inside. Claws sank into the gloves, but not into him, and as the box opened he managed to get one hand securely on the cat's ruff. 'Well, you're a big handsome girl, aren't you? Come on, out you get.'

He set the spitting cat on the treatment table, held her firmly while Hannah moved the box off the table and came to stand by his side.

'What's the plan, Dr Expert?'

He chuckled. 'You're never going to let that go, are you?'

'Not in this lifetime.'

'I vote we sedate her. Then we can check for a microchip, run some bloods. See if she's been spayed.'

Vera's voice sounded by his side. 'Spayed?'

'If she's a stray, she has to be spayed. We can bath her, too, to get rid of any fleas or other mites she may have. Sedating her will be the kindest way to do it.'

Vera huffed out a breath. 'You know I'm broke, right? I don't know if I can afford an operation.'

'Council legislation. We can't get around it.'

'I knew I hated legislation for a reason.'

Hannah interrupted. 'You know a lot about legislation, Vera? Hey ... didn't I hear along the Hanrahan grapevine that you used to be a journalist?'

Josh raised his eyebrows at his sister over the table. Where was she going with *that* question?

'That's in the past.'

Vera's tone of voice didn't invite closer questioning. He figured they could set her mind at rest about the fee, because he knew what being broke felt like. 'Don't worry about the cost of the operation. Since you're Poppy's boss, you get the family discount.'

'Don't start sharpening your scalpel yet, Josh,' said Hannah. 'She might not be a stray.'

'Can you do the honours, Han? I'll hold her still.'

'Sure.' He watched her slide the thin needle into the thick fur on the cat's neck, then held the cat until the dose began to work. When he felt it safe, he laid the now loose-limbed animal on the table.

'Can I pat her?'

He glanced at Vera. 'Sure. But she's going to be asleep for a while, and we can keep her here overnight.'

Hannah moved in beside him with the microchip reader and slid the machine around the cat's neck, along her spine. 'Flip her for me, will you, Josh?'

He pulled the cat's legs up and rolled her over onto her other side. The cat was breathing heavily, rough snorts of air coming through her snub nose. 'Anything?'

She shook her head. 'No. She's a stray all right. Just a good-looking one.'

'Okay. Let's do this then.' He looked up at Poppy. 'You want to make Vera a cup of tea or something? We won't be long.'

'Okay. Vera?'

She seemed reluctant to go, so he gave Poppy his favourite do-as-you're-told dad look and jerked his head to the door. Jokes aside, if you weren't used to the realities of slicing into living flesh with a scalpel, you had no place in an operating theatre.

'Come on, Vera,' Poppy said again. 'I can show you Maximus on the way. He's super cute. Even cuter than Dad. Who is totally available, by the way.'

Oh. My. God. He and his daughter were going to be having a serious talk on the drive to the train station.

They'd barely been gone ten seconds when Hannah started in on him. 'She's not your usual type, Josh.'

'Like I have a type.'

'Oh come on. Lily Sanders? Penelope Kanye? Giggly and pink-cardiganed and addicted to nail salons?'

He arranged instruments in a kidney dish: scalpel, suture kit, swabs. 'That was in high school. Anyone in a bra who looked in my direction was my type at high school.'

She snorted. 'Some of them did more than look, as I recall.'

He grinned at her. 'What can I say? Chicks loved me.'

She made a gagging noise. 'No, seriously, Josh. Vera seems kind of … I don't know. Prickly.'

'Yeah. You're not wrong there.'

She swabbed the cat, held it firmly while Josh used clippers to trim her belly of fur. 'So what makes you think she's interested in you?'

He ran a hand over the animal's smooth belly. 'She's told me she's *not* interested.'

'I see. Finally, a woman of sense. Maybe she and I will become friends.'

He paused as his fingers ran over a tiny bulge. 'I think she's lying.'

'And what tells you that, hotshot? Your high school history of being ogled by anyone wearing a bra?'

He shrugged. 'I'd tell you, but it's part of the blokes' code. We know what we know.'

'You are so full of shit.'

Yeah. He probably was. But underneath it all, he did think Vera wasn't totally immune to him. And he sure as hell was not immune to her.

'Feel this, would you, Hannah?'

He watched her slide her fingers over the exposed belly of the cat. 'You thinking what I'm thinking?'

She grinned. 'Oh yes. Pregnant, but not ready to pop just yet. You want to go tell Vera she's having kittens in a month or so while I do the bath and bloods? Who knows … maybe she knows nothing about animals, and she'll need your advice so badly she'll overcome her distaste for you and agree to go on a date.'

He eyed his sister over the table. 'That's not a bad strategy, Dr Cody. How'd you come up with that idea?'

'I'd tell you, but it's part of the girl code. We know what we know.'

CHAPTER

17

The woman who had been occupying his thoughts had still been in the waiting room when he'd returned from his hour-long round trip to Cooma.

He took one look at Vera's pinched face and wanted—badly—to give her a hug, despite the quiet air of 'don't touch me' she seemed to give off.

He decided he had nothing to lose by giving his sister's strategy a go, and it turned out that even though his sister hadn't been on a date for at least eight years, as far as he knew, she wasn't wrong about girl code.

The serious-faced *I'm an animal doctor and I need to talk in a deep and compelling voice to you about your cat in a quiet just-you-and-me environment* strategy had totally worked.

The wide esplanade along the shore of Lake Bogong was quiet this late in the evening, and he'd snagged a scarf of Hannah's from the hooks in the hall and wound it around Vera's neck. The forest green suited her, made her eyes gleam with as many secrets as the deep lake water they walked beside. He wandered south, in the direction of the hall where he'd be spending his nights for the next week toiling away for Marigold.

'The cat will be alert soon, so you can see her if you like, but we'll keep her for the week to get a full course of antibiotics in and make sure she's not underweight or dehydrated.'

'So the cat's going to be fine?'

He grinned. 'Well, that depends on your understanding of the word fine. And it's cats, not cat.'

Vera stopped beside him in the glow of a wrought-iron streetlamp. 'Cats?'

'Your stray is pregnant.'

'How on earth—'

'Well,' he said, dropping his voice to a purr. 'A moonlit night, the scent of wildflowers in the air … a rugged man-cat prowling through Paterson Lane catches her eye … I think we all know how these stories end.'

She punched him in the arm, and he grinned. Vera was losing her prickles at last, and it felt good.

'I should never have put out that saucer of milk.'

'A home's not a home without a pet, Vera. Maybe it's time you gave your stray a name.'

'Oh, but—'

He waited, but Vera had fallen silent. The easy mood of a moment before had disappeared. He ran a hand down her arm until his fingers linked with her hand. She stiffened a little, but then let his hand stay there.

Baby steps, he thought, and linked his fingers more snugly around hers. 'You want to talk to me, Vera?'

She sighed. 'Josh. You've been … very kind to me.'

Such faint praise. He gave her fingers the tiniest of pinches. 'I like you.'

'You shouldn't.'

He turned to face her. 'I've been looking for a reason to stop, because you don't seem to like me too much. But damned if I can see your rationale.'

She looked up at him, then away. 'It's not that I don't like you, Josh.'

Oh, at last. This was progress. 'What is it then?'

'I've got … commitments.'

'I've got commitments, too. I have a daughter. A vet career that I'm ten years behind on starting. A sister, friends, a ute that needs new engine mounts but I'm low on funds while I finish renovating our building, and I've just been roped into ripping out an old ceiling for a friend and replacing it. When I came back home, here to Hanrahan, my commitments were all I was thinking about, but then I saw you, splitting cake slices so carefully as though they were nuclear atoms, and I realised there was room for something more. I think maybe you're the something more, Vera.'

She was shaking her head. 'I'm not. I can't be.'

'You might be. And wouldn't it be fun to find out?'

She turned around and started walking back in the direction of town. 'Please trust me on this, Josh. I've got a track record of screwing things up, and I can't take another failure.'

A track record of screwing *what* up? He wondered if whatever it was that was haunting her had something to do with her reluctance to discuss legislation. Or her journalism career. And, now he thought about it, she was damned reluctant to talk about *anything* that predated the opening day of The Billy Button Café.

'Vera.'

She paused. 'Yes?'

'I trust you, Vera. I don't need to know the nitty-gritty. And you can trust me.' He held out his arm and watched the thoughts play across her face. Wariness. Reserve. And, at last, a wisp of a sad, sad smile. She tucked her arm into his and they made their way back to the clinic.

She should never have agreed, Vera thought, as she slid back the mirrored door of the teeny wardrobe in her tiny bedroom in her incy wincy rented apartment.

Not to the cat, not to the hand holding at the lake … and especially not to a daytrip, together, into the mountains.

Even as her mouth had been saying the word *yes*, the realist living inside her brain had been leaning up against the wall of a jail cell, wearing an orange jumpsuit and ankle shackles, shaking its head and saying *Vera, I'm tired of explaining it to you. Do I have to remind you what happened when you cosied up with Aaron Finch? Disaster happened. Disaster involving a possible jail term happened. DO NOT GET INVOLVED.*

Mostly, it was Graeme's fault. He'd spent the whole of the week after the cat crisis putting the idea into her head that her life was going well. That she could take good stuff for granted. Poor, deluded man … he didn't know a black cloud of unhappy endings liked to follow her from one crisis to another.

Take yesterday at the café. He'd started filling her with a false sense of *joie de vivre* after the Saturday lunchtime rush. 'We are smashing goals today, boss,' he'd said.

She'd looked up from her mandolin, where she'd been trying to turn cucumber into tendrils without damaging every knuckle on both hands. 'How so? Customers have been steady, but we've not been run off our feet.'

Graeme ticked his fingers. 'Catering event for the Women in Business breakfast in Cooma's town hall next Tuesday. Lunch bookings for Friday booked out for the next three weeks—'

'Three *weeks*?'

'And that's not the best bit, honey bunny.'

She grinned. 'It better be so good it needs a full complement of staff, because I've got to tell you, Graeme, calling me honey bunny is a sackable offence.'

Could fifty-year-old bald men with immaculately sculpted facial hair pout? Graeme was sure giving it his best shot.

She took pity on him. 'Okay, I'm sorry. Call me what you like, just tell me. What's the best bit?'

'Someone called @gravydave398 just left us a review on social media and it's going viral. Six thousand likes in less than an hour. You want me to read it to you?'

'Hell yes. Every word, maybe twice over.'

'Okay. *If you're travelling west headed for the Snowy Mountains, do yourself a solid and detour via Hanrahan. Order the cake and coffee special at The Billy Button Café. Here's what happened when I did. The coffee came out first. Crema like silk, over a coffee so dense with flavour my taste-buds started singing* Waltzing Matilda. *I joke you not. Nothing can be better than that, right?*

'*Wrong! Because that's when the cake came out. First, let's talk about wedge size. If you're a vodka soda kinda guy who only eats carbs on a full* moon in a leap year, then maybe you wouldn't care about wedge size. But everyone else? Think wingspan of a pelican. That's how much chocolate mocha rum cheesecake was on my plate. No way could I eat that much, right?

'Wrong! One bite and I thought I'd passed out and travelled into another dimension where trees were made of fairy floss and rivers flowed with Barossa Valley chardonnay. The second bite and all the blood cells in my body stampeded up to my tastebuds, because all those little fellas wanted a taste of the glory.

'One thousand freaking stars.

'Oh wait, this site only lets me leave five. Well, it's an all-caps, all-star fabulous freaking five from me.'

Vera struggled to find words for a moment. 'You're making that up. You wrote that. One of your friends from Melbourne. Your partner. Someone.'

Graeme smirked. 'If you think I'd call myself Gravy Dave on a public forum, you don't know me very well.'

'Six thousand likes?'

'Uh-huh.'

'Wow. Maybe the staff will get paid this month after all.' And maybe Jill's fees at Connolly House could be paid so far in advance it wouldn't matter if she was slung into a prison cell to rot.

Business profits! Her head spun into a rainbow-hued daydream where she could put new tyres on her car before the local police noticed the bald ones she'd been driving around on for the last six months. Take some of Jill's fabric down to the seamstress in Cooma to make cushions for the banquettes in the café. She had plenty of cake in her life now, maybe she could eat some too? Maybe—

No. She was getting ahead of herself. Building an income stream out of this café was her number one priority now. So getting too confident too soon? Nope. Not going to happen.

But still … six thousand likes!

It was the euphoria of that crazy social-media moment that had caused her current problem. She'd been high-fiving Graeme and then laughing as he did a victory dance through the tables in the café when Josh had popped his head in the door. Asked her out hiking on her next day off. *Hiking!*

And what had she said in that crazy moment of optimism?

She'd said yes.

And now it was crunch time. What did a woman having major second thoughts wear on a hiking date anyway?

Hiking boots? She was a city girl. Not much call for hiking boots in the café strips of Queanbeyan or Canberra. Her sneakers would have to do. Shorts? She shivered at the thought. No, despite the calendar telling her it was the middle of spring, the Snowy Mountains had their own idea about daytime temperature. It was brisk outside. Jeans, definitely.

Fleece. Anorak. Hat. Sunscreen. Water. Tape for a blister event, tourniquet for a landslide event, compression bandages for a snakebite event … *you're losing it, Vera.* She inspected the precisely hung and folded garments tucked away in her wardrobe then shook her head. An expedition to Antarctica to study emperor penguins wouldn't require this much overthinking.

A toot sounded outside and she walked to the window. Josh stood on the footpath, a cat-sized travel crate in his arms.

Oh. Now she remembered why she'd said yes. A handsome, caring, fun man was interested in her. And … he'd just saved her cat for free.

It was a problem. One she'd have to do something about today. She'd go on this damn hike, snakes and landslides and cat obligations and all, but she'd lay it out on the line. She was in no position to be getting involved with anyone, and the big handsome anyone down there by her front door deserved to know the reason why.

For a woman who'd promised herself when she moved to Hanrahan that the café and her aunt were going to be her only priorities in life, complications had sure started to pile up fast. Like the cat. The *pregnant* cat. How it had schmoozed its way from dumpster diver in her back alley to home-delivery service in a cushy crate from the Cody and Cody Vet Clinic to her front door ... bloody hell.

She waved through the glass, then headed downstairs to let him in.

'You know, Josh, I've not looked after a pet since I won a goldfish at the Royal Canberra Show when I was eight.' And that hadn't ended well. As an adult, she'd *never* minded a pet ... or looked after a friend's child ... she was so frazzled, she could barely recall watering a pot plant.

She'd never been the nurturing sort, so what madness had made her think she could bring home an invalid, pregnant cat?

'It's the same principles as with that long-ago goldfish. Food. Water. Attention.'

She frowned at the aggrieved silence pulsing from the crate. 'Okay, but when I have trouble flushing the body down the toilet, you're paying for my plumbing bill.'

Josh chuckled. 'Relax. You'll do fine. Which way?'

She sighed. 'Upstairs. Turn right at the top.'

'Did you get the kitty litter? The dried food? A water bowl?'

'Yes, Dr Cody. The cat's needs have all been catered for.'

He flashed her a grin over his shoulder as he headed up. 'Now, now. No need for sarcasm, I get enough of that from Hannah. I've spare in the truck if you didn't have time to get prepared. I know how many hours you put in at the café.'

Oh. Well. Now she did feel snarky. She moved past him to the front door of her apartment and held it open. 'Laundry's this way.'

'Great. I'd lock her in there for today; it'll help her work out it's her space.'

This was all happening way too quickly. She followed Josh into the laundry then remembered the room was barely large enough for her, let alone her, an upset grey cat, and a six-foot-two muscled male who smelled like leather and sunshine.

And her libido. Let's not forget *that*, she thought, because it had just rocketed into the laundry with her and started sucking all the oxygen out of the air.

Her libido needed a distraction. 'Josh, I don't think you quite understand. I'm not very good at ...' *Caring for people? Getting involved?* 'Looking after things,' she finished lamely. 'I'm not like you, Josh. You have a way with people. With animals. You like them and they like you and it's all easy-peasy. I don't have that. I ... misunderstand social cues. I—'

Shit. She was floundering now. How did she explain that she'd lost her faith in her ability to have relationships since Aaron blind-sided her?

He set the crate down on the dryer and turned to face her. 'That is so not true.'

She blinked. 'I'm afraid it is, Josh.'

'You want to know something?'

'What?'

'Before you met Poppy, she and I had been going through a rough patch. Not for a week or two, but for months.'

'Oh. She said a little bit, but I hadn't gathered it had been a big deal.'

'The eyebrow piercing? All that goth makeup she wore when she first arrived? That all started when I told her I was thinking about moving back to Hanrahan.'

'Poppy adores you, Josh. It's plain to see.'

He grinned. 'Sometimes. But for a long time, all I was getting from Poppy was the don't-speak-to-me cold face. You know when that changed?'

She shrugged.

'The night you offered her a job in your café.'

'It was just a job. I don't know how that—'

'Vera, it was not just a job. It was community you offered her. With you and Graeme, the locals popping in and out, her listening to the gossip, pinning up the garage sale notices on the display board, being part of things … you were the one who made my dream for Poppy begin to come true. I wanted her to understand why Hanrahan was important to me, and *you* were the one who kickstarted that process.'

Was she?

Josh reached a hand over and squeezed hers. 'Seriously, Vera, if you can wrangle a stroppy fifteen-year-old into doing six am shifts at your café, one knocked-up cat is going to be a breeze.'

Josh's hand on hers was doing fluttery things to her composure, as were his words. It was true, now that she thought about it. Poppy had seemed happier with every passing day. The eyeliner had grown less thick, the clothes less skimpy, and she'd bought a cute little fifties-style dress from the retro store on Dandaloo Drive that had even made her ridiculous black boots look charming.

She eased her hand from Josh's. She had a lot to think about, and her brain wasn't at its best with Josh in such close proximity.

'Er ... how's she doing back in Sydney?' she said.

'Good, I think. She's even talking about coming up for a week-end in the middle of term if she can persuade her mum to let her ditch the Friday swimming carnival.'

'That'd be so nice,' she said breathlessly. Man, oh man, she had to get out of this tiny room. 'I'll fill the water bowl,' she said in a rush, squatting so she could reach the fish-shaped dish she'd purchased from the retro store. Big mistake. Now her libido was getting an eyeful of all that well-filled denim.

She stood up as close to the sink as she could get and splashed water in the bowl, wished she could splash a bit of it over her face while she was at it.

Josh opened the door of the crate. 'Well, old girl? What do you think of your new home?'

Vera looked inside the crate. Two cross-looking eyes scowled out at her. 'She looked happier in the alley eating three-day-old salmon spines.'

'Let's leave her to get settled. Now, about that hike.' Josh eased a hip against her laundry tub, clearly not finding the confines of the space a problem at all. 'How okay are you with a last-minute change of plan?'

Oh boy. She edged backwards to the open door. She'd be okay with anything so long as it got her out of the close confines of this laundry. 'Fine. Whatever. Let's go.'

CHAPTER

19

'Horseriding?'

Vera's voice cracked on the last syllable, and she tried again. 'Josh, I know I said whatever, but the thing is, I can't ride a horse.'

He glanced over at her, took his hand off the wheel to shift gears. 'Nothing to it. Ironbark Station does trail rides and farm stays over the summer season, so they've plenty of horses that are used to beginners.'

Crap.

His hand reached over and gave hers a squeeze, before she pulled her hand away and tucked it under her leg.

'It'll be fun. Trust me.'

That was the second time he'd told her to trust him. She wanted to roll her eyes and be cynical and think *yeah, like I'd trust any guy ever again.* But trustworthiness shone out of Josh Cody the way lemon scent steamed out of a fresh-cooked souffle.

She chewed her lip for a moment. Maybe she should just tell him now about her problems. About why she was a bad bet. She could get the difficult part of the day out of the way, they could do a U-turn and head back to Hanrahan, *and* she could save herself a humiliating ordeal strapped to the back of a huge scary beast. 'This horse place. It must be a way out of town?'

She'd need at least twenty minutes to let spill the last twelve months' worth of her woes. She should have launched straight into it the second she climbed into Josh's truck, not allowed herself to be distracted by creeks burbling through the dappled shade of gum trees, tracts of wildflowers, the easy chitchat about the rocky, grass-stippled countryside Josh had regaled her with.

'Nearly there. See those weatherboard buildings on the rise?'

She looked to where Josh was pointing. A cluster of neat grey and white barns—stables, she supposed, filled with plunging, sharp-hooved beasts—clung to a green swathe of pasture in the crook of towering mountain peaks.

'Oh,' she said. 'How lovely.' How absolutely, freaking scary!

'Yeah,' he said, and swung his wheel so the truck left the bitumen and headed up a steep gravel track to where an iron gate barred the way forward. Above it, strung between posts, swung an old timber sign: IRONBARK STATION.

'Nineteen twenty-three,' she murmured, reading the date burned into the wood.

Josh followed her eyes to the sign. 'Mmm. There's been a Krauss here since just after the First World War, bar a few years there where the family were interned during the next war. Being German wasn't so popular in the forties, no matter how long your family had lived here. Horse breeding's where the Krausses started, but they own a lot of land in town, too. I went to school with Tom. Be right back,' he said, and left the truck to open the gate.

Vera sat in the truck, watching him. She realised she was in no hurry to spread her bad news and bring their day together to an end. Was it the peace of the mountains? The satisfying thrill of seeing her business blossom over the past two months? Whatever it was, her vow to stay rigidly alone was starting to lose its appeal.

'I think you've met Mrs LaBrooy,' said Josh, once he was back in the truck, the gate secure behind them, the mountain scenery again flashing by.

'Maybe.' She'd met hundreds of people since The Billy Button Café had opened its doors.

'She's the Krauss's housekeeper. She's worked out here since I was in nappies. Longer, probably.'

What an image: Josh as a sturdy toddler following a dog around in a dusty paddock. 'Mrs LaBrooy,' she murmured. 'Wears colours almost as wild as Marigold's? Drinks her coffee with milk, and she's partial to butterscotch sourdough donuts?'

'That's her.'

'We should have stopped by the café and brought her a box of them.'

Josh glanced over at her. 'Next time,' he said, and gave her a wink.

She turned away. There wasn't going to be a next time, not when she revealed the truth. Josh was building a life for himself and she wasn't about to be part of ruining that. She scrabbled around for a more neutral topic. 'Why are we here, anyway? Besides the horseriding?'

'Tom asked me to come out and see his prize mare. She's in foal, and she's been off her feed.'

'Oh. Is he worried?'

Josh pulled the truck up next to a dilapidated tractor and hauled on the handbrake. 'Let's go find out.'

The barn was warm inside, shafts of sun sliding in from high doors in the gables at either end. Shreds of hay spun in the air, and from everywhere came the unmistakable smell of horse. Brown ones, black ones, patchy ones—horse heads popped over stall doors and watched their progress as they made their way down the central aisle, snuffled at them.

'They seem curious.' And freakily large.

'Horses are intelligent. And they love people.' Josh stopped to run a hand up the muzzle of a coal-black horse with a white flash between his ears. 'Soldier? Is that you, old buddy?'

The horse whickered in response.

'I used to ride out here with Tom back in the day. I can't believe this old guy's still here. He must be getting on for twenty-five.'

A low voice came from the shadows at the far end of the aisle. 'Soldier and Bruno are in a competition to see who's going to out-last who. My money's on Soldier.'

'Tom. So, where's this prize horse you've been bragging about?' Josh leaned in close to Vera, spoke low into her ear. 'Old Mr Krauss has multiple sclerosis. He's not doing too well.'

Tom walked up to them, ignored Josh and gave her the not-so-subtle once-over with hard eyes. He seemed as unlike Josh as a man could be: all hard edges and suspicion, where Josh read like a sun-filled open book. 'You must be Vera.'

She held out her hand, nearly winced when he closed it in a vice-like grip. 'I must be.'

He turned away and headed to the far end of the barn. 'Butter-cup's down here. I'd be glad of your opinion, Josh.'

The mare at the centre of all this fuss was standing in a large clean stall, her head drooping to the floor. Her fur—Did horses have fur? Or was it hair?—was a deep red. Beautiful, in fact. The other remarkable thing about her was her size.

'She's enormous,' she said, staying out in the aisle when the two men let themselves in the stall. There was no way she was getting into that confined space with such a gigantic animal.

'Thoroughbred,' Tom said.

Josh gave her a smile. 'What Tom's trying to say is she's a race-horse. The other horses in here are workhorses, and they're built for endurance, not speed, so they're short and stocky. Buttercup here is something else entirely.'

He turned away to the horse, ran his hands over her sides, down her legs to her hooves. 'She's beautiful, Tom. I can see why you think she's special. How long have you had her?'

'Not long. She was already in foal when she arrived.'

'I'll take some blood, check there's nothing sinister going on.' He swung his hand down under the horse's bulging belly and smiled. 'Foal's kicking like a champion, Tom.'

Tom grunted. 'I'll save my cigar for after the birth.'

Josh stood up and the horse butted her muzzle into his shoulder. 'You mind if I call her previous owner? Maybe she's missing someone. Her old groom, her old stablemate perhaps. These thoroughbreds aren't called high maintenance for nothing.'

'That's a great idea.' Tom pulled his phone from his pocket and tapped its screen. 'I've sent the number to you. Flick Taylor, she's English, and as stroppy as she is successful, but she cares about her horses. If she's got any ideas, she'll share them.'

'Great. I'll take the blood samples then they'll need to go in the fridge while we ride. You still okay with lending us two of your trail horses?'

Tom nodded. 'Bridget will saddle them up for you. Make sure you call into the house on your way home, though. Mrs LaBrooy got wind you were headed this way, and she's had ovens burning ever since.'

'Will do. You ready, Vera?'

She was as ready as she'd ever be. Which wasn't saying much, as just standing in a stable with a four-foot timber wall between her and a horse was making her nerves fray. She tried to ignore the queasy feeling in her stomach and followed Josh out of the barn.

Peace. That's not what she'd expected to find on the back of a horse on a steep trail ride through the upper slopes of the mountain the locals called Old Regret. But undeniably, she felt more at peace in this moment than she had since—well—as long as she could recall.

The late morning sky was so blue and deep it shimmered to purple behind distant mountain peaks. Leaves crunched under hooves, horse-breath huffed into the crisp air … her senses felt alive, carried along on the lush scents of the long native grasses.

How had she not known such beauty existed?

Josh rode up beside her, looking romance-novel perfect in his checked shirt and battered akubra. 'Glad you came?'

She flashed him a smile. 'So glad.'

'There's a waterhole not far from here that should be running with all the early snowmelt we've had—maybe ten minutes further—and the track takes us past a grove of wild lavender. I wouldn't mind picking some for Buttercup.'

'You give flowers to horses?' Odd, but sweet.

He winked. 'Whatever works. Lavender is a proven relaxant, and horses have an excellent sense of smell. We hang a bunch in Buttercup's stall, who's to say it won't help her settle down?'

Hmm. Perhaps she could pick a sprig for herself.

'Only, the track's a little steep. You up for it?'

She rested a hand on Calypso's neck. 'You hear that, my sweet? Josh has doubts about our trail-riding skills.'

The little horse the stablehand had saddled for her was not the plunging, frothing, rearing stallion she'd envisaged the whole drive out here to Ironbark Station. Instead, she was a black-and-white pony with kind eyes and a broad back who could have carried a toddler safely through these mountain trails.

Josh looked down at her feet in their ratty sneakers. 'It's not Calypso I'm worried about.'

Was he worried on her behalf? God, how sweet that sounded. But Josh was that kind of guy. All the more reason why she had to nip this ... whatever this was ... in the bud before he got caught up in the worries she had ahead of her.

'Lead on, Cody.'

The rocky cliffside, when they reached it, had a deep cleft worn into the rock and a waterhole had formed from the run-off seeping down its mossy face. It was, she thought, just shy of heaven. Valleys spread out below them, and to the north-east shimmered Lake Jindabyne, cool and blue in the morning stillness. The river which gave the westerly mountain range its name shone silver in the wide grassed plains, and Hanrahan's church spire could be seen to the south on the ridge above Lake Bogong. The old, restored paddle-steamer was puttering along the lake, perhaps on its first run of the season.

'It's deep enough to swim. Tempted?' Josh quizzed her as he helped her down from the horse.

She brought her gaze away from the view and dipped a hand into the water. An icy spear shot up her arm and jangled in her brain, worse than nails on a chalkboard. 'Not if I was on fire.'

Josh's fingers stilled on his saddle pack. 'You know,' he said, shooting his eyes sideways at her, 'a guy could take that as a challenge.'

A challenge? Surely he wasn't going to throw her in?

'My watch isn't waterproof. My hair will go frizzy. Maybe I can't swim.' She forced herself to stop gabbling.

He smiled. 'I threw Hannah in here once, years ago, when we were teenagers. She put a striped legless lizard in my bed a few days later as revenge.'

Holy hell. She'd barely met Hannah, but made a mental note to never, ever, ever tick her off.

Josh pulled a rug from his saddle pack, followed by a battered thermos, and spread the rug out over a wide granite slab. 'Shimmy over,' he said, and sat down, his legs, like hers, dangling over the edge of the waterhole. He reached out and tucked a strand of her hair behind her ear ... lingered a second or two before he turned his attention to the thermos.

Oh boy. Was that a move? It sure felt like a move. Not that she'd been on the receiving end of enough of them to have formed a database of what did and did not constitute a declaration of man–woman interest.

Fingers skimming hair. Picnic rug. Isolated location with running water, romantic mossy melodies playing just a few feet away ... surely that had to be a move. She turned her face to look at him and froze. Oh yes. His eyes were sending out incoming kiss signals.

There was no way this could happen. No way, nuh-uh. It wasn't fair to him. It wasn't fair to her, but since when had the world been fair to her? The one thing she absolutely should not do was lean a little closer to the big, caring, hot-as-sin guy sharing the mountain air with her.

But the thin stand of gum trees was whispering a different message in the spring breeze, as was the gurgling of the melting snow. She and Josh might have been the only two people in the world. And if they were ... if everything else that stopped her living,

stopped her having choices, stopped her reaching out and taking what she needed ... if all of that was no longer there, then what *was* stopping her?

Nothing.

Nothing at all.

She leaned a little closer, reached up to slide her fingers into the tangle of hair at his collar. How long had it been since she'd shared herself this way? She had known women—friends, colleagues—who'd thought nothing of flirting with guy after guy in as little time as it took for a loaf of bread to go stale.

Not her. There was something ... vulnerable ... about resting your skin on someone else's. Your mouth. Hearing, seeing, feeling them so close your heart spoke to their heart, your breaths fused.

Yeah ... when she got that close to someone, she liked to be sure she wanted to be there.

And she sure wanted to be as close to Josh Cody as the laws of clothing and friction allowed.

She slid a hand up the rough denim at his hip, furrowed in with her fingers until she'd found the hot skin of his side. Muscle shifted over his ribs as she spread her hand over his heart. Then she pressed her lips to his.

There it was. There was no truer moment than this. His lips were on hers and she wound herself around him, wanting to press herself into that steady, beating warmth.

Strength. Heat. Kindness. They were such ordinary words when you said them one by one—but not to her. Not when you'd lost hope in ever feeling surrounded by them again.

She could drown in Josh's heat and drown happy.

CHAPTER
20

There was strength under the softness. Resolve under all that prickly reserve.

The woman who'd snuck her way into his thoughts had layers to her, all right, and Josh had no problem with taking his sweet time unpeeling them.

For now, pouring his way into the kiss she'd blown him away with by initiating was about as sweet as he could imagine sweet could be.

But sweet was just where the kiss started. Before his brain could react, strong fingers slid up his skull like they owned it, and she'd clamped her mouth to his like she'd become part of him. His heart rate flipped from steady to gallop.

He had to see her as well as feel her. He didn't want to miss a second. He pulled back his head, and she swayed into him, her lashes a sweep of chestnut brown across pale, pale cheeks.

She had freckles, he realised with a rush of delight. A dozen or more—so faint he could only see them now he was inches away—marching across her nose. He brought his hands up to cup her face and threw himself back into the kiss.

She moaned, and the sound roared into his ears and straight to his groin. He grinned, left his feast of her mouth to explore her throat, felt the thready pulse beneath her skin. He felt like a schoolboy who'd just discovered girls: eager for everything, all at once, before need drove him blind.

But he wasn't a schoolboy. He was a grown man, who'd made his share of spectacular mistakes, and he knew what that moan meant. Vera was in the grip of the moment like he was himself, and he didn't want her to have regrets.

Regrets were the devil to live with, and who knew that better than him?

He pressed his forehead to hers while he gathered up the scattered shreds of his control. If he was going to have a relationship with a woman, with Vera, then he was going to damn well do it right.

'Vera.'

He breathed out the word as softly as he could, and her eyes snapped open.

Need. It was there in her eyes, clear as the mountain creek. But hiding under it, not guarded away like it was every other time she'd looked at him, was hurt. Deep, muddy pools of it.

The loose focus of her gaze grew sharp and he could tell the moment when need was replaced by regret. And pain.

He ran his hands down her arms, back up to her shoulders. 'You want to tell me what's made you so sad?'

Bulldozing his way into the problem was one way to broach Vera's reticence. Who knew? Maybe it would work? He'd caved to temptation after that moment in the surgery, and at Hannah's insistence, to find out a little more about the woman who he couldn't shift from his thoughts.

Vera De Rossi, he'd googled. *Journalist.*

A flurry of articles had come up under the search string, but he'd only read one before his conscience gave him a good kick in the nuts and asked him what in blazes he thought he was doing stalking the backstory of the woman he had the hots for.

He'd stopped reading then, because there wasn't a Cody alive who didn't understand that bullshit on the internet didn't equate to truth. But that one article he'd skim-read had been enough to convince him that Vera was the real deal.

Honest, earnest, driven … and wounded by it.

WHO CARES ABOUT THE ELDERLY was the headline. An opinion piece in some Sunday magazine, pointing out systemic failures in care and the concerns of family members seeking answers to questions.

And maybe she needed to know that he was an ear that was willing to listen.

'Vera? You want to talk about it? Whatever *it* is?'

She frowned and shook her head, and a flush of colour surged faintly beneath those freckles.

She cleared her throat. Looked at her watch. Shifted her hips and wriggled away on the rug so she was out of reach. Evasive tactics if ever he'd seen them. She bore an uncanny resemblance to a soft-hearted pet owner in that moment, trying not to answer a question about how often she fed her furry companion a highly fatty treat.

'Nothing's wrong. That …'—she waved a hand in the air, near her mouth, indirectly in the direction of his chest—'whatever it was, shouldn't have happened.'

Like hell it shouldn't have. He took a deep breath in, let it roll out slowly, tamping down the buzz in his head as he exhaled.

'That "whatever it was" was always going to happen. And it'll happen again if I have any say in it.'

She was pale now; the colour that the horseride had brought to her face had faded. 'Yeah.' Her voice was bitter. 'Like what you want, or I want, or any of us wants actually matters a damn.'

He frowned. 'I don't get it. What do you mean, Vera?' He got the feeling the topic of this conversation had just leapt about a hundred feet out of his reach. They weren't talking about him and her and one soul-scorching kiss on a bridle trail anymore. This was about her past, about which he knew exactly zilch.

He eased back a little. If the bulldozer approach wasn't going to work, maybe patience would. Time, along with the opportunity to get to know each other a little better, because now that he'd seen—*felt*—her connection with him, he wasn't stepping away.

He could give her all the time she needed. And what better way to start than here, by the waterhole, under the warm spring sunshine?

'Okay,' he said, making his tone as friendly and unloverlike as possible. 'If kissing's off the menu for today, what are your thoughts on coffee?'

'Oh, right.'

He could see the effort it took for her to pack her feelings down into the secret place where she hid them.

'Coffee. Well, it depends.'

'Yeah? On what?'

'The barista. I've got Graeme in my life now. He's turned me into a coffee snob.'

He grinned. 'Luckily I swung by The Billy Button Café and had Graeme fill my thermos then.'

She looked at the battered grey object he'd pulled out of his pack. 'I can't believe Graeme condescended to let that grotty-looking thing within eyesight of his espresso machine.'

He winked at her. 'I think your barista has a sweet spot for me.'

Her posture eased, finally, and he relaxed. The Cody charm offensive hadn't grown totally rusty with disuse.

'Graeme has a sweet spot for everyone. He's like a marshmallow, only buffer and way more talkative.'

'And he made me donate a twenty into Marigold's community hall fundraiser.' He poured a cup of coffee into the mug-shaped lid of the thermos and handed it to her, then took a swig straight from the neck of the bottle. Coffee bounded down his throat like a stroppy kangaroo. Strong and fierce, just the way he liked it.

'So,' he said, keeping his tone light. 'You want to tell me why kissing's a no-go zone?'

She froze. 'No.'

Fine, Vera's life could be off limits for the moment. He searched for a different tack. 'Okay then. Abrupt change of topic coming up. Did you know I'm hoping to get council approvals back soon for a renovation project for the Cody building?'

Vera perched her lid of coffee in a crack in the granite. 'Oh? I thought you were underway already fixing up the apartments.'

'Hannah's apartment is done. Mine's a total mess, but no, we're going to restore the downstairs shopfront to its original condition. The building is a great example of Federation architecture, except for that dodgy plywood and glass front window. I've been researching heritage building methods—the Community Hall is home to the historical society archives—and I think it's totally doable. We might even be able to source some bluestone from the original quarry that was used in the area. It should be a perfect match for the rest of the building.'

'That sounds incredible.'

He shrugged. 'Well, as much as being a vet was always my dream, I didn't hate working construction. But this will be my first building project working on something for me. For the Codys. That building is our history, so it means the world to us.'

'You're lucky to have such a strong family connection,' she murmured.

'I know. I took it for granted when I was Poppy's age, but now? I feel like the luckiest guy to have a second chance in Hanrahan.'

'I guess kids are never interested in old buildings and heritage.'

'So true. I told you, I think, that Poppy didn't want me to move back here.'

'Yeah. And I kinda figured that after the crying episode by the skip bin.'

He stared out over the mountain ridges in the distance. 'I should be thanking Kelly Fox for making me lose my temper that day.' He glanced over to see her raising her eyebrows at him. 'What?'

She shrugged. 'You don't seem the type to lose your temper very often.'

He grinned. 'Well, I did that day. I'm lucky Braydon's guinea pig didn't go into cardiac arrest. But Poppy running off, you offering her a job, me worrying about her all afternoon ... it was like a dam wall bursting. Poppy and I talked it out, and I think she finally understood that me choosing to move back here to Hanrahan didn't mean I was abandoning her.'

Vera's voice was low. 'Nobody wants to feel that.'

He pulled on a tuft of grass, ran its length through his fingers so the seeds speckled the ground. 'Who abandoned you, Vera?'

Her eyes shot to his. 'We're not talking about me.'

'We could. If you wanted to. It's just me and the horses listening, and we can all be trusted.'

'Trust.' She said the word like she'd forgotten what it meant. 'Listen, Josh—'

No conversation that started with the phrase *Listen, Josh* ever ended well. He leaned back on his hands, turned his face to the sun.

'This you-and-me thing. Whatever it is. I'm sorry, I can't be a part of it.'

He wondered if she knew how defensive she sounded. 'You don't like having friends?'

'Of course I like having friends. I just don't like having … complications.'

He grinned. 'Honey, I'm not that complicated.'

'You know what I mean. Friends don't kiss each other beside romantic alpine waterholes.'

He reached out a hand and smoothed her ponytail. 'You think it's romantic here?'

She blushed again, and flicked her hair out of his hand. He was really getting a kick out of seeing the pink warm her face.

'I'm not joking, Josh.'

Neither was he. He just hadn't realised how totally serious he was about pursuing this … complication … until she'd told him he couldn't. But he wasn't going to push anymore, not today.

'Okay. I'm listening, Vera, I am. Even if I don't agree. You ready to hit the saddle again?'

She tipped the dregs of her coffee into the grass and handed him back the lid. 'Sure.'

He boosted her on to Calypso's back and turned his thoughts to befriending Vera. Sharing laughs, sharing problems and ideas and dreams … it would be a start, and luckily he had just thought of a problem of his own he could share.

'You want to hear something funny?'

'Funny weird? Or funny ha-ha?'

'Good question. Definitely weird and I'm only laughing about it to keep it from pissing me off.'

Vera ducked her head as Calypso walked in close to a low-hanging spruce limb and he trotted in beside her to hold the branch out of her way.

'So tell me.'

'We've been getting these complaints from town council—well, someone is complaining about us to town council, who then send us stroppy letters which we have to reply to or else they'll suspend our business licence.'

'That's outrageous. What sort of complaints?'

'Oh, one was about farming chickens, which was pretty random. The next one was about exercising dogs in a public area without them having adequate identification on their collars. The councillor we've been talking to has quashed them, but it's got Hannah a bit rattled.'

'I bet it has.'

He glanced across at her. The prickles were back in her voice, and she looked as spiky as an anxious echidna. 'Hannah said you mentioned something about legislation being a bugbear of yours.'

'Oh, well. I guess.'

'You guess?'

She shrugged. 'Before I moved here and opened up the café, my job often required digging up facts from public records. Real estate, city by-laws, federal legislation, corporate ownership structures. Boring stuff.'

'This was when you were a journalist, right?'

She took her time answering him, and when she did, it wasn't exactly an answer. 'That's in the past. I cook now. It's what I'm good at.'

Fair enough. She could keep her secrets. For now.

'Vera. You want to give me a lesson?'

Her look was startled. 'In cooking?'

'Honey, why would I need to learn how to cook? There's a perfectly good pizza joint twenty feet from my front door. No, in searching through public legislation.'

'Oh.'

'I want to get a copy of any likely laws, council or state or federal, that we need to comply with. And put a protocol in place so if any more of this nonsense comes our way we can prove we're acting like responsible business owners. We don't need this bullshit in our lives, so we want to be proactive about it.'

She shook her head. 'I can't help you.'

The tidy, busy enclave of Ironbark Station opened out on the grassy plain ahead of them, and Vera made a clicking noise to spur Calypso ahead of him down the trail. He watched her go and wondered why the day seemed a little less bright.

'Can't? Or won't?' he muttered.

His horse gave a soft little whinny, then headed down the path in Vera's wake.

She had to get away. Being near Josh, especially now with that kiss scalding her brain so badly she could barely string two thoughts together, just reminded her how weak she was. How foolish.

All he'd had to do was lower his voice and get all warm and schmoozy, and she'd melted into a puddle of want.

She knew better. When her feelings were involved, she lost her objectivity. Her judgement. She couldn't make that mistake again.

She'd resolved to tell him why she was a bad bet, but then she'd let pretty views and sun-warmed man smell override her prudence. And now here she was, acting like a monster, saying no to a simple request for help hunting through dusty filing cabinets and online databases.

Had Josh sent her a bill for helping with the cat? No. He hadn't asked for one cent. And she'd repaid him by turning her back and trotting off into the distance like a teenager enjoying a sulkfest.

She had to stop. Literally. As in pull on the straps, or whatever the hell these leather things in her hands were called, and bring Calypso to a halt.

And she had to stop pretending she could live a normal life and go on horsey dates in grassy valleys with kind-eyed hot vets.

She couldn't. She had a court case hanging over her head like a vat of boiling oil, and she couldn't risk that oil tipping down and scarring anyone but herself.

Café, aunt, solitude ... they were her goals and it was time she remembered them. She'd apologise for being a cow. She'd go home. She could spend the afternoon planning stuff she *could* do without screwing up: maybe a fun brunch menu, or a new lamb shank pot-pie. It would take her mind off the things she couldn't do, like start a relationship. Help people. Spend one damn day without this awful weight of *shame* on her heart.

Calypso finally seemed to get the hint that she wanted her to stop moving and ducked her head down to nibble on the long grass by the side of the trail.

Vera twisted in her saddle and practised what she had to say while she waited for Josh to catch up. *Oh, Josh, just in case you were wondering why I rode off like a crazy woman, here's a few reasons: the last man I kissed betrayed me and I can't put it behind me, because the betrayal led to a court case and I may end up going to prison and I can barely acknowledge that thought to myself, let alone to anyone else.*

Was that too much all in one go? Because that wasn't even the half of it. *Oh, Josh, also, my state of mind is pretty dire and I could fall at any moment down into the black pit of not-coping. My aunt's health failed because I chose a terrible aged care home for her, and then I became a vigilante and failed.*

There were also mundane worries, like if she went to prison, what would happen to the lease she'd signed on the café premises. Her loan. And the new concern she had no room for but which had piled up anyway: who would feed one cranky grey cat and her umpteen kittens if she was in an orange jumpsuit in a cement building with bars on the windows and despair in the air?

She looked back up the trail. Whatever she was going to say, she'd better work it out fast, because Josh and his horse appeared through the trees, sunlight flickering over them. He had sprigs of lavender blooms tucked into his shirt pocket, and another posy of them in his hand, but his face was shadowed by the deep brim of his hat.

Heaven only knew what he was thinking.

She waited until he'd brought his horse abreast with her in the shade of an ancient grass tree.

'Josh. I'm sorry about before.'

A dimple flickered on his cheek. 'Which is the bit you're sorry about?'

She pulled a lock of Calypso's mane through her fingertips. 'Getting huffy when you asked me for help.'

'You want to tell me why you got huffy?'

'I'm going to try. It's not easy.'

'I'm listening.'

'You're right, I am a journalist. At least, I used to be. But then I messed up my job and my life and my aunt's security in a really bad way, and the thing is, Josh, soon, like in just a few weeks, I might have to go to pri—'

A buzz went off in her jacket pocket. The café had run out of milk, she thought. Or the fridge was leaking, or old Mrs Lim had wandered in wearing her pyjamas again and was asking for help finding her way home.

'Sorry,' she muttered as she checked her screen. The call wasn't from the café, but the number was local. No reason to suppose the city journalists had followed her up here to harass her about the lawsuit.

'Vera De Rossi,' she said, bringing the phone up to her cheek.

'Vera. It's Wendy Boas from the nurses' station at Connolly House. We have you listed as next of kin for Jill De Rossi.'

Oh no. No, no, no. 'What's happened?'

'Your aunt's had a fall. It's likely she had a stroke, but we'll let the doctor confirm that. I think you should come over if you can.'

'Of course. I'll be right—'

Crap. She couldn't be right there. She was on some fool's errand up a mountain on horseback, and she hadn't travelled here in her own car.

'I'll be there as soon as possible.' Back to Hanrahan; find car keys; roar down the highway to the outskirts of Cooma as fast as the speed limit allowed. 'Maybe two hours, hopefully a bit less, I don't know. How is Jill? Is she talking?'

There was a short silence, into which Vera managed to squeeze half a dozen ugly scenarios.

'Not talking, no. She's breathing well, and she has good colour, but she's non-responsive. We're keeping her warm and comfortable, and the doctor's expected in the next few minutes.'

'What about an ambulance?'

The nurse—Wendy, wasn't it?—was kind, but firm. 'The doctor will decide the next step. Now don't rush here in a fluster; we have one of the duty nurses sitting with Jill, holding her hand. She's not alone, so—'

Vera didn't hear the next bit; her brain had stumbled on the nurse's words: *she's not alone.*

Jill wasn't. But she, Vera, would be if this was to be Jill's end. Alone. And lonely. And who would be there to hold her hand?

She choked back a sob. 'Thank you, Wendy. I'll be there as soon as I can.'

'We'll be waiting for you.'

Her fingers felt numb as she stuffed the phone back into her pocket.

Josh was frowning at her. 'Vera?'

She swallowed the numbness down. 'That was the hospice calling. My aunt— I have to go.'

He reached over as though to touch her hand and she lurched away, Calypso snorting as she jerked on the leather straps in her hands.

His hand paused. 'Come on. I'll take you back down the mountain. You think you can canter on that old slug-a-bed they've given you?'

This morning, she would have said no. 'I can do it.'

His outstretched hand closed into a fist and he gave her a friendly rap on the leg. 'I'll lead. Calypso will know to keep up. You ready?'

Yeah. She was ready.

Josh clicked his tongue and drove his heels into the sides of his horse, who grunted in surprise before obliging him by breaking into a run. Josh hauled on Calypso's bridle as his horse sped past, urging the pony to keep up.

'Keep the reins low,' he said as they raced down the track. 'Calypso knows what to do. We'll be back in Hanrahan in no time.'

It wasn't quite no time. It was about sixty minutes of time— racing helter-skelter back to the horse stud, rushing through Mrs LaBrooy's efforts to hug Josh and force him inside to the tea table she'd set up, and waiting while she bundled him up a slice of apple pie. Josh had flung the lavender he'd collected at a startled groom and told him to tie it on a post in Buttercup's stable, then they'd shot off out of the car park so fast gravel spit out behind the wheels of the truck.

Josh had tried to talk to her as they drove down the mountain. Kind words, comforting words, but she'd shot them all down. Worse, she'd been curt with him, and all he'd done was be a stand-up, all-round saint …

When had she become this horrid, bitter woman?

Forty minutes after Josh had pulled up outside her apartment block, she was clicking on the indicator of her battered little car and parking beside the sweep of lawn at the front of Connolly House. A young nurse sporting a retro hairdo and concerned eyes walked her through corridors that smelled of lemon cleaner and tea trolleys and into the quiet hum of a room set up like a hospital ward.

Jill lay there, still.

Frail as a bird—wasn't that the phrase?—she hadn't realised the truth of the saying until this moment. Her aunt's thin frame lay beneath a pale mustard waffle-weave blanket, and the ridges that were Jill, the jut of hip bones and chest and thin feet, barely showed.

Where had her brave, ferocious, fun aunt gone?

A round-cheeked woman, nearly as wide as she was tall, stood by the end of the bed tapping figures into some sort of digital chart.

'Dr Brown?' said the nurse. 'This is Jill's niece, Vera.'

Vera stepped up to the bed and took one of her aunt's thin hands in hers. A gauze bandage covered her aunt's temple, but aside from that she looked as though she had fallen asleep, although—

Her eyes lingered on the set of Jill's mouth: one corner drooped slightly, as though tugged down to her chin by some wry thought. Not asleep but unconscious.

'Your aunt's had a stroke, Vera.'

She nodded, as though she had some idea what that meant, when she had no idea. Not about this, not about anything. She asked the question bubbling at the top of her thoughts. 'Is she dying?'

Dr Brown was blunt. 'Not this minute. But Vera, this is a hospice. Your aunt has a complicated array of medical conditions, and she's here because her doctors back in the city have determined medical intervention will not save her.'

'I know. It's just … I'm not ready.'

She felt a plump hand pat her on the shoulder. 'Family is never ready. But maybe your aunt is. Does she look upset to you? Or does she look peaceful?'

Vera raised her eyebrows at the doctor, then turned to look at her aunt again. Jill *did* look peaceful. Pink bloomed in her cheeks, her grey hair was smooth and brushed. Other than the odd lilt to the corner of her mouth, her aunt could have been caught napping under a wattle tree on a lazy summer afternoon.

'I'm going to sit with her a while. Just in case.'

'You do that.' Dr Brown smiled and slipped the digital chart back into its dock. 'I'll be doing rounds again in a few hours. The nurses will call me before if they need to. And Vera?'

She looked up.

'Say your goodbyes. Let Jill hear them now, while she's still with us, so she can take your words with her when she goes.'

Vera nodded, but on the inside her thoughts were rebelling. Jill couldn't go *now*, not when she was finally safe at Connolly House. The café profits were steady, the nursing care was all that she'd hoped for and more. Jill *had* to live, so Vera could make up for sending her aunt to that terrible place near the city.

Jill had to live, so Vera wouldn't be alone.

❧

When the nurses finally persuaded her to head home and rest, hours had passed. A yowl greeted her as she opened the door of her apartment. For an old pregnant cat, who supposedly supported herself on an impoverished diet of dumpster scraps, she had a healthy set of lungs.

Kev's favourite saying floated through her head. *Hold your horses, love.*

She'd have said it to the cat if she wasn't so tired.

She turned the handle on the laundry door and an irritated eight-kilo lump of fur stalked past her into the living room.

'And hello to you, too,' said Vera.

She flicked the switch on the wall so white light flooded the narrow space, and braced herself for a scene from a horror movie: inch-deep gouges in the cupboard fronts, pillow-sized clumps of moulted fur, toxic waste where the kitty litter tray had been.

Hmm. The laundry was pristine. The bowl of water was perhaps an inch lower than it had been when she had left this morning, but other than that ... okay. Perhaps that MISSING YOUR CAT? sign she'd been thinking about putting up at the shop could wait another day or two.

A tuna sandwich. She could share it with the cat. A glass of wine, which there was no way she was sharing. And then maybe a long, long sit in the armchair by the window where she could think of nothing at all for a while.

Not her aunt's pale face propped amid hospital pillows.

Definitely not that lunatic moment up there on the mountain when she'd pressed her lips to Josh's and felt the world shift beneath her feet. She'd been so sure of her goals when she'd moved here. How had she allowed herself to become so distracted?

She pulled her keys from her jacket pocket and tossed them in the basket on the kitchen counter. Her phone was next, but with it came a crushed and wilted sprig of lavender.

She held it to her nose for a long moment. If lavender could calm a racehorse the size of a ute, surely one average sized woman wouldn't be a problem?

The aroma reminded her of her mother's sweaters, folded in neat piles within the closet where Vera had hidden as a child, giggling her way through a game of hide-and-seek. And Sunday visits to her grandparents' house, being allowed to play with the hairbrushes and trinkets on the old-fashioned dresser in the bedroom.

It had been at her grandparents' home, on the faded velvet seat of the dresser, that Jill had found her after her mother's funeral, so many years ago. *I'm in charge of you now,* her aunt had said. *Now and always.*

Vera took a last sniff of the bedraggled sprig in her hand. Maybe she could buy a pot. One pot of lavender to tuck into the window-sill where it would catch the northern sun.

Her phone gave a chirrup and she snatched it up, but the call coming through wasn't from Connolly House. Crap. Of all the times for her lawyer to call, why did it have to be now?

'Hi, Sue. You're working late.'

'Yeah. Busy week. Listen, Vera, the magistrate has scheduled your arraignment.'

She drew in a shallow breath then spent a long time exhaling it. Her trial was starting. Finally. Relief or dread … at the moment the two emotions were so intertwined she couldn't tell which she felt the most.

'Run me through that again, will you, Sue?'

'Sure. We appear before a magistrate who reads out the charges, and you enter your plea. If you were pleading guilty, you'd be sentenced, but as it is, you'll be committed to trial.'

'Yay,' she muttered.

'Now, now, I'm pretty sure the contract you signed when you engaged my legal services gave me exclusive rights on sarcasm. Hang on, I'll read you the relevant bit. *Please be advised the arraignment for plaintiff Acacia View Aged Care versus the accused Vera De Rossi will be held at the Queanbeyan Courthouse, Thursday at ten am, presiding magistrate Carmel Grant.*'

'Thursday! Like this coming Thursday?'

'Can you make it? I can delay if I have to, but I'd rather not. Sends the wrong message.'

'What sort of message?'

'Magistrates are apt to get snotty with people who waste their time. We want to be there, bright-eyed and blameless, letting her know we want this whole business behind us so we can carry on with our squeaky clean lives.'

She could make it, unless Jill's condition worsened. She was on the late shift Wednesday, which meant the dinner-before-movie set, and the craft group in the back room, then the coffee-and-cake-after-movie set. Wednesday's were busy, but they didn't run late. She could be in the car by nine that night and in Queanbeyan before midnight.

'I can make it,' she said into the phone. 'I'll meet you at the court. I'll be the one who looks like she's had four hours' sleep in a cheap motel.'

'That's my girl.'

'Is there anything I can do to prepare?' Not that any of it would matter a damn if Jill didn't pull through.

'Not unless there's something you haven't told me. We're prepared. Just relax and be yourself, that's all the magistrate needs to see. I'll see you in a few days.'

Be herself. If only it were that easy. She'd lost her idea of who she was the day Aaron Finch rolled out of her bed and announced she was being sacked. And sued. And charged with a criminal offence.

Who was she now?

A miaow had her eyes dropping to the grey cat at her ankles. She was a tardy feeder of cats, apparently … that much was clear.

The rest was a work-in-progress.

CHAPTER
22

'Tell me why I'm here again, Josh.'

He looked at the wall of cushions in front of them, colour-coded like a stadium wave. Hundreds of fringed, corded, spotted, checked, frilled cushions. Wasn't it obvious? 'My living room's painted, floor sanded, architraves gleaming whiter than celebrity teeth. It's time to pack the camping chairs away and choose real furniture.'

'Uh-huh,' said Hannah. 'And I get to choose your cushions because I don't have a Y chromosome?'

He clasped a hand to his chest as though he'd been pierced by an arrow. 'Would I be that sexist? Out loud? To a woman who owns scalpels?'

She nudged him with a hip. 'Come on, Josh. I saw your place in Sydney, it was lovely. You could do this blindfolded. Tell my why I'm really wasting my morning coffee time here with you.'

Yeah ... like there was an easy answer to *that* question.

He snagged two velour cushions in duck egg blue and another two in taupe and tossed them in the trolley. 'Okay. You got me. I need your advice.'

Hannah smacked his hand away from a beige throw rug and pointed to the navy and ruby red one. 'We didn't have to drive forty minutes into Cooma at seven am on a Wednesday morning to talk. I see you, like, eight hours a day.'

'Driving clears my head.'

She frowned up at him. 'Okay, then. So spill the beans, big brother.'

He cleared his throat. He'd wanted her help, hadn't he? He just wasn't in the habit of asking his baby sister for advice about his love life. Of asking anyone if it came to that. 'It's Vera.'

Hannah's eyes widened. 'Umm. Okay.'

'You know how long it's been since I had a love life, Han?'

His sister winced. 'Josh. You're my brother. And my business partner. Telling me about your sex life is strictly a no-no. In fact, why don't I add it as a clause to our partnership agreement? Clause 16B: no icky stuff.'

He ignored her. 'And I sure don't have time. Now Poppy's gone back to Sydney for the school term, I've started the community hall ceiling, which may take forever if Marigold keeps popping her head in and finding new "favours" I can do for her. I'll be starting on the exterior of our place as soon as the council approvals come through. This heritage reno stuff takes time, right? A guy juggling a stethoscope and a toolbelt can't handle a love life as well.'

Hannah picked up a three-pack of towels and tossed them in the trolley.

'I don't need those,' he said, momentarily distracted.

'Yes, you do. I have seen the ones in your apartment and they were woven by cloistered monks in the thirteenth century. They'd struggle to dry a hairless cat.'

Fine. Whatever. 'Problem is, Han, there's a little something here'—he tapped his chest—'that I can't get unstuck.'

She frowned at him. 'A crust of toast? A hiatus hernia? An apology for flogging food from my fridge?'

He nudged the trolley into his sister's annoying butt. 'None of the above, Hannah. And I've got a hunch this *thing* is the real deal.'

She turned to face him in the aisle. 'Josh, you barely know Vera. She's been in town, what, two months? You can't fall in love with someone in that time.'

He sighed. 'Tell that to my heart.'

Hannah's usual look of snark had softened. She leaned in and gave him a hug. 'Okay then, let's workshop this. What is it about Vera that speaks to you?'

Hannah had cut straight into the core of it: this was a question he'd asked himself more than once as he'd driven the mountain roads on his way to horse foalings, snake-bitten pigs, cows stuck in freezing ditches.

He'd seen something that first time he'd laid eyes on Vera, something he'd recognised. She'd been alone behind her counter, and she'd looked damn near crushed by some unknown burden, but she'd also looked valiant. Defiant.

There had been a time he had longed to be alone. To be a man no-one knew, who could get on with his life without feeling every move he made was under scrutiny from family, from friends and neighbours and his old rugby coach ... even the damn ticket collectors at the local cinema.

He'd pushed through that.

He'd *had* to push through his need to be left the hell alone. For Poppy's sake, and for Beth's and, he'd realised much, much later, long after he'd felt pressured to leave Hanrahan, for his own sake.

Community mattered. Having family and friends and neighbours at your back mattered.

And he'd taken one long look at Vera De Rossi, braced like a lighthouse on a lonely coast determined to withstand any storm headed her way, and he could see she had no idea how the storm would sweeten into spring if she let a few people in to share that coastline of hers. Her aunt falling ill while they were on the trail ride had brought that home to him.

'Josh? You're wool-gathering, mate.'

'Sorry, Han. Okay, did you know her aunt's taken a fall? She's elderly, a resident at Connolly House. I was with Vera when she found out.'

'I didn't even know she had an aunt. Is she a local?'

'I don't think so. I think they moved up here together.'

'You don't know?'

He shrugged. 'Vera's not exactly Miss Chatty. Thing is, Han, I've called her to ask how her aunt's going … being neighbourly, you know … and she hasn't returned my call.'

'Joshua Cody, ignored by a female. Remind me to buy a lotto ticket.'

'Very helpful. Thing is, if Vera really didn't like me, I'd know. I wouldn't bother her. I'm not a total stalker.'

'Uh-huh.'

'But she does like me, I know it.'

'You sure that's not your ego speaking?'

'Han, my ego hasn't had a say in what I do since Poppy was born.'

'That's true. I'm sorry, Josh, sometimes I'm a little too snarky.'

He grinned. 'You think?'

'Maybe this isn't about you. Maybe she's got stuff of her own going on, and she doesn't have room for a handsome daddy-vet hero from Snowy River in her life. We both know people keep secrets about themselves. Especially in a small gossip-hungry town like this one.'

Yeah. He did know. 'There's definitely something going on. She almost told me on the trail ride the other day, before she got the phone call from Connolly House.'

'She almost told you?'

'Yep.'

Hannah took a breath. 'Persevere, then, Josh. If she wants to tell you, she will. Maybe it's just taking her a while to build up the courage. Although, I gotta tell you, she still doesn't seem your type to me.'

Hannah was so wrong. Vera was the only type he wanted. 'When I look at her, I recognise myself.'

'No way. You're such a sunny person, Josh. So … happy. Vera seems a little, I don't know, stiff? Aloof? Cold? Are you sure she's the one?'

Talking this out with Hannah had been the right thing to do, he realised. Because he *was* sure, and Vera was so not cold. He'd had his lips on hers, and the heat of that moment had spiked at about a thousand degrees Celsius. No, Vera may look cool and aloof on the surface, but there was an inferno of need and loneliness and vulnerability boiling away beneath the surface, and that's what called to him. That's what spoke to his heart.

Being sunny and happy was a strategy he'd mastered over the years to cover his regrets and salve his pride. He turned to it now. 'And boy,' he said, 'she's easy on the eye, isn't she?'

Hannah made a small gagging noise. 'Point of order. That was a clear contravention of Clause 16B. Icky stuff.'

'Legs that never end. Eyes the colour of up-country moss after the spring rain. And when she wears that plum-coloured sweater? With the V-neck that plunges just a little low in the—'

Hannah dragged two of the cushions up out of the trolley and pressed them to her ears. 'La la la la la la,' she said.

He grinned. 'Yeah. Okay. Good talk.'

His sister pursed her lips. 'Can we get coffee now? And we should be heading back to the clinic. We can't both go AWOL just because you've got yourself a bad case of the unrequiteds.'

He dragged the cushions off her, then started pushing his trolley down to the check-out. 'You're such a romantic, Han.' He'd convinced himself he knew what he wanted. Now all he needed to do was convince Vera.

Josh pulled the last tray of instruments into the autoclave and set the timer to cook, then picked up his final patient for the day and headed out to the reception area.

He was beat.

'Letter for you, Josh.'

'Thanks, Sandy,' he said. He gave the ancient terrier he was holding a final pat and then handed him back to the owner waiting on one of the chairs. 'Monty will be fine, Mrs Singh. We've removed the cyst, and pathology came back clean. Pop back in a week from today and we can nip those stitches out for you.'

'Thank you so much.' She turned her attention to the little guy who was clearly thrilled to get away from the big scary vet and back to his indulgent owner. 'Who's my brave little man?' she gushed. 'You are!' She bestowed a flurry of affection on the dog, and Josh smiled as he turned back to the receptionist desk. If hugs and kisses cured pets, he'd be out of business.

'Looks official,' Sandy said.

Josh weighed the letter in his hand, his eyes on the logo of the Southern Snowy River Regional Council in the top corner. 'This is either bad news, as in another fool complaint has been lodged by our mystery vet-hater; or it's good news and my approval permit to restore the front of the building has come through. Which, I wonder?'

Sandy finished swiping Mrs Singh's credit card, then waited until the lady had made it out the front door before turning to Josh and grimacing. 'You-know-who isn't in the right frame of mind for bad news today, Josh. Maybe open it on the down-low until you know for sure.'

'Hannah? Why, what's up? She was fine this morning.'

'Been out since lunch at a foaling down near Dalgety. Foal hadn't developed properly and she had to send it over the rainbow bridge. She's pretending she's totally fine, but she was out in the back office when she got home, filing.'

'Hannah Cody, my younger and stroppier sister, was *filing*?'

'Uh-huh. You can see why I'm worried.'

'Might be time to crack the secret stash of chocolate biscuits, Sandy. Just let me know where you keep them and I'll take one in to Han.'

'Nice try. The location of the secret snacks is a mystery that I will take with me to the grave.'

He sighed. 'It was worth a shot.'

'Besides, she's gone. Walking her sad off down by the lake would be my guess.'

'It's never easy losing a patient.'

'Mmm. Listen, Josh, I have to run. The kids have soccer practice and they'll give me grief if they're late.'

'Sure, no problem. See you tomorrow.'

Quiet settled over the clinic as Sandy locked the front door behind her. The pets tucked up in the sleepover room were behaving for once, Poppy was four hundred kilometres away and Hannah was out finding some peace by the waters of Lake Bogong.

Shoot. This alone thing wasn't all it was cracked up to be.

Shrugging, he ripped open the envelope, and studied the contents within.

Applicants: Joshua Preston Cody and Hannah Celine Cody

Land to Be Developed: Lot 36 DP 129334 – 36 Salt Creek Flats Road, Hanrahan.

Proposed Development: Removal of 1970s window bay and store front and reconstruction.

Determination made under section 3.16 Land and Heritage Management Act.

Determination: APPLICATION REFUSED

What? His gaze stumbled over the words a second time before his brain comprehended their meaning. Refused? What on earth?

Reason(s) for Refusal: Council has received submission from the public contesting the compatibility of the proposed reconstructions with the character of the local area, pursuant to blah blah blah …

He stopped reading. This was nonsense; the character of the local area was currently being totally disfigured by the tacky seventies-era ply-and-glass shopfront. Which anyone with a particle of knowledge about Federation architecture would know.

Surely he could object?

He frowned down at the letter, brooding for a moment. He was out of his league dealing with bureaucracy and Land Management Acts and bullshit … but he knew someone who delighted in grinding up bureaucratic nonsense and sprinkling it on his cereal for breakfast: his old boss, Frank Gullo, loved and feared by building apprentices all over the southern outskirts of Sydney.

He looked at his watch. Perfect time to call: jobs done for the day, Frank was probably sitting in his ute on his long commute home … just one of the things about Josh's past life in Sydney which he in no way missed.

'Mr Millimetre,' he said, when the builder's gravelled voice said hello. 'How's the hard worker?'

'Josh, mate,' said Frank, drawling out the word mate so long he must have covered a good hundred metres of freeway. 'How the bloody hell are you?'

'Good, mate, you?'

'Busy. You ever get sick of shoving your hand up cow butts, you've got a job waiting for you here.'

'Thanks, Frank. Me and the cows appreciate that. Listen, I need a favour.'

'Here it comes,' his former boss said. 'Do I need a beer in my hand before you hit me up?'

He grinned. 'No, Frank, I don't need a loan or a truckload of steel girders on the cheap. I need advice about a planning application.'

'Yeah? You come to your senses and strapped on your old tool-belt, Josh?'

'Sort of. My sister and I inherited a Federation three-storey building up here in Hanrahan. It had a bodgy storefront tacked onto the ground floor that I'm wanting to rip out so I can restore it to its former glory.'

'Brick?'

'Stone. The original quarry where the stones came from a century and a half ago isn't far from here. I'm hoping I can match them.'

'Sounds like quite a project.'

'Yeah. Could be. Thing is, council just knocked me back.'

'Typical. What's the reason?'

'A submission from someone who claimed the restoration wasn't in keeping with the street.'

'Sounds like a typical first salvo across the bows, Josh. Who was the objector?'

'It doesn't say.'

'Go into council. That's a matter of public record; they have to show you the objections submitted.'

Huh. Well, that would be interesting.

'Step one, mate,' said Frank, 'is make sure you object to their refusal by the due date. Step two, you send your original application to me and I'll put some flesh on its bones. These desk jockeys in council like their steak cut up and their spuds mashed for them ... I'll give it a rewrite for you, use the lingo they're used to.'

'Frank, you're the man.'

'Yes I am. You take care, okay?'

'You too.'

Crap. What next, he wondered, would arrive to piss him off some more? Thank heavens for old mates with expertise.

He peeled off his lab coat, gave his hands a sniff, and grimaced. Still bad. No-one needed to smell where his hands had been today. He stood at the sink letting hot water and antiseptic run over them while his thoughts settled.

He wanted a beer, and food that had more love and care poured into it than a sixty-second whirl in a microwave. And—he could admit it—he had a weak-but-to-hell-with-it yearning to rest his eyes on Vera. What better time than now to start convincing her that he was the one? Besides, he hadn't seen her since her aunt's fall. It was his neighbourly duty to go and ask after her aunt, wasn't it?

Lucky for him, the woman he had the hots for worked in a café that offered dinner, so he could do all those three things at once. It was just a matter of maths, and he loved maths.

'Or it's a matter of desperation,' he muttered to himself in the mirror as he washed up.

Yeah. He had it bad for Vera. So what? It was his life, and if he wanted to have it bad for a prickly woman from out of town who barely seemed interested, then that was his choice, wasn't it? Besides, after the kick in the teeth from the council rejection, he needed to see her more than he even needed that beer.

He pulled his jacket off the coat hook and then heard the scampering claws of a dog on the floor.

'Jane Doe.'

She looked at his jacket, then she looked at the row of hooks on the wall where the dog lead was hanging.

'Girlfriend, I'm sorry. They don't allow dogs in The Billy Button Café. I'm going for a meal, not a quick drink. You'll have to stay here.'

Jane Doe sat down expectantly and extended her neck to let him know that slipping the catch onto her collar would be no trouble at all.

Josh rolled his eyes. Now he was being guilt-tripped by a dog. 'Did Poppy teach you that trick?'

The dog's tail beat a steady rhythm on the floor.

'I don't make the rules, Jane. What about a high-priced, organic roo-jerky treat instead?'

He made his escape while Jane Doe hunkered onto the floor with a generous chunk of jerky between her front paws, and thought, not for the first time, how relieved he was that seven-year-old Parker hadn't turned up yet to reclaim his pet.

The park that separated the clinic from the café over on Paterson was quiet, and the breeze kicking up off the lake hadn't got the memo that summer was only a month away. He stuffed his hands deep into his jacket pockets and kept his eyes on the lights of the café glimmering a golden welcome through its ornate windows.

Marigold was floating about the inner room, her arms waving about as though she was conducting a symphony orchestra. Of course, Wednesday was craft night. Mr Juggins was there, and Vonnie from the supermarket ... and was that Vera tucked into a corner stitching? He smiled. The babble of people relaxing together at the end of the day in a gracious old room that looked like a fancy parlour from an olden-day movie sounded exactly like what he was in the mood for. He eased his way in the door and was pounced on by Graeme.

'Dr Handsome, welcome back. Dinner? A takeaway beef bourguignon pie? Or have you finally succumbed to the lure of Marigold's Wednesday night craft group?'

'Woah.' He threw his hands up. 'I've done my share of stitching today already. Dinner. A table for one.'

Graeme looked at him as though he'd just shot the last Tasmanian tiger in captivity. 'Josh, you disappoint me.'

'I do?'

The manager shook his bald head. 'Single men never ask for a table for one. It's a rule.'

'Whose rule?'

'It's a law of the jungle type rule. Come. Sit at the counter.'

The counter was perfect. He could see into the craft room and keep an eye on Vera there, and maybe start up a little conversation if she wandered over to the till. 'Lead the way. Hey, I thought you didn't work Wednesday nights.'

'Roster changes,' said Graeme. 'For Alex, I mean. He's on call nights this week.'

Josh took a seat. A menu was propped up on the counter between a stone trinket box filled with Himalayan salt and a miniature pepper grinder, and on it he spied the magical word, beer.

'What do you fancy?' said Graeme.

'Lasagne. Beer.'

'The dinner of champions, excellent choice, mate.'

'Make it a generous helping, would you? I've been living off my own cooking and it—'

'Sucks?'

Josh snorted, and grabbed the copy of the *Snowy River Star* tucked in amongst the serviettes and sauce on the end of the counter. Vera swished by behind him and he let his eyes rest on her for a long, wistful moment as she disappeared into the kitchen. 'Does that sort of comment get you tips in the big city, Graeme?'

'Everything gets me tips, Josh. I'm an operator.'

'That's the truth. How's the house building coming along? You need a hand again, you let me know.'

'Only if you promise to wear a toolbelt and strip down a few layers.'

Josh laughed. 'Does your boss know you flirt with customers in the café?'

'Like you're not a customer who's come over here to lurk about in the hopes of having a little flirt with my boss,' said Graeme, waggling his eyebrows in the direction of the kitchen doors Vera had just walked through.

He lifted the stubby of lager Graeme had uncapped for him, and saluted with it. 'Fair point.'

Graeme tapped the dinner order into the tablet on the counter then lifted his head as the door opened to let in a guy dressed head to foot in motorcycle leathers. 'Is that—'

'What?'

'Do you smell smoke?' Graeme's nose was lifted into the breeze like a goanna who'd smelled a roast chicken.

'No, I—'

Wait. He did smell smoke. 'Not the kitchen? That better not be the last of the lasagne burning. My need is great.'

Graeme's voice was grim. 'Our kitchen's not across the street out front. Something's on fire. Let's go, handsome. That's building smoke, not food smoke.'

Josh turned his thoughts away from dinner and headed out into the street. 'Coffee king *and* smoke whisperer. You're quite the expert, Graeme.'

They stood on the corner of Paterson Street and Curlew and stared out into the night. Lights glimmered behind the upper storey windows in the old brick buildings. The moon was up, but hung low in the sky, sending silver rivers rippling down the mountains.

The breeze that usually swept up off the lake and over the town had stilled but … there *was* something in the air, more of a taste than a smell.

'Kids burning something in an alley?' he muttered.

A dull pop sounded above the moving cars on the street and the chatter reaching them from the busy café at their backs. A pop, then the unmistakable sound of shattering glass.

'That way,' said Graeme.

That way was the way to the clinic. Josh stepped off the kerb and a fist of unease settled around him. He shook it off, but put a jog in his step. The clinic was barely two hundred metres from The Billy Button Café, but set back in its lot—he couldn't see the building for the ancient alpine snow gum spreading its limbs in the park.

Shit. Now he could really smell it, and the closer he got to home, the stronger it became. 'Call 000,' he said, and broke into a sprint.

'I'm on it.'

He covered the last fifty metres at a speed he'd not managed since Year Twelve, and what he saw when he reached the clinic had his fist of unease powering up to a sucker punch.

A shattered plate glass mess covered the footpath and inside the Cody and Cody Vet Clinic's reception room, blazing bright, roared a fire the size of a bull.

Had Hannah returned from wherever she'd disappeared to and gone up to her apartment on the top floor?

Jane Doe and her pups were in there. So was Harry Newell's pet snake, a guinea pig called Porpoise, and an old and bitter cat with an attitude problem and more health problems than could fit on a standard Cody and Cody patient chart.

He heard the whoop-whoop of sirens as he bashed his way in the side door to the back office, then frantic barks from Jane Doe in the sleepover room. Sisters first. Animals second. Thank heaven Poppy was in Sydney.

'Hannah!'

He roared out her name over and over as he pounded up the stairs. 'Hannah! Hannah!'

CHAPTER

23

Vera was hiding in the kitchen like a coward and she knew it. Cooling fruit buns could only be checked so many times, and the orders had thinned; no more lasagnes just cake and coffee requests, all of which could be handled out front.

Dishwasher stacked, oven gleaming, knives sharper than an arctic breeze. She'd run out of excuses. She was going to have to go out there and say hi to Josh and try and untangle the mess she'd made of their date before her head split apart.

Her aunt was in a coma, and she was about to drive two hundred clicks to face a magistrate. Her travel bag was packed for a two-night stay, she had a boot full of indexed facts and figures and affidavits, and all she could think about was the guy sitting in the second stool from the end at her café counter.

She needed a clear head, and she wasn't going to get one before she'd explained why she'd blown so cold after blowing so hot the day he was kind enough to take her for a horseride.

She could make it brisk. Impersonal. Just stride out there to her front counter and say it. *So, Josh, yeah. I'm facing a criminal charge and I'm about to drive to Queanbeyan and I may go to prison. Rescue the cat, will you, if I'm not back by Friday? Mrs Butler on the ground floor has a key.*

God, no. *Josh, you've been kissing a jailbird. Thanks for the memories.* Nope. That sounded like a country and western song no-one wanted to hear.

She could always try the truth. She whispered the words to the refrigerator in a test run. 'I'm a fool, Josh, and the last guy I was involved with took something from me when he betrayed my trust and started this whole chain of disasters that's ended up with me shelling out a fortune in legal fees to stay out of prison. He took the part of me that could be with someone. He took my faith in humanity. And I don't know if I'll ever get that back. Even for a guy with kind eyes and a kiss factor that's off the freaking charts.'

Vera rested her head against the fridge, wishing the cold sheet of stainless steel could work its way inside her thoughts and chill them down, too.

That was the problem. Well, one of them.

Since those kind eyes had started looking in her direction … since she'd felt the brand of that kiss showing her a future she might have had if not for all the shitstorm brewing about her …

Her thoughts couldn't settle. When she closed her eyes, Josh was there. Usually undressed, and there was a part of her that kept wondering would it hurt to sample just a teensy tiny bite of what he had to offer?

She might not have a future, but she had a now, didn't she?

Josh deserved a future that she couldn't give him, but damn it, she'd tried being noble and look where it had got her.

The lonely voice inside her head kept workshopping scenarios in which it would be okay for her to be with Josh … to have him march on into the kitchen and haul her up against all that manly hotness like she was a soufflé and he was her own personal white-hot ceramic dish.

Just for a bit.

Just until the preliminary hearing pinched away at all that was left of her.

Maybe she could invite Josh over for a drink. He'd probably say no … she'd given him plenty of reasons to put her in the high-maintenance-blows-hot-and-cold basket, but …

'Don't say no,' she murmured into the silent cool of the fridge door.

'Vera? Are you okay?'

Perfect. It would have to be the town's self-appointed do-gooder, sticking her nose through the kitchen doors just while she was talking to herself about seducing the town vet. To the refrigerator. She was genuinely losing her marbles. Maybe it wasn't too late to text her lawyer and throw in an insanity plea.

She hauled open the fridge door and started clanking bottles of sauce around. She was a busy cook, not a loser who'd … well, lost it.

'Marigold. You need something?'

'Not sure, but Graeme and Josh just ran out of here and Graeme asked me to let you know. They can smell smoke. I'm heading out to see what's up, and—' Marigold broke off. 'Can you hear a siren?'

Vera reached up and killed the switch to the industrial exhaust rigged up over the grill, and into the silence fell the unmistakable noise of sirens. 'They sound close. I'm coming. Let's see what's going on.'

The diners lingering over dessert were lined up at the window, and even the crafters had put aside their projects to wander out. Before Vera and Marigold could reach the front door, it flicked open, bringing with it a waft of smoke smell and Kev Jones.

His eyes met Vera's. 'Honey, it's the vet clinic on fire.'

'What?' The clinic! And Josh and Graeme had gone down there! With two sharp claps she silenced the rising din. 'Everyone! Please, the café is going to shut. You can pay next time you're in if you haven't paid already.'

Marigold was by her side, and she grasped the woman's arm. 'Can you see the craft group safely to their cars? I have to go. I don't know if—'

She stopped there. She didn't know anything. She just knew she needed to go find out.

'Leave it to me. You got spare keys? I'll lock up when I'm done.'

'Marigold, thank you.'

'Well now. This is the first time you've leaned on me, Vera, and I'm pleased I can help. I reckon you're thinking like a local now.'

Vera grabbed for her coat then pulled the spare set of keys out of the till drawer and handed them over.

'You go on and make sure my Kev doesn't forget himself and start acting like a hero. God will snap that man up for himself first chance he gets, and I'm not done with him.'

Hanrahan's residents had congregated in the corner of the park and watched the blaze take hold. Two fire trucks blocked Dandaloo Street, their strobe lights a whirlpool of dizzying blue and red. Vera squeezed through, nudging shoulders and handbags as she made her way to the front of the crowd. A cordon had been rolled out, and she could see Alex—Graeme's partner—hauling hose equipment down from one of the trucks. A policewoman was urging the onlookers to stay back, move along, remember where their homes were and go to them.

The reality, when she saw it for herself, took her breath. The Cody building was in darkness—someone must have cut the power—but the lower storey was ablaze. It looked like a meteor had torn through the reception.

Raised voices, the crackle of radio traffic, and everywhere action, water, hoses thicker than elephant trunks, all directed on the beautiful old building. Where was Josh? Where was Graeme? She pushed forward to the cordon, ignoring the frowns from the police officer.

A man, vaguely familiar from the café, stood by a red-and-white traffic cone.

'Do you know what's happened?' she asked him.

'I know my stock will be ruined.'

She raised her eyebrows at him and he pointed to Bits and Bobs, the small gift shop that operated out of the ground floor of the next building. Vera'd been in there once searching for a book on Hanrahan's history to read to Jill.

'Has the fire spread there too?'

'Not yet, but the smoke stink will have. A lot of my stock is fabric: cushions, tea towels, scarves, that sort of thing. Worthless now, and my landlord's so stingy she won't give a damn.'

'I'm sorry.' Stock could be replaced, she thought. People couldn't … kind-eyed vets and outrageous gold-hearted baristas couldn't.

To her side she caught sight of a green corduroy cap—Kev. 'Do you know what's going on?' she said.

'I've spoken to Alex. He says they're trying to work out if Hannah was in there, and they're trying to get the animals out.'

'My god, is that safe? Alex wouldn't let them go inside, surely.'

'Hold your horses, pet. Let's not get the worry beads out until we have to.'

Vera scanned the crowd and was relieved to see Marigold swooping in on them like a hippy rescue angel. She would know what was going on.

'Keep away from the cordon, please, ma'am.'

Marigold patted the policewoman on the arm. 'Sergeant King, thank heaven you're here. What can you tell us?'

'It's too soon to know much, but the Fire Chief—' The policewoman turned away mid-speech as the radio she wore crackled to life. 'Copy that,' she said into her mike. Her face was more relaxed when she turned back to them. 'Everyone's clear of the building.'

Shouts sounded from the laneway around the corner, and Vera squinted through the smoky darkness. Was that— Not Josh, but Graeme, carrying one end of a cage. As he reached the street, she saw Hannah was holding the other end of the cage, her face covered in ash, an old oilskin riding coat miles too big eroding her of shape.

But where in heaven's name was Josh? As she thought it, the sturdy shape of the brown dog who'd adopted him came barrelling across to the park. Behind her the unmistakable silhouette of the vet. Her vet. The man she'd been having inappropriate fantasies about not half an hour ago.

She dragged in a breath of smoky air. He was safe.

Close behind Josh was a firewoman, with something—puppies?—in her hands. The firewoman herded the group over to the cordon and lifted it so they could duck through.

'Kev, grab a pup from Lorraine, will you?' said Josh. 'If we put them down out here, they'll get trampled. Vera, would you mind taking the other? I need to find a crate.'

Wordlessly, she held out her hands and the firewoman handed her a squirming yellow lump of fur. Her eyes clashed with Josh's for a charged moment. 'Josh. I'm so sorry. Is there anyth—'

'Next time I give you an order, Josh Cody,' cut in the firewoman, 'you're going to pay attention, you got that?'

He turned to her. 'Yes, Chief.'

'Now, you get those animals you've got stuck in your pockets sorted out. And if I see that snake loose, I'm gonna cause a ruckus the likes of which Hanrahan has never seen.'

'Now, Lorraine, he's harmless to everyone here except the guinea pig he's currently sharing a cage with.'

'A snake's a snake, Cody. If you don't want to see the chief of the Rural Fire Brigade—namely me—crying like a toddler in front of all the stickybeaks cluttering up this park, you keep that thing out of sight, that's all I'm saying. Now, get yourself sorted and stay outside the cordon. I'll come find you when we've got this fire contained.'

'Thanks, Lorraine. Appreciate it.'

'Meg, arrest him if he crosses through.'

The policewoman nodded. 'No worries.'

Lorraine patted Josh on the cheek then headed over to the broken windows where the main fire seemed, finally, to be losing its battle.

'Josh,' said Hannah, 'what about Max and the other pups?'

Josh reached into the jacket he was wearing. 'How many pockets you got in that coat?'

'Plenty.'

He handed three of the pups over. 'Zip them into your jacket, will you, Han? It's pretty cold out here. I'll keep Max.'

'How on earth are we going to tell Mum and Dad about this?' said Hannah.

'Hopefully they're out of range of a cell tower. We can ring them when we know more,' her brother replied.

The two Codys stood shoulder to shoulder, the smouldering shell of their home lit up before them. Vera knew what it was like to lose everything, to have the foundations you thought you could count on ripped out from under you. She knew ... but what words of comfort could she offer?

A half-date that had ended with a hot-handed kiss on a bridle trail and her charging off in tears like a crazy woman, a few charged looks over a busy café counter, a dozen midnight fantasies in the privacy of her own home ... that wasn't enough. She wasn't part of Josh's life, she was a bystander.

And she was a mess. This wasn't even her home burning down, and she could feel her eyes stinging from more than smoke. A wet nose snuffled into her hand and she looked down at the golden pup she held. His eyes were open, and regarded her like she was his rescuer, not the big capable guy standing on the kerb with his sister. She pressed her nose into his fur and hoped it would dry the tears on her cheeks. 'Don't look at me like that, big guy,' she murmured. 'I didn't run into a burning building and haul you out.'

No. But she could do something. A crate, Josh had said. She had a dozen or more fruit boxes stacked outside the back door of The Billy Button Café. She tucked the pup firmly into the crook of her arm and slipped off to the opposite side of the park.

She'd find the Codys a crate. And then she needed to get in her car and drive two hundred kilometres to see if she could find herself a future.

Josh saw Vera's face, looking as beat down as he felt, before she backed away through the crowd. He went after her, and caught the tail of her jacket by the clocktower in the centre of the park.

'Vera.'

She turned, and he froze when he saw the tear tracks down her cheeks.

'Honey. Are you okay?'

With a squirming pup in her hands, she made an unsuccessful effort to wipe her face. 'Oh, Josh. I'm not the one whose home was just on fire. Don't worry about me.'

He moved in front of her and took the yellow dog, tucking him into the large pocket of his jacket with his brown brother. 'It's bad at the front, in the clinic, but the back stairs and the apartments aren't even wet. It's awful, but the fire brigade were able to put it out and it's not a tragedy. Are those ...'

He almost didn't want to say it. The messages Vera had been throwing in his direction had been kind of confusing, and she was beginning to mean too much to him for him to get this wrong. 'Are those tears for me?'

She pulled up the apron she was still wearing and wiped her face with it. 'I'm not sure,' she mumbled. 'I just cry these days, and often I don't even know why.'

He reached for her and felt no resistance as he brought her up against him. She smelled like plum crumble and tomato relish and about a dozen other delectable things, and he rested his hand on her neck and just held her for a moment. 'I'd be okay with it if they were,' he said.

A pup let out an annoyed don't-squash-me yip and she pulled away from him. 'I'm sorry. I always seem to be saying that, don't I? Seeing you and Hannah there, together, surrounded by just about everyone in Hanrahan, and everyone was hugging each other … it made me a bit teary, that's all.'

'Don't you have family, Vera?'

She gave a half nod. 'My aunt.'

'No-one else?'

'No.'

He ran his hand down her arm. 'Lucky you moved to Hanrahan then. We take care of people here. Even when they're not sure they want to be taken care of.'

Her eyes widened. 'Is that what I am to you? A stray who needs to be taken care of?'

Woah. Where had that come from? He hooked a finger into the apron strap that rose from her breast to her neck and tugged on it until she was a breath away. 'Not at all. You are a thorn in my side, Vera. A dream I can't wake from, a feeling I can't shake. Have you not figured that out yet?'

He could feel the shiver riding her skin, and he let his finger rest on the collarbone visible above her blouse. His home and business were just on fire, he had nowhere to sleep, his dog was about to be taken from him, and yet all he seemed to want at this exact moment was her.

A sigh escaped her. 'I wish I could be the dream you want me to be, Josh. I really do.'

She was pulling back, and her eyes had grown bleak.

'Problem is, you get too close to me and you're going to work out I'm more of a nightmare. I've wrecked enough, Josh. Don't let me wreck you, too.'

'You don't think you're sounding a little melodramatic?' he said, as gently as he could.

'No,' she said baldly. 'Look, there are crates in the back of the café if you need something to keep the pups in. Help yourself. I have to go.'

She stepped into Paterson Street and disappeared into the shadows up Curlew, and he let her go. Whatever was going on in Vera's life, she wasn't ready to share it. Yet. Luckily he had plenty of practice with being patient.

The crowds had dispersed by the time he'd found a suitable crate, tucked the rescued pets into the tray of his ute, seen Hannah off to her friend Kylie's for the night, organised a room for himself at the Hanrahan Pub, and had a last brief from Lorraine, the acting chief of the local Rural Fire Brigade.

Graeme jangled his car keys beside him, his offer of a nearby shed where the animals could be housed for a few days too welcome to refuse. 'You want to follow me over in your truck? Alex will be here for a while yet making sure nothing's simmering away on the ground floor. You and I can get the menagerie sorted.'

'Thanks, man,' he said. 'You sure you and Alex don't mind playing surrogate dads for the night?'

'Of course not. I have no idea what to feed them, but I can pour water into a bowl like a boss.'

'They'll be fine for tonight. I'll collect them tomorrow and deliver them back to their owners. Gracie at the pub is letting me keep Jane Doe and her pups with me. If Alex isn't cool with minding them overnight, you let me know.'

'Mate, relax, it'll be fine.'

Relax. As though that would be possible. His thoughts hadn't been this churned up since he'd cracked his piggy bank to buy two one-way tickets on the bus out of Hanrahan for him and his pregnant schoolteacher girlfriend.

That building that currently had smoke pouring out of it represented everything he'd strived for in the years since. And the woman who'd just walked away from him in his hour of need? What did she represent, exactly?

He was damned if he knew. Or why he cared so much.

CHAPTER
25

Vera smoothed the wool of her black dress over her knees with fingers that trembled.

Walking into the local court in downtown Queanbeyan had been as frightening as anything she'd ever done. Bored faces. Impassive faces. The couldn't-give-a-damn faces of security personnel who watched her drop her phone and car keys into a plastic tub as they were scanned for bomb residue or bigotry or whatever the heck these machines were calibrated for. This bland assortment of strangers would listen and judge and make decisions about her … and there was nothing she could do to change that. She was in the grip of a system that she no longer believed in.

She found her name on a list sticky-taped to a wall beside a dull red door and hovered uncertainly. Did she go in? Did she wait outside?

'Sorry, had to pee.'

A waft of exotic perfume and nicotine draped about her like a cloak as her lawyer materialised beside her.

'Let's go in, shall we? The magistrate will be in soon, and we can get ourselves settled. We're not first on the docket, so there'll be some other charges to be dealt with before your name is called. It's better that way, helps settle the nerves.'

It was going to take more than a few minutes in a courtroom to settle her nerves. Her stomach felt like it was being cauterised by hot wire.

'How're you feeling?' Sue said, as she thrust open the door and marched in to the front row of seats.

'Sick. And like I've had about three minutes' sleep.'

'That's the spirit. Vera, work with me here. I'm going to ask you again: how are you feeling?'

She closed her eyes as she sat down. She had this. 'Okay. I'm appalled by the charges I've been called here to face. I have acted as any concerned and caring citizen would have acted, and I confirm my plea is not guilty.'

Sue pursed her lips, then gave a nod of her sleek-haired, impeccably made-up head. 'You'll do. Try not to fall apart when you're called. A tear or two, no problem. But you're a professional journalist who makes informed decisions, that's our strategy, and we don't want to puncture it by having you show them otherwise.'

'Got it. Two tears total.'

'Snarky, I like it. Better that than being too emotional. *Be* pissed off. It'll keep you strong. Remember that when they ask you to stand.'

Vera shut her eyes. 'Has Aaron turned up? What about Chris Sykes? I've been too chicken to look behind me.'

Sue started sliding notebooks and folders out of her attaché case. 'Both here. Your ex-boyfriend's standing up the back with a shiny blue suit and a fresh haircut by the looks. Going for clean-cut.'

'Clean as the devil's doormat,' Vera muttered.

'Now, where is Sykes?' Sue twisted in her seat. 'Oh yeah, nice play, he's taken a seat in the row right behind us. Mr Confidence. There's a lawyer sitting beside him with a nose like a fox. I've not run up against him before, but he's got a reputation.'

'Philanthropist? Ladies' man? Bingo addict?'

'Not that sort of reputation, no. Don't worry, I'll break him like a twig. Forget him—we're here to play our game, so let's not worry about theirs.'

'I wish I had your confidence.'

'Girlfriend, everyone wishes they had my confidence.'

The clerk of the court sounded a bell and an older woman with no-nonsense glasses and a forehead that looked well-practised in frowning walked into the court through an inner door.

'Carmel Grant,' whispered Sue in her ear. 'Smart, fair, and doesn't take any crap.'

'All rise.'

Vera stood. So she was to look like a professional journalist, was she? She wasn't one. Not anymore. Not since that rat she'd thought she was in love with fired her. But she could remember what it felt like to be confident and eager, full of questions and the resolve to find answers. She could fake professional journalist if she had to.

She breathed in, slowly, then let out a long breath. Perhaps Sue's confidence was cloaked about her as surely as her perfume and cigarette smoke was.

As the magistrate dealt with a few other cases, the words just buzzed in Vera's ears. Aaron was here, in the same room as her, for the first time since … when? Had it really been eleven months since this whole thing began?

She closed her eyes and was right there, back in his bed, reliving the moment when her world was ripped out from under her …

It had been early morning, on a fine spring Sunday with the hint of summer in the breeze.

'I'm popping in to see Jill this morning, Aaron,' she'd said as they lay in bed. He was lying against a pillow, his chest bare, but his funky reading glasses perched on his nose while he scrolled through his phone.

'I was wondering if you fancied having lunch later? Maybe a picnic down at Googong?' She pulled his glasses away from his nose so he wouldn't miss the saucy look she was giving him. 'I've bought myself a new bikini that I am pretty sure you are going to want to see.'

'Um-hmm,' he said.

His phone was more interesting than the promise of a bikini? She must be losing her mojo. Perhaps an update on her investigation would spark his interest?

'Hopefully there'll be someone who doesn't hate me on duty. Some of the staff were pretty cheesed off after my first opinion piece was published. I don't think they understood it wasn't them I was angry with. It was the system. A casual workforce, no continuity of care … I mean, it's just so poorly managed.' She looked at her watch. 'Be interesting to see if they've read today's article yet.'

'Yeah, er … Vera, look, I didn't want to get into this now, but I'd better tell you—'

She'd cut him off, too wrapped up in her own thoughts and agenda. 'Speaking of, what time does your Sunday paper come?'

Aaron was pulling on his jeans. 'You know, this is all you talk about now, Vera.'

She'd paused then. 'Excuse me?'

'Your aunt, old people, staff-to-patient ratios. It's starting to give me the shits, if I'm honest.'

'My worry for my aunt, who is potentially being neglected by the people who are being paid to mind her, is giving you the shits?'

He'd shrugged.

'And my investigation? My exposé on the aged care industry that you were all supportive and gung-ho about, is that giving you the shits too, now?'

'Vera, honey, let's not overreact.'

'This is not me overreacting, Aaron. This is me getting angry. Getting upset. Getting let down.'

'I just think we've all had enough of drama and bad news stories. I think the *South Coast Morning Herald* needs some levity at the moment.'

'Fluff pieces.'

'Hey, I don't answer to you, Vera, I answer to the shareholders. If they want levity in the Sunday issue, they get levity, all right?'

'But Aaron ... I thought you were with me on this.'

The look on his face made it clear he wasn't with her at all. A horrid thought struck her. 'Wait a minute. Did you even print my story this week?'

He came around to her side of the bed, where she was flinging back pillows and doonas and twisted damn sheets and trying to get the hell up. 'Vera, listen—'

She ignored him. She hauled on her jeans and t-shirt and took off for the front door of his house. There, safely wrapped in plastic against the dew of dawn, was the Sunday paper. She ripped through the layers of plastic and flicked through the pages. Sports, furniture advertisements, the national stories they printed on syndication from the big city papers … but on her page, where the article she'd laboured over for days should have been, was an advertisement.

For Acacia View Aged Care.

Where care and respect, she read wrathfully through the tears in her eyes, *comes first.*

She could feel him standing behind her on his front step, and she looked up. 'What the actual heck, Aaron?'

'I had to make a choice, Vera. The newspaper needs the advertising revenue, and when Chris Sykes contacted me—'

'You've been cosying up with the general manager of Acacia View and you didn't even tell me?'

'I haven't been cosying, as you put it. I've been running a newspaper. Which means earning money through advertisements so we can pay your wages, and not pissing off the businesses in town who are keen to advertise with us.'

'So you threw my article under the bus for financial gain, is that it?'

'It was a good business decision.'

She narrowed her eyes. 'Wait … how did Chris even know I was running a second article? The one that should be in this newspaper, today, where I discussed my aunt's care at Acacia View?'

Aaron raised his hands as though he was placating a wild beast. 'Come on back inside, Vera. We need to talk about this.'

'Correction. I need to talk about this. I need to talk to whichever newspaper in this country still gives a damn about reporting facts fearlessly. Which was it, Aaron? Did you squeeze an advert out of them in return for not running my article? Or did they squeeze you? I bet that was it, wasn't it? Where's your damn spine?'

'Are you threatening me, Vera?'

'I'm promising you, Aaron, the way I promised my aunt I would campaign for change. And unlike you, I keep my word.'

Of course that was when he sacked her. She'd been barefoot on the front step of his house and he'd pulled her job out from under her feet.

The prosecution charge came later, after Aaron ratted her out to his new best buddy Chris Sykes by telling him she'd hidden a camera in her aunt's room at Acacia View.

That had been when her belief in herself disintegrated.

Sue dug a lacquered talon into her leg and it snapped her back into the present. 'You're up,' she hissed.

'We'll now hear the matter of Vera De Rossi,' said the magistrate. 'Is Vera in the courtroom?'

She stood up. 'Yes, Your Honour.'

'The charge against you is brought about by private prosecution; do you understand what that means?'

'Yes. The police haven't charged me with an offence, instead a private citizen has done so.'

'Do you understand that the Department of Public Prosecutions can step in at any stage and take over prosecuting these charges?'

'Yes, Your Honour.'

'And you have legal representation, I see.'

She was beginning to feel like a parrot—an anxious parrot in a black wool dress slightly moth-eaten on one sleeve. 'Yes, Your Honour.'

'You have been charged with a crime under the *Surveillance Devices Act of 2007*, namely installing a listening device to record a private conversation. How do you plead?'

She swallowed. This was it, the crossing of the line. 'I plead not guilty, Your Honour.'

The magistrate nodded. 'Trial date will be set in due course. Dismissed. The court will take a short recess and be back in session at ten am.'

'Okay, that's done, let's go,' said Sue.

'That's it? So quick?'

'That's court for you. Wait six hours for a two-second appearance. Come on, you can buy me a coffee and we can begin our two-day strategy blitz.'

'Can we wait a moment? Just until Aaron and Sykes get clear of the building. I can't face them.'

'Vera, my pet, my love, my girl. A word of advice.'

Oh heck. Sue was going to make her be brave.

'You've got to look at that dickhead ex-boyfriend of yours, and look hard, Vera. Get used to it. The more you face him, the easier it will be for you, and guess what?'

'What?' She whispered it, because the court clerk was frowning at them.

'Here's the icing on the cake bit … the more you look at him, really look, the harder it's going to be for him. That's the thing about being a scumbag. Deep down inside, below that reptilian part of his brain where his advertising revenue means more to him than his self-respect, he *knows* he's just a scumbag now. And you looking at him is going to remind him of that every time. Use that power, Vera.'

Crap. Okay, she could do this. She stood up, turned, and her eyes looked straight into his dark brown ones.

His hair was short, almost soldier short, and his suit snappy, as though he'd ditched journalism to sell upscale real estate. The other thing that struck her was how … weak he seemed. As though the outer slickness was a showy cover to stop people seeing the lack of substance beneath. She tried to imagine him running into a burning building to bundle baby animals into his pockets and snorted. He'd never do it. Not for an animal, not for a person. Never for her.

Their relationship had sparked into existence shortly after Aaron moved to the newspaper. Flowers, drinks, a crazy Sunday date laughing their way through food trucks and music gigs at a local brewery open day. Promises hadn't been spoken, vows hadn't been said … but promises could be made in other ways, and she'd made them; thought he'd made them in return. When she made breakfast for a guy in her sun-filled apartment, wearing nothing but his shirt, she was promising 'I care for you'. She thought she was being promised 'you can trust me' in return. Why else give her flowers? Hold her hand on afternoon walks through Tallaganda National Park? Plait her hair, cook her risotto, bring her almond croissants from a bakery all the way over in Canberra?

He'd not meant any of it.

Vera wiped her damp palms on her skirt. 'Okay, eye contact made, but I think that's my bravery just about worn through, Sue. Let's get out of here.'

'You got it.'

CHAPTER
26

'Thanks for meeting us, Sergeant King,' said Josh. 'I didn't get a chance to speak to you at the fire, but Tom Krauss speaks highly of you. I've lived away for the last decade and a half. Old Reg Grady was in charge of the Hanrahan Police Station when I left.'

'Call me Meg. Old Reg still pops in to the police station from time to time and brings a batch of biscuits he's made himself. He likes to talk war stories about the good old days when no-one had mobile phones and the tracks up past Crackenback were so bad in winter he had to go on horseback.'

'He was a good guy.'

'He was a drunk for the last ten years he was in office and used to pat the office staff on the backside according to Kev Jones. He wouldn't last a day on my watch.'

'Good on you,' said Hannah.

Josh crossed his ankles under the picnic bench in the park where he and Hannah and the sergeant had arranged to meet. He was beginning to understand why Tom had suggested he call Meg

King. She might look like a sweet-as-sugar tuckshop mum, but she had the flat-eyed stare of a street cop.

'We want to talk about the fire,' he said. 'Lorraine told us it was no accident.'

'Have you seen the fire brigade's preliminary report?'

'Yeah, Lorraine rang us this morning. She said it was too soon for definitive results, but she could give me the gist of what they discovered last night. Deliberately lit, but no accelerant. Some weird pyrotechnic device was found in the ground floor.'

'Yep. First I've seen like that. Your garden variety arsonists want a light show, but they also want destruction. Your fire was different.'

'There's plenty of destruction in the front room.'

'Yes, the reception area behind the plate glass windows was ground zero all right. Smashed glass, lit device chucked in, and the pyrotechnic device thrown in with it. So the flooring and furniture caught alight, window treatments, doors, skirting, paperwork—enough to cause you a lot of heartache, but not enough to destroy the building. The pyrotechnic device made the blaze look far worse than it was—like a firework in a contained space.'

'It's nuts, all of it.'

Meg opened the file she had in front of her. 'That's not the most nuts thing.'

'It's not?'

'I spoke to the dispatchers at emergency after I read your statement. You said Graeme Sharpe, the café manager from The Billy Button Café, put in the first call to triple zero.'

'That's right. He had a sense something was up; we arrived just after the blaze started.'

She nodded. 'Thing is, Josh, he wasn't the first to call it in.'

He scratched his head. 'Crap. The arsonist?'

'We think so.'

'Because he—'

'Or she.'

He grinned, for what felt like the first time in days. He wished Poppy had been by his side to hear the sergeant correct him. Equality for all, arsonists included. 'Thank you, Meg. Because she or he wanted to make sure the building wasn't destroyed in the fire?'

'Bingo. Which brings me neatly to the other nuts thing.'

He raised his eyebrows at Hannah, who shrugged.

'Why,' said Sergeant King, 'have I been the lucky recipient of a Crime Stoppers call, suggesting that the owner of the Cody and Cody Vet Clinic might have burned their own building down?'

'*What?*'

'Something to do with'—Meg's eyes dropped to a printed page in her folder—'sour grapes because of a refused building permit.'

'No freaking way,' he said.

Hannah was shaking her head. 'That bloody council. What is up with them?'

Meg frowned. 'What do you mean? Have you had other problems before this?'

'Er, sure. A few nuisance complaints have been coming our way. They seem trivial, but we have to address them, or our business licence renewal is under threat. It's been a headache, but it's not been a problem. Some animal activist who doesn't like us working with farm animals, perhaps, wanting to stir up a bit of trouble.'

'You want to tell me why this is the first I'm hearing of it?'

'We were frustrated, sure,' said Hannah, 'but we didn't think anything illegal was happening, so we didn't think to call the cops.'

'Harassing law-abiding people in Hanrahan is always my business. The fire just makes it more so.' Meg looked down at her notebook. 'I'll have to investigate the claim that you torched your own building. I'll need alibis, a copy of your planning permit and so on. What about these nuisance complaints, have you got copies of those?'

'I can drop them round to the station.' A thought struck him. 'I've just remembered something. When the refusal came in, I rang a mate, an experienced developer. He's working on my objection letter for me. He told me—but I'd forgotten about it—that objections to a development proposal are public documents. Somewhere at the council office there's got to be a letter in from someone with a name on it.'

Meg nodded. 'It's a start, and until we get forensics back on the clinic fire, it's the only lead we've got. You get the name, and if they give you any grief, you call me, all right?'

'Will do.'

He kept his eyes on the policewoman as she strode off back to her car. She was pursuing the arson investigation, his mate Frank was writing up his objection to council's refusal, but what was he doing? Sitting here like a shag on a rock in a park in the middle of a workday with the charred ground floor of his building mocking him from fifty metres away.

His eyes wandered from the Cody building, along Dandaloo to the art deco cinema, back to Salt Creek Flats Road where the stately three-storey Victorian buildings glowed in the midday sun. *Holy sh—*

He cut his eyes across to his sister. 'I've just had an idea.'

'I hope it's a good one.'

It was. It absolutely *was*.

'Some dickhead objects to our reno on the grounds of it being out of character.'

'Yeah, I know this, Josh.'

'Hear me out. I'm going to gather some ammunition of my own.'

'Like what?'

'Between us, we know a lot of people in this town, right? Let's speak to them. Let's walk around the town park and ask the other business owners what they think of our plans. We'll ask tourists, couples eating out at the winery, the people down by the lake queueing up for sunset cruises on the steamboat. I'll show them my sketches of the restoration we're planning, and ask them to send in *their* opinions to council.'

'Sure, that's going to help with the building permit, but is it going to stop this vendetta someone has against us?'

He leaned forward and squeezed his sister's arm. 'That's why we go public.'

'I don't understand.'

'What's the one thing about Hanrahan that I was worried about when I came back here to live?'

'Being outclassed in veterinary skills by your bad-ass little sister?'

'Besides that.'

'Gossip. Everyone knowing your private business and blabbing about it.'

'Correct. And I was right to worry; the Hanrahan Chatter has splashed my personal life all over its column, and god knows what else. Well, guess what?'

'I dread to think, but that evil smirk you're wearing isn't boding well for anyone in your path.'

'I'm calling Maureen.'

'Mrs Plover? Condom guardian and gossip columnist?'

He gave his sister a wink. 'The very same. I'm going to invite her to do an article on me and my mad heritage restoration skills currently being volunteered to restore the ceiling of Hanrahan's community hall.'

Hannah sat back on the bench seat. 'Josh, that is brilliant. You can work in your plans for our building … share a bit of Cody history from the gold rush era … it'll be like thumbing our noses at whoever this idiot is who thinks they can destroy our home from under us.'

'Marking our territory,' he said with relish. Finally, something he could do to protect his family. 'You going to be okay if I spend a bit more time at the hall the next couple of days? The electrician's done, so if I can get in there now and finish the project before I contact Maureen, she's more likely to take the bait. Maybe I can persuade Marigold to perform a little ribbon-cutting ceremony or something.'

'Sure. I'd offer to help, but I'll be more use on the road visiting sick animals in their homes than mixing up plaster.'

'Thanks. Last question: you know where I'll find Kev this time of day? He and I have a deal going. I fix the hall ceiling, he does my archive research for me. I'm going to need that research done, too, if I want to track Maureen Plover down in her lair and convince her to direct her evil skillset towards a win for us.'

Hannah grinned. 'Kev will probably be down at the cemetery tending his roses. You tackle him and Mrs Plover, and I'll go rearrange your appointments.'

'Thanks.' He pulled out his phone, found Marigold's number, and typed in a message.

Time to hold up your end of the bargain, Mrs Jones. I need that archive stuff ASAP.

A message flashed up on his screen a second later. *You finished my ceiling yet, my love?*

Soon, he typed, then shoved his phone in his pocket. He had to visit city hall and get the name of whoever had objected to his proposal before he could even think about plaster and cornices and fanciful frilly fretwork.

CHAPTER
27

Vera stood in the corridor willing the tremor in her hands to still. She was dog-tired, embarrassed, and royally pissed off with just about everyone in the world, herself included. She needed a moment to herself.

'I'm ducking into the restroom,' she said. 'Back in a minute.'

The ladies' restroom was full, so she headed into the parents' room, hoping there'd be no-one in there so she could pull herself together in private. As she pushed the door in, someone hustled in behind her and swung her around.

She skidded on the heel of her boot and grabbed the nappy change table to steady herself. 'Aaron. What the hell?'

'You're looking good, Vera.'

'Don't talk to me.'

'Vera, honey—'

'You rat. I have nothing to say to you.' She took a step to the door.

'Just hear me out, please.'

'What could you possibly have to say, Aaron?'

'Hey, I didn't bring this charge against you. I'm not the bad guy here.'

'You dobbed on me, Aaron. You knew I wasn't using that recording device to entrap Acacia View. I was using it to monitor my aunt, who can't speak for herself. She has dementia. And you sure as hell were the one who sacked me.'

'I'm here for you, Vera, don't you get that? Look, sure, I was a little hasty, but only because I cared for you. I still care for you, Vera. Why won't you—'

She'd heard enough. Had Aaron always been like this? So self-absorbed that he couldn't see the damage he'd done?

She turned to leave just as her lawyer bulldozed her way in through the swinging door.

'Vera, you may be my favourite client,' her lawyer announced, 'but I don't think you've understood just how surly I can become when I have to wait for caffeine, so hurry up— Oh! Well, well, what do we have here? The prosecution's star witness engaging in a little off-court harassment?'

'Let's just go,' she muttered.

'Can I call you?' Aaron said. 'I know you've moved away, maybe I could come visit. Talk things through.'

What did he not get about how bitter she might feel about what he'd done? Did he not *know*? She wanted to scream at him, but beside her, Sue's chest was swelling up like she was a self-inflating life jacket that had just hit water. 'There will be no talking, Mr Finch. There will just be the sound of the door closing as you get the hell out of this gender-neutral nappy-changing facility paid for by the taxpayers of Queanbeyan. My client has nothing to say.'

Aaron looked for a moment as though he was going to argue the point, then his shoulders fell and he turned for the door. 'I know we can get past this, Vee. I just know it.' And then he was, finally, gone.

'Drama queen,' muttered Sue. 'Thinks he's auditioning for a role on *Home and Away*. Who in their right mind ever gets back with the dickhead who ruined their life?'

Vera drew in a shaky breath.

'Hey, come on, don't let him get to you. Want to know a little trick I learned my first year as a barrister?'

She breathed in, and out, and let her lawyer prattle on.

'Whenever some arrogant guy was giving me grief—you know, suggesting I'd like to make him a coffee because I had ovaries and he didn't, despite my law degree and having worked my arse off to get qualified at the bar, or leering down my blouse like he'd never seen boobs in the workplace before—I'd picture him naked, and work up an equally gendered backstory for him. Like, you know, when he was a small boy playing naked in the garden under the sprinkler, he had an unfortunate incident with the neighbour's sausage dog.'

Vera closed her eyes. Jokes didn't help, not today.

Sue tucked her hand into her arm and gave her a squeeze. 'Come on. Let's get you out of here. As fun as this is, the smell of yesterday's stinky baby bums is going to get into my clothing, and you do not want to know how much I paid for this skirt.' She pushed her way through the swing door and Vera followed her out.

She didn't want coffee in some grey, city bistro.

She wanted mountain air. She wanted a quiet moment in the chair by her window with a fat grey cat on her lap.

She wanted to go home.

CHAPTER

28

Josh stared at the name. He'd marched down to the council office and asked Barry O'Malley to show him the objections council had received to his renovation proposal. Now here it was in front of him.

Pamela Hogan.

Why, oh why, was that name ringing a bell?

Sandy hadn't known the name, and there were no Hogans in their client list. 'Want me to google her? Stalk her on social media? I've got mad skills online, Josh,' the receptionist had offered.

'Drop your weapons back in your holster, Kojak. Let me ask Hannah first, okay?'

'No problem. But refilling kitty litter trays isn't my only skill. Just saying.'

'Understood.'

Sandy had insisted on coming to work even though the clinic was shut and cordoned off with crime tape. She was neck deep in sorting paperwork in the back office, determined to do something useful. He'd not had the heart to say no—single mums with growing sons needed their wages same as any other parent.

He tracked Hannah down in the old shed out back, where she was looking into the engine of her car with a cranky look on her face. He moved in next to her and looked down. 'Problems?' he said.

'Besides our livelihood going up in smoke? Yeah. My fan-belt's screaming every time I start her up, the heater doesn't work, and there are so many rust spots now, some days I feel like I'm driving a dalmatian.'

He pulled the oil stick from the engine, inspected it, and shoved it back in, thereby exhausting his knowledge of all things mechanical. 'Maybe it's time to say goodbye to the old beast and fork out for a new one.'

'Says moneybags himself.'

He laughed. 'Han, if you could see my bank balance, you'd know just how ridiculous that sounds. The bulk of my savings went into buying building materials for this place.'

'We're going to be broke before long if we can't open up. There are the repayments on the ultrasound machine, the haematology unit.'

'I've put a call in to the insurer. I'm waiting on them to get back to me.'

'Yeah. You think they're going to be paying us a single dollar if the police are investigating *us* as the potential arsonists?'

'One anonymous Crime Stoppers phone call is not a police investigation.'

'It's pressure, Josh. It's pressure on our business.'

'I wonder ...' he said slowly. 'Hannah ... do you think that could have been the plan all along? Is someone trying to make us walk away from our business?'

She whacked the support strut out of its lock and slammed her bonnet shut. 'You mean, one of the other vets in the region? That's a big claim, brother, and you don't know them like I do. We help each other out, we don't sabotage each other's businesses.'

'Sorry, Han. You're right, you do know them, but if we're not being harassed by a competitor, who is behind this? Here, read this.' He handed her the copy of the objection letter he'd picked up from council.

'What's this?'

'The objection. Signed by someone called Pamela Hogan.'

'Bloody hell.'

He looked at his sister's arrested face. 'You know the name?'

'I sure as hell do,' she said. 'Quick, to the back office.'

His sister ran across the flagged rear yard of the building and through the side door like the hounds of hell were after her. What on earth?

By the time he'd followed her into the office, she was on her knees in front of the filing cupboard, hauling out a jumble of manila folders.

'You're messing up my good work, Hannah,' said Sandy.

'Sorry. I'll fix it. Okay, here it is.'

She slammed a green folder on top of the desk. 'Pamela Hogan. You remember the offer we got to buy the building, way back, after we'd just officially become the owners?'

'Um, sort of. I didn't really take much notice, to be honest, Han. Walk me through the details.'

'Okay, so the first offer came when you were on your final internship at the Dalgety Flats Stables. You hadn't graduated. It was a letter in the mail, I think. I put it through the shredder with the rest of the junk mail and lined the cages with it.'

'And there was another offer?'

'Some guy from Lake Realtors over at Jindabyne. He'd received a generous offer, one we "couldn't refuse". He came during clinic hours. Sandy found him wandering through the first floor taking photos on his phone. I said we weren't interested and told him he'd better have a sick pet with him next time I caught him wandering around my property.'

Josh nodded. 'Nice.'

Hannah grinned. 'I'm not a total coward.'

'You're the bravest person I know.'

She cleared her throat. 'Where was I? Right, so then the emails started. I printed out a few and kept them.'

'These emails, are they from Pamela Hogan?'

He opened the folder and rifled through the pages. Pamela Hogan, Solicitor from an office in Cooma whose unnamed client had apparently authorised her to send increasingly persistent offers to acquire the Cody and Cody building, month after month.

'Nothing for the last few months, though,' he said. 'Nothing since I've been here.'

'I had the computer guy block her email account.'

He had a thought. 'You know how Barry O'Malley wouldn't tell us who was behind all the trivial complaints we were getting because of some privacy law?'

'Mmm.'

'Maybe we get that cop, Meg, to ask. She may be able to convince him there's a greater good here. And if it's the same person, it's starting to paint a pretty big picture, Han.'

'Call her,' she said.

'I'll make copies of all these so you can give her the file,' said Sandy.

'Thanks, Josh,' said Hannah. 'Thanks, Sandy. I'm not sure I could be the one who … it's just … dealing with stuff isn't really my special skill.'

'No big deal, Hannah Banana. I've got your back.' Yet another reason he'd fought so hard to come home: he didn't want to leave Hannah on her own when their parents decided their retirement involved circumnavigating the country in a motorhome.

She butted her head into his shoulder so her thanks came out muffled against his shirt, but he got the gist.

She lifted her head. 'Maybe I shouldn't have just ignored the first letter. If I'd been more proactive and told them to rack off, they'd have got the message and stopped harassing us.'

'We're too nice. That's the problem,' said Josh.

'Correction. You've been too nice. I'm bitchy as hell, but only in the privacy of my own bathroom. I can't take this on, Josh. I can't do conflict.'

He put down the letter and his coffee and wrapped her in a hug. 'I know. Hannah, I've got this.'

She didn't need more pressure in her life. And damn it, he'd worked too hard to get tripped up by some crackbrained vendetta against the Cody vet business.

He'd sort this. Somehow.

CHAPTER
29

The gracious old snow gum in the centre of the town square was lit with a thousand white fairy lights. Around it, the timber and stone Federation buildings were mostly dark, their shopfronts closed and tidied away for the night; the residents of their upper storeys tucked into bed with a book, a chamomile tea, a late-night bingefest of their favourite show.

The world kept going round, even while it felt like it was ending.

Her indicator tick-tick-ticked in time with her thoughts as she slowed to make the turn into Dandaloo Drive. She had to be in the café at dawn the next morning which was—she looked at her watch—dear god, only eight hours from now. Food prep, check the catering jobs, order supplies. After the breakfast rush, she'd duck out to Connolly House and sit with her aunt for a while. Maybe she could work on the summer menu while she was visiting; tourists would be plentiful, and that would mean more slices to bake, more sandwiches to fill, more cold drinks to stock. Perhaps a line of picnic lunches for the hikers who'd flock to the Snowy River National Park over summer.

A busy day tomorrow, which was good. Busy meant no time for brooding about going to trial.

The three-storey building that was home to the Cody and Cody Vet Clinic loomed on her left and she took her foot off the accelerator. Not a crumbling ruin, then, despite the yellow crime scene tape flickering across the plywood sheeting where the clinic's front windows used to be.

She eased into the kerb and sat awhile, surveying the charred bricks and rubble tumbling down the front steps.

She wasn't the only one who'd had a crap few days, she should remember that. Movement in the narrow street that ran down the side of the building caught her eye. A man stood there, his hands shoved in his pockets, staring up at the building.

She couldn't make out his face, but she knew it was Josh. She didn't know how she knew it, she just did. Damn guy had snuck his way in past her defences while she was distracted by all that handsome manness.

Before her head could persuade her otherwise, she slid her fingers into the catch of her car door and opened it, to step out into the chill mountain night. A low woof sounded, and Jane Doe came scampering up to push her wet nose into Vera's hand.

'Hey, girl,' she said and pulled a soft ear through her fingers.

Josh turned his head and watched her as she walked towards him.

'Hey,' she said.

She stood next to him and looked up to where he was looking. Stone. Timber windows trimmed in white. The gracious acanthus brackets of a bygone era carved beneath the old parlour windows of the upper floors.

The breeze off the lake had more than a whisper of cold in it but she welcomed it. The drive up from Queanbeyan had taken two hours, but it felt like she'd travelled back through history a hundred years. City traffic, diesel fumes, crowds … she'd barely noticed the busyness of Queanbeyan when she'd lived there, but these few months she'd been living in Hanrahan had changed her.

She pulled in a lungful of air, smelled the lake water, eucalypts, a lingering curl of woodsmoke from the fire. And Josh.

'I'm so sorry about your building,' she said.

'Mmm.'

'You get all the animals out?'

'Yeah. They spent the night in Graeme's toolshed, then the sick ones went to the vet in Cooma and the rest back to their homes.'

She looked down at the dog seated by his feet, gazing lovingly upwards. 'This animal doesn't look like she'd leave you willingly.'

He shrugged. 'Unlike some. Two days you've been gone, Vera.'

She drew back. Oh, wow. She must seem like the most selfish cow in the southern hemisphere. She had a quick flash of the people who had gathered in the park when the clinic was on fire—all of them there to help or offer support. And she'd just driven away.

Sure, she'd had to … but Josh didn't know that, did he? Because she was too ashamed of herself to share her secrets.

She cleared her throat. 'If I can do anything to help, I hope you'll let me know.'

He glanced at her. 'Last time I asked you for help, you weren't so keen to oblige.'

Oh my god. The council by-laws he'd wanted her help to research to stop the nuisance complaints about the practice. A horrid thought came to her. 'You don't think … holy hell, was this fire *deliberate*? Oh, Josh, I'm so sorry.'

He frowned down at her. 'Where have you been the last few days? The gossip wire's been running so hot, I'd have thought your café would have heard all the news. It was definitely arson and the really fun part, Vera, is that someone called the cops and dobbed me in for doing it.'

'What? That's crazy.'

He let out a long sigh that sounded as tired and dispirited as she felt. 'We're just lucky the damage was limited to the reception rooms.'

'You don't need to demolish the building?'

'No. But the insurer's dragging their feet while the investigation plays out, so I'll probably have to refit the clinic myself if we want to get the business up and running again. Once we're allowed back in the front room, that is.'

'That sounds like a big job.'

'Marigold's set up a working bee to clean the smoke smell out of the upstairs apartments, and we have a smoke extractor running in there now. It'll take time, but we'll get there.'

Time. The one thing she didn't know if she had.

'Where will you stay?'

'You remember the Krauss family?'

She remembered getting the lips kissed off her on the mountain above Ironbark Station, home of the Krauss family. She was going to be remembering that moment until the end of her days, so yeah ... she knew who they were.

'Richer than they need to be, but also super happy to help anyone out. They own the old Hanrahan Pub. It's two planks of wood away from being derelict, so there's only a caretaker been living there for a couple of years now. Me and the Doe family have moved in there.'

'Hannah too?'

Josh shook his head. 'Hannah would rather sleep in a wet ditch than accept a roof over her head from Tom Krauss.'

'That sounds like a story.'

'So I keep telling her. She's not shared it with me yet. She's staying with her friend Kylie for a few days until we know what's what.'

She turned and studied his face in the low light. 'This building must mean a lot to you.'

'You have no idea.'

Her words came out unfiltered by the caution she usually had clamped tightly in place. 'I'd like to hear. Tell me.'

Josh turned to her and then cocked his head. 'You know, you blow a little hot and cold, Vera. I can't quite see my way through it.'

She deserved that. And he deserved better, but after the long days she'd had in Queanbeyan, facing court, the ugly scene with Aaron in the restroom, the endless meetings with Sue, her willpower to resist him had puffed out. 'I know,' she said quietly. 'I'm sorry I've been so all over the place. I have a reason, but it's a long and ugly story, and it's … shameful. I'm ashamed.'

'I'm not here to judge you, Vera. I like you. I don't know why, sometimes,' he said, with that easy smile on his face which took the sting from his words and made them almost, god help her, affectionate. 'And call it my highly tuned male intuition, but I think you like me too. Sometimes. When you're not busy giving me the brush-off.'

She lifted her face to the night. Cool, a hint of rain, and everything silent but for the hum from a streetlamp, and Jane Doe's snuffling as she lay at Josh's feet. Her busy day ahead seemed distant, like chores waiting for some other person. Not her. Not the Vera standing here in the moonlight with a thoughtful, handsome man by her side.

All the jobs she had lined up, the worries she had to shoulder … perhaps now, in the quiet of this November evening, *was* the time to be honest. 'Have you eaten?'

'Pizza three hours ago. What did you have in mind?'

'I could rustle up a slice of cake, if you like. Maybe we could talk if you're not too tired.'

Josh reached down and found her hand. 'I'm very partial to cake.'

She felt the warmth of his hand seep into the chill of hers. God help her, she was very partial to him.

'So where have you been these last couple of days to not hear about the arsonist?'

'I had to go to Queanbeyan.'

'*Queanbeyan?* Was this something to do with the old life you're trying to leave behind?'

She snorted. 'Trying is the right word. Turns out, my old life is gripping on to me tooth and nail. It's been a shattering couple of days, truth be told.'

They left the park behind them as they wandered to the north end of Dandaloo Drive, past the cinema and the retro store.

'Mind if we detour on the way? I'll drop Jane back to her pups.'

'Sure.' She was enjoying the walk. Her thoughts had been a scramble all day, but trudging along, with the world all quiet around them, was soothing her. She was in no hurry to stop wandering.

She stood on the footpath under the wrought-iron railings of the majestic old pub while Josh took the dog inside, and then he was back, and somehow her hand was in his again. The moon was on the wane, and low enough in the sky to throw a shimmer of moonlight across the blackness of the lake.

Josh cocked his head. 'Want to take the scenic route? We can walk along the lakefront and cut back to Cuddy Street up there by the dock.'

She nodded. 'I'd like that.'

Gravel crunched under their feet as they picked their way along the foreshore, and now and then a fish plopped, sending ripples through the dark water.

'We grew up around this lake,' Josh said.

'You and Hannah?'

'Oh, there was a great crew of us. Most have left the area. Unless your interests lie in tourism or farming, the jobs can be few and far between out here for youngsters. A handful are still around. Kylie, that's Hannah's bestie, and a few others that pop in from time to time.'

'It seems an idyllic place to grow up.'

He grinned. 'Skinny-dipping at midnight on summer nights. Bonfires, camping over the far side of the lake in the national park. Tom used to ride to school on a horse, some days.'

'Okay, the horse part doesn't sound quite so idyllic.'

He squeezed her hand. 'They grow on you, trust me.'

His words played on her mind as she stepped over an old log. *Trust me.* Aaron had flung phrases like that around like they were ping-pong balls: lightweight little bits of plastic that he'd bought in a two-dollar shop and valued not at all. Could two men be any more different?

When Josh said *trust me*, it mattered.

'When I was at the clinic with the cat,' she began, 'your sister mentioned something about trouble with council. I wasn't really paying attention … then, or when you asked me for help.'

'Some time ago, we had an offer for our building, sent via a lawyer. It was a sizeable chunk of money. The block has views of the lake from some of the upstairs windows, and two street frontages, a yard out back. We said no.'

'And that wasn't the end of it?'

'The lawyer pestered Hannah for weeks—this all happened before I moved here. But Hannah kept saying no, and the lawyer kept making offers. We'd never sell it. Not only because it's where the clinic is, and Hannah's spent every cent of her business profits kitting out the ground floor to be a modern surgery. But that building is a family heirloom. The Codys have owned it and run a business out of it since Hanrahan was a gold rush town in the 1880s. We'd never part with it.'

She didn't have a building to show for family, and heritage, and history. But she had Jill's books, her mother's jewellery, and most important of all, she had their recipes and their love of food. She could understand the Cody siblings' refusal to sell.

'Then, the lawyer goes quiet. Han was pleased; thought they'd found some other property owner to harass. But then the "concerned citizen" letters started arriving at council … the nuisance complaints that threatened our business licence.'

'Like what? What did they say?'

'Oh, they varied. One was about chicken farming in an urban area, which was clear-cut rubbish. Another was about inadequate ID on dog collars, can you believe.'

'And now a fire.'

Josh shook his head. 'It's mental. All of it. It's not as though our building is the only one in Hanrahan. There's a strip of Federation buildings on all four sides of the park, some of them have been on the market for years. Why us? Why be so damned persistent?'

She sighed. 'I wish I knew of something that would answer your questions. I'm so sorry, Josh.'

They left the lakeshore behind them and turned up Cuddy Street. Josh squeezed her arm. 'Your turn. Want to tell me what was so urgent that you took off without saying anything?'

'I'll tell you, I will, but let's get inside. It's going to take me a while to get through it.'

The cat was mewling its discontent by the time they arrived at her apartment, and she hurried into the laundry to spoon out a saucer full of fish mush. Mrs Butler had fed her last night, but she'd hoped to have been home earlier than this. The cat's grey fur brushed her fingers as she began hoovering up her meal, and Vera gave her a quick stroke before leaving her to it.

'Have a seat,' she said to Josh as she returned to the living room and headed into the kitchenette to review the contents of her fridge. Did she even have any cake?

There was wine. That was a food group, wasn't it? She pulled out a bottle of Yarra Valley chardonnay and waggled it in Josh's direction. 'Fancy a glass?'

'Love one.'

He moved over to the counter and took a sip from the glass she handed him. 'Nice. You didn't buy this at the local bottlo.'

Vera poured herself an I-went-to-court-and-will-drink-whatever-the-hell-I-want serve of the delicate white. 'Graeme's broadening my palate. Last week it was a South Australian pinot noir. He slides them into my handbag with little love notes.'

Josh took another sip. 'The man knows his beverages.'

She grinned and instantly felt better for it. God, how long had it been since she'd just … laughed? Had a silly conversation and relaxed? 'Don't tell him. His ego barely fits behind the counter of The Billy Button Café as it is.'

'It'll be our secret.'

She cleared her throat. That was a segue prompt if ever she'd heard one. 'Speaking of secrets, Josh, I meant it when I said I'd tell you why I've been so … hot and cold.'

He set down his glass and then took hers and placed it on the bench so he could take her hands in his. 'It's safe to tell me, Vera. I promise.'

She braced herself. 'Okay. I drove to Queanbeyan after the fire had settled down. I had to. I was in court the next morning.'

'A law court.'

'Yep.'

Damn it. She pulled her hands away and turned to rummage through the pantry until she could trust herself to get the words out without crumpling to her knees. Packets of rice and pink salt and pasta stared up at her from inside the cupboard. Her trusty soldiers. It would be a lot easier to share her shame with them.

She found a tin of crackers, plucked a brie and grapes from the fridge, fussed with them a little on a platter and then moved to the sofa. She met his eyes as he sat down beside her. 'You want the short story or the long?'

He stretched out and crossed his ankles. 'Better make it the long one.'

'My aunt used to live at an aged care facility in the outskirts of Queanbeyan. She was there a total of four and a half years.'

'This is Jill, who's at Connolly House now?'

'Yep. She's ... fading away. Quicker than I'd hoped. That fall she had last week—she's not improving.'

'I'm sorry, Vera.'

She realised she'd shredded a grape into pulp and set it aside on a napkin. 'When she was living at Acacia View, I would visit, and after a while, I started noticing ... stuff.'

'What sort of stuff?'

'Unwashed hair. Her bedding or clothing not being changed. Staff never the same so you couldn't be sure there was anyone there who my aunt could recognise.'

'That's terrible. Could your aunt not care for herself at all?'

'At first, yes. She could shower, watch TV, play cards with the other residents. But she has vascular dementia and problems with her heart and the decline has been steep.'

And crippling to watch. Vera sighed. 'As her ability to communicate with me deteriorated, I became more and more concerned. So I started looking out for other people there visiting relatives and I talked to them. Turned out I wasn't the only one with concerns. I spoke to the facility manager and asked for something to be done.'

'And, what, they did nothing?'

'They brushed me off. Sure, my aunt's room would be given a spring-clean, she'd be in a different nightie the next time I visited, but the change never lasted. I was upset about it. I mean, this place and her medical bills were sucking her and me dry financially, yet they couldn't even roster enough staff on duty so someone could brush her hair.'

'That's awful.'

'So I decided to take my concern public.'

'How do you mean?'

'You know I was a journalist before I moved here and became a cook?'

Josh nodded. 'Yep. Quite a career change.'

She shrugged. 'You do what you must.'

'So true. You know, before I came back to Hanrahan, I wasn't a vet.'

She smiled. 'Josh Cody. The town's prodigal son, who knocked up the high school science teacher, chucked in his uni scholarship and left town. Worked construction, came back fifteen years later with a daughter and a vet degree. His little sister Hannah let him buy into her vet practice. How'd I do?'

A cracker in his hand snapped in two, showering crumbs all over her sofa. 'I see small-town gossip is alive and well.'

'In my defence, I'm not gossiping, I'm just boxing up blueberry and limoncello cheesecakes. It's the Hanrahan residents who like to overshare *everything*.'

'I can imagine. So you decided to do a story on the aged care facility. Newspaper journalism, right?'

'The *South Coast Morning Herald*. Not a huge paper, but syndicated, so stories we wrote could go national if the interest was there.'

'Sounds ambitious.'

Yes, ambition had played its part. Her own, in particular, and that's what made her guilt so unbearable. She had hated seeing her aunt's living conditions, but at the same time, she had been congratulating herself on what a boost this exposé would give her career.

She dragged her mind back to her story. 'The first article was well received. My, um, boss received a lot of feedback from readers, so I got the go ahead to do more. That's when I started writing about the Acacia View Aged Care Facility in detail. That's when it all went bad.'

'Bad how? I'm not hearing anything so far that explains why you'd be appearing in court.'

'One day I found my aunt on the floor of her room, a big bruise on her face. She'd fallen, and no-one could tell me when she'd last been checked on. She could have been lying there on the floor for hours. So … I planted a hidden camera in her room.'

'Oh.'

'Uh-huh. And I wrote another article describing how I'd found her on the floor.'

Josh winced. 'That can't have gone down well with management.'

'It was never published.' Here it was. The Big Bad Wolf of a thing that had taken over her life. 'My … er … boss saw an opportunity. He pulled my article in return for a lucrative advertising contract with the Acacia View owners. When I called him on it, he sacked me.'

'Surely that's unfair dismissal.'

'It didn't end there. He told the manager of the facility about the camera, and they decided to prosecute. That's what I'm facing in court, a charge for installing a surveillance device which is, apparently, illegal.'

She sucked in a breath. Best to get this part out all in one go. 'So, I was jobless, my aunt's bed at the facility was suddenly no longer available, and my resumé turned out to be worse than useless, because no-one would give me a job. I sold my apartment to pay my legal bills and Jill's care costs.'

'Vera, I'm so sorry.'

She took a sip of the wine and let the cool of it slide down her throat. 'So, that's what I'm currently fighting in court.'

Josh picked up her hand from where it lay on the couch. He ran calloused fingers over hers. 'What are your chances of fighting the charges?'

She sucked in a breath. 'When I'm feeling brave? Maybe I'd say I had a good chance. But mostly, I don't feel so brave. When my, um, boss let me down—threw me under the bus, in fact—it took my confidence, Josh. I can't trust my judgement anymore.' It hurt to think it, but she'd thought of little else for months. 'Maybe I really *do* deserve to go to prison.'

Silence ticked along in the room when she stopped talking, measured by the dull click of the hands of her old clock. What did he think about her now he knew the ugly truth? Did he regret being here?

God knows, if the gossip she'd heard over the cake slices was true, Josh had fielded enough drama of his own in his day. Why would he want to rock his newfound peace by being associated with her?

'I'm sorry you're having to go through this, Vera.'

He hadn't drawn his hand away from hers. Instead, he'd curved his upwards, so his fingers curled over hers.

'You aren't … horrified?'

His mouth quirked. 'Sweetheart, I used to work construction in Sydney. I've seen more vice than you've served pots of tea.'

She felt a little bud of hope uncurl within her breast. 'I was so worried that you'd think—'

'I'd think what?'

She bit her lip. 'That I was too much trouble. That you'd had enough of being the subject of gossip.'

He smiled then, and there was more wicked in it than sweetness. 'I love a little trouble now and then.'

He'd had women in his life. Too many, his sister would have said, especially back in high school. His affair with Beth had survived a baby and the crash-and-burn of his university scholarship, but then waned over time into friendship; and he'd gone out in Sydney every now and then, but never with any real intent. Never with his heart in a flutter and his thoughts all torn up like confetti, like they were now.

Never with a woman whose inhibitions were so at odds with how she kissed.

Maybe he'd got it wrong that day on the trail. Maybe he'd imagined her response to suit himself, because he needed her to want him as much as he wanted her. But she was looking at him now with need in her eyes and he wanted—he *really* wanted—to believe it was him that she needed.

He tucked a curl of her hair behind her ear, letting his hand linger on the soft velvet of the skin he found there. Only one way to find out, and here, in the soft light of the fringed lamp, with nothing but the low purr of a sleeping cat to disturb them, was the perfect time.

He slid his hand down to her shoulder and nudged her towards him. 'Speaking of trouble, you want to kiss me?'

'I shouldn't.'

He leaned in until he was a breath away. 'Because you're not sure how you feel about me?'

He knew damn well what he was feeling: weak-kneed, starry-eyed ... with visions of him and Vera building something *real* together. Something that looked like a family, with his daughter, and a cavalcade of pets, and lazy Sundays holding hands.

She breathed in, a long shuddering breath that sucked a piece of his soul in with it. 'I'm feeling plenty. And that's exactly why I shouldn't kiss you. My life's a mess, Josh. The sort of mess that could end up in prison.'

'When bad stuff happens, we get through it, Vera. Day by day.'

She smiled, a sad little curl of her lips that made him want to gather her into a hug and hold her until all that sadness faded away.

He touched his lips to hers, lingered there until the warmth built. 'I can hope with you. I can worry with you. I can mind your cat while you make licence plates in Old Wentworth Gaol.'

She eased her head back. 'Is that what inmates do in prison? Make licence plates?'

'That and throw bundles of burning toilet paper out of their windows.'

She took a sip of her wine, and his heart eased a little as some of the worry left her face. 'I see movies have formed the basis of your vast knowledge of the Australian prison system. You do know Wentworth hasn't homed prisoners since the 1920s?'

'Come closer.'

She shook her head. 'I don't deserve this, Josh. I don't deserve *you*.'

'I'm not some stuffed koala that you just won at the fair, Vera. I'm making my own choices, here. And I'm choosing you.'

'It's not that simple.'

He kissed her again, on the corner of her mouth, beneath the tiny red stone she had clipped to her ear, in the groove of her throat where her pulse beat.

'It doesn't have to be simple, Vera. It just has to be real. Kiss me, and you tell me if what we have feels real to you or not.'

'God help me,' he heard her mutter and then her lips were on his, and it took less than a second to work out he hadn't been imagining anything back at the waterhole. Being kissed by Vera was like being doused in hot sauce and set on the grill.

She moaned and he hauled her in closer so he could wrap his arms around her and let himself feel every inch of her pressed against him.

'So soft,' he murmured, feeling the curve of her back, the swell of hip beneath her woollen dress.

Vera was vulnerable. Everything she'd told him—her dying aunt, her dobber boss—warned him to go slow, slower than pitch. But when her breathy little moan reached his ears, he forgot his good intentions.

She moved above him, twisted, her mouth fused to his, sending sparks of lightning into his brain.

'Vera,' he said, her name like a prayer.

Her hands slid beneath his shirt and swept up his back and the tide of lust that swept with it nearly blinded him.

He pulled back until her eyes, green and glittering, met his. 'Is this real for you, Vera? Because if it's not, if you want me to stop, now's the time to say so, sweetheart.'

'Don't stop, Josh Cody.'

He bit his lip. Heaven here on Vera's couch, his for the taking, but darn it, he wanted more. He wanted trust, and confetti, and oval-faced sons who aced cooking classes at school.

'I'm not a one-night stand, Vera. Don't use me to scratch your itch. If we're doing this, we're really doing this. Sex. Coffee dates. Holding hands in public. Listening to gossip about us until our ears bleed and promising each other to see this thing through.'

Those green eyes didn't waver. 'I still don't want you to stop.'

So he didn't. He dived back in, his heart in his mouth, and the future he'd hoped for finally within his grasp.

If heaven was a moonlit bed with a naked Josh sprawled across it, and her tucked snugly into the furnace of his musclebound chest, then she'd died happy.

Happy and full and soft.

She pressed a hand to her chest, to where the great icy chunk of worry usually lived, and it wasn't there. All that sunshine and optimism and strength of his had somehow chiselled into her breastbone and released all the angst she'd had stored up like permafrost.

Bits of him had chiselled in elsewhere, too, she thought with a smirk.

Deliciously.

More delicious than anything she could whip up in a month of Sunday baking. How had she been so dense to not let this man into her life sooner? He'd been supportive when she'd told him her great shameful secret, not horrified. He hadn't tried to distance himself or back out.

He'd embraced her *and* her shady past.

She burrowed her face into the smooth curve of his shoulder while hot tears of relief leaked from her eyes. She hadn't known relief could feel so overwhelming. So necessary.

She'd had no-one she felt she could confide in, and bottling up all this stuff had been eating her up from the inside out. Jill's mind was too faded to understand. Her old colleagues she'd been too ashamed to face, too worried about what nasty whispers Aaron had fed into the newspaper's back office about her sacking.

There was her lawyer Sue, sure, but Sue sent her invoices after every confession ... their relationship was based on dollars, not friendship.

A rumble sounded from within the chest she was snuggled up against.

'Josh,' she whispered.

'Mmm.' He sounded eight parts asleep.

'I feel happy.'

'Happy,' he mumbled.

Make that nine parts asleep, she thought with a smile. It didn't matter. She was here, in his arms, and tomorrow she would go and see her aunt and take the quilt project with her to finish the next section. Choose some cheerful fabric: sunshine yellow, broccolini green.

Then she'd smile at customers in the café. She'd dance with Graeme when his favourite song came on the radio. Heck, maybe she'd stun Marigold and Kev and rock up to yoga in the park.

Her future had some black spots in it, sure, but with Josh by her side?

She let her lashes flutter shut against his skin. With happiness running through her veins like liquid gold, she could face anything.

Finally, she could see a future that she could look forward to.

CHAPTER
31

The first phone call woke her in the dark. A shrill ringtone she didn't recognise nearly tore out her eardrum, followed by a muffled oath which startled her even more.

Oh right. She wasn't alone. There was six feet of man-cake wrapped around her like she was his jam and cream filling.

Josh.

A long arm stretched over her head and silenced the noise.

'This better be good, Tom,' said Josh, who kept his eyes on hers for a long moment before whatever he was being told claimed his attention.

'When did it start? Uh-huh. Nope. Crap. Keep him still, I'm on my way.'

She fumbled for the switch on her lamp and a cone of yellow light spilled over them in the ruins of her bedding. She hoped there wasn't a squashed cat somewhere in amongst the wreckage.

'Hey,' Josh said. A glancing kiss landed on her shoulder, and then he was up, hauling on his jeans and halfway into his shirt before she could remember this was supposed to feel awkward.

'Hey,' she said, unable to keep the grin from her face despite the hellishly early wake-up call.

'Cricket's got colic again. One of the breeding stock up at Ironbark Station. It's terrible timing, I know, but I've got to go.'

She pushed a hand through her hair. 'It's fine. Go. I hope it's not too serious.'

He sat next to her on the edge of the bed while he pulled on his boots, then rested a hand on her cheek. 'This wasn't the wake up I was hoping for. Let's talk later, okay?'

She held her hand over his. 'Sure.'

'Promise?'

She smiled, still bemused by the glow of happiness. 'You are one pushy one-night stand, Josh Cody.'

He pulled her hair. 'Pushy but adorable. Kiss me quick, I've gotta go.'

A quick press of his lips to hers, and he was gone.

Another phone call woke her again, but the darkness had a shimmer in it this time, and the ringtone was her own. Dawn wasn't far away.

Josh, she thought sleepily as she rolled for her phone. Maybe she could whip up a batch of pancakes before her shift started. Lashings of lemon syrup. A naughty dollop of vanilla bean ice-cream on the si—

'Vera De Rossi?'

She sat up. Josh didn't sound like a bossy middle-aged woman. 'Yes?'

'It's Dr Brown from Connolly House.'

Oh no. She pressed her hand to her mouth to keep a sob at bay. There was no good reason for them to be calling her in the cold hour before sunrise.

'My aunt. Has she …?'

'I'm sorry, Vera. Jill passed away in her sleep a little while ago. Would you like to come over now and say goodbye?'

Josh slid his ute into the staff car park of the pub. He needed a shower. Maybe an hour's sleep. If Cricket's colic didn't settle, he'd have another long night ahead after a busy day of Saturday home visits, and the constant driving was wearing him down. He was so not a fan of the mobile vet concept.

And somewhere in all of that he needed to find time to pick a bunch of flowers and deliver them to The Billy Button Café. Perhaps sneak in a slow burn kiss in the kitchen to tide him over until the day's patients were seen to.

The smell of coffee caught him and he ducked his head into the kitchen.

'Gracie?'

The pub's elderly caretaker sat at a scrubbed wooden table, toast, coffee and a newspaper before her. 'Josh, my love. You've had a long night.'

'Unhappy horse. You seen Jane Doe? She's fond of a piece of toast in the morning. I'm surprised she's not sitting at your feet practising her pathetic look.'

'If you think I'm having dogs in my kitchen, you can think again, young man.'

He clinked his coffee cup to hers. 'Yes, ma'am.'

Gracie patted his hand. 'She's in the laundry with her pups. Those rascals will be climbing out of that whelping box soon, Josh; maybe it's time they had some space to run about in before they get sold on to their new homes.'

'Yeah. I know. I've had offers aplenty, but I want to hang on to them a while yet. Poppy's promised to come up one weekend, and she'd be sad not to say goodbye. Plus, some kid rang me a while back, reckoned he was Jane's owner. I'm still waiting for him to call back.'

'Mmm.' Gracie's voice was distracted. 'I didn't know there was a new ski lift going in up past Crackenback, did you, pet?'

He took a sip of his coffee and grimaced. Graeme really had turned him into a snob. 'I haven't been up to the ski fields in years.'

'Might be the spur to the sides old Bruno needs to set this old pub to rights. Be a treat to see it open again. There's a lot of development going on and not all of it is what this town needs. Modern rubbish that looks like it wouldn't last a decent snowstorm.'

'I think Bruno Krauss has enough on his plate at the moment.'

'True. Poor man, he was skinny as a stick insect last time I saw him in town.'

The pages rustled as Gracie turned the page. 'Hello ... De Rossi. Isn't that the name of the new owner of the café on the corner?'

Josh put down his cup. 'Vera De Rossi. That's right, why?'

The caretaker spun the paper so he could see the page she was reading. The Hanrahan Chatter ... his least favourite section of the paper, useful only for lining animal cages and recycling. He braced himself and started reading Maureen Plover's latest article.

STORM IN A COFFEE CUP: *Hanrahan's newest business owner Vera De Rossi of The Billy Button Café appeared in court in Queanbeyan earlier this week to plead not guilty to a charge of illegally using a surveillance device. The Chatter hears recently returned local veterinarian Josh Cody has been ordering more than a few cupcakes from Ms De Rossi in recent weeks. ... read the full story on Page 6.*

Holy shit. He toyed with the idea of turning to page six but quashed it. His days of being influenced by gossip were so over. 'Gracie?'

'Yes, love?'

'I need some paper to clean out the whelping box. I'm taking this one.'

'What? Oh, Josh, honey, I've not read it all ye—'

He stormed off to the laundry with the pages crumpled in his hand. Shit on a stick. As much as he loved this town, he didn't love the stickybeak mentality that sometimes came with it.

He had to warn Vera before she saw that article. She'd be behind her counter at the café, slicing some delicate meringue concoction into precise strips, and she'd be blindsided if a random breakfast guest started blabbing about what she considered to be her secret shame over their toast and jam.

He cleaned out the pups' box at a lightning pace, grabbed his jacket, and hit the door.

Vera felt like she would never feel warm again. A sheet covered her aunt's face, and a hospital blanket buried her aunt's emaciated frame. Jill, hidden behind the bland beige of a facility blanket, because her niece had been too caught up to finish her quilt.

She'd been too busy for her aunt ... lost track of her goals because she'd been distracted by stray cats and late evening strolls by the lake and chocolate-eyed vets. She'd put her own needs first. Again.

The magenta swirl of Marigold Jones in caftan and beaded heads-carf swooped into the room. 'Darling Vera, Graeme called me. I'm so sorry for your loss.'

'Oh, Marigold,' she said.

'Come here, pet.'

She buried her head in Marigold's billowing sleeve and let the tears slide unchecked. 'I can't believe she's gone.'

'Just cry it out.'

She took Marigold at her word, and it was many moments before she was able to look up and focus on her aunt's still form again. 'What do I do now?' she said.

'Well, there's a question with a lot of answers, Vera. You don't need to know it all at once. I can help you with the first ones, though. When you're ready, the funeral home people have come for your aunt. You can trust them to take care of her.'

She crumpled against the bed. 'I'm not ready.'

Marigold's hands gripped her shoulders. 'I'll help you feel ready. Come on, now. Let's stand back here near the window while they get your aunt settled.'

The funeral home staff worked with the efficiency of a well-oiled machine. Her aunt's thin body was transferred to a gurney, the blankets tucked about her with neat precision, then she was wheeled off, rubber wheels squeaking faintly against the polished linoleum.

Jill was gone.

'Come on, Vera. This is no time to be alone. Let's go sit for a bit.'

But she was alone. Really and truly alone.

Marigold steered her into the garden and found a bench set where, she imagined, a score of relatives before her had faced their own sad news. How on earth had they coped?

Her friend patted her hand. 'Do you want me to call someone for you? Relatives?'

'There's no-one.'

'You don't want to be on your own packing up your aunt's belongings here and organising the funeral. You want me to be your someone?'

She nodded mutely, too wretched to speak. Her phone buzzed but she ignored it.

'You want me to answer that for you?' said Marigold.

She shrugged. Caring about anything seemed like a language she no longer spoke.

'Vera's phone. Marigold Jones speaking.'

The tissue in her hand was like fruit pulp, but she pressed it to her streaming eyes anyway.

'Aha. Yes. Hang on.' Marigold held out the phone. 'It's Josh. I don't think he knows about your aunt … you want me to tell him, or will you?'

Vera shook her head but Marigold opened her eyes wide, gave her a look that couldn't be ignored. She pressed the phone to her ear. 'Josh, I—'

'Vera, thank god. I'm on my way to the café to see you, but I just wanted to call and warn you … did you see the paper today?'

'No, I haven—'

'Shit. I don't know how that woman found out or what idiocy prompted them to print it, but you might want to take a moment to read a copy before people start asking questions.'

Vera struggled to get a thought straight in her head. 'I'm not at work. I'm sorry, I don't know what you mean. Now's not really …'

The tears were welling again and she was all out of tissues. The phone slipped through her fingers and she let it lie on her lap, Josh's voice just a faint rumble from far away.

'Vera, honey.'

Marigold was still with her, but for how long? Everybody left her in the end. Everybody. And the more she loved them, the more it hurt.

Loving people didn't work. Not for her.

She reached down and ended the call.

CHAPTER
32

'Josh.'

He looked up from the microscope, where a flatworm the size of a pinhead was busy invading the red blood cells of a champion sow named Iron Lady. The flatworm would explain why the pig had been out of sorts. If only it would be so easy to explain his own malaise.

'What's up, Sandy?'

Their receptionist had worked like a trooper since the fire, washing everything that hadn't been dragged out to the skip bin, and moving the air filter from room to room to encourage the smoky smell to get itself gone. The back office was the only undamaged room on the downstairs level, and when he wasn't working on the community hall ceiling for Marigold or measuring and sawing wood for the clinic's front room rebuild, he hid himself away in the office to brood and work on his backup of pathology testing. Who said males couldn't multitask?

'You've got a visitor.'

Finally. He knew she'd come see him after avoiding his calls, he'd just had to give her time. He'd knocked on her door, he'd sent flowers, he'd visited the café only for Graeme to send him home again with a consolation brownie, because Vera wasn't at work.

Or answering his calls.

She'd closed him out like he meant nothing and it had damn near torn his heart out.

'There's a kid out front, he's been knocking on the plywood sheeting covering the front windows. Says, and I'm quoting here, he needs to see the vet real bad about his dog.'

Not Vera, then. A thought struck him. 'Is the kid's name Parker?'

'I didn't get a chance to ask, because when he saw me he scooted in through the gap and spied the jellybean jar I was holding, and that was it for conversation.'

Had to be the same kid. 'I'll be right out.'

He'd known this moment was coming, so there was no point putting it off any longer. Parker was wearing the scruffiest pair of jeans Josh had seen in about two decades. Rips covered one knee, oil stains that he'd bet were from a bike chain coated the hems at the ankles, but the razor-sharp ironing crease riding down the front of them told him someone was looking out for this kid. 'Hey, Parker,' he said.

The boy's eyes widened. 'Are you Mister Vet? Have you got my dog?'

Josh nodded. 'I reckon I might. You got a parent with you, son?'

'My mum. She's looking for a park that isn't gonna get her in trouble.'

Josh looked through the smashed windows to where half a dozen vacant car parks adorned the street. 'These ones out front no good, Parker?'

'She's in the big truck, on account of her little car shat itself, and she's not so hot at squeezing the big truck in between those little white lines. Last time she drove it into town, the cop chick said she'd give her a parking ticket next time.'

'Uh-huh.' His lips twitched. Parker the seven-year-old was all kinds of cute.

A woman walked down the path from the corner of Salt Creek Flats Road, a tiny figure in steel-capped boots and faded overalls that had been ironed with the same military precision as Parker's jeans. 'This your mum?' he asked.

Parker shot a glance over his shoulder. 'Yep.'

Josh blew out a breath. Here goes, he thought. He walked over and held the tarpaulin back so she could step into the carnage that had once been the Cody and Cody Vet Clinic, then held out his hand. 'Josh Cody.'

She had a clear, no-nonsense look about her. 'Sonya,' she said. 'I'm Parker's mum. I'm sorry it's taken me this long to get to town, but we've had some transport trouble.'

'So Parker's been telling me.'

She looked around at the burn scars still visible on the walls. 'Seems like you've been having some trouble of your own.'

'Yeah.'

She frowned at Parker. 'Hey. How about you save some of those jellybeans for the other people who come visiting. How many have you had?'

He pulled his hand out of the jar and his shoulders wilted. 'Just a couple, Mum.'

Sonya surprised Josh by shooting him a wink. 'Okay then, why don't we see this dog you've found, Dr Cody, and we can get out of your way.'

Josh cleared his throat. 'About that.'

Sonya looked up at him. 'There a problem, Dr Cody? Because if this is about boarding fees, we pay our way, don't you be getting your knickers in a twist about that.'

'No, Sonya. That's not it.' He rubbed his forehead. 'The answer sort of depends on your definition of problem. We're going to need to walk a block over to the Hanrahan Pub, if you don't mind. We had to clear all the animals out of here during the fire.'

It became clear within a bizillionth of a second that Parker and his mum had differing views on what constituted a problem.

'Puppies,' breathed Parker, on a long drawn-out ecstatic breath, before he dived over the low gate and buried himself in the pyramid of plump, squirming fur.

'Puppies!' winced his mum.

Josh unclicked the latch on the gate and Jane Doe tottered over to him with her usual expression of feed-me-love-me-feed-me. Parker had dropped a casual pat on her head as he raced past to the furballs. 'Mum,' he said, and Josh could have sworn he heard tears in the kid's voice. 'We've had baby doggies!'

'I can see that, Parker.'

He met Sonya's eyes and shrugged. 'I delivered them by C-section. I didn't know your dog's name, so I've been calling her Jane,' he said.

'Rosie, you fool dog,' Sonya said, without heat, as she bent down to stroke Jane's ears. 'Ran off in a storm. Parker nearly cried the freckles off his face when she didn't come home.'

He nodded. 'A farmer found her in his barn, her fur full of fleas, and her belly full of pups. She's had some adventures, all right.'

Sonya sniffed. 'And not all of them PG-rated.'

He chuckled. 'So, what do we do now? She's still feeding the pups. I'm happy to keep them with me until the pups are weaned, maybe another couple of weeks … unless you want to take them all?'

The woman let out a breath. 'That's kind of you. Thing is, Dr Cody, I'm in a bit of a bind.'

'How's that?'

'My husband's laid off with a back injury. He can't drive. He can't seem to do much more than lie on the couch in front of the television snapping out orders for beer and party pies. I'm working nights down on the highway resurfacing project, and I don't think I have any more to give at the moment, if you see what I'm saying.'

'I understand. What about Parker?'

They both looked at the boy, who had all eight pups on his lap. He was busy telling them a story about how their brave mummy dog didn't get snacked on by drop bears after all.

'I've got an idea,' he said. 'Why don't we convince Parker that Jane—I mean, Rosie—is needed here a little longer so she can feed her pups. You bring him back in a couple of weeks when the pups are on solid food, and maybe you're a bit less busy, and we can both make a better decision. I've had plenty of takers for these pups, so don't feel you need to worry about them, too.'

'Dr Cody, you're being a good sport about this.'

He felt Jane settle herself over his boots. 'Call me Josh,' he said. 'To tell you the truth, Sonya, I'm in no hurry to say goodbye to them just yet.' Understatement of the year. With Poppy away at school, Vera pretending he didn't exist, Jane being taken from him too would be too damn much.

Sonya nodded. 'You ever need some fresh honey, you drop on by the Cooma markets one Saturday. My stall's always there, and there'll be a jar waiting for you, okay? We'll see you in a few weeks.'

He shook the calloused little hand she held out to him. 'See you soon.'

He wandered back to the clinic after saying goodbye to Parker and his mum, and as he cut through the park, his gaze was drawn to the pretty picture windows of The Billy Button Café. He paused when he saw Graeme coming out of the doors and crossed over to greet him.

The printed sign that had been there all week like a punishment was still taped to the glass. *Closed due to family bereavement.* Vera had made her point very clear: family didn't include him.

'You've got a frown on your face that explains how Old Regret got its name,' said Graeme.

'My shitty week just got shittier.'

'Yeah? Vera rang you, did she?'

He narrowed his eyes. 'No. A kid arrived and turns out he's Jane Doe's owner. Why, was Vera trying to call me? Did she say something to you?' He'd not missed a message, had he? Maybe she rang the clinic. Maybe Sandy had lost the sticky note. Maybe—

'She bit my head off when I told her you'd dropped by the café to see her the other day, that's all. I figured there was trouble brewing.'

'It's brewing all right. You know, she's not said a word to me about her aunt. The only reason I know about Jill passing away is because Marigold rang me to see how soon the hall would be ready.' Not Vera. Vera had just slipped away mid phone call a few hours after they'd spent the night together, and left him wondering where on earth she'd gone.

'Funeral's day after tomorrow,' said Graeme.

'Yeah. It's going to be touch and go whether I get the ceiling finished in time. I've done a little fancy plasterwork in my day, which is lucky, because there was quite a lot of damage.'

'Bog and paint, mate.'

He snorted. 'Any more of that cheek from you, Graeme, and I'll be handing you a paintbrush.'

'So hand me one.'

'Seriously? You'd give me a hand?'

'Of course. When are you planning on painting?'

'I'll finish the cornice work tonight if I get stuck into it after dinner, give it the day to dry, and we paint tomorrow evening. You up for that?'

'With two of us on the job, we'll get it done in no time.'

'Thanks, man. I mean it.' That was one problem solved. If only he knew what to do about the others. He hesitated. 'Does Vera seem okay to you? I thought we'd reached a point where she trusted me a little, but she's not answering my calls. I've been to her apartment, and no answer there, either. I'm worried about her. I don't think she's as resilient as she pretends to be.'

Graeme looked him over. 'Josh, my friend, girl trouble is not my special skill, but if you need a beer and an ear, I'm your man.'

Josh considered. 'That new place round the corner serve double cheese and pepperoni?'

'The Feldmark Cellar serve *pizza*?' Graeme gave a deep and theatrical sigh. 'Some days, I wonder how we ever became friends. We'll go to the winery, and we'll have a cheese platter, with some quince paste, grapes, bruschetta. Maybe some of their olives stuffed with goodness and deep fried in a crumb so thin and crispy you'll forget pepperoni ever existed.'

'Lead the way.' Beer, heart-to-heart, then plasterwork. Yeah, single life in the country was turning out to be pretty much as he'd expected.

∞

The olives were great. As was the platter of fruit and cheese the waitress conjured up after a lengthy and spirited discussion on the merits of every item on the menu with Graeme. He layered a wedge of double brie onto an oat cracker and gave it a try.

'Okay,' said Graeme. 'Now you have a beer in front of you, you want to tell me why you've got a hangdog look on your face?'

Josh sighed. 'You picked it before. Girl trouble.'

'With my boss.'

'Like you and the whole town don't know, man.'

Graeme nodded. 'Good point,' he said, and swirled the red wine in his glass, before tipping his nose in and inhaling as if he was a beagle after a sausage. 'You know the difference between a young cabernet and an aged cabernet?'

'Are you using a wine analogy to explain my love life to me?'

'Roll with it, mate. Do you know the difference?'

'Time in the barrel? Rainfall while the grape was on the vine? Southern versus northern growing slope?'

'All good suggestions, but no. The difference is the volatility.'

Josh took a deep sip of his beer. 'Clear as mud.'

'When a person is young, he's content to drink a young cabernet. The colour is bright, the flavours are bold, the taste is typically intense and high in tannins. The young person can afford this wine, it's sunny and warm and uncomplicated, and he'll enjoy quaffing it.'

'Uh-huh.'

'A bit like the legendary Josh Cody might have enjoyed himself dating the netball team back in high school.'

Josh rolled his eyes.

'But when the guy gets a little older, his palate changes. It's time for something a little more complicated, where the flavours and colours have had time to settle into something unique, softer, with a rich and nuanced quality. Something that requires a little patience to find.'

'I can be patient. I've *been* patient.'

Graeme lifted his glass and clinked it against his. 'Hang in there, champ. Vera's got the hots for you so bad, she's not going to care that in my wine analogy you come in just slightly above vinegar.'

Josh shook his head. He didn't know whether to be offended or relieved.

'How do you know she's got the hots for me?'

Graeme shook his head. 'Maaaate.'

CHAPTER
33

The Friday in November on which she was to farewell her aunt brought with it a bleak, grey-skied afternoon, and rain had darkened the granite of the old headstones scattered about the cemetery. Overhead, leaves shivered in the breeze, and Vera gathered her coat about her. This was all so wrong.

Jill had loved colour, and sunshine, and fun. Not drooping flowers, and grass running with rivulets of mud. The coffin she could barely recall choosing spilled dull sheets of water as it was lowered into the hole in the ground.

Marigold had organised everything, from holding Vera's hand while she sat by Jill to say goodbye, to bossing around everyone at the funeral home and announcing herself celebrant of the service.

Vera had just ... stopped. Everything, every goal she'd pursued since leaving the city, had hinged on Jill being alive.

Finding a new and peaceful aged care home for Jill: *that* had brought her to the Snowy River district. The need to find a way to earn income if she lost her case and was incarcerated? That goal had resulted in her opening a café in Hanrahan, hiring a manager who could run it in her absence, making enough profit to employ a replacement cook, and working dawn to dusk to make it all happen.

And the other goal … the secret that had been at the heart of every decision she'd made except for that mad, foolish, night with Josh … was to never get hurt again.

She'd screwed up, and now Jill was gone, and what did all her plans matter now?

She was like a knife with no blade, an oven with no heat. The only thing tethering her to the world was a criminal charge that she felt too exhausted to fight.

'May your passage be swift,' said Marigold, addressing the mourners who lingered in the rain.

Graeme had come, his partner Alex by his side in full fireman's uniform. The café was shut. Baking, usually her go-to solace for every malady, had been more than she could face.

Kev stood by his wife, dapper in a corduroy cloth cap and suede coat, holding a misshapen orange golf umbrella over his wife's head.

Mr Juggins was there, and Wendy from Connolly House; Sandy, the vet clinic receptionist, who she barely knew other than the fact she ordered a take home box of raspberry jam donuts every Friday for her sons' afternoon tea. The woman who ran the op shop, the couple from the cinema who'd been so happy to promote a dinner and movie deal, and half a dozen faces from the weekly craft group all stood, solemn faced, by her aunt's graveside.

They'd come, so many of them.

Marigold had volunteered the community hall for a cup of tea after the funeral, its doors now open to the public once more, and

Vera had shaken her head. 'There's no need, really,' she'd said. 'Jill was a stranger here.'

'Funerals are for those of us that are left behind,' Marigold had said firmly. 'Not for the departed.'

She still hadn't thought a service was necessary. She wasn't a local. And, after the notoriety of having her private shame splashed all over the community page of the *Snowy River Star*, she wouldn't have been surprised if nobody showed up: to the funeral, or to darken the doorstep of her café ever again.

Her gaze wandered of its own volition over to Josh, who had turned up at her café and apartment more than once, only to be met with her stony silence.

She should never have slept with him. He'd been open and honest and asked her for her assurance that them being together was the beginning of something more ... but her courage had failed. She'd scratched her way out of the mess she'd made of her last relationship with her self-esteem in tatters. She'd done it once, and it had broken her.

She couldn't risk that again. She was a woman who made dumb choices, and he was better off finding a decent woman to hold in his arms on moonlit nights.

Not her.

She'd never seen him in a suit before. The coal black cloth, the white shirt ... his hair combed so neatly it could have been cartoon hair, if cartoon did sexy. His face was drawn, though, and held none of the easy smile she'd grown so used to seeing.

He could have been a stranger, in that outfit, with that remote expression ... but then, when she looked at herself in the mirror, was there not a stranger standing there, too? A chicken-hearted woman who'd had the stuffing plucked out of her.

Jill, she realised on a sob, would not recognise this pathetic worm of a woman she'd become, either.

'May you know wholeness and peace,' said Marigold, in a deep calm voice.

Oh, how she wished that for Jill. Her eyes burned with the simple truth of Marigold's words. Wasn't that the most anyone could wish for?

'And now, our Vera is going to say a few words.'

It wasn't until a dozen sets of eyes were looking at her expectantly that Marigold's words sunk in. She sent the celebrant a speaking look, which was ignored.

'We've not known our Vera long,' Marigold continued, 'and sad to say, we didn't get a chance to know Jill De Rossi, but we would have liked to. Come now, Vera. Tell us a little something about your aunt. It's just us and the gum trees here.'

Vera bit her lip. She felt a hand pat her back, just briefly, one quick touch of support from Graeme.

She dragged her eyes away from the rain-drenched coffin. She used to wield words to make a living … surely she could find the right words now for dear Jill.

She moved forward a step and was surprised to see Poppy standing tucked into her father's side. Her hair was tied back in a braid, there was none of her usual eyeliner framing her eyes, and she wore a prim, old-fashioned dress that a librarian might have worn back before librarians became funky.

Poppy had tears on her cheeks, but managed to give Vera a little smile, and the sweetness of it caught at Vera's breath. Her eyes dropped to Poppy's feet, and there they were, those disreputable boots, and their incongruity with the dress pierced the hold she had over her emotions.

Jill would have adored Poppy. She took a deep breath as a memory she could share popped into her head.

'There is a De Rossi family story,' she began, 'that when Jill was about thirteen, she told her parents, my grandparents, that she was never going to have children. Instead, she was going to be the cool, rebel auntie.

'She was definitely a rebel. She was older than my mother, who predeceased her by nearly two decades, but she never let age stand in the way of her love of adventure. Camel trekking in the Northern Territory. Hot air ballooning over Kangaroo Island and getting blown out over the Southern Ocean. Jill could knit a tea cosy and change a spark plug in an outboard motor before breakfast.

'But if there was one thing she loved more than adventure, it was cooking. She passed that love on to me, and ...' She paused and waited for the squeeze in her throat to ease. 'Jill wasn't demonstrative. She didn't hug and pet and kiss, but she showed me she loved me when she taught me how to bake a crème caramel. Toasting coconut under a grill to sprinkle over hummingbird cake? I love you, Vera. Buttermilk pancakes with a vanilla pod scraped into the batter? I care for you, Vera. She deserved the world and she got it, mostly.'

Mostly. Until those corporate sharks in charge of the staff-to-patient ratio at Acacia View eroded her dignity.

She dragged herself back from the bitter edge. These kind people here weren't part of that, and Connolly House had been a haven of kindness there at the end of Jill's life. 'I think you all would have adored my Aunt Jill. I know I did. And she really was the coolest auntie ever.'

She hesitated. Glanced at Marigold, who gave her a smile then swept her arms up so the sleeves of her apricot caftan billowed like parrot wings.

'Go in peace,' said Marigold.

Vera's mumbled *go in peace* was drowned out by the sound of sods of earth being shovelled down upon the coffin.

Poppy threw her arms around her neck and gave her the hug she hadn't known she needed.

'I'm so sorry about your aunt, Vera.'

'Thanks, Poppy. It means a lot to me that you're here.'

'Dad told me and asked me if I'd be okay with ditching school for a couple of days which, you know, was no biggie.'

Vera was so pleased to have a reason to smile. 'That was a noble sacrifice.'

The girl tucked her hand in hers. 'I'm glad I'm here … especially now I can see you don't have any family with you today.'

She gave Poppy's hand a squeeze. 'I'm glad too. But the no family thing? I'm used to it.'

'Parents?'

She shook her head. 'My mum died when I was a teenager.'

'But, your dad? Cousins? Step-siblings?'

She shrugged. 'I was an only child, and Jill never had children. My dad and my mum weren't married. She met him on a trip to Italy to visit the region her parents had emigrated from. He never made it to Australia. Jill always said it started out like a romance movie but ended like a really bad cliché.'

'Wow. He never visited you? I'll never understand that.'

She smiled. 'Yeah, but that's because you have your dad wrapped around your little finger.'

'Speaking of … hey, Dad, can you come and hold your brolly over Vera? I'm going to run ahead. I promised to help Kev with the hot water urn.'

Vera took a quick breath as Josh stepped up beside her. She had to say something to him, but what?

She started with the least important but easiest to find words. 'I'm sorry about that article in the paper, Josh, that dragged you into my mess. I know how you dislike being the subject of gossip, and now I've given the people of Hanrahan something else to wonder about.'

She could feel him looking down at her.

'Gossip stopped bothering me long ago,' he said quietly. 'I just don't like it when it affects the people I care about.'

Her boots crunch-crunched on the wet gravel as she walked, the silence between them stretched tauter than an elastic band. He wanted her to say she cared about him too, she could feel it. He wanted to know why she'd promised him that this *thing* between them, this heat and need and rush meant something, but then pushed him away.

She should have tried to explain days ago—visited the surgery, knocked on the front door of the Hanrahan Pub until she found which room he was in. And if she'd known what she wanted to say, maybe she would have. Instead she'd cloistered herself away with her cat and the hot mess of quilting fabric that made her feel guilty every time she looked at it.

Her head was a mess, her thoughts clogged up together like gunk in a grease trap. How could she explain the bleakness she was feeling to someone else when she couldn't explain it to herself?

Don't let your guilt get in the way of your life, Marigold had said to her once. She glanced over her shoulder, to where smooth earth now covered her aunt's grave. She'd not been ready to hear that advice. Marigold had been a benevolent stranger then, not the accidental friend she'd since become.

Grass would grow like billyo over that new earth after this spring rain had passed. Cicadas would sing nearby on long summer evenings, leaves would skitter past in autumn, and southern stars would wheel overhead. And her aunt would be resting for eternity in Hanrahan.

This was, she thought on a rush, a tether. The funeral service was doing more than farewelling Jill, it was also connecting Vera to the community here in a way that couldn't be broken.

She looked ahead of her up the path, to where people she knew—people she'd grown to care for—were shaking rain off their coats and bundling indoors into the historic stone cottage that marked a chapter in Hanrahan's past.

Her footsteps faltered. She had a choice, she just had to make it. Did she really want to be trapped in this rain-dreary moment while the world spun on without her?

No. She'd let worry and despair drag her down long enough. She couldn't add grief to the burden. This was her day to choose to accept a little of what Josh, and Marigold, and Graeme—even that pesky grey cat that had adopted her—had been offering.

Friendship. Belonging. Love.

Josh must have felt he'd waited long enough, because he broke the silence. 'Poppy's just down for the weekend, but when the school year ends in December she'll be here for most of the six-week break.'

'You must be happy about that.'

'Yep.'

'Josh, I—'

'Listen, Vera—' His voice was low, and he stood to the side so the other mourners could bypass them and head up the wooden steps into the community hall. They were alone now.

'You first,' she said.

'I'm not going to pressure you anymore about seeing me. You've made it clear I'm not what you need right now, and I respect your decision. I just hope this—you and me thing, whatever it is or isn't—won't affect Poppy in any way. She loved working at the café, and I'd love it if she could keep doing that when she's here. There will be zero awkwardness from me, I promise.'

What? Josh was done with her?

'But I adore Poppy!' she stuttered out. *I adore you, too.* She opened her mouth to tell him so, but the screech of tyres on the wet road nearby drew her gaze away from Josh's face. A navy sedan slid into a car park. Out of it, looking as neat and pinstriped as a Bunda Street banker, stepped Aaron Finch.

CHAPTER
34

'Vera, I had to come when I heard.'

Josh scratched his head. Who the hell was this guy? Whoever he was, Vera didn't seem pleased to see him. She'd gone stiff as a board the moment the guy stepped out of his car.

'What are you doing here, Aaron?'

'I had to see you.'

'You just saw me last week. In court. Where I had to answer to an alleged crime that *you* dobbed me in for.'

This was Vera's old boss? He rested a hand on Vera's back. 'You want me to get rid of him?'

The guy—Aaron—shot him a look. 'Who the hell are you?'

'The name's Josh. I'm Vera's friend. And if she doesn't want to talk to you, then I'll be the one assisting you and your pinstriped suit back into your vehicle.'

Aaron ignored him. 'Vera, look, this has all got way out of hand. Can we just talk?' He reached out for Vera's arm in a way that had Josh's caveman instincts rising to the surface.

'I've got nothing to say to you, Aaron. Not now, not ever. Go home.'

'Come on, honey. You know I think you're a wonderful person. It's not too late to fix this. To fix us.'

Honey? *Us?* Josh looked at Vera, her pale face, her strained eyes. She was in no condition to be fielding more drama today, especially the thousand and one questions he wanted to ask her. Because describing her boss as someone who might call her 'honey' and 'us' had been singularly lacking from her recital of her problems back in Queanbeyan. Maybe he should have turned to page six and read the rest of that damn article. Everyone in town must know more about the woman he was in love with than he did himself.

Woah. Had he just thought the love word? He needed a minute, damn it, and he needed this city suit with the grabby hands to be gone. 'Kev will have the urn boiling by now. Let's go find that cup of tea.' He could check out his last-minute paint job on the ceiling in the light of day and hope like heck he hadn't missed anywhere. Standing on a ladder late at night wasn't his ideal time of day for finicky paint jobs in ornate plaster ceilings, but it had sure helped him keep his mind off fretting over why Vera had been ghosting him.

Vera shrugged away from him. 'Stop telling me what to do, both of you.'

'Vera, you're a little pale,' he said. He wanted to bundle her into his arms and carry her inside, but she was looking as prickly as she had when he'd first tried to chat with her in the café—as brittle and fragile as one of her own brandy snaps.

She didn't meet his eyes.

'I can find my own cup of tea,' she said, then turned to the other guy. 'You're not welcome here, Aaron.' Then she turned and bolted up the stairs to the hall, Aaron at her heels, and slammed the door so both men were stuck outside in the rain.

'Nice job, mate,' Josh said, eyeing the man standing next to him. He wondered how Kev would feel about him punching a stranger in the nose among his lovingly tended rose bushes. He fought back the urge.

'Your car's that way,' he said. 'Do us all a favour and get lost, will you?'

He never did get that cup of tea from Kev's urn. After staring down the man who'd called Vera 'honey', he'd felt the grip on his temper come loose.

Josh didn't lose his temper often, but when he did, he lost it like a champion bull. He decided to channel his massive desire to punch the crap out of something into the burned inner walls of the clinic. The fire chief had given him the all clear to rip it down, and now was the perfect time for some destruction. Or it would be, once he'd torn his way out of this damn suit and tie.

He was knee-deep in rubble, smashed gyprock and self-loathing when Poppy found him.

'Hey, Dad, where did you go?'

He pulled the dust mask off his face. 'Sorry, Poppy. I needed some time out.'

'Did the funeral make you sad?'

'Not the funeral as such, no.' He shrugged. 'We were there for Vera, not because we knew her aunt. No, it was afterwards. I got mad, then sad, and now I can't decide what I am.'

Poppy hoisted herself up onto his workbench. 'Girl trouble, huh.'

Wow. His fifteen-year-old daughter was getting ready to workshop his relationship with him. Parenthood was not for the faint-hearted. He swung a crowbar into a charred mass of chipboard shelving and hauled until the whole unit ripped free and crashed to the ground. 'Your dad may have been an idiot, Pop.'

'Mmm. Tell me everything.'

He frowned at her. 'Are you psychoanalysing me?'

'Dad, I've watched a lot of daytime television, and I've been scrolling through angsty teenage social media messages for years. I've got this. Why have you been an idiot?'

'Because Vera told me she didn't want to have a relationship with anyone, but I kept thinking if I was nice enough, and patient enough, she'd change her mind.'

Poppy nodded. 'You thought you knew best.'

'No! I … well, yes, I guess I did. But she did agree to get, um, involved …' He cleared his throat and hurried over the images in his head. 'But I don't think she meant it. I don't think she was *lying*, but maybe she just meant it in the moment, not for real.'

'Just a gentle heads up, Dad: I can give advice without hearing all the gory details.'

Bloody hell. Why, oh why, had he started this conversation?

Poppy crossed her legs. 'Did she tell you *why* she didn't want to have a boyfriend?'

He dropped the crowbar to the floor and turned to face his daughter. 'Well, that's the thing. She did tell me, but then today, after the funeral, I found out that she'd only told me half of it. She had another reason which is kind of a doozy.'

'Oh? What?'

'She has another guy in her life. He showed up after the funeral, and that's what made me go—'

'Apeshit?' Poppy said helpfully.

'I'm pretty sure your mum doesn't like you saying that.'

'Let's not change the subject, Dad. Maybe you should let Vera decide what she wants.'

He sighed. 'Yeah. That's what I was trying to tell her today, before Mr City showed up.' He planted a dusty hand on his daughter's knee and squeezed. 'You're smarter than you look, Poptart.'

'I know. You think it's too early for pizza?'

'It's never too early for pizza.'

'Just give me a minute to get out of Hannah's dress.'

He laughed, and it felt like the first time he'd truly enjoyed himself in days. 'Oh, honey, that's not Hannah's dress.'

'What! She got it out of her cupboard.'

'That's your grandma's dress.'

'No way. I mean I knew it was ugly, but I've never been to a funeral before that I remember. I wanted to look the part.'

'Well sure, if you thought everybody dressed up as daggy eighty-year-old grannies to attend funerals, you were spot on.'

He chuckled, and then Poppy did too, and then the two of them were laughing like kookaburras, there in the wreckage that had once been the Cody and Cody Vet Clinic reception room.

Poppy slung her arm around him. 'You're gonna be okay, Dad.'

He kissed her hair. 'Thanks, Pop.'

'But … since we're having a D & M and all …'

'What's a D & M?'

'A deep and meaningful conversation.'

'Is this another daytime TV counselling strategy?'

She gave him a shove. 'I've been thinking about what to do about Jane Doe and the pups. They'll be needing to go to a proper home before I'm back for the Christmas holidays, so it's best if we get it sorted now.'

This was clearly a day for being reminded about all the shitty things headed his way. 'I'm trying to block that out, Pop. I can only have my heart ripped out of my chest so many times.'

'Dad, that's kinda sad.'

'I know. Come here and give your old man another hug and I'll promise to be brave about saying goodbye to them all when the time comes.'

She wrapped her arms around him and gave him a squeeze. No eyebrow ring digging into his arm today, he thought, and hid his smile in her hair.

'You know as well as I do we've had dozens of offers for those pups, Dad. The second they get their last shots, there's going to be a queue at the door of people wanting to take them home.'

'Hey. I'm supposed to be the practical one. You're supposed to be persuading me to keep the whole litter.'

'Dad. Get a grip.'

'You talk to your mum about keeping one?'

'Ten kilo limit in the townhouse complex, so that's a no. Maximus is such a guts he probably weighs that already. Besides, he whispered a secret in my ear this morning when I jumped in the box to say hello to them all.'

'Maximus can whisper?'

Poppy gave him a light punch to the arm. 'You know that kid, Parker, who says his Rosie is our Jane Doe?'

'I've not forgotten him.'

'Maximus thinks Parker may prefer a young, frisky boy pup to an old dog with a grey snout who's fallen in love with my dad.'

Crazy, but he felt tears back up in his throat. Was Poppy offering to give Max up so he wouldn't have his heart broken when Jane Doe left? He cleared his throat. He was losing it. Totally, utterly, losing it.

'Dad? You're not saying anything.'

Because he couldn't speak, damn it. He buried his nose in her hair. 'Maximus is yours if you want him, honey, and that's that.'

She gave a little sigh. 'But Dad, I'll be going to uni in a couple of years, and my brothers are way too crazy to be left in charge of an animal. Besides, Maximus is a Snowy River dog. He wouldn't like the city.'

'A bit like me.' He sighed. 'Max's idea isn't a bad one. Maybe he's smarter than he looks, too.'

Poppy snorted. 'Considering he looks like a brown bathroom sponge, that wouldn't be difficult.' She frowned at him. 'Did you really hate the city so bad, Dad?'

'No. You were there, which made it the place I wanted to be. But I always wanted to come home to Hanrahan. And now you're older, you've got your own life, your own friends. You don't need me to chop the crusts off your sandwiches every second week anymore.'

She grinned. 'Or tell me off for getting my ears pierced.'

'Or rush out to the printing store at midnight because there's no ink in the printer when you've got an assignment due at eight am.'

She sighed. 'Good times, right?'

'The best. But maybe we can have different good times from now on. You can live with me whenever you want, maybe bring some friends with you and we can do a little horseriding, a little hiking. Ski season would be fun.'

'It's a deal. But hey, um, if you don't need me to rip any walls out in an act of angst solidarity with you, I thought I might go see a friend. There's a banana-choc-chip muffin recipe we're keen to try.'

'Wait, you can cook?'

Poppy rolled her eyes.

'That'll be your mum's gene pool. My role was providing the good looks and charm.'

'Humility too, I see.'

He pulled the end of her braid. 'Who's this friend?'

'Remember guinea pig boy?'

'Kelly Fox's son?'

'Yep. Braydon's kinda cute, and he likes baking. I texted him when I was back in town and he invited me over after school.'

'Bakery dating. Who knew? You think it would be okay to take my girlfriend with you? Jane Doe could do with a walk.'

'Sure thing. Oh, and Dad? I reckon Vera's going to decide she wants you, so hang in there, okay?'

He pulled his mask back over his face and set to work knocking out the rest of the burned wall with his sledgehammer. Three days to finish the refit, he reckoned. Less, if he could persuade Graeme to lend him a hand with the cabinetry.

He bashed out a splintered joist. So Poppy thought there was still something cooking between him and Vera, did she? He'd kind of thought it too. And so had everyone else in the damn town thanks to the Hanrahan Chatter. Everybody except Vera herself, apparently.

He kept bashing until the sound was hurting his ears as much as his thoughts were hurting his head. He needed a walk. If Vera was done with him, it was time he accepted it and focused on what he'd really come back to Hanrahan for: creating a home for himself and for Poppy to visit, a successful animal practice with Hannah, and restoring the Cody building to a Federation showpiece in the heart of Hanrahan.

He shucked off his toolbelt, gathered up his jacket and headed out the door.

CHAPTER
35

A suitcase, a shoebox of papers, and six cardboard cartons. Was that really all her aunt had left behind after sixty plus years on the earth?

The old photo albums Vera already had, a gift from Jill when she'd first moved out of her small home and into the dementia ward at Acacia View. Jill had given her books, pottery, trinkets, beaded earrings from Mongolia, fringed leather purses from Argentina.

She dragged all the cartons into the lounge room, the ones she'd dug through and the sealed ones, so she could tip out everything at once. This was a job she would put off no longer.

She should be ringing Graeme, too, and letting him know she was ready to reopen the café. To prep food, place an advert in the local paper announcing the summer menu, order more crockery and tableware.

Call Josh and apologise.

The look of hurt on his face earlier even as he was being kind enough to urge her to go indoors out of the rain, even when he'd seen that she'd not been honest with him, was searing her conscience like a third-degree burn.

Trust bloody Aaron to turn up just when she was about to tell Josh she didn't want him to stop wanting her.

She closed her eyes. She'd made such a bumbling mess of everything. She needed a good night's sleep and a clear head, and then she was going to make everything right. At least, she was going to try. But first, she was going to wallow in memory lane for a little while and unpack her aunt's favourite things.

She grabbed a knife from the block in the kitchen and slit through the tape holding closed the mementoes from her aunt's life. She wasn't sure what she was looking for, she just knew she needed to find it.

Clothes were in the first and second boxes. She folded them into piles on the sofa. The retro second-hand store in town might be interested in Jill's paisley shirts and henna-dyed bandanas. Next came books, both fiction and reference, well read and dog eared. *Life in the Cosmos, Mood Therapy, DIY plumbing* ... She'd keep some, ditch the others.

She slid back the flaps of the last box and found a jumble of small, wrapped parcels. A cardboard postal tube contained knitting needles of all thicknesses. Crochet hooks filled a mason jar, pale blue tissue paper peeled open to reveal metres of batik cotton, calico, some sort of fluffy wadding. Cotton reels clinked together when she opened a tiny wicker box, and mouse-shaped pin-cushions bristling with rusty pins stared up at her from down the bottom of the carton.

'Grey cat?' she called.

No answer. Not that the cat ever answered when she called. The only sound the cat regularly responded to was the whirr of her electric tin opener.

She started plucking pins from a mouse and discarding them in the rubbish pile. Surely all cats loved toys? There was bound to be a set of needles in amongst all this craft booty—even she should be able to stitch a length of elastic to a mouse.

She tipped the rest of the carton out over the floor and started gathering the bits and pieces into piles. Perhaps the craft group could find a use for all this stuff. She wouldn't need it now. Hell, she didn't even need to finish the blasted quilt she'd been working on at a snail's pace for the last few months. Her aunt's knees wouldn't be needing to be kept warm this or any other winter.

Her eye fell on the half-finished rag quilt in its calico tote under the coffee table. She pulled it out, unfolded it, and lay it across the rug. The patchwork looked back at her as though it were alive. The blue plain material in one corner she recognised from one of Jill's shirts. In the middle, a patch from a skirt. The new pieces had come from the odds-and-ends box at Marigold's craft night. Remnants from children's clothes and cushion projects and impulse buys, all lovingly stored in someone's craft cupboard before being donated so they could be given a new life.

The cat materialised through the open window and stalked over to her. She ignored the mouse Vera dangled before her nose, to settle in the middle of the quilt.

'That's going in the toss pile, cat. Budge.'

The cat blinked at her, yawned, then stretched out full length on the quilt and began to purr.

She sighed. Maybe the cat was right. An afternoon snooze did seem like the perfect way to escape thinking about the funeral, her court case, the mess she'd made of things with Josh. She rose to her feet and looked down on the sleeping cat surrounded by a jumble of fabric.

A thought struck her.

Quilts began with a mess. Scraps of unwanted timeworn fabrics, bundled away for a rainy day. But with time and effort and patience, something beautiful emerged. A patchwork quilt that a wandering cat, or its sad, two-legged owner, could rest upon.

She'd come here to Hanrahan with one goal, to stay clear of involvement, to stay clear of opening herself up to being hurt, but Jill's passing had left a hole where her goals had been.

She thought back to the warmth she'd found within the snug walls of The Billy Button Café. Involvement had given her that. People. Community. She needed to involve herself more, not less. Starting with this quilt.

She'd finish it, she decided. She'd gather more scraps from as many sources as she could, and she would finish Jill's quilt then donate it to Marigold to raffle it off at one of those community hall functions she was always organising.

Order out of chaos.

If that wasn't a metaphor for what she needed to do with her own life, she didn't know what was.

A surge of energy cut through her apathy. Finishing the quilt was only the first part of her new plan.

The second part kind of sucked, but she was on a roll now. Picking up the phone, she scrolled through her short list of contacts until she landed on Marigold's name. *Send message*, she selected, then paused, her thumbs raised over the onscreen keyboard.

Now or never. *Okay*, she texted. *I'm giving in. I'm coming to dawn yoga next week. Don't let me chicken out.*

The answer flashed up on the screen a millisecond later.

FINALLY!!!

Josh was the third and final matter on her agenda, and the most important matter of all. No-one had been kinder to her than him.

That handsome devil had snuck right in under her defences and wrapped himself around her heart six ways from Sunday. And how had she repaid him? By being snarky. By letting him think she agreed with his understanding of their relationship and then shoving him away.

He was hurt, and he had a right to be. He'd been nothing but honest with her, nothing but kind, and she'd been so caught up in her own need for space that she had let him down.

Her shame at being charged with a crime was only one of the reasons she'd pushed him aside. Ironically, it was Aaron showing up at the funeral that had opened her eyes to what was really going on.

What had he said? *I think you're a wonderful person, Vera.* This from the same guy who'd told Acacia View about the camera she'd placed in her aunt's room.

Aaron Finch was a master manipulator, and it had taken her this long to figure it out. Self-absorbed, too, because he seemed to truly not understand that she had no interest in seeing him again.

She poured herself a second cup of green tea from the pot squatting on the table under one of her aunt's technicolour cosies.

There was only one way she could think of to make up for her behaviour, and if that meant letting go of the vow she'd made to herself when she moved up to Hanrahan, then so be it.

She got up and moved over to where her laptop was on its charger at the kitchen counter. She ran her finger along the space bar until the machine hummed itself back to life, then sat on the stool and flexed her fingers.

Okay. She could do this. Whoever was messing around with Josh Cody thinking they were safe behind corporate veils and nineteenth-century civic by-laws could think again. First stop, digital register of city records, she thought. If she had to blow a few hundred bucks on corporate searches, so be it. Paper records in the bowels of the town council building was next.

❧

'Remind me again,' Vera said from her upside-down position on the scratched up yoga mat that Marigold had loaned her, 'what this is supposed to achieve?'

She should be spending the early hours of her day in a ruthlessly pressed and starched apron, proving dough or caramelising butter and sugar. Instead, her pelvis felt like it was about to snap in two, her legs refused to bend in the right way, and from her head-down, bum-up position she could see she *really* ought to have worn a sports bra.

'This is the Prasarita, just relax into it and stop your whingeing.'

'Little secret, Marigold. I'm not feeling so relaxed.'

The older woman spun deftly, like a teenage gymnast, into an odd pose that resembled an inch worm. 'Let the body relax into the position, Vera. Then let whatever it is you've got bottled up in that head of yours just float out.'

A bead of sweat dripped down her face and dangled from her chin. 'If only it were that easy,' she muttered.

'Tell me one horrid thing that you'd like to be rid of. Let's send it on its way together.'

She closed her eyes and tried to think of just one. 'I was in a relationship before I came here. I was—tricked, I think—into thinking the man I was involved with was honest. There were aspects to his personality that I was blind to. I felt like a fool when I found out.'

'What were you blind to?'

'It was like he had different personalities. When I was with him, for the most part, he was like this benevolent figure. Wise, I thought. Really smart at work. Always happy to give advice out. But then there'd be times when he'd get angry. Not at me ... not then ... but he'd disparage people who had crossed him. Call them grubs, curl his lip, that sort of thing. I was naive not to see it for what it was. I just assumed he knew more about the situation than I did, and so these people he denigrated must have deserved it.'

'Now what do you see it as?'

'He was a bully. But he was manipulative about it, always making sure he hid it under this benevolent exterior.'

'Sounds like Narcissism 101 to me, Vera.'

She snorted, then climbed to her feet so she could follow along with the next torture pose. 'Marigold, come on. Florist, yoga guru, celebrant, committee diva, craft goddess … you cannot be a psychologist as well!'

'Give me time,' said Marigold. 'I'm not done living yet. Who knows what else I can be if I put my mind to it? Now come on, stand here next to me, and look out over the lake. What do you see?'

She took in a breath. 'Water. Fields of grass on the far side with rocky outcrops here and there.' She looked, really looked. 'Oh, there's wildflowers blooming below the rocky scree on that steep part. The snow gums were just dark shadows when we started, but the sun's starting to catch them now.'

'Beautiful, aren't they? Those shadows of silver along the scree are snow daisies. When I first came to Hanrahan with Kev, I wondered if there were new words I needed to invent for all those lovely alpine colours. Greens and greys and browns don't seem profound enough to capture this beautiful patch of the world we call home.'

Vera bumped her shoulder into Marigold's. 'You're a romantic, Marigold.'

'And proud of it. Maybe you should try it some time.'

'Maybe. I do like the look of those snow daisies.'

Marigold grinned. 'I'll pick you some, make you a bouquet so pretty you'll wish you were getting married.'

Like that was ever going to happen.

'Come on,' said her friend. 'Let's whizz that bully-boyfriend thought off into the never-never. Wait for a breath of wind to stir across the lake, then whoosh.' Marigold whisked her arms away like she was wafting smoke.

'Just … whoosh?'

'Don't knock it until you've tried it. Here's some breeze. You ready?'

As silly as it seemed, she was ready. 'Whoosh,' she said.

Marigold gave a chuckle. 'Maybe we'll practise that some more next time. Give it a bit of oomph.'

Walking home from yoga, Vera tried to remember what it had felt like the first time she'd walked these streets. She'd been nervous, and emotional. And her thoughts had been dominated by commercial lease provisions and food handling techniques and budgets.

Now, she could admire the neat square of park she'd learned was the beating heart of this town. The pretty buildings with their wrought-iron railings, the tubs of flowers that the council maintained on the footpaths. Lake Bogong shimmered beneath the mountains in the early morning sun, and the heavenly smell of coffee beans hung in the air.

Her coffee beans … being ground lovingly by Graeme and served up to a string of faithful customers.

She was ready, she thought. She was feeling, finally, a little of that peace and wholeness that Marigold had spoken of at Jill's funeral.

She was ready, finally, to go see Josh.

CHAPTER
36

'That end, up two inches,' said Josh, standing back from the cabinetry he'd spent the last six hours constructing.

Sweat had pooled under Hannah's armpits, and she looked cranky as a wombat who'd lost her burrow. 'I'm going to drop this thing any second now, hotshot. Screw it in already, I don't care if it's lopsided.'

'Think of the calories you'll be able to consume afterwards, Hannah Banana.'

The counter looked good. Real good. And damn if it didn't give him a little rush to see his own design for the clinic's new reception coming to life. They'd be able to open the door again to their furred and feathered patients in a day or two … so long as that business renewal didn't get botched up by another malicious complaint.

His building permit reassessment still hadn't been resolved either, despite the objection he'd lodged and the letters of support he'd collected from the residents of Hanrahan he'd approached, and Maureen was taking her own sweet time with the renovation story he and Kev had drip-fed her.

Hannah was like a cat on a hot tin roof worrying about what council would or wouldn't do for them, but at least he had a nail gun and an impressive set of hammers handy to help him work through his own angst.

He took pity on his sister and reached under the cabinet top she was holding to screw its bolts into the backboard.

'You can let it go now.'

'Thank god for that. You're no fun to work for, Josh Cody, I can tell you that much.'

'Step back and see what you think.'

Hannah moved back beside him and they both looked over the rebuilt interior of their business. Laminate wood flooring gleamed under their feet. The receptionist desk he'd lengthened, so files and charts could be kept below bench height in a series of sliding drawers, rather than stuffed in the old shelves in the back hall.

The cabinet doors he'd scrounged from the rubbish dump and pulled apart, sanded, remade. Tasmanian oak, he'd bet his toolbelt on it, and they looked a million bucks beneath the milk-white countertop Hannah had chosen.

Their practising certificates had survived the fire and were back up on the new wall behind the counter, framed in thin copper frames. He rested his eyes on the other certificate hanging there and felt his jaw tighten. The renewal would come through. It just had to.

The police had minimal luck so far wresting answers out of Pamela Hogan. She'd claimed client confidentiality, which had totally sucked, and the council were equally unhelpful, refusing to name the complainant.

'Put an orchid in a pot and we could be on the front cover of *House Beautiful*.'

He pushed their pressing array of problems aside and grinned at Hannah. 'Is that admiration I'm hearing in your voice?'

She wrapped her arm around him and butted her head into his shoulder. 'It was a lucky day for me when you decided to bring your new vet skills home to Hanrahan, Josh. I mean it.'

Well, shoot. 'It was always my plan to come home, Han. Just took me a little longer to get it done than I'd first thought.'

'You're here now.'

Yeah. He was. He'd got it all, all he'd set out to get. A family, albeit a slightly lopsided one, settled back in Hanrahan. A vet practice, community, clean mountain air. Him, Poppy and—if Parker was onboard with Poppy's puppy-switch plan—Jane Doe.

It was the dream he'd kept in his head all those years working construction in the city. Only, why did it seem unfinished?

The arsonist was still on the loose … yeah, that was a biggie. The local council had been as supportive as a wet tissue.

He sighed as his thoughts circled back to where they began each day. *Vera.*

When had she snuck her way into his dream for the future? Not that she wanted to be: she'd been like a thorn, poking and snarling holes into his golden-eyed view of what could have been.

He'd thought they'd found something together, but he'd been wrong. She hadn't really shared herself with him at all; she hadn't trusted him with the news her ex-boss was also her ex-boyfriend, or believed him when he tried to say her court case, win or lose, was not a dealbreaker for him.

The truth was what it was, and he'd pushed through his own truth with hard work and bloody determination. He'd have helped Vera push through hers if she'd have let him.

Instead, she'd pushed him away at every damn opportunity, kept throwing her shame up as an excuse. She just didn't get it.

'Josh?'

He looked down at Hannah.

'What's up? You're looking pensive.'

He sighed. 'Soz, I was wool-gathering. I'm going to run over to Graeme's place and pick up the waiting room chairs. You want to start sorting the desk?'

She pursed her lips. 'You trying to flick all the paperwork at me?'

'Is it working?'

'I guess. Bring me back a full-fat, sugary treat, will you? I want to try out your calorie theory.'

'Sure thing.'

A knock sounded at the temporary door of the clinic he'd installed while he waited on the planning permit decision for the building's exterior. He reached for the handle to open it, and there she was: Vera. He blinked, and wondered if he'd conjured her up with his thoughts until he noticed the box full of paperwork she held.

'Can I come in?'

'I was just—'

Hannah cut him off. 'Vera, hey. Of course you can come in. How's that cranky grey beast of yours going? Might be time to bring her in for a check-up, she must be due soon.'

'Daisy.'

'Excuse me?'

'Her name's Daisy. Turns out, I have a bit of a thing for mountain wildflowers. I've named her after the snow daisies that grow on the foreshore,' Vera said, but even though she was answering Hannah's question, her eyes didn't waver from his.

He sighed. He could take a minute, he supposed, even if she had mushed his heart into pulp. He stepped back so she could move past him into the room.

She'd vowed to herself she'd never make a dumb choice again, because dumb choices ended in a swagload of grief. Her sure-fire, no-complication, one hundred per cent chance of succeeding had all revolved around one strategy: being alone.

A lone wolf, in an apron, with baking trays for company and a batch of chocolate rum ganache whenever the itch for a little sin needed to be scratched.

Her madcap café idea had been her first mistake. How does a wolf stay alone when half the darn town keeps popping in for chats and knitting bees and whatever else all those happy laughing people did at her scrubbed tables?

She'd needed the profit, so she'd needed customers. She just hadn't figured in how community-minded the customers of Hanrahan would be.

Staring into Josh's clear gaze as he held open the door of the vet clinic reminded her of what the other smack-in-the-head fault in her lone-wolf plan had been.

Him. And the coal-hot feelings he stirred up in her.

Josh Cody had made her realise that living aloof and alone might be safe, but it wasn't living.

She wasn't living.

She'd blown it, she knew that the second Aaron Finch turned up in the cemetery and started spouting his crap about 'us' and 'Vera honey'. She'd not been open with Josh, even after she'd assured him she'd told him the worst of it.

She'd been too … ashamed. Finding out she was such a poor judge of character to the point that her own boyfriend sacked her had made her feel so, so small. Admitting that would have taken a piece out of her that she hadn't thought she could spare.

She couldn't make up for not being open with Josh, but she could help him and his sister dig into the spate of harassment they'd been subjected to.

'I've found something. If you have ten minutes to spare, both of you, I'd like to share it.'

Hannah's eyes slid to Josh. They were tight, these two, she thought, and there was another thing to add to the long, long list of what she didn't know about relationships.

'We've got ten minutes, haven't we, Josh?'

'Sure,' he said. 'Here okay? The rest of the place is a construction zone.'

She took a sniff of the fresh paint. 'Can we use the counter? I need to spread this stuff out.'

'Go ahead.'

She rested the box on the counter and started hauling out the clipped bundles of paper, then paused. Turned. Faced them both.

'I just want to get this out of the way first. I lied to you, Josh. Not outright, but by omission. And not just about the fact I was sleeping with my boss when he sacked me.'

Hannah let out a soft choking noise. The younger woman looked like a rock wallaby frozen by oncoming headlights.

'Um,' said Hannah. 'You want me to step out back and change out the oil in my car or something? Powder my nose?'

'Yeah, maybe Ha—'

'No.' She cut Josh off. She was doing this once and once only, and it had to be now before she lost her nerve.

'First omission. Yes, I was in a relationship with Aaron, the guy you saw at Jill's funeral. He was my boss, and he's also the guy who blew the whistle on me to Acacia View. They then decided to prosecute me.'

'Prosecute? What are you talking about?'

Oh boy, this was hard. Harder still, because Josh had apparently not shared the Vera's-going-to-prison story with his sister, and she apparently didn't read the *Snowy River Star*.

'I installed a camera, secretly, in my aunt's room at her old home. Because it recorded sound as well as vision, it's a breach of the Surveillance Devices Act of New South Wales. Possible jail term is up to five years.'

'Five years. Oh my god,' whispered Hannah.

She wasn't going to dwell on that for a second longer than was necessary. 'The second omission, which is where this box comes in, is that I was just being bitchy when I said I couldn't help out with the council by-laws. One of the things that struck me when I started as a journalist was learning how easy it is for any Tom, Dick or Vera to search through public records. And I've not forgotten those skills.'

'Public records,' Josh murmured.

'Yes. You asked me, once, if I'd help you navigate the public records of local government and I refused. I'm sorry for that. I wasn't thinking clearly then, but I'm thinking clearly now and I've done some digging.'

Hannah clapped her hands. 'Oh, please tell me you've found something that will help us.'

She nodded. 'I think so.' Okay. The hard part was over. She wiped her clammy hands down her jeans. 'First, I wondered: why would someone bust a gut—break the law—to buy your building?

It's beautiful, it's got lake views, but it's not the only building in town that can boast them, and some of the others have been on the market without being snapped up. So I looked up who owned property in the blocks surrounding yours, and when those properties had last changed hands. There were a few noteworthy ones.'

'Such as?'

'Krauss Holdings has been busy. Bought the old Hanrahan Pub some years ago even though it's just about derelict, owns a stretch of foreshore, and most of the buildings on the eastern edge of the town square.'

'The Krauss family have always been big landowners in town. If they wanted our place, they'd have come in person and asked for it. You agree, Hannah?'

Hannah was picking at a loose thread on her denim jacket and didn't look like she had an opinion on the matter.

'What else was noteworthy?' Josh continued.

'Transfer in title of this building from Preston Cody and Shirley Marlee Cody to Joshua and Hannah Cody three years ago.'

'I'm pretty sure we know about that one.'

'But did you know a corporation called Kestrel Holdings lodged a development application with council for this building six months prior to the title transferring to you? The application was to …' Vera flipped a page so she could read the tiny print: '*hereby seek permission to reconfigure existing commercial ground floor and upper residential two-flat layout to twelve studio apartments and small commercial space suited to tourism ticketing venture.*'

The Codys stared at her, open-mouthed.

'Well, hell,' said Hannah.

'Yes. Could this have been a scheme your grandparents were considering, only to change their mind and leave the building to you?'

Josh shook his head. 'No, they couldn't have. They were neither of them alive then. Probate of their estate took a few years because our parents were driving the Gibb River Road and never stayed in one place long enough to sign all the relevant paperwork. They were the executors. The timing is all wrong.'

'The building was vacant then. It had been empty since our grandmother was moved into Connolly House.'

Vera shrugged. 'Somebody at Kestrel must have thought they had a chance to start an approval process before they owned it.'

'I ran my practice from Mum and Dad's place when I first started vet work,' said Hannah. 'Before they bought the caravan and started their grey nomad trip, they had a house just out of town.' She looked across at Josh. 'Moving in here on my own was a big step. I took my time about making it, so the place was vacant for a few years.'

'And when did the offers of purchase start rolling in?' said Vera.

Hannah pushed a strand of hair back from her face. 'After probate. After I moved in, I suppose.'

'Maybe whoever owns Kestrel Holdings got a nasty surprise when you moved into the building.'

Josh frowned. 'And an even nastier surprise when I moved in too and the practice grew even more ... because that's when the nuisance complaints started arriving.'

Vera nodded. 'Follow this line of thought through ... you then stick up a noticeboard out front, letting the world know not only aren't the Codys shifting out anytime soon, they're wanting to sink money into the building ... what happened then?'

'An arson attack designed to scare the dickens out of us but not damage anything structural.'

'Bingo,' said Vera. 'And here's the kicker ... Kestrel Holdings owns the building next to you.'

'The gift shop?'

'It's a gift shop on the ground floor, tenanted, and the guy says his landlord's pretty shady about doing repairs. Upstairs flats are empty gathering dust. The building is much smaller than this one of course, but it explains why your property was of greater interest to them than other ones that have come on the market. Shared driveway, shared common space, corner position—it would have made a studio apartment proposal very attractive.'

Hannah nodded. 'Now I think of it, with all this talk of a new ski lift going in, and the road upgrade from Cooma, there'd be dozens of city buyers keen to snap themselves up a ski weekender.'

'So how do we find out who the hell is behind Kestrel Holdings?'

'It's a shelf company. Actually, it's one in a string of shelf companies. They're a bit like termite mounds: every time you think you've found the inner nest, a mud trail leads you to a new one. Fortunately, I have a contact at a private investigative firm back in Canberra. I rang her and asked if she'd do a corporations trace for me using her software, and she found a couple of items of interest.'

'We're all ears.'

'One is a joint venture between a related entity of Kestrel Holdings and the developers putting in the new ski lift. The other big find was the names of the directors of the innermost nest.'

'Who are they?'

'A guy by the name of Brian David, and a woman. Paula? No.' Vera rifled through until she found the page she was looking for. 'Pamela Hogan.'

'Pamela Hogan!' said Hannah.

'You've heard of her?'

'Lawyer. Signed her name to a dozen requests to buy the place, but she always said she was acting on behalf of an unnamed client. Meg—you know, the local cop—has interviewed her, but she said her client's name was privileged information and she wouldn't be sharing it.'

Josh picked up the extract from the company report Vera's investigator had emailed through. 'Well, if *she* is the client, she can't hide behind herself, surely? This is gold, Vera. There is no way Pamela is not up to her neck in this. We need to get Meg here and explain all this to her.'

'Being the pushy director of a company doesn't make you an arsonist,' she said.

'Meg's no fool. If there's a link there, she'll find it. Thank you, Vera, for doing this.'

She swallowed. 'No need for thanks,' she said, her voice dry. She'd probably talked more this morning than she had in months.

'Nonetheless, I still want to thank you.'

She realised Josh was holding out his hand to her. As a lifeline? As forgiveness? She placed her hand in his and he shook it once then let go, turning to rifle through the neat piles of paper trail she'd organised across the counter.

Oh. A business handshake. The little wad of hope she'd had hidden in her heart shrivelled up and died.

She'd done the right thing.

Trouble was, she'd learned what the right thing to do was way too late.

CHAPTER
37

By late November the weather had warmed, and Graeme convinced her to place some little tables outside the café on the footpath overlooking the lake. Tourists had flocked to them like seagulls after a hot chip, and gathered in the late afternoon sunlight for glasses of wine, cheese boards, and little dishes of antipasti. Business was up, her lawyer was texting her optimistic messages like *loving our defence strategy, Vera!* and her trial date had been set for the second week of December.

She was ignoring the trial, for the most part, and when she was having trouble ignoring it, she went to yoga and Marigold helped her whizz her worries off over the lake.

Sure it was a bit hippy and nuts … but whatever. She was trying to learn not to be so rigid and loosen up a little.

She inspected the strawberry she'd just sliced. Hmm. Not so loose that *that* mangled cut of fruit would be acceptable in her display cabinet. She popped it in her mouth, then plated up three dozen of the tarts she'd spent the afternoon baking. Poppy had whimsically named them La Di Dah Tarts on her last visit up from Sydney.

The swing door crashed open and Graeme shouldered his way into the kitchen bearing a tray of empty cups. 'Marigold's asking for you, my lamb.'

Vera ran her eye over the bowl containing five kilos of choux pastry dough that wasn't going to pipe itself. 'How chatty is she looking?'

He grinned. 'She's ordered a hot chocolate to go, so maybe not too chatty. One hour, tops.'

'You mind asking her if she's happy to come back here?'

'I'm on it.'

Just as Vera was fitting a nozzle onto a piping bag, Marigold sailed through the swing doors.

'The inner sanctum!' she announced. 'I'm feeling a little dizzy with the honour, Vera.'

Vera tested the consistency of the mix with a spoon. 'That'll be the powdered sugar fumes, Marigold.' She spooned a batch of choux pastry into the piping bag and began filling her trays with short lengths of dough.

'Éclairs? Oh, poop, now I'm wishing I hadn't already had a slice of that devilish chocolate cake.'

'Relax, I'm prepping these for tomorrow.'

'My bathroom scales are scared of you, Vera, you know that? They see me coming home with shortbread crumbs scattered across my magnificent bosom, and they quake.'

Vera allowed herself a smug little snicker and pulled out a stool for her friend.

'But seriously,' said Marigold, taking a sip of her hot chocolate then resting it on the workbench. 'How are you doing, Vera?'

She looked up. 'Excuse me?'

Marigold reached over and patted her arm. 'Burying a loved one with me as celebrant gets you certain privileges. Like me coming over to check on you from time to time. And Kev, bless him. He'd have been here, but he spied an aphid on a rose bush down at the hall and went all First Testament on me. I haven't seen you at yoga this week, so I assumed you were burying yourself in hard work and dark thoughts, and I was right, wasn't I?'

She tried for flippancy. 'Someone's got to keep this town supplied with sweet treats.'

'Uh-huh. And someone else has got to keep this town feeling better by wearing epic earrings and making taciturn people like you talk about their feelings. And that person is me, Vera. Spill the beans.'

A splodge of dough erupted from the piping bag to form a fist-sized lump in her tray. It looked as pale and inanimate as she imagined her heart must look.

'I'm never been very good at sharing, Marigold.'

'You think I don't know that? Girlfriend, you're pricklier than a prickly pear. Luckily, I don't scare away so easy.'

She bit her lip, and then the words came blurting out. 'It's all such a mess, Marigold.'

'I know, honey.'

'I just wanted Jill to be happy, calm, well cared for.'

'And she was, Vera.'

'Not always. Not when those idiots in charge of Acacia View were underpaying their staff and under-resourcing their facility.'

'*Always*. Always by you.'

Was that true? She'd been so immersed in her career when Jill first showed signs she could no longer live alone. Had she taken such little care choosing a home for her because she was too involved with her career to make proper enquiries?

Vera eyed Marigold. 'I suppose you know my trial date has been scheduled for a couple of weeks from now.'

'You suppose right. This is a small town, honey. It's a miracle I don't know what colour your underwear is.'

She sighed. 'Crap.'

Marigold chuckled. 'People here care, that's all. They read the papers. They see a name they know, they sit up and take notice. They see someone through the kitchen window hanging out their washing, and they run over and share the news.'

Vera was surprised into a laugh. 'I guess I hadn't thought about that before I moved here. I came for the peace and quiet. For the promise offered up in the Connolly House brochure. For the opportunity to be an unknown person who could be left completely alone.'

'Pet, if you wanted to be lonely you should have stayed in the city.'

'Alone. Not lonely.'

'They walk the same path, Vera. But now you've set your feet in a whole new direction. How's that quilt coming along?'

'Slowly. As soon as I pull it out, the cat waddles over and plonks herself down on it.'

'Hmm. You sure the cat's not just your excuse? What's the hold-up? Fear of failure? Fear of success?'

Vera hauled open the oven door and began sliding in trays of éclair mix. 'It's not fear, Marigold. I've just, you know, been busy. I'm here before dawn most mornings. My aunt just died, and any-time that I'm not busy cooking or grieving, I'm wondering how in hell this café is going to manage with me on the wrong side of tempered steel bars.'

'You'll employ a cook. That young man Graeme may look as pretty as a peacock, but he's an operator. He'll manage.'

Vera shrugged. 'I don't know why I'm worried. The income from this place was never for me. I had to make sure I had money coming in to pay Jill's medical bills if I was ... put away.'

Marigold frowned. 'You were shouldering that burden on your own? What, Jill had no funds?'

She shrugged. 'She did, once. But they're long gone. Dementia's a brute, but for all its destructive force, it's got no speed to it. Five years of high-needs care, and live-in help before that, and Jill's money from selling up her apartment was all gone.'

'Honey, don't ever wonder if you did enough. You did wonderfully, do you hear me? *Wonderfully.*'

'I hope so. Thanks, Marigold.'

'Me and Kev would feel lucky to be so loved. Being childless has its own rules, Vera. You've done your aunt proud. But I still want you to finish that quilt, you hear? Whose fabric got cut into squares for it?'

She smiled. 'About everybody's by now. Jill's, yours.'

'Uh-huh. And that red paisley we cut up last week was out of Mrs Juggins's stash. A dozen of this town's residents have their fabric scraps in my craft box. They're all in that quilt, Vera. You have to stop messing around and finish it. Put a bit of *you* in it.'

She grinned, amused despite herself. 'You think I should cut up an apron and stitch it in?'

'Maybe. If you like. I would, but then I'm a sentimental old fool who made a quilt out of my goddaughter's flannel pyjamas. You know the craft group rule: every stitch is a good stitch, Vera, *especially* the wonky ones. Promise me you'll see it done.'

Vera swung the timer on the oven door. 'Sure.'

'Look me in the eye and say it like you mean it.'

She brushed what she could of the sticky dough from her hands. Why was Marigold so fired up about this? She looked her in the eye. 'Marigold Jones. I promise I'll finish Jill's quilt. And you know what I'm going to do with it?'

'What's that, my love?'

'I'm going to donate it to your fundraising stall. Maybe you can raffle it off, if it's good enough, that is.'

Marigold pulled her in for a quick hug and pressed a kiss to her cheek. 'That's my girl. And it will be perfect, because rag quilts stitched together with love and patience always are. Now I'd best be getting on home to Kev before he starts fretting that I've run off with that fine-looking Cody boy.'

Vera jumped, knocking her pastry bag to the ground in a splatter of dough.

Marigold dropped her a wink. 'Thought that would get your attention. When you're done stitching, you might want to bake that boy an apple pie. Quilts aren't the only things that need a bit of attention and patience.'

Vera let out a breath. 'I don't know, Marigold.'

'Shame he couldn't make it to the wake. That man worked until midnight getting that ceiling finished so we could reopen the hall. I was hoping he'd be there to see how much his hard work was contributing to this community. Kev was tickled pink when he read this week's Hanrahan Chatter.'

'Josh worked on the hall? I thought it had electrical problems.'

'Sure, but the wiring was in the ceiling cavity, and half of the old plaster had to come out, and Josh helped with the rebuild. Crikey,' Marigold added, waving a spatula in front of her face like it was a fan, 'that boy is good with his hands.'

Marigold's words played over in her head as the éclairs puffed in the oven, as she cooled them and packaged them, cleaned her mixmaster, countertops, sinks. Josh had worked his butt off to get the hall ready for her aunt's funeral and what had she done? Instead of thanking him, she'd driven him off with bitterness and lies.

Alone and lonely walk the same path.

But what other choice did she have? She was in a mess, and dragging people into that mess was not fair on them, especially when they were as lovely as the people who had befriended her here.

She thought of the world she'd found here in Hanrahan. Graeme, slipping her bottles of wine and foolish notes. Poppy, naming her tarts; the regulars who breezed in and asked how her day was going, offered her their condolences about her aunt, gave her tips on which Cooma market stall sold the freshest herbs ... Kev, tending the rose bushes he'd planted by her aunt's grave.

She didn't want to leave, she thought, as she swiped disinfectant across her workbench. And if she was forced to by the courts, she knew this was where she wanted to come home to when she was free.

She didn't want to be alone.

Marigold's words played across her mind, and she ducked out to the alley to where she'd binned the old newspapers earlier. Yes, there it was. She pulled out the *Snowy River Star* issues and rifled through them until she found this week's Chatter. What had Kev been so chuffed to read?

GOLD RUSH GLORY RESTORED BY LOCAL TRADIE-VET *by Maureen Plover*

Hanrahan's history has been given a makeover these last few weeks with a ceiling restoration project in the community hall. Local Kev Jones did the research using the Historical Society archives, and hometown vet Josh Cody strapped on his toolbelt to restore the ceiling to its former glory ...

How amazing! She'd barely noticed the interior of the hall at the funeral, but she'd have to go back, especially—

'Oh good,' said a voice from the doorway. 'The chatterbox of the Australian Alps has gone. You can get outta here now, boss. You look beat.'

'Graeme, hey. I'm just packing up.' She folded the paper and took it back into the kitchen so she could read it later in full.

'I can do that, Vera. You head on home and let me lock up.'

Now was the perfect time; foolish to waste it. She took a breath. 'You got a minute?'

'For you? Plenty of minutes. What's up?'

It was her lucky day when Graeme Sharpe answered her advertisement for a café manager. 'We have any wine out front?'

Graeme grinned. 'There might be a busty little pinot noir rosé hiding behind the organic juice. Otago region of New Zealand. So smooth on the palate, you'd think Aphrodite herself peeled the grapes.'

'Are you interested in Aphrodite, then?'

'Good point. Let's make it Thor, the Byron Bay version, because … damn.'

'I'll get the glasses.'

'And find cheese. Something sharp. And give me a second to text Alex so he doesn't think I've driven into a ditch on the way home.'

Cheese and wine glasses. If only every chore she needed to do in the limited time she had left would be so easy. She set a tray of nibbles on the honeymoon table in the front window and waited for Graeme to finish his call. The closed sign was squarely set mid-door, the oven was cooling, tomorrow's baking prep was ahead of schedule.

The day was done. Sort of.

'So spill, honey.'

Vera cut a wedge of brie and laid it on a cracker, pressed dried cranberries into the soft cheese. 'Try this.'

'Procrastination hors d'oeuvres? Don't mind if I do.' Graeme tossed the cracker into his mouth, chewed, then took a reverent sip of his rosé. 'Delicious. We should start a YouTube channel for the ultimate cheese and wine pairings.'

She clinked her glass to his. 'A business idea for another day. But actually, business is what I wanted to speak to you about.'

'Okay.'

'Marigold tells me everyone in town knows about my court case. Do you?'

Graeme reached over and took her hand. 'A little gossip isn't the same as knowing. Why don't you tell me properly? You'll get no judgement from me, Vera.'

She rubbed her face. 'Thank you. I mean that. It is true, I've had charges laid against me. I'd hoped the preliminary hearing would be enough to get them thrown out, but I was wrong. Unless a miracle happens and the courthouse in Queanbeyan is struck by a meteorite, I'll be going to trial soon.'

'What are the chances of winning?'

'According to my lawyer? A hundred and twenty per cent, but she's an operator, and she's probably done some ballsy marketing course that says optimistic clients pay their legal fees faster.'

'And if you lose at trial?'

'If I lose ... best case scenario is community service. Worst case? Five years behind bars.'

'Hell, Vera. What exactly did you do?'

'I was worried my aunt was being neglected, so I hid a camera in the bookcase of her room at her aged care facility.'

Graeme's eyebrows nearly rose out of sight over his bald head. 'That ... does sound kind of illegal.'

She choked on a mouthful of brie. 'Well, yes, it was impulsive and I didn't think it through. But as to the legality or not, it depends. I put the camera in because I wanted to know how often Jill was being checked in on. The Acacia View, of course, saw it as a gross invasion of the privacy of their nursing staff. I can see their point ... but I can also see *my* point.'

'I'm sorry, Vera. You must have been to hell and back.'

'Yeah,' she sighed. 'It sure feels that way. So, worst case scenario—I've had a plan. It's about as ready as a half-baked loaf, but here goes. How would you like to become a partner in The Billy Button Café?'

Graeme sat back in his chair. 'An owner?'

'Yep. When we're both working, we split the profits fifty-fifty. If I'm not here, the profits are all yours. I can help with menus, recipes from prison, I guess. I could probably still do the books if they let me take my laptop.'

'Wow. That's a lot to take in. It's also super crazy considering you're the one with the bank loan for the café fit-out. Loan repayments first, then the remaining profit is split between us based on hours worked. *If* I say yes.'

'Oh, Graeme, does that mean you'll think about it? These few months since the café opened ... my cooking has only been part of the reason we've been turning such a handsome profit. It's you, too. Your coffee, sure. But you're the drawcard. You get people. You're warm. People come here to get a little lift in their day and you give them that.'

'Aw, shucks.'

She grinned. 'Don't pull that humble routine with me, Graeme Sharpe.'

He threw back his head and laughed. 'I know. People love me. It's a gift.'

'So what do you say? Does your gift want a little more input into how this café is going to go in the future?'

'I'll need to think about this, Vera. Talk it over with Alex.'

'I know. I'll send you the financials since we opened. The lease is a liability you need to consider. Maybe get a finance person to advise you.'

Graeme was leaning back in his chair, surveying the dimly lit interior of the café. The Billy Button had evolved over the months they'd run it together; the newness of the furniture had mellowed, her ferns in their brass pots had grown leggy and lush, the painting of the high country she'd bought from the Cooma markets echoed the splendour of the view through the old windows.

'I have had some ideas,' he said.

She smiled. 'I bet you have. Like what?'

'Like ... a much bigger wine list. Big enough to support a wine bar in the back room on a Friday and Saturday night. Maybe Sunday afternoons, too, with a little live jazz set up in the window bay. In winter, with the fire going, we explore the reds. Cabernets from Margaret River. Shiraz from the Barossa. Grapes, mulled wine, pot roasts with dumplings and duck-fat potatoes.'

'Oh, just excuse me while I mop up my drool. Fabulous idea,' she grinned. 'This is why we make a great team, Graeme. You've got vision and people skills, and I've got a lot of angst that enjoys being thrashed out in a kitchen under a rolling pin.'

'I'll think it over. Although, worst case scenario, hon ... finding a cook to replace you won't be easy.'

Vera looked up. 'Flatterer.'

'And it'll eat into my share of the profits.'

She choked on her sip. 'Okay, also true. But I'm saving that particular worry for later.'

Graeme's warm hand rested on hers. 'I have a good feeling about the future, Vera. Mine and yours.'

She smiled. 'I hope you're right.'

'Come on. Let's lock up together. Want me to drive you home?'

'I drove today. My car's out back in the alley.'

'I'll walk you there, then.'

CHAPTER

38

Vera almost had a skip in her step as she let herself out of the kitchen and into the alley. She'd made a small move in the right direction with Josh today, and that had felt good. Offering Graeme a share in The Billy Button Café … that felt good, too.

Maybe Marigold was right. Maybe she *could* hope, just a little. Even if Josh had stopped popping into her café. Even if he just smiled politely at her now whenever they met in the street, and didn't linger to chat. She was the one who'd let him down—

A deep, sinister yowl rose up from the shadows by the rubbish bin and she paused. Surely grey cat hadn't found her way back to the alley from her apartment?

'You hear that, Graeme?'

Her bunch of keys was jangling in the door lock, but still she heard a faint scuffle. 'Daisy?'

Nothing. Of course … she'd taken so long to name the stray cat who'd befriended her, why would the cat respond? She flipped over the phone and used the screen to illuminate the rubbish bin. 'Grey cat?' Two round, yellow eyes gleamed back at her from a still, sprawled shape.

'Oh no,' she murmured. 'No, no, no!'

'What is it, Vera?'

'I think—'

She couldn't say it. The alley was cool now the sun had hidden itself behind the mountain range, and shreds of leaf litter skittered along the old brick gutter. Her handbag slipped from her fingers as she ran forward.

'Oh god.'

Grey cat's eyes were closed, but her sides heaved in distress. A low sound escaped her mouth, nothing like the tractor purr she used when she was content; this sound was terrible. It spoke of pain, and loss, and suffering. Vera recognised herself in it: her pain, her loss, her suffering.

'She needs help,' she whispered.

'Vera?' Graeme's voice was worried behind her.

'She needs help!' She all but shrieked the words. 'Get Josh. Please. And run.'

Her friend's booted feet pounded down the street as Vera bent her head to the cat's.

'Hang on, girl. Hang on. Help's coming.'

The cat's breathing was rough. Vera pulled off her gloves and rested her fingers, as gently as she could, between the cat's soft grey ears. There was no blood that she could see, but the cat's back legs looked loose, somehow, as though her muscles had given way. She'd known grey cat was wandering—why had she done nothing about it?

She could do something now, but what? God, she'd never felt so useless. A box—yes. When Josh came, he'd need something flat and stable, strong enough to bear grey cat's weight. The cat was fatter now she no longer had to scrounge for food, and heavy with the life she carried in her belly.

Vera lifted her head, wiped away the blur of tears. Milk crates towered by The Billy Button Café's service door, and beside them stood a stack of waxed boxes that her vegetables were delivered in. They'd do. They'd more than do if she tore out one of the sides.

She leapt to her feet and pulled the stack of boxes apart, searching for the cleanest one, then raced back to the cat. Should she move her?

Just as she was dithering over the wisdom of trying to lift her on her own, footsteps sounded in the alley and the broad white beam of a torchlight shone square in her face.

She shielded her eyes. 'Josh?'

'I'm here.'

Thank god. Two little words from him and that's all it took; tears she'd been fighting to hold back roared up like a freak wave and overflowed down her cheeks.

'I think she's been hit by a car. Her breathing's all funny and her tail's all still.'

'We can't do anything here. Put your hands under her head and I'll do the back. We'll lift her into the box on three. Ready?'

No. She wasn't ready, but she slid her hands under grey cat's head and shoulders anyway, lifted as Josh commanded.

The cat gave a low, low yowl, then subsided into silence.

'Is she—'

She couldn't finish the question.

'Hold the torch,' said Josh. 'Graeme's with Hannah getting a table prepped. Vera?'

She hurried along beside him, shining the torch where his feet needed to step.

'Yes?'

His voice was firm. 'This doesn't look good, Vera. You need to be prepared.'

She swallowed back a sob. 'I know.'

Lights were blazing in the vet clinic, and Hannah was in hairnet, mask and gloves when they raced into the operating room.

'Anaesthetic,' said Hannah.

'On it,' said Josh, pulling on a pair of gloves then lowering a conical mask over the cat's face.

'Back's not broken,' said Hannah, as her fingers slid along grey cat's spine and around her haunches. 'But that leg is. She's going to need surgery to pull— Oh, the kittens are still alive. There's movement.'

Vera let out a breath.

'Feel here, Josh,' said Hannah. She grabbed Josh's hand and slid it over the belly of the cat.

'But her leg,' said Vera. 'What's going to happen?'

Hannah started to answer but Josh cut her off.

'Grey cat—Daisy—is badly injured, and the leg may not be the worst of her problems. She may have internal bleeding, and if that's the case, then our job is to help her on her way as quickly and pain-lessly as possible. We also need to deliver these kittens by C-section. There's a lot of unknowns, Vera. They may well not live. You need to step out into the waiting room.'

She shook her head. 'No, Josh, please. I can't leave her.'

'That wasn't a request, Vera. Off you go.'

She looked at his face. No smile in his eyes. No look of the easygoing sweetheart she'd pushed out of her life. He looked like a stranger.

'Can't I stay? Please. She's all I've got.'

Graeme slipped his arm around her shoulders. 'Come on, honey. We're stepping out the door, and we're staying right there, close by.'

Vera walked out to the dimly lit waiting room and collapsed in a chair, covering her face with her hands. There was no way she'd be allowed to keep kittens in prison.

CHAPTER
39

Who knew quilting could be so cathartic?

Vera had stitched her way through the long hours of the night, waiting in dread for her phone to ring with the terrible news.

But the phone didn't ring.

Not until dawn, anyway, and when she answered, it was Hannah on the other end.

'Daisy's awake. She's weak, but she's accepted water and managed to muster up enough energy to sink her canine tooth into my little finger.'

'Oh, thank heavens.'

'It's fine,' said Hannah. 'I didn't need that finger.'

'So you think … she's going to make it?'

'Let's take this day by day, Vera. But'—she wasn't imagining the smile in Hannah's voice, was she?—'early signs are promising.'

'And the kittens?'

They'd let her hold the two speckled kittens for a few minutes, before Graeme had driven her home and ordered her to bed. They were so new, and their mother cat so fragile, they would need rigorous care when they were released from the clinic.

A few weeks ago she would have baulked at the prospect of taking on that role, but now, the thought of having a little family to care for warmed her.

Hanrahan had changed her.

Hanrahan had given her back her hope for a rosier future.

'The kittens are as pretty and perfect as they were last night,' Hannah said. 'Get some rest, Vera. Me and Josh have got this.'

Vera set down the phone and ran her fingers over some crooked stitching where she'd placed a fabric square askew. In time gone by, she would have pulled that patch out and worried at it until its edges were aligned perfectly from north to south, but Marigold had taught her the value of a crooked stitch.

'Leave it,' she'd said often and again at craft group. 'A few frazzled stitches are a sign that this is a homemade work of love, Vera. I adore this part of the quilt. The wonky bits are what make it personal.'

That, her need to be sure and precise and have her edges all tidy, had been the reason she'd pushed Josh away. She'd sworn to herself that her days of making dumb decisions were over; but what she hadn't taken the time to see—or perhaps had been too hurt to see—was that Josh wasn't a dumb choice.

He was a sunny, warm, joyous choice, and it was her turn now to open herself up to him and let him decide if he wanted to stick.

She'd made her decision. Court case or no, she loved him and if he was willing to ride out the rough track ahead by her side, she should stop trying to push him away.

She didn't need to know all the answers anymore and—she took a deep breath—the relief of knowing that was enormous.

Josh's resolute insistence on caring for her, despite her attempts to keep him at arm's-length, had given her faith that she *could* trust in a happier future.

Daisy and her kittens, for instance … if she had to go to prison and the cats needed a foster home, she could worry about finding one then.

She reached for the pot of tea she'd made and poured herself a cup. Another hour of quilting while she daydreamed about kittens and new beginnings, then she'd better think about work. There were cakes to be made, ganache to be whipped, perhaps a new risotto recipe to try … and a kind man to reclaim as her own.

The knock on her door surprised her into slicing Jill's ancient fabric scissors through the full thickness of the quilt and about half an inch into the flesh of her palm.

'Ouch!'

Bloody hell. Now there'd be two wonky bits in her quilt. She wrapped a fabric scrap around her hand to staunch the bleeding and was halfway to the door before she realised the buzzer to the street door hadn't sounded. So much for security. No doubt Mrs Butler on the ground floor was out of vanilla extract again. Or maybe it was Josh, come to give her an update on those tiny kittens (unlikely), or come to forgive her for being the world's greatest fool (unlikelier still).

She glanced down. Her bathrobe was as modest as a nun's habit, only fluffier and more pink, and nothing Mrs Butler or Josh hadn't seen before.

She cracked the door open a few inches and found herself face to face with her nemesis, Aaron Finch.

'How did you get in here? How did you find out where—' she gasped. No matter. She didn't need to know, she just needed him gone. She started to close the door but he held his hand up and forced it open.

'I've had just about enough of you shutting doors in my face, Vera De Rossi.'

CHAPTER

40

'This information was gold. Your girlfriend knows her stuff, Josh. Sorry I've been out of town or I could have acted on this sooner.'

Josh didn't care about a couple of days' delay. What he did care about was the pissed-off feeling churning in his gut. 'She's given me the brush-off about a dozen times now, Sergeant. Vera is not my girlfriend.'

He could feel Hannah's eyeroll from beside him. It was too early in Josh's morning for sarcasm, *and* he hadn't had a coffee, *and* he was feeling pretty darn ticked off with just about the whole world.

Meg didn't care. 'Whatever. She's given us a motive so tight all I need to do is type it up and hand it in to secure a search warrant. She ever needs a break from grilling prosciutto and baking figs, you tell her she's got a job waiting in law enforcement.'

'I don't think her opinion of the law's too high at present.'

'Yeah, I heard about that. Anything I can do to make a difference, I'll do it.'

Josh turned the words over in his mind. Every offer of help or support had been brushed aside. Vera was determined to see her troubles through alone.

Hannah spoke up beside him. 'You really think this persecution of our business is going to stop, Meg?'

'I really do. As soon as the courts open, I'll be applying to Judge Bamfrey for a search warrant. My constable's heading in to Cooma for a ten o'clock meet with Pamela Hogan, which I'll be joining once I have the search warrant in my hands. Her house, her car, her records. Every damn thing she owns, we'll be going through looking for evidence she knew about the fire in your building before it started. If she's involved and we find evidence, we'll charge her.'

'You might not find anything.'

'If she's involved and we don't find evidence?' The cop smirked. 'Yeah, we'll be putting the wind up her so high she'll be thinking twice about pulling any more stunts.'

'I hope you find something,' said Hannah. 'I'm not sure how much more of this we can take.'

Josh rested his hand on his sister's back.

'Oh, and here's a little something Barry O'Malley gave me when I stopped by his office last night when I got back to town,' said Meg.

Josh eyed the official yellow envelope she handed him. 'Crap. Not another one.'

Meg smiled. 'Open it before you start bitching, Cody.'

He slid his finger under the seal and a thick, embossed page fell out.

'Is that—'

'Our business licence renewal?'

He looked up at the sergeant, who was smiling at him like she'd just abolished global warming.

'Yep. Now look at the second page.'

He flipped the business licence over and found a letter, addressed to him and Hannah, on gilt-edged council letterhead. The most important word was in bold type, smack bang in the middle of the first line: APPROVED.

Holy shit, his building permit had come through.

'Barry asked me to let you know how much he enjoyed reading last week's edition of the Hanrahan Chatter. Seems that article about the Cody commitment to remembering the town's gold rush history struck a chord with him.'

'Well, hell,' said Hannah, reading the approval letter over his shoulder. 'Maureen came through! You think that's what got the permit approved? A bit of publicity? I wonder if Sandy kept a copy for us.'

Meg shrugged. 'He also asked me to extend his apologies for all the complaints you've had to respond to in the last few months. There was some other stuff he said, like junior officials not having more sense than a blue-arsed fly, and he hoped this wouldn't get in the way of the Cody family supporting his next election, yada yada.'

Josh shook his head. 'You are the best, Meg.'

She got to her feet. 'Much as I'd love to agree with you, in this case, Vera was the best. I'm not saying we wouldn't have found the link between Pamela Hogan and the neighbouring building, but we sure wouldn't have been on to it this swiftly.'

A squawk burst out of the radio the sergeant wore clipped to her jacket. 'Excuse me,' she said. 'Duty calls.'

'Dispatch? Sergeant King.'

The voice through the radio was loud enough to fill the room. 'There's a snarl-up on the Crackenback Road, Meg. Two cars and a ute that's rolled, spilling a ton of lucerne. No serious injuries reported, but we've called an ambulance as a precaution.'

'I'll take it. Send another car to meet me there.'

Meg gave them both a nod. 'Duty calls, team. I'll let you know how we get on with that warrant.'

Josh became aware of Hannah giving him the hairy eyeball when she snapped him on the arm with a disposable rubber glove.

'Earth to Josh.'

'What?'

'You're brooding,' she said. 'My new pot plant's going to start wilting if you don't get that glower off your face. Just go see her already.'

He dropped his head into his hands and pulled on a tuft of hair just to remind himself there were other things that hurt besides this empty hole in his chest. 'I want to and I don't want to all at the same time, Han. It's messing with my head.'

'The mighty Josh Cody, not sure if his chick magnet status has lost its allure. How happy am I to see this day.'

He knew she was joking. His sister would crawl over broken glass for him in a heartbeat ... but still, the words stung. Had he started flirting with Vera just assuming his usual brand of charm would win her over?

He was sure he hadn't.

In fact, he was pretty darned sure he'd lost his head so fast, he'd fumbled every attempt to be the wannabe charming suitor.

A paperclip, or two, smacked him on the cheek.

'I think my heart's broken, Hannah.'

His sister stopped tossing paperclips at him and dropped to her feet from the desk she'd been perched on. She wrapped her arms around his shoulders and tucked her face into his neck.

'Oh, Josh,' she said.

He closed his eyes. 'I know, right?'

'Go see her.'

'She's turned me away. How often does a woman need to turn a guy down before he actually listens? I'm trying to do what she wants.'

His sister's sweet hug shifted into a headlock. 'Josh, honey, you know I am the very last person to give advice on boy-girl stuff.'

'Agreed.'

'But even I could tell that when Vera came here the other day to offer up information about the Hogan woman, that wasn't the only thing she was offering.'

He pulled Hannah's bony wrist away from his Adam's apple so he could breathe.

'She offered us a box of paperwork and search records.'

'Yep. What else?'

'An apology?'

'I cannot believe you won a scholarship. Seriously, bro, you are the dumbest person in this room.'

Jane Doe's tail thwacked against the filing cabinet in agreement.

'You're going to have to spell it out, genius. Your brother's brain has turned to mush.'

Hannah gave his hair a ruffle and let him go so she could skewer him with her favourite my-brother-is-a-moron look. 'She was offering you an olive branch.'

He sat up. 'She was?'

Hannah shrugged and walked over to her side of the office. 'Yup. So get outta here already and go make some kissy noises in her direction, would you? I've got some *Back in Business* flyers to create.'

'What are you doing here, Aaron?'

'Vee, you're upset, I get it, but you've been through a terrible time.'

She had, yes. And the slick-haired man standing in front of her had played a part in that.

'The court case sucks, totally, but we can put that behind us. Change your plea, you'll do a few community hours pulling up weeds by the riverbank in Queanbeyan, and it will all be over.'

'I'm not guilty of the charge, Aaron. You knew full well I wasn't trying to listen in on people, but you went and dobbed me in anyway.'

'Hon, you know me, as honest as the day is long. I felt it was my duty.'

She could feel a red haze of rage welling up.

'I do know you, yes, and so I know it's just a damn sham, this honesty of yours. You telling people something is true doesn't *make* it true. The way you tell people how talented you are, how smart you are.' She choked down the frustration she had bottled up. Which part of the words she was saying did he not understand? The *stay away* part? The *I blame you for ruining my life* part?

'Vee, I'm here, you don't need to be brave on your own.'

'How *are* you here? How did you find my home address?'

'Business name registration search, of course. You're not the only journalist who can dig up information, Vee.'

'Aaron,' she said, putting so much heat into the word he finally shut up. 'I'm not guilty of the charge that's been laid against me. You know why?' She was probably spilling the beans about Sue's defence strategy, but she was past caring. 'Recording conversations *on purpose*, that's what's illegal. Guess what?'

He held his hands up in the air like he was placating an hysterical victim. Well, newsflash, buddy: she was not hysterical, she was angry. And she, Vera De Rossi, was done with feeling ashamed and feeling like a victim.

'Vee, babe—'

'My aunt had dementia. She didn't have conversations, which you would know if you'd ever bothered to visit her with me when you and I were together. I'm not guilty, I'm going to win this court case, and you and your mean-spirited mates at Acacia View can get the heck out of my face.'

She finished on a roar, and though her roar was coming out all breathy and choppy, it felt like she'd unstoppered a cork.

'You don't know what—'

'Quit bugging me, Aaron.'

'You'll regret this when you calm down.'

'Get out of my doorway so I can shut my door.' Where the heck was her phone? Was Aaron really going to not leave? Did she need to call the *police*?

The sound of a throat clearing made her spin towards the stairs.

A man stood there, one hand on the banister railing, looking like six feet of chiselled sunshine. 'Everything okay up here?'

Josh.

❧

His horrified gaze skittered over Vera, her face pale but determined, trying to get rid of the jackass lodged in her doorway.

Aaron.

Ex-boss.

Ex-boyfriend.

And soon to be ex a couple of front teeth if he, Joshua Preston Cody, had anything to do with it.

Vera looked at him. 'Aaron's just leaving. If he doesn't then—well, yes, actually, I would like your help. If you're offering, that is.'

He took a predatory step forward. 'Oh, I'm offering,' he said, his eyes on Aaron's. 'Downstairs. Now.'

The guy turned his head to stare at him and Josh felt a degree of satisfaction when the man's eyes narrowed. 'I'm going. Cool your jets, mate.'

'I'm not your mate.'

The guy, Aaron, stood stock-still for a moment, as though debating whether or not to make an issue out of leaving, then hit the stairs.

'I'll call you soon,' he called up to Vera.

'Please don't,' Josh heard her mutter.

He waited until the slap of thin-soled shoes had disappeared down the stairwell, then took a breath. 'You want to tell me what that was about?'

She slumped in the doorway. 'I think ... I think he's a bit unhinged, Josh. He wasn't listening to a thing I was saying.'

'Maybe it's time you talked to someone about that. It doesn't have to be me ...' Hell, he was the last guy on the planet who was going to be bothering her at her door like that jackass. 'But someone.'

'Josh?'

She looked vulnerable, and wretched. He stayed where he was, because it killed him to see her like that and know she didn't want his help.

'Yes?'

'You reckon you could just give me a hug for a minute and pretend I'm not the world's biggest idiot?'

Was she—

Heck.

He took two giant strides, hauled her into his arms, and rested his head on hers. 'I can hug you for as many minutes as you need.'

He held her there, his mind racing. Aaron was clearly a nutjob, this darned trial was stripping the life out of the woman he'd lost his heart to, and he didn't know where he stood in all of this.

'Vera? Honey? Are you okay?'

She nodded. 'I will be.'

He held her face in his hands and gave her a thorough inspection. She looked tired, and strain had left shadows the colour of bruises beneath her eyes. He'd bet a million bucks she'd been worrying about the cat, or the trial, or god knows what else all night instead of sleeping. He ran his hands down her arms, stopping when he reached a rough cloth about her hand.

'Holy heck, what happened?'

'Oh,' she said, holding her hand up. Blood was seeping through some scrap of chintzy-flowered fabric. 'The scissors must have cut deeper than I thought.'

'He attacked you with *scissors*?'

'No! God no. I was doing some sewing when there was a knock at the door. I was surprised because I don't get visitors. I jabbed myself.'

He ripped off the cloth and investigated. 'You need stitches.'

'Bloody hell. I wrapped it up so quick I didn't see how bad it was. Faulty pain receptors … it's a cook's hazard from all the slicing and dicing and hot pans. Hell, the scissors were rusty, too.'

'Lucky you, one tetanus shot coming right up. I'll drive you to the hospital.'

'Really, Josh, I don't need—' She paused, and he waited for her to finish.

She placed her hand—the one that wasn't bleeding—on his chest. 'Actually, I'd like that. I'd like that a whole lot.'

He tried not to let his wounded heart leap at the idea that maybe she was talking about more than a ride to the hospital.

'And Josh? Maybe you and I could have a talk. There's some stuff I need to say … that is, if you want to.'

He took a breath. 'Once the doctor's checked you out, you can tell me anything you need to.'

CHAPTER
42

'You stay out, buddy.'

Josh frowned at the tall woman in scrubs barring his way into the triage room.

'She needs someone with her, and that someone is me.'

'Sorry. Medical staff and patients only on the other side of this door.'

'I'm a vet. I promise I won't faint …'—he scanned the tag pinned to her scrubs—'Dr Pozzi.'

'You could be Dr Seuss himself, you're still not getting through these doors. We've got a backlog of patients after some idiot ran her quad bike into the middle of her own eighteenth birthday party, and we don't need any extras cluttering up our space.'

He blew out a breath. 'Okay. I'll be waiting.'

'There's black stuff in the waiting room that someone's misla-belled as coffee. Go grab a cup.'

The black stuff was as bad as predicted. He choked down a mouthful of it for something to do, and was just deciding which of the chairs in the waiting room looked the most promising for a lengthy sit when the handbag Vera had grabbed as they left her wrecked apartment buzzed in his hand. He unzipped it and looked in gingerly. A sister, a mother, a daughter and a variety of ex-girlfriends had taught him a woman's handbag was a no-man's-land that he never wanted to visit.

The buzz stopped, then set up again, as insistent as a jackhammer.

Crap.

He slid the screen to green and held it to his ear. A deep female voice was off and running in his ear before he could draw breath.

'You want to explain this crazy text message to me, Vera? Aaron Finch drove all the way out there to woop woop to harass you? In your own apartment! My busy bee antennae are whipping around like wind turbines. This is big. This is stalker big. We need to take action.'

'It's not Vera.'

Silence, then, 'Who the hell are you?'

'Josh Cody. I'm Vera's—'

Yeah. What *was* he exactly? Persistent admirer? Love-struck handbag guardian? 'I'm her friend.' He could be that, just that, if that's what she wanted. No matter how much it hurt.

'Where is she?'

'Um. She can't get to the phone right now.'

'Look, Josh Cody, I'm Vera's lawyer, Sue Anton, and she's going to want to speak to me right this goddamn second. Put her on.'

Christ. Just what he needed, a lawyer in his face.

'She's not speaking to anyone right this goddamn second, Sue. She's in hospital.'

'What?'

'She cut her hand. She needs stitches and there's some delay.'

'Holy crap. Is she all right? Oh my god, I wonder if that … how did she cut her hand? Was it that rat-faced ex-boyfriend named Aaron?'

He rolled his eyes. 'How many rat-faced ex-boyfriends does Vera have?'

'Don't get smart with me, Mr Cody. I will chew you up and spit you out like pencil shavings. Tell me what happened?'

'She was sewing and she was startled, and rammed a rusty set of scissors into the palm of her hand. It's a minor wound. But yes, then ratface showed up. He was being pretty persistent when I got there, and wasn't too keen on being told to leave.'

'Hmm.'

There was a long pause, punctuated by the snarl and horns of big-city traffic. Wherever Vera's lawyer was, it wasn't Dandaloo Street, Hanrahan.

'You know about the trouble Vera is in?'

'Trial in a few weeks, hidden camera, possible jail time?'

'I see you do. Vera tell you all this herself?'

'Yep.' About as willingly as a toddler visiting the dentist, but yeah, she'd told him, even if she'd left a few salient boyfriend facts out of the initial recital.

'Hold the line. I just need to think for a second.'

He closed his eyes momentarily as he wondered about the ethics of plucking a woman's phone out of her handbag, answering a call from her lawyer, and then talking over her criminal case. He let out a breath. He didn't care. He was all in with Vera, and nothing the lawyer could say would change that.

'Okay, let's do this. First, are you Vera's boyfriend?'

'Er … it's complicated.'

The snark in the lawyer's voice softened a fraction. 'When isn't it? Okay, Josh, here's the deal. You willing to make a statement about what you saw of Aaron Finch harassing my client at her home?'

'Sure.'

'Good. This is an opportunity, and Vera needs to seize it. We apply for a restraining order to keep him away from her.'

He looked at the sliding door through which he'd been denied entry. 'I'm totally onboard with that. But—you better ask Vera. Whatever she decides, that's what I'm supporting.'

'Huh. You as cute to look at as you sound, Josh Cody?'

He rolled his eyes. Again. Sue steamrollered on as though her question had been hypothetical. 'Get her to call me the instant she's finished there, will you? I'm having a slow day, and it would give me a lot of pleasure to ring Aaron Finch and hand him his testicles minced into teeny-weeny little pieces.'

Josh raised his eyebrows. 'Remind me never to piss you off.'

'Wise call.'

The voice in his ear clicked off and he stared down at the phone. God, what a day. What a hell of a day.

CHAPTER
43

Vera lifted her hand, wondering how on earth she was going to construct six dozen prawn and vermicelli rice-paper rolls with this bandage-swaddled club at the end of her arm. She felt as weak as a lettuce leaf. A drop of blood she could cope with, but watching a needle and thread stitch her palm back together?

Her stomach flipped. No thank you.

The doctor who'd stitched up her hand had insisted she take a seat and drink a cup of tea until her colour improved, but had then bustled off through swing doors and disappeared.

Should she get up? Find someone?

Sooner or later she was going to have to haul herself out of the recliner chair she'd been allocated and make some sense out of what had happened … but it was quiet in this little treatment room she'd been parked in.

She lay back against the vinyl headrest and closed her eyes.

Quiet and calm, like someone else was in charge and she could take a break from being Vera for a moment.

Aaron had lost his marbles, that was clear. To drive all this way to tell her she was mistaken, that he was really a great guy who could overlook *her* flaws? It was outrageous, and creepy as hell, which was why she'd texted the bare details to her lawyer on the drive in to the hospital.

Was asking for a restraining order an extreme reaction?

She wasn't sure. She just knew she couldn't face another scene like that alone.

But that moment when she'd finally had enough of being his victim, enough of feeling that he and Acacia View and the mistakes of her past were in charge of the shape of her future ... she'd had a moment then. An *epic* moment.

Staring him down and pushing back at his bullshit had done more than shut him up. Seizing that moment had been like seizing back control, and the weight she'd been carrying for months had gone. She hadn't seen the truth in her own words until she'd flung them in his face.

She'd been blaming herself, all this time, thinking she was a failure for not making better decisions, but now she knew. She took in a long breath and let it out, feeling the certainty build. She hadn't been a failure; she'd made a mistake, and she was dealing with the consequences like a responsible adult. She'd had a valid reason for her actions: she'd been worried about her aunt.

What valid reason had Aaron had for dobbing her in to Acacia View? A fat deposit into the *South Coast Morning Herald*'s advertising account?

He'd used her for his own ends, and she'd been naive, yes, but she hadn't been a failure.

What she *was* guilty of was letting her miserable history ruin her chance of a happier future when she'd pushed Josh away and kept the truth about Aaron from him.

A creak made her look up and there, holding open the hospital's swing door, was the man himself. Josh. Her heart splintered into a thousand painful needle pricks. He was carrying flowers, a great messy bunch of ... were they wildflowers? Billy buttons and triggers and daisies in pinks and yellows and silvers dizzier than Jill's quilt.

'Can I come in?'

A man with flowers. And not just any man, *the* man. The one who'd burrowed his way into her brittle lonely heart and made her feel again. Love and pain. Hurt and longing. And great deep swathes of want.

She tried to smile. 'I thought you'd have had enough of me and my dramas by now, Josh.'

He shrugged a little in a way that made her realise he was feeling as unsure as she was. 'Can't a guy bring his girl flowers when the mood takes him?'

She frowned. 'I wasn't aware I was your girl.'

'Well, shoot. Don't tell Dr Dragon that; it took a thirty-minute question and answer session before she'd let me in here. Besides. I think we both know you could be. I know I want you to be.'

Crap. The tears she'd been fighting started leaking out every which way. 'Oh, Josh, I want you to be my guy, too. I'm just so worried if I let you in, I'll mess everything up.'

'Vera, honey.'

She wanted this so badly, but she didn't know what to say.

'Vera? You've gone very still. You need me to call the nurse?'

'Josh,' she managed. 'Would you do something?'

'Anything.'

'Squeeze your way into this recliner chair here and hold me?'

She opened her eyes and he was there, next to her, his eyes all soft and kind-looking, the way she loved them, and a smile on his face bigger than Lake Bogong.

'Honey, I thought you'd never ask.'

The Queanbeyan courthouse was baking in the sun on the second Friday in December. Vera wasn't sure whether a summer heatwave was on the way or the gates of hell had been flung open. Standing on the courthouse steps on the cusp of her trial sure felt like her own personal version of hell.

She'd dressed before dawn in a sober grey suit, and had spent a quiet moment in her chair by the window with her bandaged cat in her lap and two kittens at her feet while she waited for Josh to arrive. He'd insisted on driving her to the city, and she'd been grateful.

What she hadn't expected was for Graeme to turn up on the footpath outside her building too, with a waxed box of muffins he'd cooked in his own kitchen, and two freshly made coffees.

He'd handed them over to Josh and hauled her in for a hug. 'Good luck, boss. Call me with the news, good or bad, and don't worry about the café. I've got your back.' He'd even tucked a note in with his muffins: *You need me to bake a cake with lock picks hidden inside, just let me know :) love, G xxx.*

Marigold had texted her as they'd driven down out of the alps and through the farming country of southern New South Wales, offering her love and support and a yoga breathing exercise called, of all things, Victorious Breath. Kev had been popping into the café every day for the past week to pat her hand, and even Kelly Fox, guinea-pig boy's mum, had wished her well.

'Ready to go in?' said Josh.

'Sure.'

She placed her hand in his just as Sue barrelled up the steps towards them.

'Sue, you're here.'

'In the flesh, my lovely. And why have I not laid eyes on this handsome beast before? I'm your lawyer, Vera. I insist on knowing every detail of your life. Especially the inappropriate ones.'

Vera would have rolled her eyes if her anxiety levels weren't at breaking point.

'Josh, my lawyer, Sue Anton. Sue, this is Josh Cody.'

'We've spoken on the phone,' he said, holding out his hand.

'Yes, we have,' her lawyer said in a voice that resembled golden syrup. 'Now I'm wishing we'd held our strategy meeting in person out there in woop woop where you've hidden yourself away.'

'It's an historic alpine town, not woop woop,' said Vera. 'Hanrahan, population of four thousand, birthplace of The Billy Button Café.'

'Whatever,' said Sue. 'I have news. Let's clear security and find somewhere we can have a huddle. My news has a capital N and you're going to want to hear it.'

Vera raised her eyes to Josh who cocked his head towards the entrance.

'Come on,' he said. 'The only way forward is to get this day over and done with, so let's get started. You're not alone, and I'm not going anywhere no matter what the verdict.'

She held his hand close to her heart for a moment before dropping it to clear security.

The guards were just as brisk and impersonal as the first time she'd been here, and within a few minutes she was inside, where the air conditioning was battling to cope with the blistering conditions.

'Follow me,' said Sue, and marched them through a foyer, through a beige door clearly marked No Unauthorised Entry, and outside again into an enclosed courtyard where one dead pot plant sat beside an old paint tin filled with yellowed cigarette stubs.

'Smokers' hangout,' her lawyer said. 'No-one will disturb us here; turns out nicotine addicts like me are going to be the next dinosaurs in the evolutionary chain.'

Vera took a breath. 'What's this news, Sue? The trial's scheduled to start in less than an hour. Has there been a postponement? Is that it?'

Sue smirked. 'You know that restraining order I slapped on Aaron Finch?'

'Yes.'

'Well, I dropped a word in the ear of the DPP—that's the Director of Public Prosecutions—and suggested that Acacia View had commenced a private prosecution based on the evidence of a witness who had turned out to be not so shiny. They've had a word with Acacia View's lawyer.'

'What sort of a word?' said Josh.

'They think the proceedings should be discontinued.'

Vera took a breath. 'Can you repeat that in plain English?'

'They don't want trivial matters cluttering up the courts, and they can't see any public benefit to this case.'

'Bloody hell.'

'Yes, that's what I said, only with a string of truly naughty adjectives. Acacia View weren't pleased at all, but I sweetened them up with a deal.'

Vera felt cold suddenly, despite the sweat trickling down her back. 'A deal,' she said.

'An apology, in person, from Vera for installing a camera in their aged care facility without their permission. In return, they will agree that Vera's intent was to record her aunt's movements and the presence of staff, not to record private conversations.'

'But this is ... well, it's—'

She could barely stutter, she was so relieved.

'The truth?' suggested Sue.

'Yes! The truth! My god, is this deal really a possibility, Sue?'

'It's a lot more certain that that. We have a meeting room booked for ten-fifteen. I'll have to go see the judge and make sure she knows the DPP have taken your case off the docket, then we make our formal apology, and then ... well. Then we say goodbye and I toddle on back to my office to type up my bill for a job well done.'

For a moment, the only sound in the grubby courtyard was the hum from the air conditioning motors running themselves ragged in the corner.

'I'm having trouble taking this all in,' said Vera at last.

Sue grinned. 'You're free, Vera. It's over. The case of Acacia View Aged Care Facility versus Vera De Rossi is in the past.'

'Oh my god.'

'Girl, we've covered this. God does not have a licence to practise law in this state.'

Vera turned to Josh. 'Did you hear that, Josh? I'm free. It's over.'

He wrapped his arms around her and spun her in a hug that had her laughing and crying all at the same time.

'Weeping will not reduce my bill,' Sue said dryly. 'Nor will public displays of affection with handsome men.'

Vera wriggled out of Josh's arms so she could hug her lawyer. 'You're the best.'

'I know. Now, I'll go work my magic on the judge, and I'll meet you both inside for the formal apology.' And with a nicotine-tinged kiss on her forehead, her lawyer was gone.

CHAPTER
45

One sneaky text mid-afternoon to Graeme was all it had taken.

Josh turned off the old highway just as the setting sun was stippling the upper crags of the Snowy Mountains in gold and orange and pink. Vera, thankfully, was in such a tizz of delight she had barely noticed when he pulled into the alley behind the café instead of driving her home.

He walked round to her side of his truck and opened the door for her.

She gave him a half-smile. 'I don't have a work shift tonight, you know. We could go back to my place ...'

Man oh man. The glimmer of flirt under those words stripped the blood from his head. Perhaps he'd been a little rash sending that message to Graeme, but given the hubbub leaking out from between the brick and timber of the café walls, he was too late to cry off.

But he could have a moment.

And—if he played this right—he could maybe have a lifetime of moments.

Vera cleared her throat. 'Umm, are you going to say something?'

'I'm about three seconds away from planting my lips on yours, Vera, I just ...' Woah, this was a heck of a lot harder in reality than when he had been practising it in his head. He blamed it on the skip bin and the food scrap smells lurching out of it. Could he not have used his brain and pulled over by the lake reflecting the sunset? Under the majestic snow gums in the town's heritage-listed park?

To hell with it. He'd waited long enough and he wasn't waiting a second longer. Love was love, no matter where he proclaimed it.

'I love you, Vera.'

'Oh, Josh.' Those green eyes had smudged into smoke, and the lips he was about to kiss trembled. 'You have to know I love you too.'

He couldn't stop the grin from spreading across his face. 'Yeah. I figured.'

Her eyebrows snapped together. 'You figured?'

He hauled her in close and swivelled so she was pressed up against the dusty length of his old ute, and he was pressed up against the prim, grey-suited, jasmine-smelling length of her. 'I'm kind of irresistible,' he murmured as he ran his hands up into her hair and held her face there, just inches from his own. 'Just ask Jane Doe.'

She gave a little giggle that made his heart spin cartwheels in his chest. 'Okay. You are indeed irresistible.'

He brushed the tiniest of kisses onto her mouth.

'Oh,' she moaned.

'I'd kiss you again,' he said, 'but we need to get some things settled first.'

'Yes to anything. Kiss me quick.'

He hovered a breath away. 'So that's a yes to my question?'

Her lashes were dark against her cheeks, and her cheeks were flushed, and her mouth was doing things to the stubble on his chin that ought to be outlawed in a public place like an alley.

'What's the question?' she murmured against his cheek.

'I want to get married. To you. Say yes and I'll let you kiss me properly.'

Those dusky lashes shot upward. 'You want to get married? To me?'

He shrugged, all kinds of insecurity tightening around his gut. He had everything riding on this moment. His life. His happiness. His desperate desire to have the whole of that future happiness tangled snugly with Vera's forever and then some more.

'I want it more than I've wanted anything. What do you say? You got room in your life for a small-town vet with a fifteen-year-old daughter and an old brown dog?'

She ran her hands up his chest and all sorts of unquenchable fires started burning.

'I have all the room in the world. Yes, Josh. Yes!'

That was all he needed to hear. He gathered her close and fastened his mouth to hers.

It took a while, but eventually he remembered there was a café full of people waiting to join in the celebration. He rested his head against hers while he lowered his, um, heart rate enough to brave the crowd.

'Let's get out of here,' she murmured.

'I'm with you a thousand per cent on that. Small problem.'

She smiled. 'More questions? Let's just fast-forward and pretend I've said yes to everything.'

'You hear that ruckus going on inside The Billy Button?'

She lifted a head. 'You're right. It does sound a little rowdier than usual for a Friday evening.'

'That'll be the welcome home party.'

'For … me?'

'If you're going to get mad with someone, get mad with Graeme,' he said gallantly. 'Come on.'

He shepherded her round the side of the building and in through the front door and the blast of laughter and cheering nearly lifted the roof off the place.

Marigold was first in line, a blur of tangerine lipstick and beaded earrings. Alex was there, dusty and tall in his fire brigade outfit, clapping him on the back, and Kev must have dug deep into his endless drawer of ties, because he was wearing a yellow swirly number that could have stopped traffic.

He ducked to the side so the wellwishers could throng around Vera, and was heading for the counter to sweet-talk Graeme into selling him the coldest beer in the fridge, when a squeal nearly took out his eardrum.

He turned, and there was Poppy.

'Dad!'

'Popstar, I wasn't expecting you so soon.'

She looked smug. 'I had a secret plan going. The school year finished at noon today, so I caught the first train out and Hannah collected me from Cooma.'

He wrapped her in a hug. 'Huh. Where is my secret-keeping sister?'

'Oh, some sheep fell off a truck and she took off. Graeme's in charge of me in your absence.'

He held her away from him so he could look her over. Was this the same girl who'd barely looked in his direction without rolling her eyes six months ago? He kissed her on the cheek and hugged her again until she squealed.

It was a lucky day for him when Vera offered his daughter a job.

It was an even luckier day the day she agreed to be his wife.

He held Poppy's hands in his. 'Poptart, I have some news.'

She grinned. 'Oh yes? It's not lovey-dovey news, is it, Dad, because I have my limits.'

He pinched her hand. 'I just asked Vera to marry me.'

This time her squeal got buried in the lapel of his jacket before his eardrum was perforated.

'Dad, that is so amazing only ...'

She pursed her lips.

'Only what?'

'Who's going to break the news to Jane?'

He pulled her ponytail. 'You working here tonight or what?'

'Of course I'm working. I'm Graeme's right-hand girl.'

'Well, go find me a beer, will you, kiddo?' he said, his eyes roaming the crowd until they found Vera's smiling face. 'Your dad's in the mood to celebrate.'

ONE YEAR LATER

Vera scrolled up to the first page of her manuscript and sat for a moment before typing out the word.

D–E–D–I–C–A–T–I–O–N

She felt a little teary. Was this what closure felt like? She hoped so. God, how she hoped so. How many months ago had it been when she had made that rash promise to herself and to Jill that she could make a difference?

The shame she'd felt when she'd thought she'd let her aunt down had made her life so very bleak.

A deep purr rose from under her desk and she nudged her slippered feet against the plump sides of her old grey cat.

'You're right, Daisy,' she said. 'That's all behind me now.'

The cat had snoozed beside her—at her feet, across her keyboard, sprawled across the reference book she most particularly needed to read—for every word of this guidebook for families trying to navigate the aged care sector. As Vera had typed, Daisy's injuries had healed and word-by-word, month-by-month, she had finally come to believe that her own wounds had healed, too. She had fulfilled her promises; to her aunt that she would campaign for change, to the bundle of fur she'd once offered a saucer of milk to in an alleyway. A publisher had put their faith in her and offered her a contract; aged care workers and facilities and families had helped her with research so the guidebook contained perspectives that differed from her own.

She was proud of it. She was proud of herself, for seeing it through.

To my Aunt, she typed. *You lived a full and fearless life and deserved to be safe, respected and cared for in your final years. This book is for you, Jill, and for all the other fierce and fabulous women who grow old before their time.*

A large pair of hands slid over her shoulders and she leaned her head back into the warmth that was Josh.

'I think I've finished.'

He leaned down and pressed a kiss into her temple, letting his hands slide down and around the swell of baby belly pushing out her dress. 'I'm proud of you.'

She covered his hands with her own and took the moment to just be. 'You know what, Josh?'

He pressed his cheek to hers. 'What?'

'I'm proud of me, too.'

'I've got something to show you.'

She smiled. 'Is that a line? Because I'm pretty sure I've seen what you've got to offer, Josh Cody, and I am one hundred per cent in.'

'Don't distract me with saucy talk, Vera Cody. Come on.'

She followed him out of the large open-plan room he'd made in the second storey of his grandparents' apartment block, then down the hall with its polished timber floors and extravagant trim. They passed the doorway to Poppy's room, then to their room, then he halted at the door to the other as-yet-unused bedroom.

'Shut your eyes.'

She shut her eyes and held her hands out to the man she trusted more than life itself. 'Show me.'

She heard the door open, its timber humming over the newly laid carpet. The faint smells of paint and turpentine lingered in the air, overlaid by the cleanness of lake and mountain roaring in through the open window.

Josh's hands found her waist and moved her forward a few paces. 'Okay. Open your eyes.'

A cot stood where, until yesterday, bare carpet had been the only comfort in the room. Its sides gleamed white, its legs were turned in shaker style, and above it, spinning in the breeze, hung a mobile of gaily painted wooden animals.

Tears ran unchecked down her cheeks. 'You made this?'

He grinned. 'Graeme lent me a corner of his shed so I could get it built on the sly.'

'It's perfect. So perfect.'

'Our first family heirloom.'

She reached a hand to the mobile and sent it spinning. 'You made this too?'

'I cut them out. Poppy and her brothers painted them. They wanted to be involved.'

So, so perfect. 'Josh.'

He smiled. 'I know, I'm pretty awesome,' he said, then he put his fingers to his mouth and blew a short, sharp whistle.

Jane Doe trotted into the room dragging a large paper sack with her.

'We thought you might like this to go on the cot.'

She could barely make out the knots in the ribbon, the tears were running so swiftly. She gave up, and tore the paper off the heavy parcel, until a mass of dense, coloured fabric flowed out of the wrapping and landed on the mattress of the cot. Jill's quilt!

'I don't understand! How did you—'

'I put in an outrageous bid in Marigold's community hall fundraiser. She's been keeping it for me ever since.'

The rag quilt. She ran her fingers over the ruffled squares. Ones Jill had stitched. Ones she had stitched from material given to her around the craft table at The Billy Button Café. Every stitch had brought her further along in her journey from a confused, lonely woman to the woman she was now.

'You've given me the world, Josh. You know that?'

He wrapped his arms around her, so the two of them stood at the foot of the cot, looking down to where their child would sleep. Jane Doe's tail thumped against their legs like a heartbeat.

'You've given it right back, Vera.'

ACKNOWLEDGEMENTS

Hanrahan, where this book is set, is of course a made-up town. The cakes I've baked over the years haven't been works of art like Vera's, and the quilts I've cobbled together have had more than their share of wonky stitches. I think Marigold would approve.

What is not made up, however, is my love of small towns and rural settings and characters who take the time to *really* introduce themselves on the pages. The small town I grew up in didn't have brumbies in the high country or gum trees tangling their limbs over snowmelt creeks. It had coconuts, not snow. It had kids messing about in canoes, and mango trees lining the main street, and a grocery store where you could only buy a potato if the ship had been in.

It was the kind of place where returning after a long absence felt like coming home and that was the feeling I wanted Josh to have after his long absence away from Hanrahan.

His love for old buildings and his interest in their preservation mirrors my own. I went to boarding school in a regional country town in Queensland where the streets are home to stone and brick buildings that have survived a century and a half with varying degrees of success. Sadly my in-person visit to reacquaint myself with the historic buildings in the Cooma district was "covidated" so I had to content myself with the websites devoted to sharing the long and diverse history of the Snowy Mountains region. I particularly enjoyed reading about the restorations done by the volunteers of the Kosciuszko Huts Association.

Also … I may have watched the movie, *The Man from Snowy River*, about a thousand times as I wrote this book. That music! Those wild skies! Clancy! My book also owes a nod to the bush poetry of Banjo Paterson and John O'Brien. The humour and affection they could portray as they described their country characters' antics is a skill I very much admire and hope (think the guinea pig scene!) I was able to match. I have a swag of bush poetry of my own hiding in a folder on a shelf and can confirm that my rhyming skill is right up there with my wonky stitches.

What is not wonky, however, is the support I have received as I have deviated from my life's path (mother, accountant, dog lover, reader) to embrace the wonderful world of fiction writing. Thank you to my writing group, Jayne Kingsley, Megan Mayfair, Marianne Bayliss and Anna Foxkirk, who have cheered me on through many a manuscript.

Thank you also to the Australian Society of Authors and HQ Fiction. Their generous sponsorship of the 2020 ASA/HQ Commercial Fiction Prize, in which an early manuscript of *The Vet from Snowy River* was shortlisted, resulted in my story receiving a publishing contract from Harlequin MIRA. My journey with Harlequin's editorial and cover teams has been a dream come true, and that phone call from Rachael Donovan at HarperCollins to tell me my book had attracted their interest ranks as one of my Very Best Days Ever.

Thank you to the back gate girls; you know who you are.

Thank you to my family.

Thank you to Romance Writers of Australia whose competitions, community, and conferences gave me the confidence to pursue a career as an author.

And, finally, thank you to the readers who have chosen this book from all the wonderful books out there. I hope you enjoy *The Vet from Snowy River*. If you do, please tell your friends.

Happy Reading!

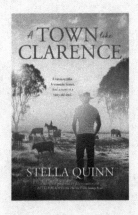

Turn over for a sneak peek.

A TOWN like CLARENCE

by

STELLA QUINN

Available July 2022

mira

PROLOGUE

Kirsty sat in the back seat of her mum's ancient hatchback, drawing a getaway route on a rumpled paper map with a glitter pen.

She was good at drawing getaway routes, even when she had a banged-up arm. Besides, concentrating on the neat glittery line was keeping her mind off the hot vinyl seat. And the broken aircon. And the fact she'd been stuck waiting for *ages* in the car.

She was good at other things, too, like fobbing off cranky landlords with hard luck stories, and she was especially good at buying yesterday's loaf of bread for like twenty cents or whatever.

She could make her brown eyes go all sad and droopy and hungry-lost-dog-looking. The man at the bakery at the last town—William Creek? Or was it in Oodnadatta?—had been a sucker for sad, droopy eyes. He'd snuck a sticky bun into a white paper bag and handed it down to her along with the day-old bread.

She had to be good at all these things—and more—because of the family curse.

Kirsty snuck a peek through the car window to check her mum was still in the hotel-motel office and (phew) out of earshot. 'Bad s–h–i–t happens to Foxes,' she whispered.

The words were chiselled into the headstone of every dead Fox since the dawn of time, according to her mother. And yet, Kirsty still wasn't allowed to say the s–h–i–t word, or spell it out loud. It didn't even count that everyone at school (when she went to school) said worse. Eleven-year-olds aren't allowed to swear, not until they're eighteen, her mum would say.

Kirsty traced her pen along the squiggly line of Callie Creek Road but it came to a dead end. 'Fudgebucket.' That wouldn't do … what if that mean-eyed woman from behind the hotel-motel counter came after them in her ute? It wouldn't be the first time they'd had to empty their suitcases by the side of the road and hand back teaspoons and fluffy towels and some of the money from Mum's lucky tin.

She leaned down to check. Yep. The old biscuit tin was still there, safe as anything. She reached for it but winced when the plaster cast on her arm went clunk under the car seat. Stupid thing.

Stupid her.

Stupid *arm*, which she better stop thinking about because that was in the past, and she and Mum didn't do that.

Her attention now back on the map, she saw a yellow line that looked promising; maybe it was a highway that would take them someplace new. When bad s–h–i–t happened to Foxes, they upped stumps and took off. Finding themselves some new luck, her mum called it. Mum was always happiest in a new town, because it meant she had new pokie machines to try.

Kirsty nearly jabbed her glitter pen through the map when her mum ripped open the driver's door and leapt in.

'Let's go,' her mum said, panting.

'Are they after us?' Kirsty said, having another stickybeak through the dusty car window.

'Not this time, sugarplum. She let me write her a cheque from the bank, but no point hanging around tempting fate, right?'

Totally right. Fate, lady luck, whatever her mum called it, *loved* chasing down the Foxes. 'But there's no money in the bank, is there, Mum? You said I'd get sneakers when we had money in the bank.' She could say that with just Mum there, because Mum would *never* get mad and grip her until she had purple fingerprints spotting her arms.

Crunching the gears with a hand that was trembling a bit, and revving the engine, her mum dropped her sunglasses down her nose and twisted towards the back seat. 'The hotel-motel lady doesn't know that, does she?' she said with a wink, before pulling the little car out onto the cracked road.

Kirsty grinned. 'What about Colin?'

Colin was the love of Mum's life. At least, he had been for about three weeks, and he was okay. Before that, Stew had had been the love of Mum's life, for ages and ages, and he had not-at-all been okay.

Her eyes wanted to look at her arm, but she couldn't let them. No going back … that was the rule.

Before him it had been the one with the gold tooth who played the harmonica all the freaking time. Donny? Danny?

'Turns out, Colin won't be joining us, sugarplum. It's you and me again. Want to climb through to the front?'

'What about Colin's jacket?'

Her mum grabbed the plaid fleece that was sitting on the front seat and chucked it out her car window. 'I don't see a jacket.'

All right then. Kirsty undid her seatbelt with her good hand and squidged her way through the vinyl seats until she was plonked next to her mum. 'I reckon the town we should try is Marla, Mum. It's two hundred and nine kilometres away, and I saw a notice stuck to the door of the laundromat saying a cattle station out there needed a cook. You know, just in case the pokies are ganging up against you again.'

'Well, aren't you the clever one,' said her mum. 'A new town, a new job, and no-one hunting us down for unpaid rent … you know, you might have broken the curse, Kirsty Fox.'

Maybe. Kirsty grinned. She was kinda used to it now—breaking the curse every time they took off for somewhere new. When the bad s–h–i–t happened, she and Mum always got to go off on another adventure somewhere and forget all about it.

Running away from bad s–h–i–t was kinda fun.

CHAPTER

1

Twenty years later

Kirsty Fox strode through the Mediflight West hangar. Four years on at the Port Augusta headquarters, she still wasn't over the thrill.

As far as adventures went, this one was a cracker. She'd even broken her never-hang-around-for-long rule for this job.

'Where's my clipboard?' she said.

John, retired paramedic, head sausage-turner for the monthly barbecue, and logistics legend of the two aircraft and ten personnel who connected patients from remote South Australia to the hospitals in the city, stood up from behind the clutter on his desk.

'Emergency pick-up of Mrs Ullrich,' he said. 'She's gone into labour a month sooner than she'd planned, and her husband's having kittens by the sound of him.'

Kirsty lifted her eyes from the flight plan long enough to shoot John a grin. 'Isn't that always the way? You know I'm supposed to be off duty on Fridays, right?'

'Missing out on a hot date, love?'

'I wish. No—I'm supposed to be in Adelaide. Mum's been calling me nonstop and wants me to go see her. She's probably behind on her rent again and needs me to negotiate.' Or pay it.

Terri had been three years off the pokies, but her ability to stick at a job was a work in progress.

'You're a good daughter, Kirsty.'

She smiled. 'True. And bad luck doesn't follow me around the way it follows Mum.' Because she didn't let it. 'So, who's on board with me today?'

'The new doctor. Don't freak him out with turbulence this time,' John said. 'It took maintenance a week to get the smell out of the carpet.'

She snorted. She had a perfect flight record, as John well knew. She gave him a wave, then set off for the gleaming King Air B200 aircraft and began her walkaround. Tyres, excellent. Rivets on the newly repainted wheel strut looked good as new. Propellors were free of nicks, the windscreen was free of cracks.

'We getting in the air anytime soon, Fox?' said a voice behind her.

'When my checklist is ticked, Carys,' she said, leaning forward to swivel the cargo hatch lock. Righty-tighty, lefty-loosey … the lock was secure.

'You and that bloody clipboard.'

Kirsty turned and grinned at her friend. 'I'll take that as a compliment. All right, on you go. Let's get this ambo in the air.'

The rookie doctor was already aboard, clutching an airsick bag and looking greener than his Mediflight uniform. Kirsty hauled the stairs up, locked them, and made her way up front to the cockpit.

She rested a hand on the doc's shoulder as she passed. 'Forty minutes' airtime,' she said, 'and John's weather printout is saying clear skies all the way. It's a perfect day for a perfect flight.'

'Great,' he said weakly. 'I love flying.'

Yeah, she thought. If he kept telling himself that, one day it might even be true.

Unlike her. She'd loved flying from that childhood moment when she'd scabbed a ride in a crop duster, on that Marla property. The day she'd earned her pilot's licence had been the luckiest day of her life, and everything had been bang-on perfect since.

Well, mostly perfect, if she discounted the occasional financial bail-out of her mother.

She squeezed her way into her seat, scanned the dashboard left to right—trim tab controls set, flight tracker on, oil pressure perfect— and fired up the twin Pratt & Whitneys.

The rumble and whine filled the plane, and she reached for the headset she'd left on the empty co-pilot's seat. Just as her fingers hooked into the headstrap, her phone lit up with a call from a screened number.

The boss, she thought, with some last-minute plan change.

'Kirsty Fox,' she said, pressing the phone close to her ear to drown out the propellors spinning only a few feet from her.

'This is Constable Farrelly, from the Gindarra Street Police Station.'

What? That was the cop station near her home. 'Can I help you?'

'Do you live at 16 Barbery Street?'

'Yes.'

'A woman has been apprehended breaking into your property via a window. A neighbour alerted us and we caught her in the act.'

'Oh my god. Has anythi—'

'The woman says she's your mother and has your permission to be there, but we wanted to confirm that with you. We ran her ID … turns out she's got a record.'

Her happy pre-flight buzz evaporated. 'Terri Fox,' she said. 'Short for Theresa. Is that who it is?'

'Yes ma'am.'

She sighed, then switched into the explanatory mode she'd developed all those years ago living out of the hatchback, from country town to country town. 'Look, she doesn't *really* have a record. There was a misunderstanding about some unbanked rates when she was working at a local council, and she did her community service and everything was paid back. Every dollar.'

'So, no need to charge her with break and enter, then?'

'Of course not, Constable.' But ... Kirsty pressed her fingers into the crease that had decided to cut her forehead in half.

'Wait ... she wants to talk to you.'

She listened to the scramble as a mobile phone changed hands.

'Kirst? Is that you, sugarplum?'

'Yes, Mum. It's me. What's going on? I sent you a text: I'll come see you tomorrow.'

'Tomorrow would have been too late, Kirsty.'

'Don't tell me; something bad has happened to you.'

'Well, I am a Fox, darling. It was only a matter of time. And ... well ... the thing is, Kirsty, this time it involves you.'

What?

Terri hadn't finished. 'Of course, it's probably nothing, or good news even, so I'm freaking out for nothing, but I won't know until you open the letter.'

'I'm about to get airborne, Mum, but I should be home after lunch. Put Constable Farrelly back on, will you?'

'Sure, dear.'

'Tell her she can stay,' she said when the policeman returned.

'Rightio,' he said. 'Maybe hide a key under the doormat next time, hey?'

She ended the call and looked through the thickened perspex of the B200's windows. Next time. There was always a next time with Terri, wasn't there?

And each time was getting a little bit harder to shake off.

She reached down for her headset and noticed her fingers were trembling. Actually, not just her fingers. Her hands were shaking. Her lungs felt tight and she closed her eyes for a moment.

'Pull yourself together,' she muttered. 'Terri has the bad luck, not you. You are totally fine. You do not have the curse.' But had she made a mistake buying a house? Staying at the one job for so long?

She took a long breath and blew it out the way she'd seen Carys instruct patients who were about to lose their cool because of some farm accident where they'd lost a finger or whatever in an auger.

She was fine. She was about to fly off on an adventure, and she was a thousand per cent fine.

And the roar of the propellors reminded her today wasn't about her. She was on a rescue mission, and a young woman was counting on her. 'Fuel gauge, oil gauge, tachometer,' she said, chanting it like a good luck charm. 'Fuel gauge, oil gauge, tachometer.' She slipped the brake, cranked up the throttle, and cleared her mind of everything except the voice of the control tower operator in her ear.

'Delta-one-six-eight-Charlie, you have clearance to runway one.'

That was good. That was excellent. As the B200 flung its way skywards, its speed pressed her deeper into her seat. There was no freaking way the curse of the Foxes was finding her up here.

Only … the curse did find her.

At least that was the one thought she had in her head forty-three minutes later when she brought the plane down in the rough red dirt and the starboard landing gear buckled beneath her.

Her head whacked a cockpit panel even as her hands fought for control, and there was a breathless moment while the world went sideways and six million dollars' worth of aluminium and high-tech gear ground its way to a halt.

She blinked.

Engine off. Check fire. Check fuel leak. Check passengers.

'Captain Fox?'

That was the newbie doctor behind her, bless him.

'I'll be right with you. Is everyone okay back there?' She slewed around in her seat, but getting up was weirdly downhill and her ears were buzzing as though desert flies had taken up residence.

Was *she* okay?

Maybe not, but she could worry about herself later.

As the buzz in her head cleared she heard yelling, but it wasn't coming from her own mouth … she could work that out because hers felt like it was full of cottonwool.

She fought her way to the rear of the plane. Carys and the doctor had opened the door and evacuated—emergency landing procedure 101—and the empty cabin was a mess of strewn baggage and shrink-wrapped bandages and shortbread biscuits.

Okay, so the curse hadn't totally messed with her. No-one was dead, but now the yelling had stopped, she could hear a female crying out in the paddock. She took a breath and hurtled down the stairs, only to be stopped by a large freckled hand gripping her arm.

Her arm. Right there, between wrist and elbow. Right where—

Her lungs seized. So, it seemed, did everything else, because her arms and legs and thoughts stalled.

'How hard is it to land a fucking plane?' yelled an angry voice in her ear.

She forced herself to get breath back into her lungs. She wasn't a kid. This man was a stranger, not one of the loves of her mum's life. People were relying on her, so she needed to pull herself together right this second.

She wrenched her arm away. The man with the angry voice wasn't the rookie doctor; it was a big, sunburned fellow with an ancient felt hat and a mouth so grim it looked like it had been carved from concrete.

Shaun Ullrich, imminent father. Patient medical notes weren't her purview, but she knew the basics of who she was here to collect. Janey Ullrich, thirty-five weeks pregnant, possible breech birth, high blood pressure.

Shit. The B200 wouldn't be flying anyone out now. She breathed out as the farmer turned back to the utility parked beside the strip of red dirt where she'd landed.

Well. Crash-landed.

'Kirst, honey? Can you give me a hand?'

Carys, the thirty-year nursing veteran who she'd flown with for the last four crash-free years, was kneeling beside a first-aid kit. Blood was gushing from a cut in her eyebrow.

'Thank god you're okay. How's the doc?'

'He's fine, unlike our new father, who's got himself in a bit of a state.'

The new father wasn't the only one. Kirsty was feeling as unlike herself as she'd ever felt. 'Understandable,' she said, her voice quavering. Perhaps she'd damaged her throat in the landing. 'Want me to grab you a bandage?'

'I've got one, I just need a hand with the tape. What happened? I was about to unclick my seatbelt when everything went topsy-turvy.'

'I'm so sorry, Carys. We had a problem with the landing gear.' And when she could pull herself together, she'd go check out what that problem had been.

'So ... no take-off, huh?'

'No take-off,' she confirmed, ripping off tape with her teeth and securing a pad of gauze to the nurse's eyebrow. And they both knew the other of the two Mediflight West planes was en route to a vehicle roll-over five hundred kilometres south. Patient critical, blood loss … that'd take priority over a birth, breech or not. 'I'll radio John.'

John Mann would ring everybody he knew in the district who kept a set of wings in their shed. If anyone could find a plane to get Mrs Ullrich to hospital, it would be him.

Another cry made her jerk, and she looked over to the back of the farm ute parked by the old airstrip. 'Poor woman. Is our new doctor up for this? He looks as though he started shaving about three weeks ago. And how are you feeling, Carys? Dizzy? Loss of vision? Nausea?'

It was easy to name the likely symptoms, because they were the ones she was feeling herself.

'I'm good,' said the nurse. 'Haul me up, will you, lovey? Sounds like I'm needed.'

Kirsty's hands had a tremor when she reached out to help Carys. That must be the bang to the head making everything around her judder.

Yes. Juddery was the word. She felt off, and sick, and *juddery*. 'You sure you're not concussed?' she said. She wanted to ask Carys to check if *she* was concussed, but she wasn't the patient here. She wasn't the one wailing in the back of a ute.

Carys—bless her, too, for surviving—was back in action mode. 'Right. Let's get ourselves a little organised, shall we? Young master Ullrich seems to be in a hurry to arrive, and he's setting our time-table here. Looks like we're having a baby in a paddock today, bum first. You reckon you can get into the cargo hold?'

Kirsty forced herself to check out the B200. The plane's body and wings were intact, so long as you didn't dwell upon the sheered strips of paint and aluminium where the wingtip had furrowed a new rut in the old airstrip.

The nosecone looked like it had been hit by a freight train, and the starboard propellor—what was left of it—would never see service again.

'I can get in,' she said. 'Tell me what we need.'

'The humidicrib and the duffle marked INFANT, and the jerry can of sterile water.'

'I'm on it.' Busy was good. Busy could fix anything.

But then anything she could do was done, and the medical team were a hundred per cent focussed on the young mum trying to deliver her baby in the back of a ute. She stood in the red dirt, cradling her bruised arm with one hand, and over the agonised noises coming from Janey Ullrich, all she could hear was her mother's words.

Bad shit happens to Foxes.

Only … stuck out here on a red dirt airstrip, running away wasn't an option.

talk about it

Let's talk about books.

Join the conversation:

 facebook.com/romanceanz

 @romanceanz

romance.com.au

If you love reading and want to know about our
authors and titles, then let's talk about it.